MICHAEL FOLEY was born in Derry in 1947 and was educated at St Columb's College, Derry, and Queen's University Belfast. He was joint editor of the *Honest Ulsterman* from 1970 to 1971 and contributed a regular satirical column 'The Wrassler' to *Fortnight* magazine throughout the early 1970s. His first novel, *The Passion of Jamesie Coyle*, was serialised in *Fortnight* and published in book form in 1984; his subsequent novels were published by Blackstaff Press – *The Road to Notown* (1996) and *Getting Used to Not Being Remarkable* (1998). He has also published a collection of translations of French poetry, and three poetry collections with Blackstaff Press. He currently lives in London where he lectures in Information Technology at the University of Westminster. He is married with one daughter.

ALSO BY MICHAEL FOLEY

FICTION

The Passion of Jamesie Coyle
The Road to Notown
Getting Used to Not Being Remarkable

POETRY

True Life Love Stories
The GO Situation
Insomnia in the Afternoon

TRANSLATION

The Irish Frog
(versions of French poetry)

beyond

MICHAEL FOLEY

THE
BLACKSTAFF
PRESS

BELFAST

First published in 2002 by
Blackstaff Press Limited
Wildflower Way, Apollo Road
Belfast BT12 6TA
with the assistance of
The Arts Council of Northern Ireland

ARTS
COUNCIL
of Northern Ireland

Typeset by Techniset Typesetters, Newton-le-Willows, Merseyside

Printed in Ireland by ColourBooks Limited

A CIP catalogue record for this book
is available from the British Library

ISBN 0-85640-718-6

www.blackstaffpress.com

1

When Marie was single she craved the imperium of the wife and, the moment she was married, the insouciance of the maid. Custom, teamwork and alcohol carried us safely through the wedding day but it was obvious from the morning after that Marie had grievous second thoughts. Apparently unwilling or unable to dissemble, she spoke only rarely and then in a listless, indifferent tone. For once the Irish weather was not to be blamed. By day we drove along the west coast in sunshine, which was less of a benediction than a rebuke to our discontented silence. Evenings were even more difficult. Neither of us had brought anything to read or could suggest an alternative to sitting in lounge bars attempting to think of something to say. After a night of morose drinking in Westport we had a furious quarrel in the hotel. I have long since forgotten the issue but not the end of the argument – my flinging of a new watch against the wall.

Next day came a symbolic failure. We ran out of fuel five miles short of Clifden. It took a minute of stomping the accelerator to bring this truth home. Marie had been carefully painting her nails and now, to help the polish dry, held out both hands with the fingers splayed.

'What's the matter?' A lazy, detached enquiry, eyes still on her hands.

'If you'd read a map or a signpost once in a while' – my tone undeniably tart and pent-up – 'I might have time to keep an eye on the petrol gauge.'

As though seeking the recipient of this remark, Marie looked out at the hillside, then up at the sky. Failing to discover an alternative addressee, she had to assume that she had misinterpreted the message. Inclining her upper body a little, while not moving her hands, she said calmly but sharply: '*Come again?*'

'We're completely out of petrol.'

'I see.' A sagacious nod. 'And of course it's my fault.'

In the rear-view mirror was the face of a petulant bookkeeper with the pinched mouth she had once compared to 'a camel's arse in a sandstorm'. An attempt to mitigate the tone was only a partial success. 'All I'm saying is that you could help with the navigation once in a while.'

We sat on in silence, blind to the sunstruck beauty of a scenic Connemara back road. Still no other car had passed – and a five-mile hike in midday sun was not an attractive prospect. Ignoring the crisis, Marie calmly proceeded to paint her toenails.

Seething in confined space is difficult. I got out to sit by the side of the road – and twenty minutes later an American couple in a hire car stopped to offer assistance. But it was a further hour and a half before the arrival of a breakdown truck. Sore from the unforgiving Connemara stone, I was back in the car by this stage. A mechanic emerged, paused to appraise us with leisurely relish, and sauntered across to lean down at my window and stare past at Marie's sun top, pink shorts and brown legs.

'Bit of bother . . . *ah?*'

'Didn't the Americans tell you we need a gallon of petrol?'

He glanced at me suddenly, as though only just aware of my presence. 'Yees'd be from the North . . . *ah?*' And, in case Marie felt excluded, he leaned even further down and across.

'On our honeymoon,' she told him.

I could have strangled her with my bare hands. The phrase was a reminder, a mockery, a betrayal and, worst of all, an invitation to intimacy. Such abrupt and compelling mirth possessed him that he had to step back to accommodate it and beat on the car roof to aid its release. Shaking his head at the wonder and absurdity of it all, he looked around at the hills and sky – and for some reason the sunshine seemed to heighten the joke. 'Yees are gettin' the weather for it anyway.' After another hearty slap on the roof he came back down for a bold reappraisal of the bride. But again the question was for me. 'And what would ye be up in the North?'

The delay in responding was to register disapproval of his impertinence. 'I'm an accountant.'

Entirely unchastened, he chuckled knowingly at my cunning in obtaining such a lucrative sinecure, then knowingly at Marie for *her* cunning in hooking such a fly boy. 'And how much would that pay ye in a week, like? I mean, how much would ye get in your hand at the end of the week?'

I established direct and persistent eye contact. 'What do we owe you for the petrol?'

Immediately he straightened up and looked in the direction of the invisible ocean, his eyes adopting the thousand-yard focus of those about to overcharge.

Even Marie was aghast. '*What?*' As she leaned across in outrage a thigh came away from the sticky seat with a tearing sound.

'Like, it has to be brought out.' In accordance with long-range absorption, his voice was distant and detached.

Anxious to put the incident behind us, I paid up and took off at speed – but he overtook us just outside Clifden, his joviality restored and perhaps even enhanced, waving and yelling and sounding his horn.

'Why did you have to tell him it was our honeymoon?' I hissed.

The newly built luxury hotel was on a hill outside the town. All modern amenities – but the room was not ready. An unctuous desk clerk suggested that we wait with a complimentary drink in the lounge. Outside was some of the most splendidly rugged scenery in the island, perhaps even in Europe – but the lounge was windowless and softly dim. Ireland still lacked the confidence to look out of the window at itself. Bars provided not natural grandeur to rouse the soul but a perpetual twilight conducive to oblivion.

We sat in a well-upholstered alcove, a cosy den within a den, and, fiddling with beer mats and halfs of Smithwick's, pondered the circumstances which had brought us to this.

It was less than three years since I had met Marie in Belfast, where she had come to help an older married sister with the latest in a succession of babies but, with typical irrepressibility, had insisted on getting out to the Royal Showband on Saturday night in the Boom Boom Room. I was teaching geography, hating it, and studying accountancy part-time, by now almost qualified, so that the years of monastic self-denial were coming to an end. So too was my tolerance for a certain type of girl, fellow teachers and accountancy students and other similar daughters of the swanky end of Catholic West Belfast. In the way of embattled enclaves this Protestant-surrounded district was more Irish Catholic than Catholic Ireland itself. Involvement with one of its bourgeois daughters meant taking on much ancient baggage, as well as submitting, like a medieval troubadour, to the code of the inviolable high-born lady.

Marie was from the other end of the province, a Catholic town comforted by proximity to the Irish Republic and taking to its unthreatened heart Hollywood, rock and roll, rococo beehive and duck's arse hairstyles, white stiletto-heeled shoes and blue bumfreezer suits. As Brendan Bowyer crooned 'Love Me Tender' Marie floated into my arms and revealed, with the casual ease of an intimate, that she had sat through three successive showings of the Elvis film with this title song, entering the cinema at two o'clock and emerging only when it closed at eleven to go home and be 'battered soft' by her outraged father. Something of the original ensorcellment recurred in the telling and her innocent rapture softened and moved my bookkeeper's heart. So many nights wasted on dry accountancy books! There possessed me a rage for erotic enchantment in smoky dark places – cinemas, dance halls and singing lounges.

'I just cried me eyes out.' Marie sighed for the imperious passions of youth. 'Almost made meself sick. Just as bad every time.'

This emotional ease seemed exemplary. And in her sister's house later she disposed her body on the sofa in a comfortable abandon which revealed, like the cream at the top of the milk bottle, a band of sumptuous naked flesh above a stocking top. All about us was the ineluctable verity of a Glengormley living room – imitation brushed-velvet suite, shagpile littered with toys, framed photographs of children on the television, over our heads the groans and sighs of an overweight and disgruntled man and wife. A setting which repeated an old message: life is banality, boredom and burden. Yet here at its centre was the crème de la crème, apparently offered without inhibition or artifice. It was too much for one so inexperienced in love. As soon as my trembling body touched hers I shot off violently and copiously in my pants.

Then an even more profound wonder – Marie seemed to accept ignominy as part of the fun. When, in the hope of avoiding a tell-tale stain, I surreptitiously pulled out my trouser front, she issued a laugh that was high and ringing but entirely without malice.

'That's your good suit ruined.'

It may have been just at this humiliating moment, trapped in my seeping congealing shame, that I fell in love with Marie. For it was surely now that charm would evaporate and the disguise of the masked ball come off. Yet there was not a trace of impatience, disgust or scorn.

She was also surprisingly free from the pieties of religion and nationalism. When I went up to visit her in her home town one of the first people she pointed out was a plump man with long hair. 'I had to go to that character for Irish dancing. He claims he'll never get his hair cut till Ireland's all free.' And at the absurdity of this pledge she shrieked with laughter. 'Actually, I think he's a big jessie. He was always pawing over the boys.'

While I marvelled at a casual sacrilege unthinkable in my own circles, Marie suddenly clenched her arms to her sides and, looking straight ahead with a grim, tense expression, cried, 'But he taught me "The Sweets of May",' and proceeded with a parody of Irish dancing, managing to kick up her legs in spite of the tight skirt and heels.

'Very good,' was all I could mutter, astounded and shocked. 'You must have been a great success.'

'Naw. Thanks be to God I got too big on top. You have to be flat-chested for that.'

This problem had been apparent even in the brief demonstration. She was certainly not a colleen but a child of the modern carnal age.

Yet she was devoted to her home town – as were the majority of its daughters and sons. Many small towns imagine themselves to be the centre of the universe. Here the belief was the core tenet of a fanatical cult. And, even more unlikely in one so young, she was entirely happy in her job. Nominally a shop assistant in Colm O'Kane's pharmacy, she virtually ran the business while Colm drank and played golf. Not an unusual arrangement in small towns, but Marie seemed to appreciate that her freedom would be difficult to replicate elsewhere.

Hence two rare and priceless gifts: autonomy and the wisdom to value autonomy.

My plan was to leave Ireland as soon as I qualified – impossible to contemplate a career with local accountants – but that was before Marie's intoxicating cocktail of gaiety, mischief and sensuousness. The compromise was a job with a multinational chemical company which had opened a plant on the outskirts of Marie's town but had headquarters in the USA and other plants across Europe. In this way it seemed possible to maintain links with Marie and the equally alluring wide world.

Immediately there was a problem with accommodation. The chemical plant was on the Protestant side of the river and Marie informed me that if I chose to live in this area, as did all the non-local staff, visits from her would be as likely as if I were in company HQ in West Virginia. But the Catholic town on the opposite bank had a low opinion of flats. Only incomplete or broken people could live in an incomplete or broken house; flats were by definition dismal and squalid. On a cold rainy night in October I moved into new quarters which did nothing to challenge this assumption. But, just as I was succumbing to the desolation without and within, Marie arrived with a pink transistor radio and, brushing aside my protestations of physical incompetence, moved the dingy furniture to the dingy walls, kicked off her stilettos, took my limp hand and forced me to gyrate in time with her. Yes, she accomplished the near-impossible: she taught me to jive.

In Manhattan or Rio or Monte Carlo we might have danced the nights away for ever – but in an Irish town in the early sixties perpetual blitheness was not an option. After a year or so the issue of marriage came up. Marie presented it not as incarceration but a daring and ingenious escape plan. For the last daughter left at home with a widowed mother, marriage was the only way out. But to leave home and town at the same time would break the poor widow's heart. Marie was willing to quit both – but only one at a time. I agreed to a contractual amendment postponing escape from the town till well after the marriage. Needless to say, we would not acquire property to burden our fleet limbs. My shabby rented flat would suffice.

Now, from her freshly painted toenails to her washed, conditioned and lacquered hair, Marie was, as always, exquisitely well turned out. Moreover, in the gloom of the hotel lounge her tanned skin assumed a deep tawny glow that should have stirred the blood of any pale Northern keeper of accounts. But instead of the dazzling girl, I saw a torpid fat woman like Marie's mother and sisters. Her town encouraged a terrible reverse metamorphosis: butterflies turned into swollen larvae.

Already the marriage was becoming dull. Already our contract had been broken. My dingy flat had not been good enough after all. Marie had got wind of a new conversion which transcended the prevailing seediness and, with no apparent awareness of inconsistency, immediately signed up for less space at a much higher rent.

Suddenly she threw down her beer mat decisively and turned to me a determined face. 'Let's go back.'

'*Ah?*' Did she not realise that no one can ever go back? 'To where?'

'Back home.' For once, she refused to be irked by my disagreeable tone. 'Back for a good drink with Helen and Neil.' In her face purpose, commitment and enthusiasm blazed.

'But we'd be laughed out of town. No one comes back from a honeymoon early.'

She shrugged elaborately and slowly, lifting both shoulders high and gradually letting them fall back in a movement that gave me a sudden fresh sense of her warm-breathing casual voluptuousness. '*We* can. *Why not?*'

It took a moment to recall that Marie was a strange mixture of conformity and revolt – and that the latter impulse frequently prevailed. If she was prepared to curtail a ritual as sacred and binding as a honeymoon, then any other convention could be as readily flouted. In an instant the shackles of wedlock were broken. Marie was a free spirit after all and the spectre of the sluggish matron faded in the radiance of the mettlesome maid.

Wild-eyed and elated, we rushed at the lobby, where, despite the protection of a sturdy desk, the clerk drew back in alarm.

'We're not waiting.'

He studied each of us in turn to determine if this was a mere ploy. Such a frenzy of departure could never be feigned. 'But your room . . . it's almost ready . . . ' He gestured feebly at the ceiling.

We seized the cases and blundered joyously to the exit. A final look back showed him leaning over the desk with the ashen and nauseated glaze of a man kneed in the groin. Joy of the exultant riposte to the smug! Impossible to resist a *coup de grâce*.

'Thanks a million for the drink.'

Sunlight smote us in the face with Dionysiac force. Hills and sea blindingly glittered. Paganism had recaptured the island from Patrick. Surely the Great God Pan was abroad today in the Twelve Pins.

Marie took the road map. 'I'll navigate.'

How peevish my earlier carping now seemed! 'You don't need to. It's easy on main roads.'

Magnificent oddity – abandoning our honeymoon with the manic zest we should have had on starting out.

Elation subsided a little in the course of a monotonous homeward journey by the unscenic route. Doubts and practical problems arose. What *would* we say if we met someone we knew? And we had eaten nothing since breakfast. Should we stop for a meal and risk arriving too late for a convivial evening – or, even worse, to find that Helen and Neil had gone out? The brilliance of the coup depended entirely on the Quinns being home.

We settled for crisps and chocolate in the car, and our

self-denial was handsomely rewarded when Neil came to the door of his flat and looked from Marie to me and back in gaping incomprehension and terror.

Radiant and resolute, Marie took a step forward into the hallway. 'We're not a pair of ghosts, Neil. Flesh and blood . . . and *gasping for a drink.*'

Helen appeared at a door down the hall. '*You didn't come back early!* How long are you back?'

Marie's momentum swept us all into the flat. 'Just arrived this minute.' And then, to the unspoken but overwhelming question. 'We were bored out of our minds!'

'But those luxury hotels?' Helen regarded Marie for a moment and then turned to me, perhaps expecting me to confirm a suspicion of sexual fiasco.

I made a sceptical face. 'Wacky fun at crazy golf?'

Marie shook her head decisively. 'There was no craic, Helen.'

At last the touching simple truth: we had abandoned honeymoon luxuries in order to be with our friends. Marie adroitly circumvented embarrassing emotionalism. 'And of course the weather was *terrible.*'

Helen laughed gaily. Neil, at first struck dumb by the possibility of disaster and then overcome by evidence of a deep and compelling bond, finally managed to speak, though only in a low obstructed murmur. 'You got a bit of sun somewhere.'

Marie, now comfortably seated with crossed legs, glanced frowningly down at her brown arms, lifted for inspection a brown foot, and was finally obliged to confess: 'I suppose I got a wee bit.'

In a dark armchair, against a drab and dim flat, Marie's skin and light clothes were more lucent and sumptuous than at any time on the honeymoon. She was certainly in dramatic contrast to Helen, a tall thin pale girl in a nondescript turquoise blouse and skirt, wearing no make-up (or none that I could detect) and with anyhow hair that was neither fair nor dark, long nor short, and from an imprecise middle parting fell, at first perfectly straight and then increasingly unstraight, though not in a manner sufficiently defined to be classified as curls or waves. Yet Helen was not without distinction – large blue eyes in a frank countenance (entirely devoid of Catholic cunning, torpor and scorn) gave her a permanent look of eagerness and enthusiasm.

'Neil, get everyone a drink.' Then to Marie and me, with penetrating intuition. 'Have you two had anything to eat yet?' We sketched dismissive gestures vague enough to be themselves dismissed. 'I'll get you something.'

Now our gestures were of protest – but equally vague and as easily dismissed.

Neil distributed glasses of gin, apologising for the lack of choice.

'To the newlyweds!' Helen cried.

We raised our glasses and muttered solemnly in a toast which was nominally to marriage but really to a friendship stronger than tradition.

Very soon after meeting the Quinns it had been apparent that here was the near-impossible dream of compatible couples. All the relationships among the four were good, or at least not bad, though Marie at first dismissed Helen as 'dootsie'. This key adjective summed up women who neglected their hair, did not use make-up and favoured conservative clothing and footwear. In Marie's philosophy, such a combination, or any significant subset of it, was incontrovertible evidence of humourless repression. And initially I too had been inclined to reject Helen as a typical example of the circumscribed bourgeois type I was desperate to avoid. Yet Helen soon turned out to be anything but dull. If anything, the problem was her relentless effulgence – always exhausting for Irish Catholics.

Now she astounded us afresh with impromptu culinary wonders. Actually, cold pie, salad and bread – but what a pie, what a salad, what bread!

'It's just a bit of left-over onion tart,' Helen explained.

But Marie and I had never seen or heard of onion tart. Nor of salad chopped small and tossed in a tangy vinaigrette dressing (our experience was whole tomatoes, lettuce leaves and scallions, the only garnish a bottle of Heinz salad cream). Most amazing of all was the bread which emerged from tinfoil steaming hot, with a crunchy crust and moist succulent pith. Apparently this was garlic bread.

Of course the food was merely the product of resourcefulness and expertise but there was an element of sorcery in the way a delicious meal was conjured so swiftly from virtually nothing – onions, salad and stale bread.

As we ate, Marie revealed the truth of the dispiriting honeymoon.

'*Listen!*' Helen cried. 'Wait till I tell you. *We* went camping . . . or *tried to* . . . on *our* honeymoon. Neil borrowed a tent but of course never got any instructions or bothered to try it out first. The whole thing kept falling down round us.'

'And a great help *you* were,' Neil accused Helen before turning to us. 'She stomped off and said, I'm away to sleep in the car. I spent the night alone in a sleeping bag with a collapsed tent lying on top of me.'

'And *that* was the first night of *our* honeymoon.' Helen regarded her husband in fond amusement. 'First a violent row and then sleeping apart.'

'That's even worse than us.' Marie gazed upon me with equivalent and gratifying tolerance.

Something miraculous seemed to have occurred. The mysterious alchemy of friendship had transmuted the lead of humiliating failure into the gold of anecdote and laughter. This process was entirely beyond comprehension – but obviously alcohol was an essential ingredient.

Now that the gin was finished, Helen, so unjustly accused of dootsiness, was revealed as a votary of Bacchus. After rooting in the kitchen she returned with half a bottle of cooking sherry. Unfortunately this too was swiftly consumed.

'We'll have to go up to Mullen's,' Marie boldly declared.

Neil was excited, then alarmed. 'Someone's bound to see you there.'

'So what! Let them see! Just as long as I can change out of these shorts first.'

I fetched a suitcase from the car and there was an affecting little interlude while Marie changed in the bedroom, the rest of us falling silent, as though in respect for a solemn ceremony. Neil sat with his head vaguely cocked, unconsciously harkening for the rustle and fall of flimsy things.

Mullen's was the watering hole of young professionals – teachers, civil servants, bank staff, nurses. How it had achieved this was a mystery – it looked no different from other establishments – but there was no denying its pre-eminence. For anyone with social standing this was the only bar in town.

As sharply defined as its clientele was its culture. In general, women dressed up (though never revealingly), while men dressed down (greasy trousers, baggy sweaters, anoraks and cracked shoes); and whereas the women were positive and ebullient, the men were cynical and surly. The local concept of virility seemed to require a total absence of enthusiasm.

It was fortunate that the bar was practically empty. For Marie had changed into a low-cut sleeveless dress and Neil was bright-eyed and flushed, bursting with unmasculine animation and excitement. I may well have been unsuitably jocund myself. Certainly, I bought the girls double spirits (large gin for Helen, large vodka for Marie) with a pint and a short each for the boys.

The bar extended over several storeys and, thanks to the current lack of patrons, we were able to appropriate a secluded alcove on a landing. There was a moment of near-sublime harmony in which we knew ourselves to be invested with mysterious grace. Neil bore aloft his pint with the reverence of a priest raising the chalice at the consecration of bread and wine. 'This is the life.' Then, possessed by the Mullen's ethos or some personal demon, his face suddenly clouded. 'But work again on Monday.'

The world which we currently held at bay would soon claim us back. Neil had perhaps most to fear. He taught in St Patrick's, a rough Christian Brothers school, and already his handsome face had the baffled embitterment of those who endure rather than enjoy. Could there be such a thing as congenial employment? Neil spoke with wondering envy of a guy he had once met in London who was paid to smash up furniture. I recalled a girl who worked for a cuttings agency and read newspapers all day.

'Cybernetics.' Neil's tone was suddenly decisive.

'*What?*'

He chose to interpret Marie's hoot as a serious question. 'I'm not sure exactly . . . but I think you just sit in a room and come up with brilliant ideas.'

This was indeed an attractive scenario – all the tedium of work eliminated by attaching electrodes directly to the brain.

Helen piped up. 'I'd like to be a systems analyst in Australia.'

To be a new kind of magus in the new world – a bold dream.

Neil regarded his wife in amazement. 'I thought you were determined to be the first woman bank manager in Ireland?'

Helen ignored this. 'And Marie's the only content one among us! Happy to work with Colm O'Kane.'

'He pays me well and lets me run the shop.' Marie seemed to hesitate, then opted for candour. 'I even do prescriptions now.'

This removed Helen's patronising smile. 'You fill prescriptions . . . that only a qualified pharmacist should do?'

'Colm comes in if it's anything difficult.'

'And when he wants a grope.' I was keen to repeat the pleasure of seeing smug Helen shocked.

Instead, Neil was shocked. He stared long and hard at Marie

– and eventually seemed to decide that the allegation was true. 'You actually let him touch you . . . *that wee baldy bastard?*'

'Aw now.' Marie gave the rest of us a mischievous look. 'There's quare goings-on in the back dispensary.'

Helen laughed – but Neil's white face obliged Marie to make excuses.

'Colm's very unhappy. And I can't say I blame him. His wife's an absolute bitch. And he's always been very good to me.'

Neil's outrage was untempered. 'It'll have to stop now you're a married woman.'

Marie, tolerant so far, shrieked at this sudden invocation of matrimonial duty. What had attracted us to the Quinns was their avoidance of the prescriptive and coercive effects of wedlock. They appeared to have discovered an exciting way to subvert marriage – conduct an illicit affair with your spouse. Where the norm was for couples to become joyless business associates, Helen and Neil exulted in the sexual delirium of adulterers and startled us with shameless accounts of frequent, enthusiastic and multiform intercourse. This example had undoubtedly been a factor in convincing us that we too could marry and live.

Neil's naked turbulence was impossibly tempting. Leaning intimately towards him, I murmured, with a show of concern, 'He only squeezes her wobblies,' then glanced swiftly sideways at Helen, who threw back her head in a gratifying laugh.

Marie was happy to prolong the torture. 'And only through me shop coat.'

Neil blundered to his feet, shaking the table, and made off downstairs.

There was a contrite and awkward silence.

'You shouldn't have mentioned that,' Marie accused me.

Helen made a blithe dismissive gesture. 'Neil gets too worked up about everything. Don't worry about it. He's probably only gone for cigarettes.'

For cigarettes and alcohol. He returned with a packed tray which trembled and tinkled like the duty-free shop on a continental car ferry.

As soon as the double round was distributed he turned to Marie with a troubled and penitent expression. 'I'm really sorry, honey.' Lifting her right hand, he enclosed it gently between his own. 'I've no right to tell you your business.'

Marie regarded him with affectionate amusement. 'That's OK, Neil.'

'No ... but I've ruined the whole evening now.' Emotion seemed about to overwhelm him again. He lifted one hand in a hopeless gesture, as though at some scene of frightful carnage, then replaced it on top of Marie's hand which he squeezed in tender but desperate entreaty. 'And such a lovely evening too. It was *great* to see you back ... just great to see you back so soon.'

Marie herself was now too moved to speak.

Someone had to say something. I turned briskly to Helen. 'So ... systems analysis in Australia or bank managing here?'

My ironic expression made it clear that the question was merely the vehicle for an intriguing subtext. Helen enjoyed a slow draught of gin, then turned untroubled eyes full upon me and gave a slow shrug freighted with a complexity as rich as anything expressible in words.

Among its manifold meanings was certainly the suggestion that everything was possible and choice an outdated and unnecessary restriction. Were we not in public but also in private, employed but also independent, bound in wedlock but untrammelled and free?

2

The Quinns' first late-evening visit was an exhilarating surprise, a sudden dramatic galvanising of the torpid time before bed, Neil commanding centre stage to declaim, with passionate sincerity: 'This fucking town is the fucking arsehole of the universe.'

'My husband's language' – Helen spoke precisely and slowly, as if to compensate for Neil's intemperate coarseness – 'is just . . . *choice*.'

Neil flung himself onto the sofa and fumbled desperately for cigarettes.

'A hard day at the office?' I softly suggested.

Removing the unlit cigarette from his mouth, he came forward abruptly. 'This fucker in 4E spat on me yesterday when my back was turned. A big gob of phlegm down the back of my trousers. So I grab him by the shoulder and march him to Brother Claud's office. Business as usual in St Pat's. But this morning I saw him and his da coming out of Claud's office . . . and the two of them smirking all over their faces.

So I went in to Claud and demanded to know what had happened. Apparently they claimed I tore the seam of the jacket and . . . *wait till you hear this* . . . Claud gave them twenty quid. *Twenty quid!* No money for books – but he gives *them* twenty quid. As it happens, I know the da too. A chancer from Katanga.'

'*What?*' I have always been a bit slow on the uptake at night. '*Katanga?* You mean the father is *black?*'

Neil stared at me blankly. Marie and Helen simultaneously laughed.

'Katanga's a council estate,' Marie explained. 'These two new estates were built during that trouble in Africa and they're known locally as Katanga and the Congo.'

Neil continued as though there had been no interruption. 'I said to Claud, So this is the way of it now, there's a twenty-pound reward for anyone who spits on your staff. *He* suggested I come back when I'd calmed down. *I* suggested he pay for dry-cleaning my trousers. The bastard refused – so I stormed out.' Neil paused to replace his cigarette, light up and treat himself to a long appeasing inhalation.

'*Did* you tear the jacket?' Marie asked.

'I don't know . . . and to tell you the truth I don't fucking care. That's not the point. The point is that Claud is a useless fucker. A principal has to support his staff.'

'So,' Helen said drily, looking from Marie to me. 'You can see why Neil is still on Scale One.'

Inhaling savagely, Neil stared without affection at his spouse.

Marie brightly suggested the universal palliative. 'I'm sure yees wouldn't say no to a wee cup of tea.'

Neil fell back in a more relaxed and ruminative mood. 'Phlegm is one thing that turns my stomach. *Greeners*, they're known as in St Pat's.' He shuddered a little. 'The ultimate victory is to land a big greener on someone. *Greasing*, they call that.'

'What a charming accomplishment.' Even Helen was taken aback. There was silence while Neil smoked in reflective bafflement.

'We're keeping you out of bed,' Helen suddenly said to me. 'Neil would sit up to the clouds of the night . . . and he thinks everyone else is the same.'

'No no no no . . . not at all.'

This was a remarkably convincing denial from one who was just beginning to wonder how long Neil would stay. My American masters had decided to build a second plant and I was assigned to the planning group. The project leader was a beefy Protestant from Culladuff but he had been to the US headquarters to train and, like so many of the born-again, had developed a zeal even more fanatical than that of the original hierophants. Above a Bri-nylon shirt of dazzling whiteness his eyes blazed with visionary fervour as they anticipated creating the temple of a second synthetic fibre facility (this was a time of strange new pagan gods – Orlon, Vincel, Vyrene, Crimplene, Terylene and Courtelle). Behind his head as he expounded his dream was an icon he had brought back from the States, a framed print of a magically snow-silvered tree with the inspirational message: Snowflakes are among the most delicate and fragile things in Nature – but just look at what they're capable of achieving when they co-operate with each other.

The fragile snowflakes of the planning team were required to assemble at 8 a.m. and co-operate all day. Is it possible to glitter on inadequate sleep? Such negative thoughts were dispelled by Marie's dramatic entry with a tray of tea things and a leaning tower of toasted sliced pan. This extravagance was both an expression of gratitude for the visit and an attempt to alleviate Neil's despair. And certainly his sore-vexed heart was touched.

'*Honey*,' he murmured, 'you shouldn't have gone to such bother.'

It really was no bother. Late nights did not trouble Marie, who walked to work for nine thirty and had no superior to face since she opened the pharmacy herself. Nor did she share the bourgeois achiever's need to be tucked in at a sensible hour.

Two days after the late arrival of the Quinns she proposed a return suppertime visit. After all, their flat was not that far away. This time it was Neil who was vouchsafed unexpected rapture, in reward for which he made not merely toast but grilled bacon on toast. On the Monday evening of the following week the Quinns turned up at ten twenty, unannounced and unabashed. Marie flashed me a significant and unequivocal look. Although far from enchanted, I made grilled sausages on toast with a dollop of piccalilli on the side and even added a sweet course of Tartan shortbread.

Soon there was a late visit on all but the drinking nights and the supper snacks continued to grow in both sophistication and size. The baroque splendour of those three-course late-evening collations! First came a hot savoury (usually grilled meat on toast, though Helen astounded us with mushroom vol-au-vents and Marie contributed to variety by introducing sausage rolls); then something baked (wheaten bread, baps, farls or scones – Helen once again impressed us by baking her own bread and scones); and finally a dessert of biscuits or sweet buns (the Quinns often served Tunnock's Traditional Tea Cakes, chocolate-covered marshmallows individually wrapped in silver paper, but Marie preferred biscuits and, as well as old favourites like chocolate wholemeal, experimented with novelties like Jacob's Golf and Abbey Crunch). On every course we were effortlessly (but tactfully) outclassed by the Quinns – even (no, *especially*) on dessert. It was a great night when Helen's home-baked almond slices first appeared.

Some of the socialising was instigated by me. My black time is not late at night but late on Sunday afternoon. Worst of all, the chill and foreboding of Sunday afternoons in autumn which whisper of perishing radiance and splendour and the inexorable encroachment of darkness and cold. On one such afternoon there arose before me the spectre of the project leader, monstrously immaculate in Bri-nylon, a contemporary leviathan with teeth exposed to smile rather than devour but all the more frightening for that. Marie's advice on existential dread was to stay put and wriggle down deeper in the burrow. I could understand the wisdom of this but was possessed by an overpowering urge to flee. And so, in great uncertainty and trepidation, we ventured forth in the ashen twilight of extinguished possibility and hope.

The Quinns lived near the centre of town in a side street which led off a main thoroughfare but ended in the grim bulk of the Protestant cathedral. Perhaps Catholics shunned it for this reason. Certainly the street was mostly silent and deserted. Even the businesses at the commercial end had a moribund air – an ancient, elegant but unused man's umbrella shop (although this was one of the wettest towns on the planet, the local culture forbade men any protection other than a turned-up jacket collar) and a cramped disorderly philatelist's frequented by pasty-faced obsessives whom Marie dismissed, with a shudder, as child molestors or panty thieves. The cathedral end of the street became a Victorian terrace of tall dilapidated houses subdivided into apartments rented by the town's tiny population of unaffiliated marginal people. Here the Quinns had a ground-floor flat with black iron bars on the windows. Inside were high-ceilinged rooms with elaborate cornices and mouldings and, below these, a frieze of old damp stains, which, like the masterworks of modern art, provided unlimited possibilities for study, analysis and interpretation.

The two main rooms were appropriately decorated with dark discoloured wallpaper and furnished with ancient pieces too broken-down to be valued as antique. Yet, as reassuring as the decrepitude of the street was the sempiternal gloom indoors. Where a bright modern home would have exhorted and accused, here the faded opulence and dimness provided a sanctuary from the synthetic future. And a further balm was the gentle breathing of a gas fire. But, best of all, the smiles of Helen and Neil on the battered old sofa which bore their only contribution to decor – an abstract expressionist splatter of come stains. Neil had informed us that, when Helen came home from the bank, he was often overcome by desire and possessed her immediately on the sofa. How better to forget work than in the vertigo of divine frenzy and what better insult to furniture than joyously soiling it with life?

Neil rose and, with a mock grandiloquent gesture, offered us the freedom of his sofa and home. 'Welcome to Come-Stain Hotel.'

Adopting a suspicious frown, I took an armchair instead. 'Some of those stains might still be damp.'

Helen laughed in delight, though more at her own sexual audacity than my feeble joke. 'Last Thursday teatime. Should be well dry by now.'

Marie took the other armchair with a sigh. 'I don't know where you find the energy after work.'

Neil leaned across to me with a grave mentor's mien. 'It's every man's duty to corrupt his wife.'

Helen threw back her head in a high satisfied laugh.

Could there have been any better antidote to the creeping horror of Sunday in autumn?

But Sunday was not to be so easily vanquished. Always a formidable foe, it fought back by launching upon us Helen's sister Celia with her husband Lexie and two children. All were in full Sunday regalia but, whereas Lexie seemed ill at ease in his grey suit, Celia was thoroughly at home in a nubbly tweed two-piece over a beige blouse with a long-tailed bow tied at the neck. The girl, of four or so, had a dress with a lace collar, white ankle socks and black patent shoes, and her younger brother a short-trousered brown suit. Neil and Helen moved to hard chairs, leaving the sofa to the family.

Celia rested a hand on the sofa arm, only to withdraw with a

cry from a spring that had almost burst through the uphol-
stery. 'Glory be to God, Helen, how do you stick this place?'
She looked round, renewing an old and unassuaged wonder,
pausing for a collusive grin at Marie and me. 'It's like the black
hole o' Calcutta in here.' Now she laughed heartily. 'Ah'd
have to be worked with after a week in this place. Ah'd end
up in Gransha, so Ah would.' A sudden shiver possessed her.
'And draughty too. Aren't you foundered with cold?'

As the object of Celia's cheerful gaze, Marie felt obliged to
respond. 'Where do *you* live?'

'Oakfield Park.' Already the established camaraderie of
long-time, close and forthright friends. 'Out the Strand Road,
past the industrial estate.'

Celia was clearly the type who advocates a blunt candour
but fails to explain (or perhaps even realise) that it operates in
only one direction. To express for her Oakfield Park semi a
contempt and revulsion equivalent to hers for this flat would
surely provoke her to outrage and Lexie to enquire, with a
countenance of thunder, if you wanted your melt knocked in.

'Helen, I had to call round to give you the craic about the
wedding.'

Our hostess uttered a sharp cry. '*Una Casey was married yesterday.* I completely forgot.'

'Och it was brilliant, Helen.' As though she had exchanged
her tweed suit for a favourite old cardie, Celia settled back with
a sigh of contentment. It was obvious that we were in for a
lengthy account.

Lexie produced a packet of twenty Rothman's, held it up
for all to see and raised his eyebrows at each of us in turn. Neil
and Marie nodded and were casually but accurately tossed
cigarettes. Neil rose and went round with a lighter.

'It was Father McWilliams and he was the best laugh,' Celia
was saying. 'They're going to Majorca for two weeks for the
honeymoon, so he told this story about another couple he
knew that went there for a fortnight. They had a great time

for a week but then the funds began to get low. So they decided to eat this local dish ... some sort of cheap thing with mushrooms and milk. But when they went into this wee café hadn't they forgotten the name of the dish. And of course the waiter spoke no English. So the husband has a brainwave ... gets out a pen and draws a mushroom and a cow. The waiter nods and off he goes. Fifteen minutes go by. Half an hour. The two of them sitting there famished, stomachs thinking their throats have been cut. Finally the waiter turns up all apologies ... and what does he hand them?' Almost overcome by laughter and anxious not to spoil the punch line, Celia turned to her husband for assistance. 'Lexie, what's this it was that he brought them?'

Obviously an adept of silent strength, Lexie frowned in dark annoyance and was forced to exhale prematurely. 'A parasol and two tickets for a bullfight.'

Celia clapped her hands in rapture. 'Father Harry's great value. He's real with-it. He's real mod. What's this he said about marriage, Lexie?'

Without looking at his wife or indeed at any of us, Lexie leaned forward to flick his ash into an ashtray on a glass coffee table, an incongrously modern item among the ponderous old pieces (later we learned that it had been a wedding present from Celia). Then he paused to study his cigarette, and when he finally spoke it was in the curtest and most grudging of tones. 'He said, A lot of people are putting in oil-fired central heating these days ... but marriage is still the best central heating of all.'

Celia cried out in renewed admiration. 'And the best man was great craic too. You should have heard him about the groom.' Apparently oblivious to her husband's reluctance, she turned to him once again. 'What did he say about Liam Boyle?'

For a long time it seemed as though Lexie would fail to reply – or indeed respond in any way. He was rigid and still as the bust of a Caesar. Only when the silence was becoming unbearable did he finally relent. 'He said, Liam's very frank and earnest with the girls ... when he's in Portstewart he's Frank and when he's in Letterkenny he's Ernest.'

We all laughed again, though less heartily than before. The reserves of goodwill were large but finite. Even the obedient children were becoming restless. The girl shifted against the boy, who lunged petulantly back. Placing the cigarette carefully in his mouth, Lexie leaned across his wife and daughter, slammed a heavy hand on his son's bare thigh and, in an action more eloquent than words, lifted and held an index finger close to the young delinquent's face.

Helen leaned forward confidingly to the children. 'Were you two at the wedding?' Diffidently they shook their heads. '*What?* You mean, you never got any of that lovely food?'

'Sure you couldn't take them to a wedding at that age,' Celia came in. 'Though Concepta Timoney did bring a wee one with her. But what was he not like anyway? Wasn't he as through-goin', Lexie?' The look on her husband's face convinced even Celia that his co-operation had been exhausted. 'Oh he was *desperate altogether*. If he was mine I'd have *battered* him.'

Helen, vibrantly empathic, continued to smile on the children. 'I'm sure *you two* would never be badly behaved. And I have just the thing for you.'

Brightly she jumped to her feet and went into the kitchen, returning with a tin of Tunnock's tea cakes and kneeling in front of the children to whip off the lid in a splendid *coup de théâtre* which revealed a profusion of glittering hemispheres like a colony of geodesic domes.

'They'll have their clothes destroyed with chocolate,' Celia complained.

'No they won't.' Helen leaned close to the children in complicitous intimacy. '*Sure you won't?*'

Suddenly Celia came forward urgently to lay a hand on

her sister's arm. 'But wait till I tell you the best of it, Helen. Talking about little ones . . .' She paused to glance at her own children.

Helen was instantly and brilliantly perceptive. 'Now before you open your tea cakes there's something else you can have. You can both go out to the kitchen and take a piece of fruit from the bowl. And eat everything at the kitchen table so as not to stain your good clothes.'

Celia waited till the door closed behind them. 'Una Casey's *that way*.'

'What?' Helen's acuity deserted her – but only for a moment. 'She's not . . .?'

Celia nodded. 'It was a question of *have to*.'

'*No!*'

Finding Celia's grim countenance without hope, Helen turned so desperately to Lexie that even this stern devotee of the taciturn was obliged to respond, albeit laconically. 'Shotgun job.'

'But *Una Casey?*' Sorrowfully Helen rose to her feet and turned to explain to us her shock. 'Una lived just down the road from us. She'd be a daughter of Doctor Casey's . . . you know Doctor Casey? And she was in Celia's class at the convent. Mind you, I wondered why she was marrying one of the Boyles. They're not . . . you know . . . But if you knew Una you would think she was just the *last one* . . . the *last* one to *ever* . . .' Renewed disbelief caused her to trail off in mid-sentence.

Celia, her face a turbid storm cloud, glanced instinctively towards the kitchen, as if even there her daughter was imperilled by the rampant depravity of the age. Then she turned back to the room. 'Sure it's love on the doorstep nowadays.'

We hung our heads in silence, appalled by a future in which the mighty pilasters of tradition, so long our unshakable support, would soon be eaten away to collapse and lie about us in rubble.

The visit never recovered its initial animation, not even when Neil brought the adults tea and scones and tea cakes. As we set aside our cups I flashed a significant look at Marie and she made as if to rise and go. Neil, who was collecting dirty crockery, turned his back to the sofa and, with a grimace of desperate entreaty, nodded her back into her seat. Eventually the others had to leave, though clearly askance at the impropriety of strangers outstaying kin. Marie and I stood up to see them off and the commotion at the flat door seemed to restore Celia's earlier high spirits.

'Did I tell you the craic about Gerry Brady, Helen? The photographer at the wedding? Oh he was desperate. Took over the whole thing, bossed everybody all day. But anyway when we were driving from the church to the hotel he takes a notion of doing a group portrait on this wee hill . . . you know, just past the old slob road before you come to the new bridge . . . gets out into the middle of the road like a B-man and starts stopping cars and ordering everybody up this hill. And, like . . . *elderly* people . . . most of the women in high heels. But nothing will do Gerry only get us all up this hill. Though, right enough, it was a lovely day and a gorgeous spot . . .'

Celia's unhurried progress recalled my mother's protracted leave-taking from relatives – the interminable series of lingerings, first at the sitting-room door, then at the front door and, last but longest of all, at the front gate (the agony in the garden).

'So anyway, Gerry takes the snap . . . I'm sure it'll turn out lovely . . . and when we're going back down Mrs Casey stops and shouts out of her, Where's Mrs Boyle? Where's Mrs Boyle? God of Heaven, we've missed Mrs Boyle. I was behind her and she grabs me by the arm' – Celia seized Helen to demonstrate the intensity of the grip – 'Jesus Mary and Joseph, Celia, she'll think I left her out on purpose.'

As the departure moved to its final stage at the front door of the house Marie and I retreated to allow the sisters a private moment of valediction, though Celia appeared to have no need of intimacy. We could hear her clearly from inside. 'See you during the week, Helen ... DV ... ,' she shouted, '*and if I don't see you through the week I'll see you through the window.*'

Helen came back behind Neil and took up a stance in the centre of the room. 'Celia,' she began with a decisive finality that failed to live up to its promise, 'is just ... *just* ...' And she waved her arms in a wild but ambiguous arc.

Neil took Marie's hands and fervently squeezed them between his own. 'Thanks for staying. Thanks for staying.'

This recalled Helen to her duty as hostess. 'Oh I'm sorry to you two for having to put up with that gang. I'm sure that's the *last* thing you were looking for on a Sunday.' Together the guests made extravagantly dissenting noises and gestures. '*You'll stay for something to eat.*'

Having begun at such a high level, it was difficult to intensify the pantomime of refusal. Nevertheless we succeeded somehow. Not that there was any objection to eating with the Quinns. The problem was having to reciprocate later. Marie and I had lamentably primitive skills; we could do little else but grill chops and boil spuds.

Our vehement protests were in vain.

'You're eating here,' Neil commanded, uplifting a palm to still the tumult. 'And I don't want to hear another word.'

'I'm sure you're both *starving* at this hour,' said Helen.

Marie hesitated, then opted for full and frank disclosure. 'Actually, Ah could eat a scabby wean.'

Exactly the right tone. The happy Quinns looked to me. It was necessary to be equally forthright and colourful, never easy for accountants.

'I could eat two men and a wee boy,' I said.

Marie interrupted the joyous laughter. 'But we'll give you a hand.'

How wise to reduce our obligation by making the cooking a communal effort! Helen explained that she was making chop suey (a *Chinese* meal – Marie and I exchanged a look of renewed inadequacy and terror) and that we could help by chopping vegetables.

In the kitchen Neil opened a cupboard and produced a bottle of gin. 'But there's no tonic or bitter lemon, Helen. Could we drink it with water?'

Helen frowned – but almost immediately strode to another cupboard and returned flourishing a bright plastic lemon. 'A bit of lemon juice and ice and it'll be grand.'

The authority, resourcefulness and certitude of this woman! She was not merely a votary but a high priestess of Bacchus. An inspiration to all who served her. Certainly her team was exemplary in its selfless acceptance of menial tasks and harmonious sharing of scarce resources. Any project leader would have been proud of us. It takes a team to make the dream.

'So,' Marie commenced, after a period of quiet industry, 'is Celia much older than you?'

Helen had to put down a saucepan and lean, spluttering helplessly, over the sink.

Neil explained. 'Celia is four years younger. Helen is twenty-eight and Celia's twenty-four.'

It was hard to know which fact to marvel at first – that the heavy matron was still in her twenties or that the slim girl laughing over the sink was actually a woman nearing thirty. Work was suspended while we pondered these conundrums.

'Celia is *twenty-four*,' Marie repeated at last in a wondering trance. 'Only a *year* older than me.' Sheer astonishment pushed her over the bounds of propriety. 'But she's as *dootsie*, Helen.'

Instead of taking offence, Helen fell over the sink in a fresh paroxysm of laughter. Beaming with pride at his wife's youthfulness and tolerance, her reversal of the local norm by retaining a narrow waist and broad mind, Neil moved around happily splashing gin into glasses.

Over the meal Helen attempted to explain the anomalies. 'I was always Daddy's favourite because I was good at school.

Celia failed the eleven-plus ... had to be paid for at the convent. And she couldn't get into the bank or the civil service. So I think she decided to become as different from me as possible ... in other words, a housewife and mother.'

'But why weren't *you* a *housewife* and *mother* first?'

'Helen's a career woman,' Neil came in. 'Doesn't want children or a house because of her great future in the bank. Wants to be free to move around. And this is a *Protestant* bank. Good luck to her wit.'

'I'm half Protestant,' Helen protested. 'I may have been brought up a Catholic, but Daddy was Protestant. And I've kept my maiden name in work ... Helen Boyd has a good Protestant ring to it. Anyway, all that religious carry-on is dying out now. And a woman would have no chance at all in a Free State bank.'

Marie was still having difficulty with the concept of *home-cooked* Chinese food. 'This is *absolutely gorgeous*,' she breathed in awe.

Helen summarised the recipe and promised to write it down later. Marie listened – solemn, respectful, submissive.

Suddenly reaching down under the table, Neil squeezed Marie's knee. She drew back with a startled cry. Neil leaned further down. Marie pulled away from the table in alarm. Straightening up, Neil tossed onto the table a large red eating apple from which a single bite had been taken.

'*Children*,' Helen softly chuckled.

Neil leaned into Marie who recoiled slightly, resentful and suspicious. 'What you need is a few children. Remember Mrs Plummer from Sutherland Terrace? Used to always be in Beesie Fox's shop? You must know her ... a big fat loud-mouthed stupid midden. She had this line she was always coming out with in Beesie's – Patsy never gave me any more bother after me fourth.'

Helen issued a laugh, abrupt and surprisingly deep, that tailed off into a series of half-suppressed snorts. It was suddenly obvious that she and Neil were quite drunk – but it took a moment to apply the equally obvious corollary. The condition had to be universal. We were all four drunk.

Neil grabbed the gin bottle. 'Let's go back into the living room.'

It was time to go home – but the dim rundown living room was encompassingly seductive. As caressingly as a lover, the gas fire suspired. Easeful shadows offered balm for the afflicted spirit, and commodious armchairs provided support and rest for the weary bones. Helen extinguished the main light and switched on a tall standing lamp with a scallop-edged shade of pleated beige and maroon velvet trim. Circumambient dark cradled a soft core of light. At its heart Helen kicked off her shoes and climbed onto the sofa, tucking up her legs and leaning an elbow on Neil's shoulder.

We sipped gin in ruminant silence, entranced by the breathing plaque of fire and the lamp with its endearingly dilapidated shade – several pleats were undone and the mouldy velvet trim was hanging loose in two places.

Here was the healing peace many seek but few find. Each of us was in touch with the deep still self beneath the fretfulness of daily life.

'Monday's my worst fucking day.' Neil was first to break the spell.

Helen punched him with fond lightness. '*Neil.*'

'Not only have I two fourth-year classes . . . fourth years are always the worst . . . but I'm giving up a free period to cover Tommy Peoples. Cover him so he can go and screw this woman in the Congo.'

Helen rolled her eyes at us. 'This is the way with Neil. Can't say no to anyone. But then complains about it to me. Why didn't you tell this character Monday's your worst day?'

'He needs a free period after lunch to give him enough time. Has a wife and children of his own of course . . . so it has to be during the day. He kept on and on at me. What could I do?

The male organ must be satisfied, that's Tommy's motto.'

Helen turned on us a wondering expression. 'My husband knows ... the *most charming people* ... has the *most charming friends.*'

'Tommy has genuine claims to distinction.'

'Such as?'

'He says he's the only man in Northern Ireland to ride a woman with his nose.'

Helen gave everyone an emphatic QED look.

Undeterred, Neil concentrated frowningly. 'The man's completely horn mad. He's screwing at least two women regularly and still he's going wild about a student on teaching practice at the moment. An art student ... only eighteen or nineteen ... wears these mad-coloured blouses and short skirts. If she leaves any stuff on the staffroom table Tommy pushes it back against the wall so she has to lean over for it. Needless to say, he's in a seat opposite the table.'

'And you too?' suggested Marie with a sharpness that caused Neil to break off and frown into his drink.

'It's not as if Neil's *deprived*,' Helen said. 'He gets it every night of the week.'

'*Every night?*'

'Every night.' Helen shook her head, though not without a touch of pride at such unremitting homage. She took hold of Neil's ear lobe and playfully wagged it. 'So there's no need to be looking up young girls' skirts.'

Neil turned to her a perplexed countenance and Helen placed upon his lips a tender kiss. He considered her for a moment – and then moved for a second benison, which Helen willingly bestowed. This one was longer and deeper. Again he perused – and again moved for more, his increased pressure forcing Helen to lean back across the sofa. When her angle to the vertical grew too great she turned her head aside: '*Neil.*' Gently he cupped her face and returned it to his, sealing her lips with his own and pushing her all the way back till her head was resting on the sofa arm (luckily not on the side where a spring had almost come through). Helen seemed prepared to suffer this ardent embrace but when he slipped his hand between her thighs she snorted, lunged violently, and made three fierce but unsuccessful attempts at reversal – to push away his hand, pull down her rucked skirt and remove his imprisoning bulk from her chest. Instead of desisting, Neil firmly took hold of her tights-covered genitals.

'Neil . . . for Christ's sake . . .'

His only response was an urgent gurgle. And now he manoeuvred his body between her legs.

As a station platform trembles at the approach of a train, I experienced a disturbing tremor of imminence, an exaltation tinged with fear. For the forthcoming penetration was dual: not only was Neil about to enter Helen, something new and momentous was about to enter our lives.

Did Marie appreciate the solemnity of the occasion? Her face was contorting in some sort of furious signal. It appeared that she wished me to *act* instead of humbly bearing witness. Did she expect me to break their clinch like a referee at a boxing match? No, she was nodding at a point to the side of the sofa. The lamp – she wanted me to switch it off. Surely better to illuminate fully this extraordinary scene. We accountants like to see transactions clearly. Nevertheless, I fulfilled her wish – and immediately understood its wisdom. Reduced light appeared to reconcile Helen – or at least to lessen her agitation – and made the room vaulted and holy. All that could be heard was the fire's accepting susurrus, its yellow-streaked red burning as steadily as a votive light. Everything was shadowed, softened, blurred. Emboldened by the complicitous breathing dark, Neil reached under Helen's skirt with both hands and, in a single fluid movement, drew down her tights and pants. Helen lifted a leg – long and lucently white – to permit Neil to remove the entanglement from her foot. Kneeling between her parted legs, Neil undid his belt.

Not only admitted to the inner sanctum of the temple, itself a rare privilege, we were now about to witness the secret love rite of the High Priestess. Motionless silent awe was the only appropriate posture.

So why was Marie fidgeting and whispering with maddening insistence? It appeared that she wanted me to do something else. Rising from her seat, she nodded down at the floor. She wanted me to join her there – though not from passion, that was clear. This was an exercise in manners. She wished to put the Quinns at ease.

No sooner had we broken free of convention and crossed the threshold of the unknown, no sooner had we attempted to pass beyond, than etiquette had immediately reappeared and made us its creature once again.

3

'Barry Hinds here.'
The name was uttered with tremendous familiarity and confidence, as if, even over the phone, it would surely provide encouragement or solace. It was indeed one of those resonant, *inevitable* names which insist upon universal recognition. But, after being called out of an important meeting, I was able to resist its claim. '*Who?*'

'Listen, you don't know me from Adam . . . but *I* know *you*. And I know about a deal that should interest you.'

Some words should be handled only with tongs and even then at arm's length. '*Deal?*'

'I work for T.J. McCormack . . . the accountant. This is to do with an opportunity in accountancy.'

T.J. was the town's leading Catholic accountant – and widely believed to be a crook.

'I don't want anything to do with Mr McCormack.'

'It's nothing to do with T.J.'

'Then what *is it* to do with?'

'I can't say over the phone. Can I meet you after work in the White Horse Lodge?'

This was a new hotel close to the chemical plant, which used it to accommodate illustrious visitors.

'What about Mullen's instead?'

'I don't want to discuss this in Mullen's.'

Even accountants can be seduced by mystery. And anyone can be seduced by the tribute of being chosen.

The White Horse foyer was a split-level open-plan area with white hacienda-style arches and, distributed casually at wide intervals, oyster-grey leather sofas and armchairs of astonishing commodiousness and luxury. From one of these a man arose to turn on me the luminescence of a salesperson desperate to meet targets. Youngish, probably in his late twenties, he obeyed the letter of the accountancy dress code while flouting its spirit in every way. The suit was grey but of shiny light-weight mohair, the shirt white but with a tiny collar whose wings were drawn together by a gold bar passing underneath the tiny knot of a tie which was plain navy blue but uncon-ventionally slim. Even his extremities were deviant – the shoes of black leather but slip-ons with a silver buckle at the side, his black hair irreproachably short but swept straight back and built up in the style of fifties pop culture. Finally, his plumpness and pampered sheen were affronts to the austerity of the profession.

Taking my right hand firmly in his, he guided me solici-tously with his left towards a leather armchair. Between us was a coffee table with a half-full spirit glass, a twenty pack of International Dunhill and an enormous ashtray supporting a burning kingsize cigarette.

'This'll be worth your while.' Barry sat down, taking up the cigarette with his left hand for a sharp pull and with his right offering the packet which I brusquely waved away. 'This is the chance of a lifetime. Believe me.' He was striving to appear casual but radiated restless excitement. Taking a swift gulp from his glass, he imperiously summoned (not merely raising an arm but impatiently snapping his fingers) a waistcoated youth with an Irish face and contemporary hair but the time-less manner of international vassalage – attentive, respectful, grave, subdued. 'Another vodka and white . . . *and* . . . ?'

The craving for liquor was overwhelming – but it was more astute to play the ascetic accountant. 'Coffee.'

'No bad habits, eh?' His broad grin vanished when he turned back to the waiter and repeated in a sharp tone: 'Coffee.'

As soon as the youth was out of earshot Barry came forward in sudden intimate eagerness. 'It's Dominic Dunbar,' immediately glancing about in apprehension to check if anyone had overheard. Security appeared to be an overriding obsession. It was probably fortunate that the town had no zoo or we would have had to meet at the monkey house like characters in an espionage film. Leaning across to lay a hand on my arm, he looked earnestly into my eyes. 'Now this is between you and me and the wall.'

The offer, when it finally emerged, long after our drinks had arrived, was of a half share in Dominic Dunbar's accountancy firm. As yet no one in the town knew of Dominic's wish to sell up and emigrate to Australia. Barry was an old friend of Dominic's, his preferred successor, and could raise much of the asking price. The only snag was that Barry had yet to pass his accountancy exams. He needed a fully qualified partner but for various compelling reasons could not consider local talent. An out-of-town accountant was needed and reliable sources had pronounced me competent, affable, discreet and tired of 'all that desperate company shite the Yanks love to hear'.

'If the business is doing so well why does Dominic want out?'

'Woman trouble. Dominic's a wild man for the weemen.' Barry seemed to ponder the ethics of disclosure, drawing deeply on his kingsize for counsel. The decision to testify was so sudden that he had to expel smoke into his own eyes and grimace even as he chuckled. 'Listen ... Dominic'd get up on anything that moved. He's rid most of the married women in this town at one time or another. Probably all of the good-lookin' ones. But, like, he's not too careful at the best of times ... and he's a wild case altogether when he has a couple of drinks in him.' Barry paused for a drink himself and shook his head in helpless admiration. 'The worst carry-on was with Jean Coll ... Ernie Coll's wife ... you know, Ernie Coll the bookie? Jean's a good-lookin' woman and Dominic was buckin' the arse off her for six months ... that's a long time for him. But this night they were ridin' away in the back of Dominic's car ... both of them full of course ... and they fell asleep afterwards and lay there bollock naked till morning. If he'd at least had the sense to park somewhere quiet – but they were out in the street just round the corner from Coll's and they were seen by children on their way to school. Dominic says he nearly shit himself ... first thing he seen was all these weans lookin' in at him and laughin'. Thought he'd died and gone to Limbo or some fuckin' thing.' As though witnessing the scene himself, Barry laughed and threw back the rest of his drink. 'Another coffee?'

'I'm all right.'

'Naturally this was taken a dim view of. Didn't go down well at all. Least of all with Ernie Coll. And Ernie has backings ... *ye know?* He's a bookie. Anyway that was a few months ago and now Dominic's met this young virgin ... from Galway or somewhere ... and wants to get married and settle down. Says it's time anyway, he's had a good enough innings. And fuck *me*, so he has ... *eh?*'

Barry paused briefly to appeal for amused agreement. I concentrated on replacing the empty coffee cup in its saucer. Apparently unaware of equivocation, he continued as happily as before. 'But he doesn't think he'll get peace in this town. Doesn't want his girl to hear the stories ... or possibly even get attacked. There's a lot of angry women around.'

For the first time he studied me anxiously, concerned that his enthusiastic indiscretion was not eliciting an appropriate response. As though blaming the Dunhill for offering ill-advised encouragement, he suddenly crushed it out in the ashtray with vicious disgust.

'I'll have to think about it.' In fact, one look at Barry had sufficed but I had no intention of providing even the satisfaction of a clear refusal. Perhaps my seigneurial detachment was overplayed. 'I'll make a few enquiries ... discreetly of course.'

'It's only cheap because Dominic wants a quick deal.' In Barry's face was the resentment and anger of those who have just realised the naivety of opening their hearts to a cold fish. 'There's plenty of accountants who'd snap it up.'

His peevishness did not encourage warmth. I shrugged, displaying upturned and open palms in maddening equanimity and indifference.

'Well, tell Marie I was asking for her.' No doubt this removed my superior look. 'She still in Colm O'Kane's shop?'

In small towns where everything is common knowledge the high and mighty may be swiftly brought to earth.

Fortunately Marie knew Barry only as a customer at a time when he lived near the shop. As well as being a hypochondriac obsessed with prescription drugs, he had realised that presentation was the key to modern life and (remarkable in a town enamoured of its own fetid miasmas) took a keen interest in breath fresheners, deodorants, aftershaves and *eaux de toilette*. So vivid was the memory that Marie could do an impression of Barry applying aftershave – the liquid first distributed evenly between the palms, then transferred to both cheeks with simultaneous rapid-fire slapping, and the residue distributed over jacket and trousers with equally rapid light pats.

'He was always on at me to give him a wee splash of aftershave free – Ah go on, Marie, go on, go on. Just a wee splash. *Go on.*'

In the evening the Quinns seized on the Barry Hinds incident with an avidity that suggested a desperate need to avoid
mentioning the recent development in the Temple of Eros.
Marie and I were more than happy to go along with this. Only
alcohol could give us the courage to approach such enormity.

'I was at school with Barry.' Like all the locals, Neil was a
walking biographical dictionary. 'In fact, I met Helen through
Barry. He went out with her before me.'

Consulted for a denial, Helen raised her hands and laughed.
'One night. And it was – '

The demands of nightly conversation had made new anec-
dotes priceless. Neil came forward with such eagerness that he
almost overturned our sofa, a lightweight 'contemporary'
piece with skinny black plastic legs, flimsy low wooden frame
and a stretched spring back and seat concealed by foam
cushions covered in a supposedly jaunty tartan material. 'I
went to London with Barry for summer work.'

'Listen to him!' Helen cried, though without genuine griev-
ance. 'He goes *mad* if *I* interrupt *him* . . . but *he* interrupts *me* all
the time.'

'We got taken on as barmen in this Irish pub in Archway.'
Neil seemed not to have even registered Helen's remarks. 'And
the first night we started Barry develops a nose bleed. So he's
running round the bar holding a cold bottle to the back of his
head with one hand and a handkerchief to his nose with the
other. Convinced he's bleeding to death of course.' Neil
paused to light up and deeply inhale. A good yarn and a
leisurely smoke in the company of friends – after intercourse
and alcohol, these were his main consolations. 'This was on a
Friday night with the bar jammed. So Barry goes up to the
manager and *asks for a lift to the nearest hospital.* We were both
sacked . . . and couldn't find another job. Had to come home
without a penny. Then on the plane Barry decides he has to
have *a wee vodka* – this is what cool dudes do on planes – but
he hasn't any money so I have to pay for it with the last of

mine. As a result we have to hitchhike home starving . . . not
even a sandwich between us.'

At this mention of food Marie made hectic face signals. She
wanted me to slip out and place in the oven what would surely
prove a happy innovation – four large Cornish pasties for the
savoury course. But for once our living room felt truly congenial, although, unlike the dark vault of the Quinn flat, it
was small, bright, utilitarian and aggressively contemporary.
One of the walls had paper of a different pattern from the other
three, the carpet was a bright synthetic orange with a swirling
irregular abstract design, and the floor-hugging furniture was
flimsy and minimalist with the skeletal structure and tapering
splayed legs of 'the long low look'. Tonight there was even
comfort in our electric fire, whose bulk derived not from its
two functional bars but from the monstrous simulacrum
which blossomed above them   a backlit coloured-plastic
representation of burning coal.

Neil stared into the painted plastic as though it had genuine
mesmerising flames. '*A wee vodka*,' he murmured musingly,
almost to himself.

To disturb his meditation was atrocious but necessary.
'Dominic Dunbar?'

'A chancer.' Neil emerged from his ruminations to look at
us. 'The stories about women may be true but I'm sure it's not
the real reason he's selling. Things have probably got too hot
for Dominic in every way. He owns a big hotel in Donegal
that's not doing well. In fact it's falling to pieces. And he's
heavily involved in property development in the town. His
speciality is getting a big site by buying up little shops one at
a time for practically nothing. He always says he'll keep up the
business but then lets it go derelict, so the site goes downhill
and it's easier to buy up the rest. If somebody won't sell and
Dominic owns property next door, he has his property
demolished – not from the top down the way you're supposed
to, but with a wrecking ball, as violently as possible. Usually

the business next door has structural damage and has to sell up. And if wrecking doesn't work he has buildings torched ... that's the way he got Beesie Fox shifted.'

'Ah, Beesie's,' Marie murmured. 'Me brother Don used to send me down with an empty Domestos bottle for one Park Drive. *A single Park Drive!* A returnable bleach bottle for one cigarette!'

Neil leaned across to touch Marie's arm in a solidarity of the deprived. 'Listen, *I* started off smoking single Park Drives from Beesie's. Though at least I paid cash.'

He seemed only too happy to prolong the contact – but Marie broke away with a sharp exclamation. I was sure she had remembered the Cornish pasties. Instead she turned eagerly to Helen. 'But what about you and Barry? *Tell us the craic.*'

Never had it been so difficult to leave this little room. I darted out to the even tinier kitchen, impatiently parting the curtain of multicoloured plastic strips, slammed the savouries in the oven and rushed back, pausing only long enough to hiss in Marie's ear: 'You can make the tea.'

'He took me to this party,' Helen was saying. 'I didn't even want to go ... knew nobody there ... and got left in a corner while he drank with his cronies. Then when I asked him to take me home – he had his uncle's car – he drove straight into this low stone wall he didn't see in the dark. Of course, all he's worried about is the car ... jumps out shouting, Tony'll kill me, Tony'll kill me ... and doesn't even notice that I have blood pouring out of my head. Neil was the only one to pay *me* any attention ... helped me out of the car and got me cleaned up. So then, of course, Barry persuades Neil to come along when he's taking me home, and even to take me to the door. Very brave of Neil, actually. Daddy wanted to kill him ... until I explained.' Helen regarded the modest hero with renewed gratitude and love. Then suddenly rose out of her seat, presumably to reward Neil again. Instead, she abruptly leaned her face close to mine. 'I've still got a scar.' She pulled aside hair to show me her scalp – but I was more conscious of the unflawed and fragrant remainder of her person. And of an innocent physical spontaneity Marie could never have shown.

Helen moved on to display the scar to Marie, then resumed her seat and looked at me. 'So that's the story of your new partner.'

There had to be some underlying irony – but none was apparent.

'*Partner?*' I shouted at last. 'You can't believe I'd have any dealings at all with the likes of *Barry Hinds*. He looks like a cheap Italian gangster, for Christ's sake.'

It was difficult to know which of the two of us was more shocked.

'Wait till I tell you.' Helen's calm tone was belied by her rising and advancing on me with outstretched hands, as though itching to wring my misguided neck. 'You've a chance to get your own practice when you're still in your twenties. *You'd* be the idiot if you turned *that* down. This town has been run for years by a bunch of doddery old fools. Anyone with a scrap of intelligence and energy could take over the whole place. If you don't, someone else will. Now if *I* had an opportunity like this ...' The frustrated hands jerked up, then flapped in a gesture of hopelessness as the outburst subsided and she returned to her seat. 'But it's not me. I'll shut up. I'll say no more.'

We were stunned by this vehemence. For a time no one spoke. Then Marie rose apologetically. 'I'll put on the tea.'

There was another long silence. Neil busied himself with lighting up and smoking a fresh cigarette.

'Helen,' he began, carefully, slowly. 'Barry Hinds.' Allowing this to sink in. 'Dominic Dunbar.'

'I wouldn't expect *you* to understand.' Helen flung this out with a disgust as surprising as her earlier passion.

Practically nothing more was said until Marie returned with a tray bearing tea things, Cornish pasties, Fleming's baps (one of the few authentic local delicacies) and a plate of chocolate bourbon creams. Then, scarcely credible, the ground-breaking savouries were consumed *without comment.*

'But Dominic's a *crook,*' I had to burst out at last. 'He could be selling a worthless business. For some reason he doesn't even own the building it's in ... I could end up paying a fortune for a few ancient filing cabinets and clapped-out adding machines. Barry and Dominic could be in it together ... after the deal Dominic returns Barry's money and the two of them share out mine. Leaving *me* in debt for the rest of my natural. Or else there *are* clients and they'll expect me to be a crook like Dominic. As soon as they find I can't or won't they'll disappear like morning mist.'

'Look.' Helen attempted to control her impatience. 'Dominic only took over this firm himself a few years ago. And it was run for a lifetime by strait-laced Protestants. Willman & Rosborough, that's still the name of it. Dominic's up to his neck in crooked deals ... *yes* ... but there's probably still a huge clientele of perfectly ordinary small businesses. Anyway, I could find out for sure.'

A monster was drawing me inexorably into its lair. 'How?'

'Our assistant manager ... Leo Patton. Leo knows everything about business in this town.'

Neil interrupted with a harsh laugh. 'An admirer of Helen's ... wee fat baldy guy. Only in his thirties but looks over fifty. Married fifteen years but no children ... and the wife lives in Belfast while Leo lives here.' Neil leaned forward, apparently to flick ash into a saucer, but really to savour the defeat of a rival. 'I think he's some kind of eunuch.' Then he inhaled casually as though he had said nothing unusual.

Helen regarded him for what seemed a long time. Finally she spoke in a measured tone. 'Leo Patton has always been most kind and helpful to me.'

Neil addressed Marie and me. 'He's in the Knights of Malta. You can see him in uniform outside the cathedral any Sunday. Wee fat baldy guy.'

There was another awkward silence, which Marie filled by collecting dishes. 'Finished?' she brightly enquired of Helen, who had eaten little.

Helen took her hostess by the arm in a sudden efflorescence of gratitude. 'Thank you *so much*, Marie. That was all *really lovely*.' Marie made to retreat but Helen gripped her arm more fiercely and brought close a face once more blazing with passionate belief. 'And what do *you* think of this? What do *you* think, Marie? Ten years in business could set you both up for life. Ten years of hard work is all it would take. Neither of you would ever need to work again.'

Marie was the product of a town where fantasies were endlessly rehearsed but almost never realized (as Neil put it, When all's said and done, there's more said than done). Now that she knew Helen was in earnest, her features were transfixed by terror at the prospect of change. But a change which would avoid the ultimate trauma of leaving town.

It was crucial to prevent her from dwelling on this. 'Look, stop this nonsense. I have no money.'

Helen: 'I'll get you a loan.'

Neil (with a wild caw): 'Leo Patton!'

This was a Thursday. It was agreed that Helen would make enquiries next day and, since she and Neil were meeting Celia and Lexie that evening, report to us in Mullen's on Saturday night.

Even uncommitted investigation can be dangerous. All day Friday I was haunted by the possibility of rejecting leader and team.

On Friday evening Marie informed me, as though only just recalling it, that Colm O'Kane was a client of Willman & Rosborough. 'And Colm's as straight as anyone in this town.'

'That's why he plays golf and leaves you to write the prescriptions.'

Saturday night began with a stroke of luck – we were again able to appropriate a landing alcove in Mullen's, a recess with a six-seater banquette and stools by the table at the open end. We secured it against all comers by removing the stools to the ground floor, spreading ourselves around the banquette and plugging the gaps with coats and bags.

But Helen was too excited to maintain a purely defensive posture. Almost immediately she came up to my side and turned on me those blue eyes unclouded by disappointment or doubt. 'Leo says it's a going concern ... well worth the money. And Dominic's in a bad way ... though Leo wouldn't say why. You could probably beat the price down, and if you do Leo'll give you the loan. All you need is a couple of hundred to take the bare look off the thing.'

An overwhelming sense of relief flooded through me. 'I don't have it.'

Untroubled eyes resolutely held mine. 'Sell your car.'

Helen was richly endowed with what have since been identified as the crucial E-factors – Empowerment, Enthusiasm and Energy. If she was like this with all her clients (and who could doubt it?), her dream of becoming a branch manager would surely soon be realised. By contrast, Marie and Neil seemed without vitality or vision, slumped in silent concentration on alcohol and cigarettes.

It is always dangerous to dream – and especially dangerous to dream in bars. The deal was beginning to seem like an adventure, a game, a cunning way to foil Life and its plan to extinguish me slowly over forty years in the bowels of large companies. Of course the role of corporate zero would merely be swapped for the new and equally absurd guise of small-town accountant. But there was this crucial difference – the new mask would be too temporary to fuse to the face. After ten years it would be discarded and never replaced.

One of the cornerstones of accounting philosophy is the 'prudence concept': financial planning must never anticipate revenue and always assume maximum loss. Many questions remained to be answered. As I turned once again to Helen a figure appeared in the opening of the recess.

'How're ye doin' there, Quinn? Still ridin' away?'

Neil stirred from his torpor. 'How're ye gettin' on yourself, Dessie?'

The interloper, youngish but podgy and pallid, checked that we were all paying attention, then lifted his plump right leg and swung it over the table. 'Same way as always, Neil ... *eh?*' Lowering himself heavily onto the edge of the bench, foolishly left vacant by Helen, he placed a full pint on the table. 'Nah, I'm all right, actually. As they say in Russia, I can't complain.'

When no one responded he withdrew from his coat a folded copy of *Ireland's Saturday Night*.

'Did ye see City were beat again today? Three wan. What a shower o' wasters ... *eh?* After they got hammered last week Willie Ross reckoned it was the passing. So he gets these eleven bins and puts them on the pitch ... as the other team ... right? City were supposed to practise passing between the bins. But what d'ye think happened? *What d'ye think happened, eh?*' He looked invitingly at each of us, but seemed undeterred by the lack of response. 'Fuckin' bins won five nil.'

As with interest and enthusiasm, so for laughter – Dessie himself was happy to provide enough for all five. Then he took a deep pull on his pint, which, instead of further raising his spirits, left him surprisingly morose. 'City should never have dropped Jumbo Crossan.'

It seemed to take an eternity for Dessie to go to empty his bladder. Helen angrily turned on Neil.

'What can I do?' he protested. 'Dessie Duddy's been giving me a lift every day for four years.'

Helen was typically decisive. 'We can leave.'

'Dessie's a sad case. Drinks seven nights a week. Can't get a woman.'

'He should lose a few stone,' Helen snapped.

'Not everyone's as skinny as you.' Neil adroitly created a diversion and engaged Marie and me. 'Helen eats Wate-On, ye know.'

'*Wate-On?*' Marie was genuinely incredulous. 'We still sell that stuff – but hardly anyone buys it these days.'

'I … may … have … tried … it … a … few … times.' Words squeezed out of Helen's lips like clothes from a mangle. 'But it was *ages ago*.'

Neil had succeeded in spreading the discontent. Soon we were standing apart in the cold instead of huddling together in warmth. Helen proposed the City Hotel but Neil violently refused to pay exorbitant prices for the 'wee skittery' bottles of mixer required to temper pungent spirit (itself far from cheap in hotels). For him the only alternative was the Pop Inn – but under no circumstances would Helen endure loud country music.

The Quinns stared at each other, defiant and resolute. Marie and I looked up and down the street, as if there might suddenly materialise a comfortable and well-appointed estab-lishment full of animated and interesting young people but with a vacant well-situated table for four. Finally Marie sug-gested buying drink and taking it home. A sound idea – but no one could think of anywhere convenient that would be open at this hour. The local culture was almost entirely based on alcohol and supplemented the already rich list of synonyms for drunkenness with a host of original terms – blootered, wankered, rubbered, stocious (speculative spelling of an oral term), palatic (possibly a corruption of 'paralytic'), well-on, well-lit, half-cut, plastered, steaming, rotten, wrote (presum-ably an abbreviation for 'wrote-off'), rammed, tore and (my own favourite) arseholed – but the alcohol had to be con-sumed in bars. It was surprisingly difficult to buy the means of getting arseholed at home.

There appeared to be nothing for it but one of the working-class places. In great trepidation we entered the lounge of the Electric Bar and were surprised to find it not at all dilapidated and filthy, as Helen had feared. In fact, it was more contemporary than Mullen's, with denlike Dunlopillo-covered booths intimately lit by conical lamps brought low on long metal rods and served by low-set wooden tables with tapering diagonal legs. Apart from the high stools round the mahogany-topped bar, all the fittings were perfect examples of the long low look. At the moment all the booths were occupied and all the stools free. Either the patrons were unused to high stools – or afraid to get too far off the ground. For, unlike the fittings, the clientele bore marks of wear and tear, from the temporary dissolution of drink to the permanent ravages of age, neglect and manual work – and often all of these and more. As we pondered the wisdom of tarrying, we were hailed from behind the bar and made to await the approach of a heavy proprietress, wheezily beset and vexed, who led us to a booth and practically dragged out its elderly and inebriated occupant.

'Och don't be botherin' me head crakin', Jimmy,' she cried, dismissing his feeble protests, 'just come on outa that and give decent people a seat.'

It was certainly a relief to sit down but as we tried to relax she returned, toiling and rolling like a freighter in heavy seas, sorrowfully apologetic, forcing us to cringe into the leatherette as she leaned over the table and, enormous bulk aquiver and breath emerging in a strained whistle, attacked its surface with a damp cloth. '*Now*. Sure that's a wee bit better for yees. There yees are now. An' Ah'll get yees a drink in a wee second.'

This was far from putting us at ease – but it certainly created a craving for strong liquor. All of us drew hungrily on our glasses as soon as they arrived. Then Helen looked up and around at the bar and its patrons, finally bringing her eyes to rest on me and shaking her head in accepting laughter, marvellously tolerant of all the marvellous absurdity.

'OK,' I said to her, an obsessed man. 'What if Barry qualifies? He could dump me then.'

'Not if there's a proper partnership contract.'

'Anyway he won't qualify.' Neil offered this in an uncharacteristically grudging tone. 'Barry couldn't sit down with a book for five consecutive seconds. When he was doing his Senior he read *Oliver Twist* in the comics ... on the back page of *The Topper*.'

Marie had been studying the clientele in covert fascination and wonder. 'God there's as many here I know really well. There's Nassie Kelly I haven't seen in a lifetime. He used to go round the doors with bundles of sticks in an old pram. And that old guy she threw out of our booth ... that's Jimmy Wells Fargo McGrenera. Used to be the delivery boy for the All Cash.'

To Helen I put the oldest and most fundamental query. 'Why *me?*'

'Barry's scared a local accountant would cut him out of the deal.'

'That still gives him plenty of choice.'

Neil made another reluctant contribution. 'Barry collects people on a Hall-of-Fame basis. He wants *you* because you came fourth in Ireland in your accountancy exams. Numbers one, two or three would of course have been better ... but they're probably not available.'

This had an unpleasant undertone. Was Neil sneering at accountants? At examination success? Whatever the reason, an equivalent tartness was required.

'In that case why did Barry choose *you?* What's *your* claim to the Hall of Fame?'

Our eyes met – just for an instant, but long enough to register a sharp and mutual antagonism. Then Neil looked away, shifted and resumed his normal self-deprecating manner. 'Barry thought I was a hard man because I came from Limewood Street. I may well have *looked* like a hard man. You had to look hard to survive.'

Neil was indeed stocky and muscular, efficiently assembled, with tight curly hair remote from the effete idiocies of fashion and the set look of one who would brook no interference.

But Helen threw back her head in an incredulous laugh. 'Neil that's as gentle as a baby. Neil that wouldn't hurt a fly.'

Marie too was reassessing Neil. 'The Limeys were all hard men. No one from our street would go near the Limeys.'

Always uneasy at personal attention, Neil tried to shrug it off. 'Barry was obsessed with hard men. Talked about them all the time. Wanted to *be* one . . . but hadn't it in him. A hopeless coward.' Neil reached for the tin ashtray on the table. 'Always fantasising about it. I remember him lifting a big glass ashtray and saying to me, Jesus, you could hit someone a great smack with that.' Neil hefted the tin ashtray in imitation of Barry, then replaced it and produced twenty Gallaher's Blues.

'*Son!*' A low urgent whisper came from the table in front of our booth. '*Son!* . . . *Son!*' Its source was an old woman in a tattered overcoat and plaid zip-up slippers. Between footwear and coat were bare measled legs. All her attention was focused on Neil. 'Could ye spare us a fag at all, son?'

Neil rose and went across with the packet. Then she requested a light, seizing his hand and holding it close to her face as she hungrily sucked at the flame.

Helen rolled her eyes at the ceiling. 'These people always make a *beeline* for my husband.' And, when Neil resumed his seat, 'Did you *have to* give her a cigarette? Must you *always* encourage them? You know she'll pester us all night now.' She looked Neil up and down, as if for evidence of contamination. 'She'll be over to torture us . . . and she probably stinks to high heaven.'

Neil drew deeply on his cigarette, perhaps in search of the

strength to answer calmly. 'She does not stink, Helen.'

But Helen's prediction was accurate. The old woman observed us keenly – and eventually shuffled across to sit opposite Neil. At close range her features were even more devastated – but her wits seemed intact. Ignoring the rest of us, she looked at Neil. 'I read hands.'

Helen released a high derisive exclamation. But a man faced with momentous choice will take advice from any quarter – and the ancient sibyl's eyes were penetratingly alive. 'I've a big decision to make,' I cried jocosely from the back of the booth. 'Can you tell me what to do?'

She glanced at me – briefly, dismissively – then turned back to Neil and, without awaiting an invitation, took his right hand in hers and began to study it intently, turning it back and forth and every so often looking up to peer into his eyes. At first she paused regularly for deep inhalations but soon her absorption was so complete that the cigarette was left to burn down in the ashtray.

Finally she grunted. 'There's something in your life ... a difficulty ... an obstruction ...' Once again the soothsayer looked up, scrutinising Neil's face with even fiercer concentration. Neil did not move or speak. Nor did anyone else. Even Helen was still. 'And it goes deep ... *very deep* ...' Suddenly taking up his left hand, she examined it closely, as if for contradictory evidence, musing, 'Something preventing you ... *something* ...'

'Will it ...?' When Neil attempted to speak, the aforementioned obstruction seemed to have lodged in his throat. 'Will it ever clear?'

She returned to his right hand but now stroking rather than studying, in a gesture more of consolation than divining.

Before she could answer, the landlady bore down in wheezy outrage. 'Bridie, would ye get away outa that. Get away outa that, look see.'

Bridie sprang to her feet with a snarl so malevolent that

even decisive righteousness was briefly taken aback. 'Get away outa that an' don't be torturin' everyone, Bridie. Can ye not give decent people peace for a quiet drink on a Saturday night?'

Spitting venom but no match for a tank, Bridie was bundled off to the other end of the bar. Our protectress returned and, though whistling dangerously from the strenuousness of her exertions, flung herself over our table with renewed despair and a damp cloth. 'Och sure isn't that terrible . . . yees couldn't even have a drink in peace.'

Neil seemed incapable of speech, so Marie and I protested that Bridie had not been a problem. In my case this was certainly true. I had been planning another attempt to consult the oracle, though it would obviously have been difficult to distract her from Neil (a tragic destiny is more interesting than a business plan).

'Ah but ye need to watch Bridie. She's a terrible bad tongue on her. And she would even take a wipe at ye, so she would.' A pause – and then, as though contradicted. 'Oh the same one would think nothin' of takin' a wipe at ye all right. Oh she would. She would. The same one *would*. She would take a good wipe at ye if she took the notion.'

Neil was staring across the bar with preoccupied, occluded eyes. There seemed to be little chance of establishing a convivial mood.

But Helen chuckled and, leaning across to lay a hand on her husband's arm, addressed him with good humour tempered by firmness, like a parent indulging a childish whim which has now gone far enough. 'Neil, go and see if you can find somewhere to wash those hands.'

Neil turned slowly and looked at her in astonishment, as one would at a complete stranger daring to adopt the tone of an intimate. His speech was also slow and measured. 'There is nothing wrong with my hands, Helen.'

They regarded each other for some time. Everything

seemed to take some time now.

Then, abruptly taking a swift drink and groping for the Gallaher's Blues, Neil leaned towards Marie and me. 'So it's three o'clock in the morning ... *yeah?* Helen wakes me up and says, Neil, did you put the bin out? So I get dressed and put it out ... on a freezing cold pissing wet night. I put the bin out and get undressed and back into bed. Thought Helen was asleep. Not a bit of it. Says she, Did you wash your hands after that dirty bin, Neil?' To brace himself for the story's conclusion, Neil took another swift drink and lit up a cigarette, turning then to include Helen. 'I did not wash my fucking hands then and I have no fucking intention of washing them now.'

There was another long silence. His position fully explained, Neil surrendered himself once more to the twin consolations of alcohol and tobacco.

It was as though a great hand had seized Helen's face and was squeezing it ever more tightly. Colour drained away; cheeks, nose and mouth were pinched and unnaturally white. But the blue eyes blazed with frightening intensity. She began to tap Neil with her right index finger, now the parent who has been driven too far and retains control only by drawing deep on reserves of principle and self-discipline. 'Well listen till I tell you this. Listen till I tell you this. You may believe your hands are fine ... but you can keep them to yourself tonight, OK? Is that understood? Is that all right? OK? Don't even *think* of assaulting me on the sofa tonight.'

4

A provincial town will often betray itself by obsessive use of the word 'city'. Here it featured in the titles of the soccer, rugby and golf clubs, in the widely used sobriquet 'Maiden City' ('Matron City' would have been more accurate) and in the names of many local businesses – the tiny town centre had a City Hotel, a City Café and a City Picture House.

All these metropolitan aspirations were forgotten in the torpor of a damp October Saturday morning. The old buildings seemed to hunch defensively into themselves, as if to forestall any summons to awaken, and to shrink from the sky that turned above them, a turbulent kaleidoscope of grey. In contrast to the rigidity of everything below, the sky here changed ceaselessly, almost frenetically, and seemed at peace only when it achieved darkness and rain. Though today's rain was also indecisive and vague. Every now and then a barely perceptible drizzle would commence, the moisture appearing to emerge from pores in the air instead of falling from the clouds, and then as suddenly cease, like a tentative thought that can never progress.

This town was committed to dreaming but not introspection. It could never see itself from the outside. And few curious travellers had ventured to the outermost rim of the outlying island. Discoveries and revelations surely awaited the sharp of eye and keen of mind. I experienced the exhilaration of Marco Polo, an explorer entering the unknown, and the novelty of walking with purpose but no destination.

Marie was at work and I had all day to wander and get the measure of this town. Mission statement: observe, analyse, comprehend.

The core was an old settlement on a hill with a still-intact wall round its base. On the summit of the hill was the Diamond, actually a square, in its centre a grandiose war monument, and on its perimeter and radial streets grey Victorian buildings whose ground floors housed businesses, where, above wooden-framed windows displaying quality goods, there gleamed brass plates inscribed with the names of the Protestant owners: Austin, Edmiston, Phillips, Scott, Spear. Inside these sombre emporia, ignorant of the new-fangled 'walk-around' and 'self-service' concepts, merchandise was separated from the vulgar herd by imposing counters of polished wood and mature men in dark suits who resembled not so much local shop assistants as Harley Street heart specialists.

At the foot of the hill was the low-lying Catholic area known as 'the Bog'. Marie and Neil had grown up at the far end of this quarter, in the tough terraces which clung to the steep slope of the next hill. Here they had shared unimaginably tiny rooms with unimaginably numerous siblings, eaten pork skirts and sliced pan and carried Domestos bottles to Beesie Fox's for a single Park Drive. It was a world more alien and strange to me than that of the distinguished Protestant outfitters on the summit. Below the walls on this side there wandered crookedly downhill a narrow street of Catholic businesses – betting shops (described as 'Turf Accountants'), bars (including the Electric Bar and Mullen's), a religious fancy goods shop (Child of Prague and Blessed Martin statues, wall plaques of the Pope and the Kennedy brothers, prayers to St Anthony for help in finding lost articles and to St Jude for help in passing exams), a secular fancy goods shop (cigarette lighters in the form of tiny automatic pistols, globes which when shaken snowed on cute winter scenes, bulky ballpoint pens capable of writing in four different colours or with liquid-filled compartments which tilting and tapping made tigers or racing cars sluggishly traverse), and at the bottom of the hill the Discount Stores, a tiny shack with the assertiveness so typical of the undersized, its windows covered with details of astounding reductions, its frontage festooned with the actual cut-price clothes and above its door a loudspeaker harshly blaring pop music into the street. Most of the redevelopment was taking place in this area; there were many derelict build-ings and stretches of weed-covered waste ground, much of it still possibly in the ownership of Dominic Dunbar.

In contrast to the moribund somnolence of the Diamond this quarter was wide-awake, busy and booming. Catholic businesses (and hence Catholic accountants) would have no cash-flow problems. Where the Protestant establishments had been cavernously empty, the Discount Stores had a queue of women in shapeless coats and hats of fake fur over frizzy tight perms. These were the unsung heroines of Matron City, the storm troops who would eventually take the hill. In an earlier siege Protestants in the walled town had shut the gates and suc-cessfully defied Catholic forces – but no defence can withstand an army of women with shopping bags.

A walk back around the base of the old town led to the main city gate and the highest and most impressive part of the wall, authentic old cannon pointing from its embrasures at the Guildhall across the square. Along the top of the wall was a wide cobbled walkway where few seemed to walk (though Marie had told me it was a useful resource for post-dancehall lovers – many the pleasant hour she had spent there with such as Fuckso McCallion) and which the Corporation was proposing to make a municipal car park. This town, so full of itself, had yet little or no sense of its genuine assets.

Behind the Guildhall, obscured by buildings and entirely out of sight of the town, was an even greater marvel, a majestically sullen grey river wider than the Thames or the Seine but undemeaned by heritage or leisure use, with no *bateaux mouches*, floating restaurants, old sailing vessels or retired cruisers serving as naval museums. There was not even a public riverside area, though it was possible to walk (with care) along old rotting wooden docks. Here I communed for half an hour with the Grey River God.

'Ancient Wise One,' I cried (there was no one in sight), 'Could a man fruitfully live for ten years in this place? Is this the Maiden City of song and legend – or the squalid arsehole of the universe? Should I stay here and lose what remains of my youth – or go with you to the ocean and the wide world beyond?'

For a long time the only reply was the derisive shrieking of gulls (surely the true spirit of the town) and occasional gusts of wind, which flung moist mist into my face.

Inscrutable Wise Ones are not to be rushed. The River God pondered deeply and eventually replied in a grave oracular tone: 'Investigate further. Discover more. Buy the local paper and study it in a café somewhere.' As I turned away, nodding in gratitude, it added a helpful afterthought: 'Why not Morelli's on Strand Road? You can't beat the Italians when it comes to coffee and ice cream.'

Morelli's was full of women shoppers tucking into banana longboats, knickerbocker glories and cream fingers heavily coated with sugar. The town's tongue was acid but its tooth was sweet.

On *The Journal*'s front page the lead story was a report on the latest speech by the Lord Bishop. 'In matters pertaining to domestic government,' His Lordship informed us, 'the wife is, as a rule, to yield. To claim for completely equal authority is to treat woman as man's equal in a matter in which nature made them unequal.' A swift scan of the female customers revealed no obvious desire to yield. And behind the counter Signora Morelli, a ferocious tiny woman with a perm tight and white as a cauliflower floret, was violently berating in Italian a big hapless sack of a man who slumped over the counter and hung his white head. Signor Morelli did not appear to have enjoyed his sojourn in the Maiden City.

Inside the front page 'The Question Box' answered the tricky queries with which pseudo-intellectuals love to goad the True Church. 'Are there not too many relics of the True Cross?' one such smart aleck enquired. 'In fact, enough to make over three hundred of the original?' Rev. Bertrand L. Conway responded with impressive erudition: 'In 1870 Rohault de Fleury made a careful study of all the relics and found that they would make two-fifths of a cubic foot out of the six and five-eighths cubic feet of timber required for a full cross.'

The next page was entirely taken up by 'An Irish Layman in Africa'. 'The long dark shadows of Mohammedanism are stretching south from the Sahara. Communist agents are feverish in their activity. I invite you to join the regiment of Christ's lay troops in Africa.'

And on every page were grainy photographs of leading local laymen – self-important, heavy citizens who bore their massive bellies like symbols of office. Helen was surely right to dismiss them as laughably irrelevant. Any astute younger person could push these fools aside. And the old Protestant businesses seemed to be equally unable to adapt. The entire town was ripe for takeover.

And at the thought of Helen there arose a vision of alabaster limbs in the Temple of Eros. Perhaps the wildest adventure of all was not in the wide world but here. Marvels appear under the microscope as well as in spray-wet binoculars. Exploration may be inner as well as outer.

The offices of Willman & Rosborough were in a mysterious quarter just behind the Diamond, only yards from the shops but eerily deserted and silent. Here were the Protestant cathedral, an eighteenth-century Protestant church and the Memorial, Britannia and Freemasons' halls. The architectural style was fantasy defensive, with ramparts and turrets and belvederes (even the cathedral had crenellations), but the buildings had an aggrieved and brooding look, as if aware that a Catholic occupation was inevitable and imminent. The only houses were in a tiny cul-de-sac with a single-sided terrace of four dwellings, one of which was occupied by the accountancy practice. In all his attempts to interest me in the business, Barry had never mentioned location. It was likely that he regarded it as a disadvantage. To me it was its greatest selling point. Immediately the cul-de-sac whispered the seductive promise of sequestration: Forget Time and Time will forget you.

A sudden memory assailed me. On a sunny morning two weeks before (the last valiant rally of expiring summer) two of the project clerks had called in sick. Seated before the rest of the team, our Leader grimly tapped a pencil (the anger of a prophet is as terrible as his zeal is inspiring). Weren't the missing pair fishing and drinking buddies from way back? There was a silence. Finally one of the accountants cleared his throat and acknowledged that this was the case. There was a longer silence. Then a second accountant said that he had borrowed a tent from one of the clerks – it would be easy to return it after work and see if there was any truth in the sickness story. This was the man who had revealed to me, with no trace of unease, that he billed his own wife for all personal purchases made from their joint account. Now he looked round at us and chuckled. The Leader chuckled. We all chuckled.

Surrounded by venerable churches and halls, the little terrace seemed to offer sanctuary from contemporary corporate ruthlessness.

But when I returned ten days later with Barry I discovered that the interior was not so alluring. Between discoloured walls and tattered carpets pungent mustiness flourished. Dominic Dunbar was a further shock. A legendary seducer would surely be well-dressed and satanically handsome, with sleek black hair, boldly transgressive eyes and a cleft chin where women would dip their fingers as in a holy water font. But Irish bulls do not resemble Cary Grant. Dominic had tousled reddish hair, already thinning, and sullen eyes in a mottled complexion, as charmless as puddles in a muddy field. Nor was there evidence of sophistication in his apparel – cracked black slip-on shoes and an undistinguished brown suit over a black nylon roll-neck sweater with a sagging neck. The only clue to his sexual history was an aura of fiercely appetitive impatience, which, even when he was slumped behind a desk, surrounded him like a turbulent force field.

And the legendary deal-maker took an equally unexpected approach to negotiation. Instead of singing Barry's praises, he stared angrily at me. 'So you're thinking of going into partnership with this comedian ... *this eejit?*' He turned to remind himself of Barry, today in a lightweight, bottle-green suit with a flap over the breast pocket and cloth-covered buttons. Then back. 'He tried to get in with *me* when he was going round the town for a job first. Came down to the golf club with me one Saturday night. Saturday night and the clubhouse packed. So what does he do, *eh? What does the stupid cunt do?*' My head shake admitted to imaginative failure. 'Cunt gets stocious, takes his welt out and pishes all over the carpet.' Here Dominic turned to Barry for a longer look, as if he could still scarcely believe what had happened. Barry chortled, though rather uneasily, and glanced swiftly in my direction to see if the revelations were being accepted as earthy regional humour.

'That was neither today or yesterday,' Barry suggested with the utmost mildness, attempting to distance the incident and bathe it in a warm nostalgic glow.

But Dominic addressed me once more with an outrage un-dimmed by time. 'Right in the middle of a Saturday night. Takes his fuckin' welt out and pishes all over the floor.' Then he leaned conclusively across the desk. 'This is the sort of comedian you're taking on as a partner.' Another brief glance at Barry – and disconcertingly back. 'The price is good.'

'I know it is. But my hands are tied. The bank will only lend me so much. Which means that the best we can do is a lot less than you want.' I named what I considered a ridiculously low starting offer.

Dominic grunted savagely. 'Who're you dealing with?'

'Leo Patton.'

'*Uhhrr.*' He grunted again and slumped back. '*Leo.*'

In fact, Leo would certainly lend more if asked. The so-called interview had been a lackadaisical chat in the course of which he enquired how I liked working for the Yanks. I held out my right hand, level, steady, palm down, then wiggled it and issued a long equivocal *hmmmmmn* . . . Scepticism con-strained by professional etiquette was the right response. 'There's not many can stick the Yanks for long,' Leo laughed and pushed a form across his desk. 'Fill in whatever you want there, look.'

But did I wish to buy into this business even at a knock-down price? Dominic's office had the same shabby carpet as the stairs and its rudimentary wall shelves were lined with cardboard grocery boxes full of grubby dog-eared folders whose contents were not difficult to imagine – wadges of invoices, receipts and indecipherable notes. On the floor to Dominic's left were two more of these boxes and on his right a gigantic mechanical calculator that looked like a model of a combine harvester or a machine for knitting Aran sweaters. The Yanks might be overzealous but at least their equipment and furnishings were up to date. This purchase would buy nothing but the nebulous commodity of goodwill.

Dominic and Barry badly wanted the deal but my obvious detachment gave them pause. In a world almost entirely predicated on desire, not to want anything confers extraordinary strength.

'So that's my gettings?' Dominic thrust his head forward aggressively and, spreading his arms wide, placed a palm on each side of the desk. '*All right.*'

The colloquialism and adversarial posture made me misunderstand. It took a moment to realise that an accountancy practice had just changed hands. Why had Dominic let it go so easily? He must have had more than enough salted away. His time in the practice, the early sixties, was the golden age of financial fraud. The old traditions of integrity had crumbled enough to encourage an unscrupulous new generation but not enough to alert everyone of the need for safeguards. People still had faith in professionals – and chancers like Dominic were free to invent as extravagantly and exultantly as God in the Void.

Nothing disconcerts desire like being given what you say you want. I was immediately consumed by the fear – no, the *certainty* – of being swindled, but the momentum of the transaction caught me up and swept me along. Barry was already on his feet proposing a celebratory drink. Dominic impatiently refused. Yet Barry's admiration for his mentor remained undiminished. On our way to subsequent meetings to arrange the handover he regaled me with stories.

'Dominic's a wild case altogether.' Barry first shook his head, as though overcome by wonder but reluctant to share the evidence, then leaned close to confide, 'He had a whole crowd of us in stitches the other day doin' Doreen Tinney. Doreen's a grand-lookin' big girl – but she has a wee bit of a lisp. So Dominic leans back with his eyes shut and goes, Ye're not gonnay ttthhsquirt in me, Dominic, ttthhsure ye're not now.'

'What's the secret of his success?' In the end it was impossible not to ask. 'Certainly can't be his looks.'

'He explained to me once – If ye tell women ye're in love, they cry and then ye can ride them.' Barry chuckled, though with a touch of perplexity, as of one for whom this simple strategy had not been effective. 'But you need the nerve as well. Another time he says to me, Ye need to walk right up and grab them by the lapels o' the cunt. See if you go for a drink with Dominic and there's a woman behind the bar . . . *any* bar . . . swanky hotel or anywhere . . . Dominic goes up and says to her, Have ye a wee Black Bush? Not laughing or anything, you know, looking her straight in the eye. He says the best ride he ever had was this barmaid in Sligo. You wouldn't think it in the Free State but she was brilliant, he said. Big mush the size o' yer fuckin' hand.' Barry lifted and brandished his own open hand. 'And she gave some kind ay a wee twist made him fire straight away.' His hand fell in sudden distress. 'But you need the nerve. I mind one time we ordered steaks in the City Hotel and Dominic says to me, Watch this. Steak arrives . . . *beautiful* . . . fuck all the matter with it . . . but Dominic goes mental. Points to some wee spot or something and sends it back. Gets a completely new steak. Next time we were out he tried to get me to do it . . . but I hadn't the nerve.'

Barry's ruthlessness was limited both by lack of temerity and inadequate attention to detail. By and large he let me have my way on the partnership agreement and it was fun to nail his scrotum to the floor. To give the impression of magnanimity I agreed to let his solicitor draw up the contract.

On the day of the signing Barry picked me up after work, happily springing out of the car to lay a hand on my suit jacket. 'Jesus you're all dressed up.'

'Look who's talking.' Today Barry was in a navy blue two-piece, of soft rich material that may well have been cashmere, set off by a blue shirt, a blue silk tie with red polka dots and, in his breast pocket, a handkerchief matching the tie. 'Isn't the handkerchief in the pocket a bit old-fashioned?'

'A *folded* and *pressed* hanky looks like fuck all. The natty way to wear it is just roughly stuffed in.' Abruptly he whipped out the accessory, crumpled it with stylish authority, like a stage magician prior to conjuring a dove, and shoved it back into the pocket, tugging out one of the loose ends to complete the casual effect. Then he chuckled delightedly – an awareness of the absurdity of contrived carelessness was an interesting part of the attitude.

Why were we both in our best suits? Suddenly it was obvious: we were dressed for a wedding. Formally entering into partnership was as solemn and binding as the sacrament of matrimony and, albeit unconsciously, we were both appropriately attired. Barry, however, seemed to have forgotten that this was a marriage of convenience. On the drive to the town centre he talked intimately and effortlessly, as if to his lifelong sweetheart from next door. Nor did he seem to harbour doubts. As we walked the last stretch he happily buttoned and unbuttoned his jacket, adjusted his tie knot, snapped his fingers and popped his right palm against an echo chamber formed from his loosely closed left hand. At regular intervals he issued to acquaintances lavish greetings and waves and there were several detours to point out businesses which used the services of Willman & Rosborough.

'The town's really coming on,' he announced with pride.

The prudence concept recommended silence – but even accountants are occasionally human. 'I'm just not sure I want to spend a large chunk of my life in it.'

'What would take ye off gallivanting?' Barry laughed with the tolerance of one who had already passed through the pseudo-sophistication of departure and journeyed on to the higher wisdom of remaining at home. To the naive, his position might resemble chauvinism; in fact, it was complex, ironic, detached. 'Sure isn't it a great wee town on a Saturday night?' With a sweeping gesture of his left arm, he looked about him and found it good – a philosopher king entirely at ease in the heart of his realm. His right hand patted me reassuringly. 'And anyway where would ye go?'

'London for a start.'

Withdrawing his right hand, Barry uttered a sharp cry of disbelief. '*London!*' Obviously I was even more simple-minded than he had imagined. 'Listen . . . I worked over there . . . in a bar in Archway. Travelling in the Tube, ye know? . . . everybody with their nose in a newspaper or a book.' He opened his right hand and brought the spread palm close to a face puckered in hermetic intensity. 'Nobody would speak to ye. Nobody would *even look at ye.*'

I did not forget that the terms of the contract were largely mine and that I was using Barry's lawyer only as a meaningless concession. Nevertheless, I was scandalised. Entirely lacking in professional gravitas, this solicitor was a wild-haired, unkempt woman with a loud familiar tone more suited to haggling in a country market than elucidating fine points of law. And her office was a dimly lit cubbyhole packed with the now-familiar cardboard boxes. News of the invention of the filing cabinet had obviously not reached this far north. In fact, this office had yet to make use of folders. The boxes held wads of crumpled papers secured by string and elastic bands.

'How's your granny keepin', Barry?' Her concern was immediate, sincere and deep.

'Grand. Grand. Aw she's grand.'

'Isn't she *wonderful* for her age?'

'Oh she is. She is. She is.' But there was a reluctance in Barry's manner.

His interlocutor seemed not to notice. 'What age would she be now, Barry?'

'Eighty-two.' An unmistakable curtness – also ignored.

The woman turned cordially in my direction, leaning sideways to see round the obstruction on her desk – another large

cardboard box, now overflowing with dog-eared papers but
bearing, in heavy black type, the name of its original contents
– Celtex Super Soft Feminine Towels: Size Three. 'Eighty-
two years of age and she still makes Barry his dinner. As long
as Barry's in the town he'll get his dinner at lunchtime. Every
day a bit of dinner . . . a good warm bit of dinner. Isn't that
right, Barry? A powerful woman, altogether.'

The mammy's boy syndrome is well known but perhaps
even more extreme is the phenomenon of the granny's boy,
the child reared by a grandmother due to the inadequacy or
unwillingness of the parents. It was useful to know that Barry
might be such a child – though it did not make the prospect of
a partnership with him any more inviting. It was in deep
trepidation that eventually I took up a pen to render us 'joint
and severally bound'.

Naturally Barry insisted on a nuptial celebration in
Mullen's, where he set out his plans: immediate repainting
and recarpeting of the premises, gradual introduction of
original oil paintings as profits permitted. The artist he had in
mind specialised in paintings of Irish folk musicians – but of
course in a suitably contemporary and minimalist style ('Just a
few natty squiggles, ye know?').

'Can I make a suggestion, Barry?'

'Fire away.'

'Half a dozen new filing cabinets.'

Barry laughed inordinately, as though at some tremendous
witticism.

'I don't fancy doing business out of cardboard boxes . . .
although it seems to be the style around here.'

'Did ye see that on the desk?' Barry laid a hand on my arm
and assumed the unnaturally straight face that in Ireland is a
prelude to uproarious laughter. '*A fuckin' jam rag box!*' Merriment burst forth with a gusto enhanced by the earlier restraint.
'But that's the kind of Eileen. She's a character . . . a character.'
Suddenly his expression grew solemn and he tightened his grip

on my arm. 'Don't be gettin' the wrong idea though. Eileen may look like a gyppo but she's sharp as a needle. Sharp as a needle, the same woman. Ye'd want to get up early in the morning to put one over on Eileen.'

Well satisfied, Barry finished his drink, sat back in his seat and produced a twenty pack of International Dunhill. I had taken the precaution of buying the first round so that when 'the same again' was proposed I could leave without appearing mean. But, of course, it still looked mean. To abandon a spouse *on the wedding day* – and *even before the nuptial feast*.

'I was thinking of going round to the Chinese,' Barry muttered, bereft.

Worse still, he attempted to plan for the weekend ahead. He had met this classy girl from Belfast, a judge's daughter who was also a beauty queen, though she had entered for Miss Ireland only on the urging of friends and had failed to make the final eight not because of physical deficiencies but as a result of instinctive modesty which prevented her from tossing it up to the panel. This lovely but chaste maiden was visiting Barry at the weekend – would Marie and I like to go out with them?

The plan had been to hold my new partner at arm's length. As well try to stem the esurient sea.

'I thought you had a local girl?'

'So Ah have.' Barry rallied at the opportunity for insouciance. 'As Dominic used to always say' – he paused to command my full attention – 'It's a dirty duck that paddles in the one pond.'

5

Weeks of bargaining had produced an overwhelming sense of confinement and asphyxiation. It was essential to escape from the Maiden City. Over toasted bacon sandwiches and Abbey Crunch I proposed to Marie and the Quinns a Saturday trip to Belfast. It was as though I had offered to take them all on a South Sea island cruise. Marie and Neil, who had been rather bemused and surly about the Dominic transaction, were suddenly enraptured and profoundly grateful. Helen, continuously enthusiastic and supportive, was now even more elated. So much so that she insisted on driving us in her vw Beetle and came to our door at the appointed hour in what was obviously her sporty ensemble – a three-quarter-length sheepskin coat, bright tartan box-pleated skirt and a turquoise woollen sweater with a neck the shape of an inverted teardrop but the size of a carthorse's halter. The combination was disconcerting but, as so often, Helen's radiant self-assurance overrode any negative effects. Indeed, as if to compensate for the outfit, she had extra exuberance and élan. Yet another brace of empowering E-factors! And rare V-factors too – vitality, vivacity, vibrancy and verve.

Shrieking with laughter, Helen rushed through our flat on 'a quick visit to the loo'.

Marie shook her head in dismay. 'That *neck*.'

'Dootsie?' I softly suggested.

'And a *Gor-Ray pleated skirt . . . awhh . . . and turquoise again.*'

So great was Helen's preference for this colour – she usually wore at least one turquoise item and often several – that Marie had conferred upon her the secret title of Lady Turquoise. The obsession was possibly a bid for the tastefulness of beige without its familiarity. Turquoise combined the advantages of individualism and conformity.

Marie herself wore a charcoal grey pencil-line skirt with a tight-fitting maroon sweater and, over these, a black PVC coat which she had mischievously informed me was of 'finger-tip length' and in the 'swing away swagger' style. It was typical of her that, despite the time of year, she rejected the traditional winter coat for a lightweight fashion garment in shiny synthetic material.

Neil certainly seemed impressed and leapt from the passenger seat to help her climb into the back, never an easy manoeuvre with a Beetle and especially difficult in a tight skirt. We were used to the front of my roomy Wyvern, greatly lamented, and this exceptionally cramped accommodation required some adjustment, with much exclaiming and rasping of nylons from Marie. But it was accomplished without annoyance and indeed in a spirit of adventure and fun, as though we were getting a lift into a village on the back of a farmer's hay cart.

'It's a bit of a squeeze in there!' Helen cried gaily, though in a tone which implied that such constriction was a privilege.

Neil was genuinely solicitous. 'You'll be crushed to death by the time we get there.' He continued to regard Marie with concern. 'You're looking very well anyway, dear.'

Even the usually morose Neil was in high spirits today. His face was animated and flushed and he sucked hungrily and hectically on a succession of Gallaher's Blues. Every few minutes he would turn right round to speak directly to us and when we had climbed to the top of the desolate Glenshane Pass, with a dark rampaging sky above and the east of the province spread out below, he suggested making use of the facility on the summit – the Ponderosa, a new bar named after the ranch in a TV western series.

As so often, Helen was obliged to remind her husband of practical constraints. 'Neil, we're trying to arrive in time for the business lunch in the Chinese, remember.'

The business lunch for four and six – viscous grey soup like wallpaper paste, watery, beansprout-rich chop suey or fat-rimmed steak and gigantic chips (each the size of a quarter potato – surely the fattest chips in the world) and, to finish, a scoop of vanilla ice cream in a tin dish or a tiny cuboid of custard-cream tart with a smidgin of fake cream on top (surely the most bijou dessert in the world). Yet more exciting than many a candle-lit gourmet dinner since. While the others opted for chop suey, I indulged a fondness for fat chips. Not a wise choice on the day. Neil had cleared his plate and was smoking almost before I had trimmed the steak of its fat (a huge irregular border like a country hedgerow) and Marie and Helen also finished well ahead of me.

Marie directed attention to my plate. 'See the way he keeps a wee bit of everything for the end. A wee bit of steak, a few chips, a wee bit of veg.'

'The accountant,' Neil suggested to Marie, with an apparently respectful expression.

'The *planner*,' she corrected with similar gravity.

Then both burst out laughing. Helen did attempt to smother her snigger – but with none of her customary conviction and efficacy.

'What if we stole his last bite?' Marie cried. 'His last bite with a wee bit of everything on it!'

This was probably a reaction to the business deal. The Maiden City was cutting me back down to size.

Over vanilla ice cream the afternoon shopping was discussed. Neil, a careless dresser indifferent to clothes, wanted to visit Smithfield market to search for second-hand books.

'Neil, you haven't a decent *stitch*,' Helen cried in outrage.

'I said I'd look for books for Kevin.'

'Oh . . . *Kevin*.' Helen turned to us to explain. 'Neil's family are all a bit odd. He has this brother Kevin who lives with his sister down the Bog. Doesn't work . . . or do anything much . . . just sits in this wee house reading books about the Second World War. Nothing else but the Second World War. Really odd.'

'Kevin is *not odd*.'

'Neil, he's as *odd as two left feet*. Though, mind you, the town seems to be full of oddities like him. Useless men that sit about the house doing nothing.'

'Noel McDaid,' Marie came in. 'Except that Noel only reads books about black-and-white Hollywood musicals.'

Whereupon there came, soft as a fluttering descent of doves, a vision of disinterested scholarship uncontaminated by academy, religion or commerce, proceeding unsung by the slacked fires of parlours in small terraced houses all over the Bog. A life of dreamlike absorption, with no disturbance save the ticking of clocks, the turning of pages, an occasional shifting of coals in the grate.

Not for Helen this idyll. 'Odd as two left feet. And of course his sister Josie has to do *everything* for him. Washing, cooking, cleaning . . . even redecorating the house. Last time we were down there Josie was up a ladder in the bedroom and Kevin was sitting in front of the fire with his nose in a book about the Eastern Front.' Now her tone had a note of triumphal relish. 'He's *especially interested* in the Eastern Front.'

Like Mount Fuji with its summit obscured by bad weather, Neil sat grimly silent in a cloud of cigarette smoke.

On the street Marie and Neil fell behind in what appeared to be a deliberate split into human dreamers and inhuman achievers. Not for the first time I was uneasy about my classification.

Helen had no such qualms. 'Actually, the whole family's odd. Josie's hardly ever been out of the town . . . I think a pilgrimage to Knock was the only time . . . and you can never get Neil to go anywhere or do anything. That's why it's *great* having you two.' She gave me an affectionate glance. 'He would never come up here with me on my own.'

Despite the intimacy, it was impossible to ask the overwhelming question. Why was high-flying team player Helen married to reclusive loser Neil? It could only have been a consequence of violent sexual attraction. Hence a complementarity of sorts: she was full of go and he was full of come.

Helen moved closer and lowered her voice to a husky murmur. 'You and Marie are the only two people Neil has ever wanted to see.' There was a promise here of further avowals – but we were immediately distracted by a sharp cry from Marie.

Crossing the road in front of us was a provincial sports commentator who appeared on the Saturday teatime screens to recount the exploits of Ballyclare Comrades and Ballymena United. Hardly an exotic or glamorous figure (a dour elderly newspaperman with no flair for the new medium), he nevertheless provided Marie with her first live sighting of a television personality. Not in itself a great event but surely a harbinger of metropolitan marvels.

Despite this, Marie was unprepared for the impact of a contemporary department store. What she saw is now so commonplace that it is difficult to communicate her awe. But at that time she had never encountered the 'walk around' concept of open access. And hitherto, women's clothes had been in drab browns or greys or ladylike pastel shades. Now there stretched before her row upon row of racks ablaze with the new 'heatwave' colours – as though the vastness of the American prairies had been filled with the teeming brilliance of the tropics. Stranger still, this exotic plumage was *cheap*. The store lived up to the promise prominently displayed in the window: Fashions Ride High but the Prices Stay Low.

Marie lost her mind and ran about with broken cries, tearing open racks, yanking out and holding up items in a potentially limitless astonishment curtailed only by the sight of even more dazzling raiment further along. '*Stay with me!*' she commanded in fierce impatience, even though it was impossible to keep up with her darting zig-zags, as abrupt and disconcerting as those of a demented housefly.

After an hour of this madness she had bought a skinny-rib sweater, three blouses, two skirts and, at the blazing peak of frenzy, a minidress in glowing tangerine (most hectic of all the heatwave colours) with dramatically cut-away armholes and a circular keyhole on the back of the neck.

Gradually the rest of us experienced a disturbing tremor of her delirium. We had always assumed that we were fifties people, too old and staid to participate in the sixties revolution. But here was Marie, a married woman, daring to leap a generation. Though we had yet to see her in the dress – she lacked the nerve to come out of the changing rooms to show us – the mere idea of the purchase created an electrifying sense of potential. We might even be more privileged than teenagers who could never know the value of what they possessed. Youth is wasted on the young and, as mature students better appreciate education, so we married folk could more truly enjoy the freedoms of the age.

Marie exhorted me to follow her lead and invest in the bright two-tone shirts now available for men. As if an accountant could bedeck himself! As if an accountant could participate in the peacock revolution! She responded by exclaiming that a man with his own business could dress as he pleased. This was an intriguing thought – but the men's boutiques were still too daunting for one whose only break with convention had been a tie with a straight edge and horizontal stripes instead of the usual V-shape and diagonal pattern.

It fell to nondescript Neil to make the crucial breakthrough. He was even more scornful of expensive boutiques with double-forename titles like John Patrick and Mark Anthony ('only for fuckin' nancy boys'), but in North Street he paused before the window of a traditional Gents Outfitter (as dated as the shops round the Diamond) and turned to me with a strange and uncharacteristic exaltation. The window advertised a sale of those old-fashioned two-piece shirts where the collar is attached by a stud at the back of the neck. Why was Neil excited by a garment too awkward for the busy contemporary world? Like all great ideas, his proposal was stunningly simple – to buy these coloured shirts but replace the original collars with the equivalent in white (available for purchase separately), thus creating fashionable two-tones infinitely superior in quality to, but a fraction of the price of, those in poncy boutiques.

We rushed inside, only slightly subdued by the dim interior and the dignified presence behind the counter of a darkly suited hierophant in late middle age. Behind him, from floor to counter level, was an impressive and enigmatic expanse of large wooden drawers and, above these, another expanse of smaller drawers whose glass fronts revealed monstrous underpants, heavy vests and thick dark woollen socks. Gravely he opened one of the lower drawers and laid on the counter a pile of striped shirts; then, from another drawer, a second pile in exquisitely tasteful plain colours – velvety pastel greens and pinks as well as the conventional beige and blue. Either the manufacturers had made a failed late attempt to break into the youth market or the local gentry had been sporting brightly coloured shirts for years. But the reason for the sale could never be known – to enquire about such a thing would have been unthinkably impertinent. It was embarrassing enough to have to mention separate white collars. Without a murmur of protest, the aged servitor produced two of these from an upper drawer. Neil the barbarian grabbed two shirts, one striped and one plain, and substituted white collars for the coloured originals. Before us lay a pair of elegant two-tone shirts whose stiff pointed collars added a sophistication and sharpness unavailable in boutiques.

Not only were the shirts beautiful in themselves, there was an eerie exhilaration in creating a contemporary marvel from traditional components – an early example of postmodern glee and all the more potent for being nameless and new. It must have been difficult for the old haberdasher, torn between the satisfaction of making a sale and the sadness of seeing his wares ransacked and disassembled by savages. He leaned across the counter to lay a hand on Neil's arm. Neil looked up, startled, expecting a rebuke all the more devastating for being gently delivered. But the man was pointing across the shop. On the back wall was a thin vertical glass case displaying a range of white collars – wing, butterfly, rounded, pointed – so far behind fashion they were now years ahead.

Marie turned to Helen. 'It's all hours already. You'll never get shopping yourself now.'

'Och it's no odds about me!' Helen was the self-effacing aunt indulging boisterous young nephews.

Neil and I each bought four shirts, six separate collars in a variety of styles and a dozen disposable white collars of cardboard that looked almost as good as the real thing. Now I was consumed by the acquisitive fever that had earlier taken over Marie. Despite the numerous purchases (never so many at one time before) and the fact that it was Neil who had seen the opportunity, I bitterly resented his blithe appropriation (without discussion or apology) of the only pink shirt in the shop.

But Neil too was in the grip of irrational frenzy, reluctant to abandon the cave of treasures and gaping at maroon brocade waistcoats, yellow polka-dot cravats, enormous ties of patterned silk.

Helen took him by the elbow and led him to the door.

We were shocked to discover that it was dark outside.

'What about your war books?' I asked Neil.

He stared at me with the wild incomprehension of the possessed and, after a moment's pause, aligned himself firmly with the new age. 'Fuck the war.' As though seeing it for the first time, he looked about in rapture at the darkening city of closing shops and homeward-bound huddled figures. 'Let's go for a drink.'

In the Crown we were lucky to get a snug to ourselves, the ancient wooden bench hard but a relief from the long low look. (Provincial towns had yet to realise that the most sophisticated strategy for old bars was leaving them just as they were.) Exalted and radiant, Neil bought a double round.

'I've never seen him in such good form,' Marie said to Helen.

'Don't be talkin'!' Helen was in immediate and overwhelming accord. 'He's always a face on him. Everyone says so. It's always the end of the world with Neil.' She squeezed and shook her husband's knee. 'Maybe now you'll learn to brighten up for a while.'

'I was born crying,' Neil admitted. 'Cried nonstop for months. Nearly drove my parents mad. My mother kept taking me to the doctor and begging him to do something.' He sighed and took a long supportive drink. 'Eventually the doctor decided I was crying because my foreskin was too tight.' He sighed again, wearily. 'So they had me circumcised.'

Marie released an almost involuntary sigh of commiseration. 'Aaaahhh . . .'

'Worse than that . . . they botched the job. Left me with a dog ear . . . actually more like a dog's breakfast. I've always been so ashamed of it . . . you know? Used to always stay home on the day of the school medical.' Neil took another long leisurely drink. His audience maintained a compassionate silence. 'And I saw in the paper recently . . . circumcision removes thirty per cent of your erogenous tissue.'

Marie sighed again and leaned a little towards Neil, as if to compensate for the lost percentage with extra empathic concern. 'And did it stop you crying?'

'I was worse than ever.'

His rueful fatalism made us laugh. Briskly he finished off his drink and laughed himself – a man unjustly mutilated but bearing no grudge, only too well aware of the random maleficence of fate. 'Sure there's all sorts of things, isn't there? It's all in a lifetime. Helen has a hooded clitoris, for instance.'

'Oh . . . *really*, Neil.' But a ritual protest with no real force.

'And her cousin Attracta has an inverted nipple.'

'*Oh!*' Still, incredibly, no rancour. 'Are you going to go through the medical oddities of *my entire family?*'

Shaking with laughter, Marie regarded Neil in gratitude and tenderness.

He reached across and laid a gentle palm on her knee. '*Try on the dress.*'

'What? *Here?*' The poor child could never have expected a call on her goodwill so soon. '*In the toilet of a bar?*'

'Actually, it's not too bad.' Helen had been to the toilet as soon as she arrived – but her willingness to facilitate this trans-action was intriguing.

Deep attachment to Marie's style of dress made me uneasy about the radical purchase. Like the Jesuits, sexual fetish seizes its innocent victims early and makes them its creatures for life. Formative experiences in the fifties had left me forever in thrall to stiletto heels, pencil-line sheath skirts and elasticated girdles. At our first meeting Marie was wearing all three, the girdle immediately apparent as we moved out to dance and, in ritual exploratory trespass, my left hand drifted down to rest at a

point well below her waist (but not so low as to give the
impression of blatantly feeling her ass). Most girls grabbed the
transgressive hand and yanked it up with a furious N-O-spells-
NO look but Marie permitted it to remain, so that, as we
shuffled round to Brendan Bowyer's crooning, I thrilled to
the feel of the taut integument encircling her hips. The glory
of girdles was the mixture of elasticity and stiffness, their
creaky, arcane complexity, like the canvas and rigging of old
sailing ships.

But Marie had already abandoned the girdle. Now her
sheath skirts would go the same way.

She took along the PVC coat for protection and wore it
over the dress as she hurriedly re-entered the snug and
slammed shut its door. But the coat of fingertip length did
not extend below the dress and served only to emphasise the
unnerving exposure of her legs. There was no denying the
dramatic effect. The tight defining sheath was gone but the
notion of a user-friendly interface was possibly even more
startling.

Neil was first to find words, though murmured with difficulty and after long silence. 'Aren't you taking the coat off?'

'Me upper arms look too fat.'

Again Helen was the sensible aunt who reproved, though in
mild tones, the excitable child. 'Don't be silly.'

In the enclosed dim the tangerine blazed like a delinquent
sun. From its monstrous energy there was no protection. We
were all irradiated to the core.

It was what has come to be known since as a paradigm shift,
a momentous revelation, rich in complex reactions. At the
time we could scarcely have described how we felt. Elation
contended with dread for mastery of our stirred and troubled
souls. Marie was most afraid – and with reason. The poor angel
was *driving the paradigm shift*. Tittering nervously, she flung herself onto the wooden bench, desperately trying to minimise
her volume and pull down over the exposed thighs protective

material which did not exist. These attempts to diminish impact only made it more intense. And merely by sitting next to Helen, Marie had created a dramatic contrast with the bulky 'smart'n'tartan' look – nothing in fashion is sadder than out-of-date jauntiness. As though further to point up the distinction, Helen's driving restricted her to orange juice when I went to the bar for another double round.

Time and unguent alcohol were needed to help us assimilate and accept.

Eventually Marie too was reconciled – and even contemplated further change. Raising her right foot, she regarded it sceptically. 'High heels just don't go with this kind of dress.' Holding the shoe with her toes only, she allowed the stiletto heel to drop from her foot in a symbolic gesture of renunciation. 'Ah'd need a wee pair of slingbacks to go with it.'

Of the Three Graces (Girdle, Stiletto and Sheath), two were already banished and the third now marked for banishment.

Desperately needing comfort in the back of the Beetle, I pulled my overcoat across our legs and slipped my hand between Marie's thighs. She reciprocated by opening my flies and taking hold of me, peaceably but firmly, as though it would always be her trusty staff in the journey through a turbulent and perplexing world. Mutually reassured, we returned in silence over the desolate mountain, where even the Ponderosa was dark.

When we stopped for fish and chips on the outskirts of the Maiden City, Marie stirred from her dream. 'Come to our place tonight.'

Our flat was certainly no Temple of Eros but in the absence of authentic grandeur it is often necessary to improvise. As soon as we threw off our coats Marie turned out the light and switched on the electric fire. By the glow of its bars and backlit plastic she then threw down side by side a pair of tartan cushions from the sofa and another from each of the armchairs (perhaps after all there was jauntiness left in the smart'n'tartan look). Gratefully, tenderly, couples lay down and created the sibilant temple music – slither and rustle of clothing, sighs of wonder and contentment, friction of palms on warm skin.

It had been a long, fatiguing day at the end of a fatiguing few weeks. Accumulated tensions swiftly dissipated, I rolled over and fell into untroubled sleep.

6

'You picked a great time to fall asleep' – Marie over Sunday breakfast at lunchtime on the tiny table in the kitchen.

Like a heavy vehicle with its back wheels embedded in mud, my brain strove without purchase or progress. '*What?*'

She acknowledged my obtuseness by leaning forward to speak slowly and distinctly. 'Neil was at me the whole time.' Entirely lacking human warmth, her face was a monument of Carrara marble – correct, imposing, polished, cold.

'*At you?*'

'At me,' she repeated with tremendous finality, falling back in her seat.

Behind her, clearly visible through the multicoloured plastic curtain, was a cardboard box of dog-eared folders containing the accounts of Dominic Dunbar and a sample of his clients. Needless to say, the box was due to be returned first thing on Monday.

'What do you mean' – I made little attempt to disguise deep

reluctance – '*at you?*'

'What do you *think* I mean?'

'Did he finger you?'

'YES!' Her pretence of detachment swept away by a renewal of outrage, she lunged forward angrily once again. 'The whole time you were lying there snoring like a turd.'

Beyond the window were dark buildings, silent and brooding on Sunday, and above them a sky which offered no consolation. Rain was about to resume its commentary on the absurdity and futility of human endeavour.

'Why didn't you stop him?'

'With Helen probably lying awake?'

'Let me get this straight.' Hamming like a barrister, I closed my eyes and made as though to ease the pain of concentration by grimacing and pinching the bridge of my nose. '*Neil* gropes your fanny. *You* permit him. It's *my* fault.' I opened upon her eyes of atrocious lucidity. 'Is that an accurate summary of your argument?'

For a long cold eternity we regarded each other. Both of us could play the marble monument game.

Finally Marie snorted and looked away. 'I should have known there was no point in telling you.'

'That would depend on your *purpose* in telling.' Pedantic ratiocination always infuriated Marie. 'If the intention was to chastise me for negligence, I'd say you've achieved it very well. On the other hand, you may wish me to assault Neil with a hurley stick. In which case . . .'

Marie interrupted with an alacrity and sharpness that jolted me out of my pose. 'I don't want a word of this breathed to Neil. *Is that understood?*'

Unwilling to condone Neil's advances, she also feared a denunciation which would terminate the sexual excitement and perhaps even the friendship.

'You enjoyed it,' I suggested.

'I'm fond of Neil. He gives me compliments.'

Throwing back my head, I released into the cramped space above a bitter disabused laugh. 'Not so long ago you couldn't wait to get hold of me. Couldn't wait to make me sign on the dotted line.'

Every marital dispute leads to Grievance Central.

'And as long as I live I'll never be allowed to forget it.'

Her departure from the table was understandable but a tactical mistake, for it left me free to claim the mantle of righteousness by clearing up and washing the dishes. And while Marie read the Sunday paper on the sofa (reclining on the tartan cushions which had supported her wantonness of the previous night), I made much of hoisting onto the table the box of fat folders.

But it was impossible to concentrate on accounts.

'That wasn't the first time with Neil, was it?'

She turned a page and straightened the paper. 'I'm not discussing this any further.'

Harsh, mirthless laughter is often required by the adult. Already fairly adept, I practised mine once again.

'What's so funny?'

'I was thinking of Neil's righteous indignation at Colm O'Kane.'

My turn to commit a gross tactical blunder. Not only offered a change of subject, Marie could now protest innocence with passionate sincerity. 'Colm has never laid a finger on me from the day I got married.'

In the evening, exhausted by scrutinising accounts (and unsure whether to be pleased or alarmed by a failure to uncover irregularities), I was desperate to forgo the ritual visit to the Quinns. Staying home even had an extra attraction: failure to show would punish Neil without alerting Helen. But of course Marie insisted on going.

In any case, Helen may already have known, though her demeanour was neither more nor less vibrant than usual. She had the crucial bourgeois talent of maintaining a shining veneer. Neil, though, seemed edgy and distributed Garibaldi biscuits in an uncharacteristically servile way. I took advantage of his vulnerability to propose a drink after work on Monday, supposedly to celebrate my giving notice to the Yanks (since Marie and Helen were not free at four, no one thought the invitation odd).

In fact, giving notice was far from the jubilant experience I had anticipated. First, the Leader accepted it with surprising equanimity – and it is always a shock to discover that you are dispensable. Then came the disquieting thought that a bright sanitary environment might after all be more congenial than the small-town grubby-folders world.

So I was unexpectedly equivocal in Mullen's – and Neil was unexpectedly jovial, elated by a successful subterfuge. 'Had to tell Dessie Duddy I was going to the shops. Otherwise he'd a been here. Telling us the rest of the story of his book.' He slid contentedly onto a stool, at the same time holding up to the barman two hands separated by the height of a pint. 'Dessie reads these big fat paperbacks and tells me about them in the car. The latest is about this American senator . . . handsome, gifted, ambitious . . . but ruined by scandal. Goes demented, lives alone on this island with his son and trains the son to kill successful politicians. When the boy is still a child the father breaks both his thumbs in two places and resets them as these sort of *talons,* rigid as steel, that can *disembowel with one swipe.'* Neil displayed menacing hooked thumbs. 'Just what *you'd* like to do to the Yanks.'

'Actually, I didn't suggest a drink to celebrate giving notice.'

Instantly Neil's grin was replaced by his habitual wariness. Wordlessly he turned to accept his pint, which he set before him like a loaded weapon.

'Should we move to a table?'

'I'm all right here,' he said. In his manner there was a sudden obduracy and resentment, as though he suspected I was about to use ingenious trickery.

In fact this was the case. During negotiations with Dominic and Barry I had acquired a strong theoretical underpinning from articles in American accountancy magazines in the well-endowed library at work ('Negotiate like a Pro', 'Deliver the Deal', 'Goal Redefinement in WinWin Negotiating') and had adopted the maxim of John F. Kennedy quoted by all three of the authors ('Let us never negotiate out of fear. But let us never fear to negotiate.')

Neil, though, seemed to have an instinctive grasp of the theory – for instance, the foolishness of talking too much and giving information away. He took a small sip from his pint and impassively waited for me to begin.

'The thing is . . . *I know you've been at Marie a bit.*'

Not even a granite man could have failed to respond. Neil lurched forward abruptly, searching my features with keen eyes. 'Marie tell you this?'

'No no no no. We haven't discussed it. I just couldn't help noticing.' My warm chuckle was meant to convey understanding and tolerance ('Don't aim to get even – in anger you'll make the best deal you'll ever regret'). 'You'd need to be blind and deaf not to.'

Here my nerve broke and I reached for my glass. Fortunately Neil was frowning at the floor. But when I eventually replaced the glass he failed to look up or speak. This was a problem addressed by the test at the end of 'Negotiate like a Pro'.

When the other side suddenly *goes silent* do you:

a) go silent yourself?
b) ask a question?
c) start a conversation with someone else?
d) talk to break the silence?

'Is Helen aware of what went on?'

As though working from the same set of guidelines, Neil

encouraged doubt by refreshing himself with a long draught – and failing to answer the question. 'Helen knows I like Marie . . . and has no problem with that. She knows I'm not about to run off with Marie.'

Earlier Helen's ignorance had seemed a virtual certainty. Now the only certainty was my own ignorance.

This time I was silent and Neil put the question. 'So what are you saying here – lay off . . . *or what?*'

To demand a cessation would mean taking a win–lose approach and a victory secured in this way would be fleeting ('Their revenge will come soon and be sweet'). Wiser to go for a win–win outcome.

After a long meditative drink I inclined earnestly to Neil. 'What I'm saying to you is this . . . *there's nothing much in it for Helen and me.*'

He stared in astonishment – and issued his version of the mirthless laugh. 'Listen to the accountant.'

Such personal attacks should be ignored ('Never take on the person instead of the problem').

'But there *is* something that'll have to stop,' I said sternly, gratified by Neil's alarm. I paused, as if to allow a response, though I knew he would wait for my explanation. 'We can't be seen together wearing two-tone shirts.'

It was thrilling to add a new stratagem to the manual – disorient the adversary with what appears to be a threat but is only a well-disguised joke. However, for my final touch I returned to established practice – concluding the negotiation on a generous feel-good note ('Offer something of value to the other but of little consequence to you').

On Neil's shoulder I laid a hand in virile bonhomie. 'Same again?'

7

It was one of those heady times when constraints become opportunities. If Mullen's was no longer safe (Barry was now a regular there at weekends) and the alternatives infeasible (no one wished to repeat the unsettling experience of the Electric Bar) then we could shine all the more intensely away from the gaze of the dull herd.

On Friday evening the Quinns received us in excited amusement at the novelty of dressing up to stay indoors. In fact, we seemed to have taken even greater pains than on one of our nights out. Neil and I were in suits. Marie wore her tangerine dress, as powerfully inspirational as Van Gogh's sunflowers. Even Helen was more elegant than usual, in a sleeveless charcoal grey shift more suited to a dinner dance than an evening at home. And there seemed to be something else different about her – but its source was not immediately apparent. Perhaps it was merely heightened animation. Immediately she approached to lay a hand on each of us, as if for support in the event of collapse on release of the laughter effervescing within.

'Wait till I tell you.' She paused to struggle for control. 'Celia came into the bank today and *wanted to know where we're drinking tonight*.' At last she could throw back her head to let pent mirth escape.

'Celia and Lexie!' Neil too turned his face to the ceiling as if, on hearing these terrible names, the Celestial Sadist might relent.

Yet in all our protests at harassment there was also a note of satisfaction. Though no one would mention it, or perhaps even consciously entertain the thought, we were aware of becoming a numinous group. Somehow we had assumed the mysterious effulgence of the chosen.

'So!' Helen was once more capable of speech. 'They'll be out looking for us tonight. And will very likely call here.'

'*Here?*' Marie looked about wildly, as if the couple might spring from behind the dark curtains.

'This town,' Helen lamented. 'We'll have to get out of this town. Wouldn't it be great to get away together somewhere? Completely away. To somewhere *lovely*. Paris, for instance. *We must get to Paris*.' We regarded her with amazement and admiration. 'But meantime we'll have to go somewhere nearer.' Helen leaned on Marie for support against imminent breakdown. '*We'll just have to drink in the bedroom*.'

I stole a glance at the door to the secret chamber. 'The *bedroom*.'

'It's at the back of the house, so you can't see a light from the street. And Neil lit a wee fire, so it shouldn't be cold.'

Before we could come to terms with this notion, possibly even more exotic than a trip to Paris, Helen ushered us into the private quarters, her chuckle of hostess satisfaction becoming a shriek as the threshold was crossed. Exclaiming and rushing ahead, she snatched from the back of a chair a matching brassiere and pants. But not before they were revealed as small of size, lacy of texture and strikingly unorthodox in colour –

powder blue instead of the customary white or peachy pink (how did this revolting colour dominate lingerie for so long?). Was Helen dootsie on the outside but *daring within?* I sat down heavily on the chair, touching in reverence the back which had supported the exquisite filigree.

'More chairs, Neil!' Fully recovered from, and perhaps even elated by, the underwear incident, Helen boldly commanded her husband who was frowningly crouched before the fire, working a poker with his right hand and delivering peat briquettes with his left, eyes tightly screwed up against smoke (not so much from the fire in the grate as the cigarette in his mouth).

'Sure we'll sit on the bed!' Marie immediately did so, bouncing to indicate enthusiasm and gaiety.

'I'll need more briquettes.' Neil considered Marie for a moment and then turned to Helen. 'You get the glasses and drink.'

When the Quinns left the room Marie turned to me with a patronising laugh. 'Did you see it? *The state of her.'*

'What?'

A familiar snort of annoyance at my habitual blindness. 'Helen's wearing lipstick tonight. I've never seen that before. But it's a desperate colour – Strawberry Kiss. I used to sell loads of it in the shop . . . but nobody'd be seen dead in it nowadays.' A glance at Marie's dismissive mouth revealed that she favoured pearly translucence. 'And she doesn't know how to put it on.'

'What's wrong with it?'

Marie grunted again at the tedium of explaining the obvious. 'It's just slapped on any old way . . . smudged all over her mouth.' For me the idea of a gauche daub was touching but Marie was affronted by the lack of skill. Eventually, though, her scorn became compassion. 'Has she never heard of *lipliner?* Helen just *hasn't a notion.'*

Our genial hosts returned bearing, respectively, fuel to heat the shivering body and fuel to heat the frozen soul – and creating the illusion of an outlaw encampment in a mountain cave. For this room was even more sombre than the outer chamber, with heavy, dark wallpaper and an ancient wardrobe and chest of drawers like Monument Valley outcrops. Here was a near-ideal hideaway, certainly the ultimate inner escape – and enhanced by complicity, danger and awe.

'It's like being in a priest's hole,' Helen breathed, immediately covering her mouth at this unfortunate remark.

'My wife,' Neil informed us happily, 'has a talent for unconscious *doubles entendres*. She comes out with the most *unbelievable things.*'

'It's true.' Helen was not only unabashed but proud. 'I drove to work the other day and I was still in the car getting stuff when this character from down the country . . . in an old wreck of a Vauxhall . . . tried to park in front of me and then behind me and hit my bumper both times. So I went in to work and announced to all and sundry, This old farmer just banged me from the front and behind. Well . . .' Helen searched for words adequate to the reaction. 'The whole bank just . . . *erupted.*' Her hands rose as though flung aloft by a violent explosion. 'It just *erupted*. Leo Patton was still nearly wetting himself *ten minutes later.*'

More than happy to tell a joke at her own expense, Helen laughed as lengthily and lustily as Leo presumably had done, eventually regaining sufficient control to pour everyone gin. However compelling the distractions, she was always a diligent bacchante. Then she sat on the bed next to Marie, leaning back on the giant headboard and stretching her legs out on the quilt. For some reason this position accentuated her Strawberry Kiss.

Unnerved, I half rose. 'Did you want a chair?'

'No no no no.' Gaily she waved me back, painted lips parting in another high laugh.

'We're grand,' Neil said with satisfaction, though still on his feet, a fag in one hand and a drink in the other, considering Marie who was considering me.

'Sit where you are,' she commanded. 'If you have a drink on a bed you'll pass out for sure. Talking of which . . . can I go into the living room for my bag?'

'As long as you don't put on the light.'

She returned without the bag but carrying a tiny dark bottle, from which she tapped out on her palm several heart-shaped lavender pills. With a fine sense of theatre she displayed them in silence for a moment. Then she held out the hand to me.

'*What are they?*'

'Purple hearts.'

'*What?*'

'I give these out by the dozen in prescriptions every day. And keep a few meself. Just like sweeties. One for you . . . one for me.' She laughed at the horror contorting my face. 'They're for people on diets. I took them myself to lose weight . . . and then I found they kept me going all night.'

Kept her going *at what?* Marie's past was steadily becoming more lurid. But there was an even more urgent consideration.

'You'll be caught. There'll be an audit.'

Marie threw back her head and laughed so hard she had to close her hand to avoid dropping the pills. '*What?* On a golf course? The only audit Colm does is checking who needs a glass filled.'

Not only was I married to a dope fiend but one apparently inured to the ways of theft and deceit. And not only a user but a pusher. Her eyes bright with roguery and tenderness, she stretched out the pill hand. 'Won't do ye a bit of harm. Take one, look see.'

Obedient as a child, I accepted a pill and washed it down with a swig of gin. Without taking her eyes from me, Marie did the same. And continued to hold me in a penetrating gaze. This was some sort of solemn rite – a bond of beyond.

Neil perched on the bed by Marie. 'Give us one.'

Helen turned to him. 'Neil, you're always up to the clouds of the night as it is. You need something to put you to sleep instead of keeping you awake.'

But Neil was not to be denied a stimulant.

Finally Marie looked to Helen, who alone held out against the pills, though not in an angry judgemental way. In fact, she appeared to approve and was herself more euphoric than the actual junkies. She had a remarkable talent for vicarious pleasure.

And her commitment to transgression was proved later as the childhood of Barry Hinds was being fleshed out for me. His joiner father had worked mostly in England and his mother had taken to drink as an escape from chronic depression. Barry had become a granny's boy because his paternal grandmother hated her daughter-in-law and indulged the child to the full to wean him away from his mother. Marie and Neil took turns to tell the story and when we were pondering it in silence the now-forgotten threat was suddenly made manifest: with shocking discordancy the doorbell rang.

Helen leapt from the bed and adopted a tense animal crouch.

Like pain intensified by anticipation, the second ring was harsher, more accusatory and insistent.

'It's your sister, Helen,' Neil whispered. 'Let her in, for Jesus' sake.'

Marie's nerve broke next. 'It's Celia and Lexie.'

'*Fuck them!*'

The soldier's word was perhaps the most heavily used in the vocabulary of the town but we had never thought to hear it pass a bank girl's lips. For a moment we were too stunned to appreciate what had happened. Possibly contaminated by Strawberry Kiss, Helen had unequivocally rejected tradition and joined us in espousing contemporary values.

No! We had never given ourselves to the new age. It was more a case of slipstreaming behind it. And what a wonderful technique is slipstreaming – cunningly tucking in behind the cutting edge and enjoying the benefits of its penetration but avoiding involvement when it runs into trouble. In fact, what is accountancy but official slipstreaming – entrepreneurs take risks and accountants slipstream behind them taking percentages.

In this most torpid and rooted of rooms there was a sudden sense of breakneck plunge in which we were nevertheless protected from collision and damage. A *double* slipstream was operating. Four of us were slipstreaming behind the zeitgeist and three of us were also in a second slipstream behind Neil.

Instinctively we looked to Neil for leadership – and were not disappointed.

'*Helen!*' he cried in gratitude and wonder, leaning across the bed to seize her and pull her against him. True to her new abandon, Helen fervently threw herself into the embrace, actually drawing up a long leg in involuntary hunger for fusion. Grunting with pleasure, Neil seized the zip on the back of her dress and, in a swift fluid motion, took it down to its limit. Like skin from ripe fruit, the dress fell away to reveal a black brassiere as lightweight and minimalist as the earlier blue. These were in dramatic contrast to Marie's long-line cathedral bras with padded reinforced cups and substantial side and bottom panels of heavy-duty power net encasing stay bones. It was possible that Marie was the opposite of Helen – daring on the outside and dootsic within (though, of course, Marie could argue that a more substantial congregation demanded an equivalent edifice).

Even more moving was the second revelation. Helen's upper back was lightly asperged with spots. My similar disfigurement created between us a bond like a secret betrothal – but even without being a fellow sufferer, my heart would surely have been touched. For where may perfection be found except in contrived images? Blemish is fullness and life; perfection is nullity and death.

There was enormous scope for observation and pondering – and I was blessed with a front seat, excellent lighting and a nearly full glass. But leisurely study and rumination would not be permitted. Life demands the actor and abhors the voyeur.

What precipitated my involvement was that Neil suddenly broke off from Helen and, perhaps concerned that Marie felt rejected, leaned across to plant on her pearly lips a Strawberry Kiss. He immediately returned to Helen but Marie now felt the need for a partner and rose to draw me to the bed.

Neil had moved round to align himself with Helen so that couples were now side by side. Soon all four of us were in similar disarray, with clothing still attached but hanging open for access.

As so often with defining moments, what happened next is unclear. Memory seems to preserve only the meaningless and trivial and to draw a veil over the actions which change the course of a life. And perhaps it has good reasons for so doing.

On this occasion the missing detail is how my right hand came to rest on Helen's lower abdomen – so close to her pubic hair that I could almost feel its bristle and charge. I could have placed the hand there myself – but a persuasive voice whispers that it was lifted and laid.

So who was my secret facilitator?

Who moved my hand?

8

Sexual captivation usually operates on a win–lose basis; homage to the new is at the expense of the old. But the current situation appeared to be miraculously win–win. My attraction to Helen enhanced desire for Marie – and Marie's involvement with Neil seemed to have a similarly tonic effect. On Sunday mornings Marie and I would lie late and indulge in astonishingly effective foreplay – discussing the shenanigans of the previous night. After one such intense engagement Marie made the sweetest remark I have ever received or am likely to receive. Now in late middle age and regrettably disposed to dismissiveness and disgust, I have only to recall her words then to know that I have been illuminated by glory. 'Ah God that was lovely,' she groaned, 'I was sort of half coming *for ages* before I came.'

But not even ecstasy could dispel her natural tartness. 'And you tell me you don't fancy Helen?'

'You know I've always detested that kind of bourgeois girl. That's why I married *you*, isn't it?'

Women's fondness for flattery has been greatly exaggerated. Correctly sensing evasion, Marie ignored the compliment. 'But you detested them because they were teasers. Helen doesn't tease . . . in fact, she lets you *finger* her.'

Here was a wonderful opportunity for sincere and passionate denial. 'I've never once fingered her. I stroke her bush, that's all. Locating a hooded clit would be much too demanding.'

Facetiousness was no more effective than flattery. 'And you're trying to tell me you *don't enjoy it?*'

This was the time to reply to a question with another question. Or, in this case, the same question. 'And what about you? Don't *you* enjoy what *you* do?' Marie adopted the simple stratagem of silence. 'And anyway, what choice do I have? You're furious if I try to sit it out. You're even worse if I fall asleep. What else can I do but join in?' Having established my own accommodating passivity, it remained only to reaffirm Neil as prime mover. 'This is all about Neil and you. Neil's the one pushing for it – and I don't hear any objections from you. Are you trying to tell me *you* don't enjoy it?'

Only so many questions may be ignored if a conversation is not to die. 'It's all a bit frantic, isn't it?'

'What do you mean?'

'What do you think I mean? *All those hands.*'

Certainly it was often hard to believe that there were only four male hands at work – and this hyper-activity was counter-productive. Only mystics and very young men associate pleasure with frenzy.

'And Helen's shouts and fanny farts.'

'*Fanny farts?*'

'You know what I mean.'

It was true that when Helen was aroused her vagina often expelled air with a loud liquid *tttthhhh* . . . but I would never have mentioned such an embarrassing phenomenon and was shocked that a woman could do so. Then I realised that Marie saw divine retribution in this visiting of a gross indignity on the posh. She smirked with evil relish. 'Did you enjoy those too?'

Chivalry spurred me to defend Lady Turquoise. 'More sublime than Mozart.'

Marie detected an element of sincerity in the quip. 'You *do* fancy her.' Leaning across the bed, she delivered a pre-emptive punch to my shoulder. 'Don't you be tossing off.'

'The way things are going I haven't any fluid to spare. You're sucking me dry . . . like a vacuum cleaner.'

Marie's laugh became a groan. She curled up. 'Oh God.'

'What's wrong?'

After another groan she offered my life's second sweetest remark. 'I'm going all funny downstairs again.'

But the weekend evenings in flats were beginning to lose their excitement. It was not so easy to renounce the bars. Youth demands to be seen. And, though the final half hour at home was diverting, it was preceded by several dull hours in dull rooms. However glamorous the attire, there was no longer any sense of occasion. Another problem was lack of development in the floorshow itself. Like other less abstract stimulants, transgression requires an increasing dosage to produce the same intoxicating effect.

None of this was ever discussed. Neil's trigger was action not words. And there had developed a post-coital etiquette, whereby the women would spring to their feet, hold a bunch of clothing against their breasts and a bunch of underwear against their groins (not just for protection but to catch escaping semen) and, awkwardly hunched over in modesty, scamper for cover, the hostess to the kitchen or bathroom and the guest wife to the bedroom. Husbands dressed silently at opposite ends of the living room and when everyone was ready the guests departed, with all the intimacy, gratitude and wonder expressed through farewells in a complicitous whisper, as though the forces of reaction were listening and explicit remarks at a normal volume would put us all at risk.

'Goodnight. *See you tomorrow.*'

Hands on arms in solidarity. Brief but fervent cross-couple cheek pecks.

'Goodnight. Goodnight. *See you tomorrow.* Goodnight.'

If the departure was early on Sunday morning Neil might turn back to whisper, 'Call round earlier tomorrow', and the shamelessness of his affection would draw from Marie a bright peal of laughter, hastily and guiltily suppressed, a hand on her indiscreet mouth.

'You mean *today.*'

Not to be outdone by her husband, Helen would often add, 'Come round for something to eat, sure', and we would pledge ourselves to an extra commitment in spite of the danger.

Further progress required overt action or words. Without relinquishing the protection of the slipstream, I created propitious situations. On drinking nights I would wait till Helen went to the toilet and then leave the living room myself on fabricated errands or chores. Neil was alone with Marie and free to initiate – but never went further than moving beside her and talking with fierce intensity into her face. Since the Quinns' flat had a separate toilet as well as a bathroom and it was common for two drinkers to seek relief at the same time, on our evenings as guests of the Quinns I took to going for a pee shortly after Helen in the hope of encountering her on her way back. Both toilets were off a great gaunt gloomy hall, entirely without decoration or furnishings, which offered a space outside convention and history. It was a beautiful moment if the timing was right and we arrived here simultaneously but from opposite directions, like legendary lovers meeting in a dark forest glade. Helen would release her high nervous laugh – but then rush past in confusion.

Of course there were opportunities to speak to her at the bank. On one of these visits I paused inside the door, transfixed and illuminated by ravishment. At a desk behind the counter Helen was poring over figures, her upper body leaning forward with intense concentration, while her lower half twisted sideways to profit from the space by the side of the desk. For work she had remained in turquoise mode – a dark turquoise pleated skirt and a lighter turquoise blouse with a bow, the very panoply of dootsiness – and yet the sight was deeply affecting. Men are presumed to prefer frank or coy sexual display, but infinitely more moving is unconscious absorption, the primal innocence of limbs and features concentrated on a task. Even when the tableau came to life it did not destroy the effect. With her left hand Helen abstractedly pushed her hair behind her ear, allowing the hand to linger on her head in enchanting absentmindedness. And then there was an exquisite final touch. The heel of her raised right shoe came away from the foot, so that the shoe – a dootsie black court shoe with a small leather bow – was held only by the toes. Even the grim God of Calvin would have issued a sigh. My buried stone heart was exposed, melting, liquidly full – a cherry brandy liqueur chocolate on a warm open palm.

Yet all I could share with her was business. I had come to borrow more money.

For, as newlyweds employ sexual frenzy to blind themselves to the enormities of cohabitation, so the new accountancy partners commenced their union by ecstatic immersion in refurbishment. This was undoubtedly Barry's finest hour. He supervised every aspect of the alterations, from design and choice of materials to the most trivial details of the work, ceaselessly moving about with a brusque confident stride, importance and purpose irradiating his solemn features like sun on an imposing mountain range. Only with the secretaries did he display his habitual familiarity – but when it was necessary to deal with workmen in the presence of the women he was suddenly imperious and domineering, determined to demonstrate his power in a spectacle simultaneously laughable and sinister, like that of a drunken sailor flexing tattooed biceps in a bar.

The term 'secretaries' suggests young women but Alison and Roberta were middle-aged Protestant matrons (not merely Christian but 'saved') retained by Dominic from the Willman & Rosborough era, though not for ecumenical but for brutally practical reasons ('They work like dogs and never moan'). Barry ought to have been anathema to such women. In fact, they adored him and did most of his work, for which they received scant gratitude. At the end of the first week he showed me a photograph of Roberta in *The Sentinel* (the Protestant equivalent of *The Journal*) as a member of 'The Drumahoe Women's Institute team which won the table-laying competition in the City Hotel'.

'She's all allured with herself about this. Alison showed me and Roberta went like a beetroot. Table-laying for fuck's sake! *The Drumahoe Women's Institute!*' Chortling happily, he went downstairs to return the newspaper.

The offices of Willman & Rosborough were on the middle and top storeys and, in line with my strategy of ascetic remoteness (Calvin's God has always been a major role model for accountants), I had urged upon Barry the big office on the middle floor, next to the secretaries, while I took the smaller upper office by a storeroom. Here there was only one luxury – a state-of-the-art calculator, the compact and elegant Olivetti Programma 1a (though it is surely not an indulgence for a worker to invest in superior tools).

The accuracy of Helen's assessment became increasingly apparent. Most of the clients were ordinary small businesses and only a tiny minority were dubious. We could easily afford to shed the chancers if we retained the solid core – and Barry was tirelessly assiduous in reassuring doubters. Even better, Helen had instructed Leo Patton to spread throughout the business community the news that the practice was under the supervision of the soundest of sound men (me). This kind of support is the advantage of living in small towns: the problems come later when favours are called in.

The Olivetti was in service day and night but work was frequently interrupted by troubling visions. For rectitude I would have to look out of the window at the top of the Protestant Memorial Hall. Especially difficult were the evenings of working late alone, when night whispered seductively of tenderness and abandon and it was no longer possible to distinguish the Mem with its obdurate message of No Surrender. Undulant, impalpable, mysterious, a pale body fluttered before me like a candle flame. But, not only denied relief by Helen, I was not even in a position to relieve myself. Sex with Marie was now so frequent and demanding that I dared not squander desire.

Late one Friday evening in December an erotic reverie was broken by Barry bursting into my office and rushing straight at my desk. First, I had thought I was alone in the building. Barry had disappeared early in the day and I assumed he was visiting a distant client (another congenial division of labour – Barry loved to travel as much as I hated it). Second, he was wearing a cream roll-neck sweater which not only belonged to me but was one of my favourite garments. Third, there was something crazy about his hair. Fourth, he was obviously distraught. All these factors must be listed sequentially – but their impact was shockingly parallel.

He was already talking as he crossed the room and sat down – but the wealth of compelling visual data made it impossible to grasp his words. Most dramatic of all was the top of his head.

'Christ, Barry, what have you done to your hair?'

Some phrases began to get through. 'She shot me down. She shot me down.'

'Your *hair* for Chrissake?'

He stared at me as though I were the crazy one – and in the pause we both realised the need to find an appropriate starting point. But consideration of his tragedy from the beginning overwhelmed Barry afresh. He buried his face in his hands. 'Jesus . . . *Oh Jesus*.' This posture offered a full view of the top of his head and it was obvious now that he had combed his hair forward to conform with the new style of the age. The borrowing of the sweater probably had a similar motivation. But, combined with his mohair suit and plump form, the innovations were absurd.

'You've just seen your girl?' I suggested. He nodded without removing his hands. 'And the new hairstyle was supposed to impress her . . . *she's young?*'

He lifted his face in sudden outrage. 'She said I looked like an old ted.' Repeating the insult reopened the wound. His face crumpled in anguish. 'A *teddy boy* for Chrissake. A fucking *ted*. An *old* ted.'

It was difficult not to feel satisfaction. In the fifties the crucial male initiation rite was the achievement of 'getting your hair back', removing the childish side parting and brushing hair up and back in a quiff like those of Fabian and Elvis. Big hair was one of the attributes which separated the men from the boys – but my own hair kept subsiding into an altar-boy flop. Now such floppiness was the height of fashion. All I had to do was not cut my hair. Barry's towering advantage was suddenly an embarrassment – but it was doubtful if he could manage a radical relaunch. Like Marie, he had given himself completely to the fifties and, though no one likes to admit it, there is usually only one giving.

'What age is she, Barry?'

'Nineteen.' He laughed bitterly. 'Thinks Ahm a fuckin' geriatric at twenty-eight.'

'This is the judge's daughter . . . the beauty queen?'

'Aye.'

Barry scrabbled for cigarettes, nervously lit up, sucked hungrily on a kingsize, retained the consoling smoke for as long as possible and finally blew it at the ceiling in relaxing release. This appeared to settle him for a moment. What he did next unsettled *me*. Frowning reflectively, he placed the cigarette in his mouth and shoved his hand under the sweater to scratch himself, violently distending the vulnerable roll neck. In such a sweater a sagging neck is as fatal as a ladder in nylon stockings. And this was an almost new garment, purchased in Belfast a few weeks before.

'Barry for Chrissake,' I snapped, *'don't stretch the neck.'*

He yanked out his hand like a guilty child – but it looked as though the integrity of the roll neck was already fatally compromised.

The sharp reprimand banished his momentary calm. He leaned towards me in renewed desperation. 'What am Ah gonay do? What am Ah gonay do?'

'You're sure it was final?'

'She blew me out,' he said in bitter amazement, pausing, baffled, at the inadequacy of the words to convey her contempt. 'Blew me out like a fuckin' wet fart.'

My most grievous fear was being realised. Partnership was turning out to be as intrusive and demanding as marriage. First, the shocking familiarity of borrowing my clothes. Now the horror of involvement in his private life.

Hesitant, tentative, observing me closely, Barry uttered the words I least wanted to hear. 'Could you speak to her for me?' His tone was broken, wheedling, weepy. I dared not look at his face. All the planning in the world will not protect us from life. I had tried to predict every conceivable partnership problem – but what business plan would allow for a heartbroken partner in tears? 'She's from the Antrim Road . . . same as you.' How our destinies pursue us! Not only is it impossible to protect ourselves from the future, it is also impossible to protect ourselves from the past. 'Her da knew your da.'

'Barry, we're up to the eyes at the moment . . . and then Christmas. I've no time to –'

Before I could finish, Barry was leaning over the desk,

actually plucking my sleeve. A bolt of terror transfixed me. 'She's downstairs in my office.'

As though expecting me to make a run for it, Barry kept a light hand on my back as we descended the stairs.

'What's she doing *here*, Barry?'

'I brought her in to see the place now it's all fixed up.'

'You know there's nothing I can say?'

Ignoring this defeatism, Barry ushered me into his office and, astonishing in one so near breakdown but a moment before, introduced me with jovial assurance to his girl. Then he directed me to his own seat behind the desk and retired to make us all 'a nice wee cup of tea'.

Emer had many of the conventional attributes of beauty – regular features, large liquid eyes, dimples, almost waist-length blond hair – and was fashionably dressed in one of the new tent-style minidresses and high-heeled, knee-length suede boots; on the chair behind her was a mini-length fun coat in which bands of black leather alternated with fake fur. And yet, as so often with career beauties, the effect was entirely unattractive. Perhaps it was her smirk of superiority and dismissiveness, her certainty of always creating an impression while never herself being impressed. This was an overpowering disincentive to acknowledge her charms. Beauty, like goodness, must never declare itself.

Now she withdrew cigarettes and a lighter from a shoulder bag on the floor and, without offering one, proceeded to light up herself. Leaning forward had caused her hair to fall over her face. She pushed it back behind her ears and tossed it impatiently, like a thoroughbred shaking off troublesome flies. It was obvious that she was not prepared to make conversation and that whatever she heard would be contemptuously rejected, most likely by those stock remarks ('Little amuses the innocent', 'Sarcasm's the lowest form of wit') in which the lack of originality is compensated by the virulence of the scorn.

I have never been fond of 'my-da-knew-your-da' slabber and her atrocious manners did not dispose me to familiarity. But someone would have to say something.

'Look.' I spoke without warmth, never difficult for accountants. 'This is an embarrassing situation. Neither of us has any desire to be here. I've known Barry only a few weeks and only as a business partner.'

She tossed her hair and laughed unpleasantly. '*He* seems to think *you're* the bee's knees.'

Both partners annihilated in a single short sentence. Obviously she had inherited her father's talent for judgement. Even if he managed to survive this evening, Barry would surely end up on the gallows.

'All I can tell you now is that the business seems secure.'

She released a shrill laugh and once again tossed her head. Irritating horseflies seemed to pester her continually.

Many a weaker man would have lost his nerve in the frigid silence that followed.

To add to my alienation, Barry had decorated his office in violent ultra-modern style. Each of the walls was a different colour, the curtains had circles of different sizes and colours, randomly positioned, and the swivel chair in which I sat had a circular base, a narrow stem and a goblet seat of dark hide. I felt like the cherry in a cocktail glass.

Barry re-entered, beaming happily, as though to the convivial hubbub of a bar. I firmly declined tea and rose. Gesturing and mumbling with optimistic gratitude, Barry accompanied me to his office door.

At least it provided material for an anecdote later. Says I to him, hold on a minute, Barry. Says he to me, she's sitting downstairs. Christ, I nearly shat a brick. Helen, concentrating intently, was obliged to put down her gin and tonic to accommodate a gratifying spasm of laughter.

And when we met in the hall later she did not rush past with lowered eyes. Instead, she paused and our lips met with the delicacy and tenderness missing from the frenetic floorshows. As, in Japanese art, a few sublime brush strokes convey the bulk of a mountain or the depth of a gorge, so this fleeting touch of the lips revealed a yearning intense and profound. Alas, she would not let me hold her. Although I would shortly be tweaking her nipples and fondling her pubic hair, now she would not even permit me to touch her through layers of clothing. It is too much to expect etiquette to be logical – but this inconsistency was surely bizarre. She pulled away with an apologetic whisper, leaving me alone in the forest glade, enchanted, trembling and bereft, lingering in one of the expensive fragrances she now wore at weekends.

She was also extending her use of make-up – though, according to Marie, still without knowledge or skill. 'Does she not know to keep away from shiny eye make-up?'

'Why should she do that?'

'It makes your eyes look all watery.'

I wished Marie would spare me these merciless technical analyses. When Helen offered her consenting mouth I did not wish to notice the track of foundation cream under her jawline.

Helen's next innovation was even more startling. One Friday evening she bounded into our living room, limber and buoyant, sporting a trouser suit in heavy tweed with a large and brightly coloured check. This was obviously an attempt to combine traditional material with contemporary style – but, as with many such initiatives, the combination succeeded only in discrediting both. There was no need to wait for Marie to declare it a grievous mistake.

'Green and purple.' Stunned by the assertiveness of the check, I could think of nothing else to say.

'Pistachio and damson,' Helen gaily corrected.

Marie would instantly have detected a negative reaction (and consigned the failure to a wardrobe for ever) but Helen seemed convinced that we shared her enthusiasm. 'I ordered it from Celia's catalogue. I was hoping it would arrive for the weekend.'

Helen must have had misgivings later, however, for the suit never appeared again and her purchasing policy underwent drastic change. On one of our Saturday trips to the Belfast department store Marie bought a sleeveless off-white roll-necked minidress in a soft woollen material. We were familiar with Marie's clinging sweaters and tight skirts – but the seamlessness of the clinging dress produced the shock of aesthetic unity. And where synthetic fibres often seemed vulgar and harsh, wool had the warmth and authenticity of womanhood itself. Here was a successful marriage of old material and new design, for as well as a fashionably high hem, the dress had armholes cut deep into the shoulders. Marie looked at me, then at Neil, then at Helen, then back at me. No one spoke – but words were superfluous. The most profound homage is silent. Always alert to the comic power of understatement, Marie threw back her head with a laugh. 'I think maybe I'll take it.'

As in any form of hunt, early shopping success has an intoxicant effect. As soon as she had removed the garment Marie plunged back among the racks like a boar hunter into the heart of the forest. Helen and Neil conferred solemnly, standing very close together and looking into each other's faces in a way that implied a momentous discussion. Had Helen finally objected to Neil's naked admiration for Marie? Together they went off to the women's changing rooms, where Helen commanded Neil to wait.

Her eventual reappearance was fleeting and partially blocked by Neil – but there was no mistaking the radically cut-away armholes. *Helen was trying on the roll-necked minidress in black.* She was about to make the leap of faith. The dootsie bank official would be born anew as a dolly bird.

Conversion is a mysterious and intriguing phenomenon. There is usually a long incubation period – but something must actually trigger the change. In Helen's case the facilitating factor may have been the roll neck of the dress. Helen had a taste for dramatic caparison – her winter coat had a shawl-like embellishment in fake fur which extended right across the shoulders and almost down to the waist. And the human neck is constantly aware of encirclement (for me an intensely uncomfortable sensation endured in the interest of fashion). For the wearer of this minidress the high roll neck may have worked as an insulator, its persistent intrusive grip suppressing awareness of exposure below.

One of the saddest experiences in a relationship is discovering that what has excited one partner provokes wrath in the other. At what should have been tidings of joy, Marie's face flushed with rage. 'What?' she hissed through clenched teeth. '*The same dress as me?*' And among the racks where she had so recently romped she now turned back and forth in desperation, no longer the hunter but the cornered beast.

'It's flattery,' I argued. 'She obviously thinks you have good taste.'

Marie's anger was indeed tempered – but only by bitterness and sorrow. 'The *bitch*.' Twisting and turning, she stamped her foot in near-tearful anguish. 'That *bitch*.'

'Maybe Neil made her buy it. To try to make her look like you.'

Blame was not to be transferred. A woman should know not to violate the code. For Marie many requirements of etiquette had the status of axiom. And, as after our quarrels, her disillusion was absolute. Every infringement was the end of civilisation as she knew it. Henceforth, only desolation, darkness and silence.

In her heedless hands were several garments.

'Aren't you trying those on?'

Marie glanced down without interest. 'She'd probably buy those as well.'

It struck me that this was entirely possible. 'Go and try them all on – *but don't come out of the changing room*. Never worry about what I think. Buy the whole lot if you want. Just don't come out wearing any of them.'

When the four of us met again Marie's rage had subsided into a surliness which Helen was too excited to notice. More surprising was Neil's failure to recognise the problem. In the bar he asked Marie to try on the new dress and, when she snappishly refused, he put the same request to Helen. It was obvious that Helen was sorely tempted and unaware of the continuous affront the dress would offer Marie. Fortunately she declined. But almost immediately she did something as foolish.

'What else did you get, Marie?' Without waiting for an answer, she actually snatched up Marie's bag to root in it as excitedly as a child at Christmas, drawing forth a violet Lycra blouse with a dramatically long pointed collar and leg-of-mutton sleeves. Even more incredible, she then stood up and, holding the garment boldly against her, turned to her husband. 'What do you think?'

Helen had a curious blindness to social conventions other than her own and, even more crippling, an inability or unwillingness to register mood and response. Although the only one not drinking (she was always a responsible and disciplined driver), she was easily the most skittish now, exhorting us constantly but vainly to 'show a bit more jizz'. Impossible to reconcile this demand for gaiety with Marie's silent pressure on me to join in her sulk. It was fortunate that another of Marie's binding conventions demanded good humour in bars. With each sip of alcohol her mood recovered a little.

Only patience and precision timing permitted me to benefit from Helen's high spirits. She strode out of the ladies with marvellous boldness – then bent over in laughter at the now-familiar ambuscade.

'Can't wait to see you in that new dress.'

Helen's seizures of merriment were remarkably expressive. This one seemed to suggest that my wish was absurd but understandable and, all in all, rather sweet.

But it was perhaps just as well that the new dresses were not worn that night. Even Neil's ardour might have been defeated by the logistics of removing a roll-necked dress in company in a horizontal position in the semi-dark.

Helen's exuberance persisted into the lovemaking, which she punctuated with immoderate exclamations, snorts and, it has to be admitted, fanny farts. Despite this increased abandon and the frenzied flitting of Neil's hand over Marie, to explore Helen yet again seemed furtive, seedy and crass. It was time for something more spiritual – *an act of communion.* When Helen rested her hand on the carpet I laid my own over hers to register a sensitivity beyond animal lust. Immediately she issued a loud caw, though perhaps more in response to Neil's vigorous ministrations. Interpreting the sound as encouragement, Neil redoubled his efforts. Another unspoken convention was parallelism, so that although Marie and I would have preferred a more leisurely pace, we were obliged to match our rhythm to that of the Quinns. Soon Helen uttered that most exquisite ascending triplet of notes and on the top note squeezed my hand so fiercely, actually gouging it with her nails, that a massive charge immediately surged through my loins.

With a trill of girlish laughter, Helen gathered her clothing and dashed for the bedroom – we were in our flat this time. Marie's surly mood seemed to have returned. When Neil went to the bathroom I touched her in tender apology and concern.

'You didn't come, did you?'

'With the noise of Helen?' Herself a silent lover, Marie grunted in fastidious disgust. 'She was worse than an Orange band tonight.'

When the Quinns were both dressed they did not leave as usual. Instead Neil sat down with a grave expression and, without consulting anyone, poured out four gins in a deliberate manner that seemed to presage difficult negotiations or revelations. Then he turned to Marie.

'You didn't enjoy yourself tonight.'

Marie had a range of shrugs as varied and expressive as the laughter spasms of Helen. The shrug she made to Neil now was particularly uncooperative and curt.

'*I* did.' Helen threw back her head in a laugh of startling heartiness and volume and responded to Neil's concentration on Marie by casting me a bold collusive glance. This was another inappropriate reaction. In this town you did not congratulate anyone and least of all yourself. Advertising personal fulfilment would be like flaunting an advanced case of leprosy.

Neil seized Marie's hand. 'What's the matter, honey? You've been in terrible form all night.'

Under the pretext of straightening up, Marie withdrew her hand. 'It's just so . . . all so *mad* . . . all so . . .' She paused, lost for a moment, then inspired by sudden eloquence. 'It reminds me of being groped by Fuckso McCallion up the walls after the Mem.'

'That's this character's fault.' Helen leaned across to punch her husband on the shoulder. 'You're so *rough*, Neil Quinn.' Then she turned to us to explain. 'He's so *rough*.'

My tender hand-holding strategy had surely been vindicated. A little after-tremor sweetly claimed me.

Neil sat back in rueful penitence, turning for solace first to gin and then to Gallaher's Blues.

I looked at Marie. 'I've always wanted to ask you this. What exactly did Fuckso McCallion do?'

Neither Marie nor anyone else paid me the slightest attention.

Neil came forward again in sudden animation. 'But this is just the point I was about to make. This is the problem. You women just lie there. You never do anything . . . or even *say* anything. How is anyone to know whether you're enjoying it or not? How is anyone to know what you want?' He looked at each of the women – but neither responded. 'You'll have to *say* what you want.' He stared directly at Marie. '*What do you want?*'

This was the verbal equivalent of a head butt. Marie drew back in shock and outrage.

He turned instead to Helen. '*What do you want?*'

Sitting comfortably and contentedly, with her legs crossed and her right foot playfully swinging, Helen issued a deep, richly ambiguous laugh and gave me a look that triggered a succession of delightful yieldings, a diminuendo of after-comes.

9

Our continuing absence from the local bars was arousing suspicion. One Monday morning Barry came into my office, sat down decisively and demanded to know why he had been unable to find me on either the Friday or the Saturday evening. Requiring me to account for my movements was yet another attempt to make the partnership a marriage. My vague gesture encompassed a multitude of possible activities and locations – and I deflected further interrogation by a cunning counter-query.

'Why were you so anxious to find me?'

Immediately his irritation changed to smugness. Pinching up the right knee of his slacks, he laid a moccasined right foot across his left thigh. 'I'm marrying Emer in the New Year.'

My response emerged with too-obvious reluctance after too long a silence. 'Congratulations, Barry.'

'You don't think much of her.'

The accusation had a bitterness that would have to be neutralised. 'No no no ... we hardly spoke two words. You shouldn't have thrown us together like that. It was late ... I was tired ... and I'm prejudiced against swanky Catholic girls.'

'Aw surely ... ye'd rather have scrubbers.' Barry shifted in annoyance at what he took to be perverse affectation. '*Why?*'

'They always give the impression of being something they're not. Pretend to be daring when they're really conventional and conservative.' This kind of explanation was all wrong for Barry. 'I've just seen too much of them, I suppose. But Emer looked like a genuine free sixties girl. And if I didn't think she was right for you how come I gave you such crucial advice?'

He remained deeply sceptical. 'What was that?'

'To comb your hair back again.' Barry had regained his fifties glory, with swept-back coiff, hound's-tooth jacket, black worsted slacks and black Italian moccasins, soft and supple as gloves. 'I presume you've met all the family.'

He snorted in sovereign disgust. 'Fuckin' Declan. Fuckin' Conal. Fuckin' Gráinne. Fuckin' Maeve. And that's only the half of them. Irish names. Irish dancing and feises. All that old Irish shite.'

'And the da?'

In fact, the man was a magistrate not a judge – but the latter term was more appropriate to his punitive zeal. Not merely a legend for his pitiless sentencing ('I will not tolerate teddy-boy behaviour in my district'), he was a leading figure in the St Vincent de Paul Society, chairman of the Committee of the Friends of Handicapped Children and a prominent Knight of Saint Columbanus. It would be interesting to know how he liked the prospect of a teddy boy like Barry for a son-in-law.

'A *cunt*.' Barry issued the monosyllable with explosive venom – and yet still seemed to find it inadequate, frowning with effort in the search for a suitably expressive qualifier. '*A cunt up the back.*'

It was difficult to know which avenue to explore – the etymology of this curious phrase or the behaviour of the judge. Barry made the decision for me. 'They have this big room ... sort of L-shaped, like. Fucker puts me round the corner so he can see Emer but not me.'

But why was a Knight of Saint Columbanus entertaining a cornerboy at all? There could be only one answer. The judge was compelled to accept Barry because Emer was pregnant. No sooner had I attained this detachment of insight than Barry pitched me back into emotional turmoil.

'Anyway,' he said, deceptively casual, as though proposing a return to work. 'Will you be my best man?'

Not merely an onerous duty in itself, acceptance brought further demands for socialising with Barry and Emer. It was necessary to invent weekend visits to Marie's relatives.

The Quinns were under similar pressure from Helen's sister Celia. Nevertheless, the four of us continued to drink in secret at each flat in turn. To while away the early part of these evenings, Helen suggested board games. Marie and Neil were fiercely opposed – they had no tradition of happy families engrossed in Monopoly and Scrabble. Board games were middle class, silly, effete.

Neil would countenance only virile blackjack and poker. But these gambling games were pointless without money stakes. Helen suggested bridge which was loudly rejected by everyone else; to be childish was one thing, geriatric another. Undeterred, she proposed canasta, a game of almost equivalent complexity but unburdened by negative associations. Like bridge, it was played in teams of two, so that, as spouse- or gender-based teams could encourage acrimony, Helen and I were pitted against Neil and Marie.

At first accountant and banker enjoyed a series of crushing victories, although the pleasure of winning was secondary to the thrill of intra-team communication. Overt discussion of play was forbidden, so it was necessary to resort to significant looks; eye contact was now prolonged, conspiratorial and heady. Never had Helen's blue eyes been so rich in meanings and promise. A crack team, telepathic in co-operation, fiendish in strategy and merciless in execution, we seemed virtually unbeatable. But our triumphalism was too naked. The honour of the working class was threatened. Understanding at last that this was no mere game, Marie and Neil gritted their teeth, applied themselves with greater concentration – and were eventually a match for the top pair.

Thus interest and equilibrium were restored and the problem of early evening solved. Canasta not only passed the time but provided a bonus. The mute but expressive signalling of partners was a kind of foreplay.

One Friday evening just before Christmas we settled down in the Quinns' flat with sighs of relief and expectation. Before us sat large gins, in which lemon slices floated like astringent water lilies while bubbles of tonic rose to the surface in lazy sinuous lines.

'This is the life.' Marie contemplated her raised glass before solemnly bringing it to her lips.

In harmony the rest of us also enjoyed the exhilarations of fire and ice.

This was the liturgical hour of evening when the compromised spirit is purified and healed.

'Oh by the way.' Helen turned to me. 'Celia asked me to speak to you. Lexie wants to go out on his own. He's fed up working for that crowd.'

Neil cut in angrily. 'I told you not to ask this.'

'I'm only *mentioning* it. I said to Celia I'd *mention* it. The thing is that Lexie needs equipment and a van . . . and they haven't much money. She was wondering if you could give him . . . you know . . . *some advice.*'

Neil intervened again. 'That's the kind of Celia. Always looking for something for nothing. Always looking for favours.'

Only now was it clear what Lexie wanted. 'I'm only starting out myself. We'd be happy to advise Lexie . . . but on the usual terms. We can't afford not to charge.'

'That's all right. That's all right. I just said I'd *mention* it.'

Helen conceded swiftly and with no apparent ill will. But it was obvious that she wanted me to work for her brother-in-law unpaid. Was this in return for facilitating a loan? For permitting me to stroke her pubic hair? Whatever the reason, the sacerdotal purity of evening had been contaminated by the toxins of day.

'Let's play cards.' Neil tossed a pack onto the coffee table.

'Three anythings and an ace!' Marie was determined to be jocund and bright.

'Canasta?' Helen regarded me anxiously. 'Usual teams? The two of us?'

'Sure.'

But there was none of the collusive gleam that would normally have accompanied such an exchange.

'What about Strip Jack Naked?' Neil frowned tremendously at the cards on the table.

It was obvious that he was in earnest and that here was a possible *way forward*, the breakthrough awaited so long we had practically given up hope. Though it was surely odd to choose so unpropitious a moment. Perhaps Neil had planned this before hearing of Celia's request. Or the incident had provided him with the necessary aggressive energy. The proposal certainly seemed to have taken a lot out of him. Lifting his glass, he downed three-quarters of it with the desperate avidity of a man dying from thirst.

Helen released a laugh which was probably meant to be blithe but came out forced and shrill. 'My husband is drunk again, folks.'

In this kind of situation a measured neutral tone is essential. Neil was appropriately grave and calm. 'I had two drinks after work, Helen.'

In the pause which followed, Marie and I tactfully applied ourselves to our gins.

Marie continued to hold her glass in the air, apparently

absorbed in the lemon slice. 'You mean . . . *actually peel off?*' She spoke without looking round – and immediately had another swift drink.

Her question suggested cautious interest without offering commitment. I wished I had thought of it first, for now Neil turned to me. Someone was going to have to make a decision. Even without leaving the slipstream, I felt the chill wind of the void.

'How would it work?' The speculative 'would' was a nifty touch. Even so, the question was significantly more affirmative than Marie's.

'I don't know.' Neil shrugged to emphasise the absence of premeditation and planning. 'I suppose you take something off each time you lose.'

How fortunate those who had already commented!

The responsibility of the veto now fell upon Helen. Her normally bright features were unusually drawn and when she finally spoke her voice bore the strain of duress. 'I can't very well spoil the party.'

'No one's forcing you.'

She subjected Neil to a darkly intense look. 'Aren't they?'

'It's only fun, Helen.' Neil waved his arms to suggest airy lightness, though the effect was rather spoiled by his abrupt consumption of the remaining gin.

The problem was that this game smacked of the vulgar depravity of the golf club set. Only the utmost delicacy and tact could make it seem merely a profane conduit for the sacred. Total purification of the spirit was certainly an essential prerequisite. Without waiting to be asked, I freshened everyone's gin.

The need for decorum was understood. Neil dealt cards with the gravity of a Chaldean magus and we gathered them with the diffidence of novices taking instruction. There was no sound but the regular respiration of the gas fire, an exemplary steadfastness at such a fraught time. Measured breathing is the key to calming the agitated spirit.

It was appropriate that Neil should be the first to suffer, removing his shoes in rueful resignation, as though martyred by an obligatory rite not of his choosing.

'You should have kept those to the last.' Helen's tone had an unfortunate asperity. 'The hum'll be nothing ordinary.'

At first Neil responded with the serenity of a true spiritual master. 'I had a bath after dinner, Helen. And these are clean socks.' Unfortunately the tolerance of the adept was followed by the retaliation of the husband. 'By now I understand your obsession with personal hygiene.'

Like the balm-scented hands of a masseuse, the gentle suspiration of gas spirited tension away. Also mollifying was the equal distribution of penalties. Soon there were four pairs of empty shoes – which was as it should be. Initiates should enter the temple barefoot.

In shockingly rapid succession Neil lost socks, tie and shirt. Despite this, he remained unperturbed and even displayed extraordinary nobility in shedding both collar and body of his two-piece shirt when he could easily have claimed these as separate items. This was leadership by example. But Helen chose not to follow, ungraciously removing a single earring.

Injustice always provokes me to outrage. '*Both!*' I shouted. 'No cheating.'

These days Helen used the soldier's word with local gusto. 'Fuck off.'

Neil surrendered his trousers while gamely insisting it was good fun. In the dimly lit late-night frenzies there had never been an opportunity to consider either Neil's underwear or its freight. His baggy white Y-fronts made me glad to have rejected the frivolity of the lurid new jockey shorts. But less reassuring was the bulk of his beasthood, alarmingly powerful despite its loose cover, like a battleship under camouflage lying at anchor in a secret fjord. Neil was also stocky and heavily built, with a powerful torso in dramatic contrast to the long weedy frame which had earned me so many childhood jibes ('Ye big string a misery ye', 'Ye big drink a water').

No sooner these morale-sapping thoughts than I too was obliged to lose trousers and shirt.

The girls were fortunate in not wearing dresses, for the separates gave them an extra life. Marie now lost her blouse and compensated as well as possible by hunching and covering herself with her arms. This was in spite of wearing her favourite brassiere, the classic Formfit Confidential, a fifties model with hard latex-lined cups that provided 'built-in emphasis'. In truth it was the least confidential of garments. This bra had such self-assurance it could stand up without a woman inside.

It was interesting that, faced with the same choice, Helen opted to remove her skirt instead of her blouse. The realisation that she was hiding her spots gave me a sweet empathic throb. I myself kept my back to my chair to conceal an equivalent shame, the residue of a virulent teenage acne which had brought the most wounding insult of my life ('Ye've a face like the door of a jail with all the nails pulled out').

Helplessness always attracts the bully. Now Helen's vulnerability inflamed the worst bully of all – fate. After losing again on the next round she flung down her cards and pulled open her blouse with such angry abandon that one of the buttons sprang off. Marie and I simultaneously half-rose but the velocity of the projectile made it impossible to trace.

'I'm keeping the blouse over my shoulders,' Helen defiantly informed Neil. 'I don't see why I should have to *freeze* as well as everything else.'

'But it's *roasting* in here.' Neil sought corroboration from Marie, who wisely turned away and kept her counsel. 'The heater's been full on *for hours*.'

Shivering as though at chilliness, Helen draped the blouse over her shoulders in a subterfuge that quite won my heart. Then she copied Marie's protective hunch, so that, given the impossibility of staring, there was little to be seen. Yet this rendered what could be glimpsed all the more moving. Perhaps enchantment must be elusive – a nymph flitting through trees. Helen was wearing the powder-blue brassiere that had once been hanging on a bedroom chair. To see it supporting her now was like meeting an old friend who astounds with unsuspected sophistication and elegance. For this was my first experience of a design which would later be popularised and mass-produced – the underwired cutaway brassiere that creates for smaller breasts 'the basket of peaches effect'. It seemed a miracle of delicacy and engineering skill, at its lacy heart a tiny satin bow and at the heart of the bow a tiny pearl, like the secret pearl of yearning on the male sexual meatus. Not that this was in any way *superior* to the Formfit. The world was immeasurably richer for both.

It would perhaps have been wise to remain as we were and sip gin with no further shedding of clothes. A glimpse of nymphs should suffice. But when has human avidity been content with a *glimpse?* Besides, no one had the authority to suspend the rules. After a brief uneventful lull, maleficent destiny pursued Helen once more.

'*Fuck you anyway, Neil Quinn!*' She sprang up, knocking aside the card table, and stamped off to the bedroom, blouse billowing like the cape of an imperious queen.

With a fierce exclamation Neil rose and plunged after her. To the sound of raised voices from the bedroom, Marie and I dressed in silent haste. Words and sense could not be distinguished – but the righteous fury in Helen's tone was a new and terrible thing. It was obvious that the exhilarating journey was over. The runaway train had ploughed into a wall.

Marie touched me with a guilty whisper. 'Let's get out of here.'

'You'd better tell them.'

Cautiously Marie approached the bedroom and, standing a few feet from the door, called out in a diffident appeasing tone,

'We're off now, OK? See the two of you later.'

The bedroom door jerked open. Neil, still in his underpants, a powerful bull goaded to the limit, advanced threateningly on Marie, who fell back before him. 'You're not going anywhere. Sit you down there. Sit the two of you down for your supper. You're going to get your supper now.'

Marie and I did as we were told.

Neil turned back to the bedroom and issued an authoritative command. 'Get out here now and make these people their supper.'

Helen appeared in the doorway, tying the ends of her dressing-gown belt as though garrotting a rapist. Her face was bloodless, white, taut, a mask of implacable fury. '*You make it.*'

Neil appeared to have difficulty breathing. His chest heaved and his nostrils dilated in a desperate attempt to inhale. He took a single step towards his wife. 'Ahm still in me *fuckin' underpants.*' The struggle for air forced him to pause. 'Get out to the kitchen and make the supper.' He took another decisive step. 'Or do Ah have to *keek your fuckin' arse all the way out there?*'

There was a fraught silent stand-off in which each considered the other. Then, yanking her belt even tighter, Helen went to the kitchen.

Neil came across for his clothes and made a promise of hospitality that was anything but cordial. 'You'll get your supper in a minute now.'

From the kitchen came angry rattles and bangs.

'I'll give Helen a hand.' Marie's offer was more of a plea.

Neil gripped her shoulder. 'You'll sit where you are.'

He went back to the bedroom to dress, leaving us alone with the clatters and crashes, and in due course returned to resume his seat with an air of calm expectation.

Helen came from the kitchen bearing a sumptuous tray. Along with the tea things there were floury ham-filled baps, wheaten scones sliced and buttered and a plate of the finest

Scottish shortbread – Paterson's Petticoat Tails. But our appreciation was merely visual. As Helen turned to kick the door shut behind her, the tray slipped from her grasp and fell in a percussive symphony of chaos that was amplified and prolonged by the high vault of the room. Then, as happens so frequently, the ensuing silence was even more terrible than the noise of destruction.

Helen stared blankly at the wreckage. Then, seizing a fistful of hair on each side of her head, she pulled savagely downwards, threw back her drained face and screamed.

10

O n Saturday we lay late but without realising the dream of youth – that if sleep is sufficiently long and deep the sleeper will awake to a world cleansed and renewed. Instead of rebirth there was torpor, desolation and loss. Nature herself seemed to be permeated with catastrophe and disinheritance. Lacking the will to venture out, we sat in our living room before the electric fire and gazed at a sky dirty, thin and discouraged – like a cake of soap after a week in a busy bar toilet.

Marie blamed Helen for overreacting and provoking Neil. Not that Helen was under obligation to undress in public, but she could have declined in a more tactful way. My theory on the importance of Helen's back spots might have disposed Marie to sympathy. Yet I failed to propose this, partly out of apathy and partly because it would have revealed a keen observation of and interest in Helen. Then again, such caution was scarcely necessary now that the whole thing was over.

Perhaps this was just as well. There was something incestuous and claustrophobic about huddling together in darkened flats. It occurred to me that Neil was using us to reproduce his own neurotic and reclusive family life. So many of our attempts to make a new life unconsciously re-create the patterns of the old. But there would now be an enormous emptiness in our lives. How would we get through this bleak afternoon? And what of the interminable Saturday evening with no Helen and Neil?

Indeed they did not arrive in the evening. They arrived as we were finishing a dismal lunch of baked beans on toast. With Neil trailing in her wake, Helen swept into the flat on a tide of apology and contrition. Her carry-on had been *beyond belief*. It was *unforgivable*. It was *stupid*. She had spoiled the whole evening for *everyone*. And what made it especially absurd was that she had been *thoroughly enjoying herself*.

Neil flung up his hands and rolled his eyes. 'This is what she claims.'

No, no – it was *true*. Hard to believe perhaps – but *true*. Her reaction had been due not to disapproval but to *excessive enthusiasm*. Far from enjoying it *too little*, she had been enjoying it *too much*. In the highly strung and overwrought, excitement can easily turn to panic and *attack the very thing cherished*. Throughout the explanation she continually turned from Marie to me and back, her blue eyes desperate for understanding and forgiveness. Still torpid and numb, we could offer little in the way of response.

'But of course Neil was dreadful too,' she added at last.

Neil released a heavy sigh. 'I can't manage any objectivity or balance in fights.'

'Or any restraint,' Helen prompted.

'It's always the bitter end,' he had to admit.

Marie nodded gravely. 'I'm the same.'

The Quinns regarded each other in penitent communion. Already Helen's radiance was surging back. She was bright and wholesome and positive as an educational toy.

'Listen!' she cried. 'We're thinking of going a run over the border.'

'*Donegal!*' Astonished at the thought of crossing into the wilderness at any season other than high summer, Marie turned to stare at the lowering clouds which a valetudinary sun lacked the energy to pierce.

Helen explained that the desolation was at its most beautiful in winter and that, as a consequence of regular family excursions in childhood, she was familiar with all its secret wonders.

With a woman who blazed like a thousand suns, who needed Nature's rays? Bewildered but docile, Marie and I donned heavy clothing and permitted ourselves to be ushered out into the back seat of the Beetle.

Our own Donegal trips had never gone beyond the trashy resort towns near the border with the North. Helen bypassed all these, making for the vast and untamed North-West and delightedly pointing out a symbol of the county's freedom from regulation – its first and last set of traffic lights. As we left towns behind to climb through the mountainous interior, there was a thrilling sense of lighting out for the territory and abandoning civilisation's discontents and travail.

'I ought to be doing my Christmas shopping,' Helen laughed, 'but I just couldn't face it today ... and would you look at Muckish Mountain ... isn't it *gorgeous?*'

Suddenly aware of our isolation, I snatched a look at the petrol gauge and discovered that the indicator was stuck well past maximum. The Quinns must have filled up before calling on us. Not for them the shabby trick of stopping at a petrol station to shame the passengers into paying their way.

Our hearts too were full. Just as reconciliation releases in lovers a flood of generosity and tenderness, so this unexpected reunion moved the four of us to the verge of tears.

Further revelations and intimacies were to follow. We descended to the coast and a village which had none of the careless vulgarity of peasant Catholic culture, the amusement arcades

128

and gift shops and garish Marian grottos, but instead was a model of Presbyterian primness and displayed in its well-maintained centre an imposing memorial to the agent for an ascendancy landlord's estates.

Helen was gratified by our consternation. 'There's these little pockets of Protestantism all over Donegal. Most of them have thriving Orange Orders ... they even march on the glorious Twelfth. Naturally Daddy gravitated to these places.'

The village was intriguing but hardly cordial. Helen drove on through and shortly afterwards turned down a side road which eventually brought us to an astounding strand which stretched out in each direction without a single person, vehicle or even building in sight. Into this exposed and windswept grandeur we stepped with the diffidence and awe of pilgrims entering the cathedral at Chartres.

Marie took a few hesitant paces and stopped to gaze at the strand under her feet. Unlike the usual loose, uneven beach surface, this was porcelain-smooth, firm, and of a delicate hue between beige and pearl grey.

'Even the sand is swanky,' she marvelled.

Neil nodded in grave accord. 'Protestant sand.'

Helen led us to the site of her family picnics, where a stream clove the high dunes and provided protection from the wind. Celia had once pushed the young Helen into this stream, provoking in her father an uncharacteristic wrath. 'Daddy was always so encouraging and *supportive*. Everything we did was just ... just ...' Helen raised her arms and opened her hands as if to equate her father's support with the immensity before them. 'Just ... *wonderful* ... you know ... absolutely wonderful.'

'He didn't think *I* was so wonderful,' Neil said.

Helen immediately refuted the slur. 'That just isn't true, Neil. Daddy was always perfectly civil to you.'

Neil turned to the ocean a countenance inexpressive apart from a slight downturn at one side of his mouth. '*Perfectly civil.*'

Helen punched him – but without real resentment and we faced into the wind with the intoxicating sense of a return to the pure source, the cold and desolate northern Arcadia of the Gael.

Cleansed and renewed after all, we drove back by a different route, which led through another plantation village, this time inland, with austere buildings of grey stone facing a decorous river. Here Catholic peasants had partially overrun the settlement and established trashy shops and singing lounges. Helen pulled up at a tiny old bar, empty except for a white-haired but spry leprechaun, who immediately rushed to pile turf on the fire.

Such a prolonged exposure to winter demanded the solace of hot whiskeys. Helen cried out in alarm that she was unable to drink the fiery national spirit – but almost immediately, plucky as always, agreed that she was willing to try it hot. Then our tour guide was vouchsafed a revelation in turn – the astounding transformation of whiskey when mixed with hot water, lemon juice, sugar and cloves. Our day was a paradigm of Mother Ireland: grandeur and harsh winds without, cordiality and sweet warmth within.

Neil turned to order another round – but the aged leprechaun had disappeared. Possibly spirited away by fellow little people, he was not behind or under the bar or indeed anywhere in the tiny building. Alcohol, cigarettes and money, all the desiderata of the Gael, had been left for the customers to plunder at will.

'The fucking *Marie Celeste*,' marvelled Neil, scanning the premises once more.

But unlike the Great Unsolved Mysteries of the Sea, the conundrum of the vanishing proprietor was presently explained. He burst into the bar, cackling with glee, and bearing an aromatic parcel wrapped in newspaper whose sodden petals he carefully unfolded to reveal four steaming bags of chips. A gift to the strangers from Ireland of the Welcomes (though typically marred by vulgarity – a heavy lather of tomato ketchup covered the chips). This was his way of expressing gratitude for the custom of youth. All the young people nowadays went to the big singing lounges for American country-and-western music and chicken in a basket at ten o'clock. And if it was not the singing lounges it was dinner dances in new hotels. No one wanted to drink in the traditional bars any more. Helen expressed outrage at this frightful apostasy – and Marie too murmured in protest – but our genial innkeeper was resigned to his fate. Soon the old bars would be gone . . .

We ached to reassure him further – but Helen had perilous mountain roads to negotiate. By now it was completely dark, the boundless and exorbitant wilderness dark which makes us appreciate company. In this infinity of bleakness intimacy seemed no longer a claustrophobic indulgence but a necessary survival stratagem. Another consolation was hot whiskey. Helen insisted that we would have to go to her flat since only she had the essential cloves. This was surely another of those endearing ploys by which her generosity was disguised. In matters of hospitality the Catholic half of her character certainly came to the fore. At least she allowed us to buy the whiskey.

While Neil made the hot drinks, Helen prepared another of her miraculous impromptu meals, a salad with thick slices of ham, which, as she explained with typical modesty, had been boiled in cider flavoured with onions and cloves and then baked in a coating of mustard and honey.

'That's why I've loads of cloves,' she laughed, deflecting gratitude and praise. 'I always like to have a ham in the house at this time of year.'

Even the occasional recalcitrance of her materials seemed to be a source of pleasure to Helen. 'Why is it,' she called out gaily from the kitchen, 'that *some* hard-boiled eggs are so *easy* to peel while others are *just impossible?*'

When we had finished eating we moved easefully to the living room, already heated by the gas fire. Helen placed on the coffee table a pack of cards.

'Canasta?' Marie divined, with the bright-eyed enthusiasm of the grateful guest.

Helen shook her head, in her eyes a deviant gleam.

'Ah *no!*' Marie cried. 'There's too much bother with that. There's no call for that, Helen.'

'I was *enjoying myself.*' Helen appeared to be unequivocally firm.

We sought guidance from Neil. His sagacious eyes focused intently on his glass. 'This is what she tells me.'

Apparently untroubled by doubt, Helen began to deal cards.

'Wait a minute.' It seemed to me that, as always, a little fore-thought and planning would prevent a multitude of problems (an apothegm on the wall in my former place of employment: 'If you fail to plan you plan to fail'). 'To make this fair, every-one ought to be wearing the same number of items to start with. And there ought to be rules about what constitutes a single item. I mean . . . do two earrings count as one? That kind of thing.' Before they had time to consider these preliminaries my foresight engaged with the endgame. 'And when someone's completely naked do we stop there? Or play on till everyone's the same? Or make the naked person do something else?' Sufficient questions to be going on with. 'Do you see what I mean?'

Helen issued a violent plosive.

'I see someone's been thinking about it,' Marie tartly remarked.

Neil looked to Marie. 'The Chartered Accountant.'

'He'd be even better as a contract lawyer.' Helen studied me with quizzical tolerance.

'Don't be talkin',' Marie burst out. 'You should have seen the small print I had to agree to before we were married.'

As so often, a plea for justice was rewarded by contumely and scorn.

'I was only trying to be *fair*.'

To this richly deserved reprimand, they responded with wild howls of mirth.

But there was no need for me to retaliate. The gods invariably punish hubris.

Almost immediately the girls discovered that, without their usual weekend jewellery, they had dangerously few items to surrender. And Marie was wearing a dress instead of separates, which further depleted her panoply. Soon she was exposed in a mismatched long-line bra and washed-out big knickers, which she would never have worn on an evening out, much less an occasion of total exposure. She concealed these as best she could by crouching forward with folded arms until her shoulders almost touched her knees – although, for a sophisticate of lingerie such as Neil, mismatching and homeliness may well have enhanced the charm. Certainly he reacted to Marie's predicament with gallantry and fondness – and seemed glad to express solidarity by removing his own trousers and shirt.

I was wearing a vest but derived little advantage from this extra garment. Only in women is homeliness charming.

'Christ!' Neil shouted in unconcealed impertinence. 'I didn't think anyone under thirty wore those any more.' He turned to Marie. 'It's a wonder he isn't wearing a liberty bodice as well.'

'*A liberty bodice!*' Laughter at the memory of this childhood monstrosity made Marie forget herself and throw back head and shoulders to reward Neil with a clear view of her Silhouette Young You, a heavy control structure in elastic power-net which claimed to 'provide secret support' and 'smuggle years off the figure'. 'With white rubber buttons and a miraculous medal sewn onto the side!'

All this was merest diversion. Fate's true design was to test Helen's resolve. She accepted with equanimity a rapid reduction to bra and pants, perhaps because this evening she had cannily protected her back in an old Queen Anne wing chair (she had been on the sofa the night before) and was better prepared in a matching set like the powder blue but this time in black.

The next crucial loss again fell to Helen, who accepted with remarkable fortitude, her expression rueful but resigned as she undid her bra and leaned to drop it on the floor. 'This game should be renamed Strip Helen Naked.'

There was a long moment of silence and stillness. Another significant milestone had been passed.

Neil inclined confidentially to Marie. 'Don't you think Helen has marvellous nipples?'

Barely time to acknowledge one milestone before another flashed by. This was the first overt reference to sexual parts. Not only intoxicating in itself, it provided a licence to stare. Indeed it would have been rude *not* to stare. Neil himself gazed with leisurely proprietorial fondness. 'They're like cigarillo butts.'

From Helen came a noise between a gasp and a laugh. 'Really, Neil.'

But it was clear that she was not displeased. And indeed the simile was accurate, if inadequate. Would any cigarillo have a subtle suggestion of amethyst? Nor did it take into consideration the surprise of discovering robust nipples crowning small girlish breasts.

Marie had the opposite configuration – large breasts whose tips were flesh-coloured and soft. This may have been why she was so reluctant to lose her Silhouette Young You. Or it may have been simple embarrassment at size. The poor child was acutely aware that large breasts were going out of fashion and was suffering the agony of the fading exemplar who sees a popularity taken for granted slowly but surely ebbing away. In vain did I reassure her that, however tyrannical the fashion for paucity, there would always be secret admirers of plenitude.

Nor did it help for Neil to lay a sympathetic hand on her bare arm. 'It's all right, honey.'

'*Get lost!*'

Things might well have turned nasty if Marie had been forced to shed more – but this evening Fate had other plans. It was Helen who was obliged to make the ultimate sacrifice, which she did now with startling calm, even indifference.

'There you are now. That's all there is. I may as well go and put on the tea.'

This forthright approach to nudity made it all the more shocking. We were floundering, disoriented, lost – as when a long-attacked barrier suddenly yields and the attacker is pitched into space. Not for the first time men were more flummoxed by female co-operation than female resistance.

'Can I get dressed now?' Helen turned to Neil as though to a GP after a check-up.

'Hold on a minute.' Neil could scarcely comprehend how swiftly enchantment dissipates and quotidian banality returns. Forgetting the earlier contempt for planning, he turned to me now in his hour of need. 'Didn't you say there was something else people should do?'

Sensing Helen's eyes on me, I looked away and, although neither resourceful nor quickwitted, was equal to the challenge. 'A naked person who loses again should recite a poem standing on the coffee table.'

Neil rushed away and returned with a tattered schoolbook, which he placed on the table. Then resumed play and threw down an ace to Helen. 'Sorry, honey. Really sorry about that.'

Helen played her cards slowly. Six of diamonds. Two of clubs. Nine of clubs. Four of hearts. '*Fuck!*'

Neil solemnly handed me *A Pageant of English Verse*. 'Pick a poem.'

The exultation of power was overwhelming and sudden. Entirely at my mercy was a naked young woman. Now I understood the divine ebriety of inquisitor and tyrant.

'*The Rime of the Ancient Mariner.*' I remembered this as longish, half a dozen pages at least.

Helen stood up, atrociously casual, finished off her glass of whiskey (her newfound ability to drink whiskey cold may well have been the key to this extraordinary evening), then climbed onto the table with the anthology and found the relevant page.

'It is an ancient mariner and he stoppeth one of three.' Suddenly suspicious, she flipped forward. 'It's *over forty pages! Fuck away off!*' And with that she flung the book at me.

Although the bulky hardback caught me full in the chest, I experienced no pain.

'Something else instead,' Neil demanded – but a sudden awareness of our relentless momentum left me too stunned to respond. We had actually crossed a threshold apparently attainable only in dream.

It was Marie who found inspiration. 'The catechism.'

Everyone regarded her in amazement. Again Neil rushed off.

Helen could easily have climbed down but chose to remain, still partially bent in laughter at the coup of almost KO-ing me with eight centuries of verse. And when she straightened she actually began to stride up and down – as though the tiny table were a catwalk, a podium, a dais. There could be little doubt that she had passed beyond. She was out there, beating powerful wings, exulting in the infinite. Not only no longer necessary to avert the gaze, it was now compulsory to marvel at the cigarillo butts and the tangle which created a locus of attention as compelling as a target bull's eye, each of these heightened by a background of white skin as candent as snow in bright sun.

I did not stir – and hardly dared breathe. It was crucial that nothing disturb the sensors. If properly recorded, this vision would illuminate and warm an entire tepid dim life.

Neil returned with the catechism, little more than a pamphlet. Helen opened it at random and enquired in a ringing tone: 'How many sins cry to Heaven for vengeance?'

Neil and Marie chanted in unison: 'Four – wilful murder, sodomy, oppression of the poor, defrauding the labourer of his wages.'

Helen looked at them, startled, then selected another page. 'Why does the Bishop give a light blow to the confirmed?'

Again immediate joint response: 'To give him to understand that he ought to be prepared to suffer affronts and injuries and even death itself in defence of the Faith.'

'Say the twelve fruits of the Holy Ghost.'

'Charity, joy, peace, patience, forbearance, goodness, benignity, meekness, faith, modesty, continence and chastity.'

Frowning in frustration at their mastery, Helen flipped the pages in search of more abstruse questions. 'Do fathers and mothers, masters and mistresses, sin by obliging their children or domestics to work and omit Mass on holy days without necessity?'

'They are guilty of mortal sin and withal bring a curse upon their families.'

Marie added a personal comment. 'God I used to think *withal* was something even worse than mortal sin. They are guilty of mortal sin ... *and withal.*'

Helen had surely fulfilled her obligation but instead of relinquishing the stage possessed it even more fully, striding boldly back and forth, cigarillo butts delightfully aquiver, scouring the pamphlet for killer queries. If her Protestant father could see her now – proudly posing naked on a table and reciting with gusto from the Catechism of Rome. Such was the terrible consequence of marrying Catholic white trash.

A swift glance at Neil gave me a shock. On his face was not wonder or lust but *fear*. Men implore women to break free, only to shrink back in terror at what is unleashed.

Helen howled. 'Are smutty discourses, wanton looks and lewd kisses forbidden?'

Neil reached forward and grabbed her ankle. Helen screamed and, tottering on one foot, desperately beat at his head with the catechism. For a glorious instant there was the spectacle not merely of naked young beauty but *naked young beauty in jeopardy*. Then Helen fell on top of Neil and the two of them rolled over on the floor.

Marie and I lay down beside them. After the stimulation of Helen's performance there was little need of foreplay.

Eventually I became aware of someone shoving my shoulder. '*Uhn?*'

Neil's face was dark with concupiscence. His voice was strangulated and hoarse. 'Move over a minute.'

'*What?*'

Before I could comprehend, he pushed me aside and fell upon Marie.

Helen was stretched out on the carpet like a long white glove. I seized her, donned her – and shot off.

Ejaculating prematurely can be a guilty pleasure all its own – like stealing food from the fridge instead of waiting for dinner – but there has to be *some* delay between entry and climax. This response was as instantaneous and involuntary as a child's startle reflex. Instead of helpless arms flying up, helpless fluid shot out.

I fell back beside Helen, desolate and drained. Displaying no sign of annoyance, she laid a tolerant hand on my chest. 'It's all right.'

I felt like a child who has shit his pants at the start of the first day at school. What made the experience all the more shocking was that nowadays there was never any problem with Marie. When our orgasms were not simultaneous it was invariably she who came first and, though she gamely continued to toss it up, I would sometimes still have difficulty coming, occasionally so much so that she would have to sit on me and/or jerk me off.

Behind me Neil grunted and Marie released a smothered giggle.

'Someone's enjoying it at least,' I remarked bitterly.

Helen patted me in consolation. 'I enjoyed it too.' And she leaned forward to place on my disconsolate lips a reassuring kiss. Then she leaned back, apparently in no hurry to rise, and even, in a swift discreet motion, retrieving her pants and placing them beneath her to catch the impetuous spermatozoa which, after their recklessly precipitate entry, were now surreptitiously oozing back out. Nor was she upset by continuing giggles and grunts. It did not seem to occur to her that, whereas she and I were weedy bourgeois children, big drinks of water, Marie and Neil had been built for carnality and reared on promiscuous back streets. If both of them were capable of rutting in alleyways, what would they do in a well-heated room? It had been folly to permit them to couple and absurd to have imagined that two drinks of water could ever enjoy an equivalent frenzy.

Gradually there developed within me a bitter black rage. It was obvious that I had been duped and that Helen had been part of the plot. In return for whatever pledges or services, she had been willing to grant Neil his way with Marie. This was the only explanation for her equanimity at my failure and acquiescence in the noisy fornication next to us. It was difficult to prevent myself from rising and yanking Marie away from Neil.

'What's the matter?' Helen murmured.

'*Nothing*,' I snapped.

Eventually Marie rose, still laughing, and began to dress in front of us. 'It's too cold to go anywhere else. I got freezing lying there.'

I dressed swiftly and with unconcealed anger. Normally Neil would have questioned my fury – or at least attempted to neutralise it with convivial chat. Tonight he permitted curt goodbyes and a hasty departure.

As soon as we were outside Marie turned to me. 'What happened?'

'*Nothing* happened,' I ground out. 'But I'm glad *you* had

such a good time.'

Instead of expressing apology and contrition, Marie threw back her head and howled with laughter.

'What's so *fucking funny?*' I could have slapped her stupid face.

The paroxysm intensified. She crossed her legs and leaned on my arm for support. 'If only you knew ... *oh God I'll pee myself.*' With an enormous effort of concentration and will-power she straightened up and released my arm. 'Neil couldn't get it up.'

'*What?*'

'He couldn't get a hard on.'

'Not *at all?*'

'*Flat as a pancake.*' At this she seemed in danger of once more losing control. 'He was at me the whole time to do something for him. Do something for me, Marie. Do something for me, Marie.'

'And did you?'

'YES!'

'But it didn't work?'

'NO!' She was off again. 'And of course he was ragin' at me for laughin'. Absolutely livid, he was. I've never *seen* Neil so angry. But I couldn't help it. I just couldn't help it.'

This extraordinary day offered yet another revelation. Now the evening no longer seemed a plot of Neil's but a demonstration of male inadequacy, almost schematic in the way it revealed the two extremes. The lesson was conclusive and chastening. Men invariably frame the problems of sex in terms of female willingness – but the real issue is often male ability or its lack.

Ignominy is the most faithful handmaiden of Eros.

11

Just when relations between the couples were at their most vulnerable and fraught, most in need of protection and delicacy and least in need of disruption and tumult, at precisely this crucial juncture our little group was torn apart by implacable social demands. The terrible juggernaut of Christmas rolled over everyone, devotee and sceptic alike, preventing solitude, reflection, analysis and even a quiet companionable evening with a few chosen friends.

Helen and Neil were involved in endless outings with colleagues, during which Leo Patton reaffirmed his love for Helen (by tearfully confessing to an unhappy marriage) and Dessie Duddy his bond with Neil (by sharing his pride when his poem 'My Heavenly Mother' won third prize in a Christmas competition. Barry Hinds proposed an evening with the secretaries and had to be reminded that, since Alison and Roberta were saved and did not drink, the occasion was likely to be rather sedate. No sooner was this project aborted than he wanted to produce for clients diaries in supple Moroccan leather displaying the sonorous soubriquet Willman & Rosborough, in elegantly slanting gold script.

Marie had few social obligations but this was her busiest time in the shop, which extended its opening hours to accommodate the demand for cosmetics and toiletry gift packs. It was certainly not an appropriate setting for intimate and harrowing revelation, but Neil arrived here after work, soulful and troubled, and began by making Marie promise never to repeat a word of what he was about to disclose. Marie swore a solemn oath of eternal silence and as soon as she got home gave me such a vivid and detailed account that only a tinch of speculation is needed to re-create the scene.

Neil's need to talk must have been intense ('He was *past himself*', was how Marie put it) for the shop at this period was intimidatingly feminine. Not only were most of the clientele women, but female cosmetic products and advertising dominated the display space. And Marie favoured the new assertive strain in marketing for women. On one wall, next to the counter, a placard showed lipsticks in 'eight fabulous shades, any one of which could lick any man in the room'. On the opposite wall was a giant ad for false eyelashes, in which the life-size head of a menacing blond with a white face, glistening pearly lips and cavernous dark eyes glowered at the waiting customer over the disturbing legend: Bring Back the Lash. (However, it could have been worse for Neil because Colm O'Kane had ordered Marie to remove her favourite poster, the one which explained a dolly girl's pout: Annabella isn't wearing panties today. No! She has something much better. She's wearing Charnos Hold-me-Tights).

Marie did not notice Neil until he was standing before her at the counter.

'God save us!'

'I had to see you,' he whispered brokenly.

'Colm's in the back dispensary.'

'I have to explain.'

'We're really busy now, Neil.'

'But I have to explain.'

'You don't have to. *It's all right.*'

'It's not all right at all,' he hissed. 'You don't know what it's like for me. You don't know what it's like to be mad about someone for ages ... and then when you get the chance *not to be able to do anything.* You just can't imagine what a *torture* that is. To have a hard-on all the time except the one time you need it.' He paused, bitter, distraught. 'I get hard-ons for you all the time. *Really ferocious ones.*' He paused again to master his dark drives. 'I have a ferocious one now.'

Instinctively Marie glanced round. Another customer had come into the shop but was rooting with a preoccupied air among the shelves near the door. Colm was working at the far end of the dispensary with his back to the open connecting hatch.

'Neil,' she pleaded.

'I want to see you. I want to be with you. I want to see you every day.'

'*Neil.*' No reproof could have been more tender.

'But it's true. It's *true.*'

A woman approached the counter, casting suspicious looks at Neil, and enquired of Marie in a querulous tone, 'Have ye Revlon Moon Drops Lotion at all?'

Instantly Marie switched to local-shop-assistant mode, a combination of intimacy, collusion and vernacular with heavy use of the key word 'wee'. 'Just hold on a wee second.' Darting swiftly from behind the counter, Marie went to the shelves and returned with two bottles. 'Now are ye sure it's the lotion ye want? Ye see, there's Moon Drops Toning Lotion and Moon Drops Moisture Balm as well.'

The woman uttered a sharp cry of gratitude. 'God, it's the Moisture Balm Ah want right enough. Me head's away wi' it altogether.' She turned apologetically to Neil. 'But sure aren't our heads all addled at this time o' year?'

It was fortunate that this was a sentiment with which Neil could concur. He nodded immediately and vehemently, on his face the very confusion of which the woman had complained.

When at last she had paid and turned to leave, Neil resumed, with undimmed ardour, his position directly in front of Marie. But just as he opened his mouth to testify, the woman scurried back with a mischievous grin. (In this town a common technique for creating the illusion of intimacy was to turn back conspiratorially after a conversation appeared to have ended, as though scruple and restraint had finally been overcome by the overwhelming need to confide). 'Know what Ah like best of all? When the whole Christmas carry-on's over and ye can get a bit of a lie-in.'

Marie was quick to nod agreement. 'A wee lie-in's hard to beat all right.'

The interruption had set Neil to brooding on the parallel perversities of Fate and Man. 'You know what I think about all the time? That we grew up only a few streets from each other. But I hardly remember seeing you. Do you remember *me?*'

'Not that much,' Marie had to admit.

'We could have been seeing each other all that time. And for years you were ... you were ...' He completed the sentence with a vague gesture.

Marie was instantly suspicious. 'I was *what?*'

'You went with Fuckso McCallion ... and a whole load of others.'

'What are you saying ... I was *a good thing?*' Her face tightened and paled. '*A slag?*'

'No, no.'

'You could have been having a good time with a *slag?*'

Neil reached out to touch her arm, on his face the plaintive look of those whose noble intentions are forever misunderstood. 'It's not just sex. You must know that, Marie. It's not just the sex. You know the way I feel about you. You know how long I've felt this way. And I'll *always* feel this way about

you. I'll always feel this way . . . even . . . even . . .' Desperately
he sought a pledge of eternal devotion that was not a ridiculous
cliché. 'I'll feel like this *even when you're fat*.'

Marie pulled away with a fierce exclamation. 'Oh well
thank you very much. So Ahm going to be really fat, am
Ah? Ahm going to be a big fat heap.'

Neil reached after her, stricken, scarcely able to comprehend
how such a passionate avowal could have had such a negative
effect. 'I didn't mean that.'

'Not half you didn't. Get lost, Neil.'

'Promise me one thing at least,' he begged. 'Promise you'll
let me try again.'

A stirring in the back dispensary suggested that Marie's
reaction might have alerted her employer. 'You'd really better
get lost, Neil. Buy something for the look of it.'

'I don't want anything but you.'

'I THINK WE HAVE THAT.' Adopting a loud professional
tone, Marie came out from behind the counter and returned
to place on it something which resembled a giant chocolate
bar. 'Strawberry-flavoured SUPER WATE-ON. That'll be
twenty-two and six.'

'I didn't mean you'll be fat.'

'Feed that to Helen if you like fat women so much.'

Remorseful and broken, Neil paid up and took the bar.
'Before I go, tell me just one thing at least. Just one thing.'

'Well?'

'What colour of pants are you wearing?'

Her expression remained stern – but there was a softening of
tone. 'Look, would you *get lost*, Neil.'

While actually in front of this hapless suitor Marie had
succeeded in holding back laughter – but in her subsequent
account of the conversation she surrendered completely to
mirth. 'It was a sin making him buy Strawberry Wate-On.
Stinging him for *twenty-two and six!* If I'd even given him the
Regular at seventeen and six. But I couldn't resist it. He really

got my goat saying I'd be a big fat midden.' Suddenly her face clouded over. 'He obviously thinks that's what I'll be. And it's true. It's *true*. I'll be fat as a fool with all the food over Christmas. Isn't it well for some that have to eat Strawberry Wate-On? There's Helen without a pick on her.' She paused, scowling. 'I'm fat as a fool as it is.'

'You're not fat.'

'I'm not wearing any more polo necks ... or that stupid polo-necked dress.'

'Your new dress? But you've hardly worn it at all.'

'I'm like Two-Ton Tessie in those tight things.'

'You look sensational in them ... as you very well know. You should have seen how Neil looked at you in that dress.' I paused and added, almost casually. 'He's not about to give up, you know.'

'But sure, what's the point?'

'How do you mean?'

'All I got out of it was a sore fanny. I was as sore afterwards with him pushing himself against me.'

'You must have felt *something* before it went wrong?'

She withdrew into sullen silence. I came and sat beside her on the sofa in a way that could not be misconstrued.

'Oh for God's sake.' She rose impatiently. 'We haven't even eaten yet.'

Despite his personal failure, Neil continued to push forward – and I was happy to follow an impotent pacesetter who would create opportunities but be incapable of doing any damage himself. Now he had established the thrilling precedent of the clandestine visit. The Quinns' flat was close to the Protestant cathedral, only a few streets away from the offices of Willman & Rosborough. If Neil was out for the evening I could work late at the office and in less than five minutes be alone with the pale priestess in the Temple of Eros.

Such risk-taking was not in my nature – but an opportunity presented itself soon enough. Helen had been giving us

cooking lessons and urging us to borrow the large pot needed
for many of her finest recipes. We kept forgetting to bring it
from their flat and finally Marie asked me to fetch it one
Saturday morning while she was at work.

Helen herself came to the door – and was uncharacteristically nonplussed. 'Neil's gone down home for the day. He's
putting up bookshelves for Kevin.'

So much together were Helen and Neil that I had never
entertained the possibility of finding Helen alone. Both of us
were startled and alarmed by the revelation – but the homeliness of my errand seemed to reassure Helen. She drew me
into the living room – and immediately scurried off to the
kitchen, returning with the absurd monstrosity in her arms.

'Aw that's great.' I accepted the pot with the humility and
gratitude befitting an honorary degree.

Concluding this transaction left us cruelly exposed. The flat
was silent and dark as the cosmos, utterly removed from the
phatic communion with which the town shielded itself.

In the absence of company and chatter, fundamental truths
forcefully impinged: that this was our first time alone together
in private and sober; that each body ached to entwine with the
other; that, given the recent behaviour of spouses, such
entwining could well be legitimate; and that the spouses were
sufficiently engaged for us to enjoy entwining at leisure.

The face of a yearning woman is surely the most beautiful
thing on earth (at least to the object of yearning). But to a
timorous man it is also a terrifying sight.

'Cup a tea?' Helen asked.

One of the abiding mysteries of life is the way the most
banal of phrases can convey the most profound and singular
of feelings. It was as though Helen had sweetly enquired if she
could take out my cock.

'*Yeah.*'

Once more she rushed off to the kitchen, leaving me alone
in the solemn chamber with a painfully palpitating heart.

Unable to bear the oppressive emptiness, I followed her and stood in the kitchen doorway. Helen emitted a strange grunt-laugh combining apprehension and gladness. Her preparation of crackers and cheese, already agitated, now became manic.

'No need to go to such trouble.' Nowhere near as resonant as Helen's offer of tea, the remark was still rich in vibrato and meaning.

She repeated the peculiar laugh and speeded up even more. Now was the time to put an end to this nonsense with crackers. Sexual tension warped the shimmering air like heat haze. And none of the usual obstacles inhibited fulfilment. There was justification, willingness, propitious occasion.

Unfortunately I also needed someone else to make the first move. But even a dynamic executive like Helen found it difficult to initiate love. Eventually her abrupt movements began to assume an air of impatience. *What's keeping you?* her body language seemed to repeat.

In a small provincial town even Manifest Destiny finds it hard to clear space. And no space may be held clear for long.

Harsh as a klaxon, the doorbell rang.

Instead of rushing to respond, Helen continued to butter crackers with another equivocal grunt-laugh.

She was giving me a final chance to seize the moment.

But something alien had made me its creature. 'Shouldn't you see who that is?'

As unforgettable as the earlier yearning was the look she flashed at me now: a mixture of disappointment, anger and – it must be admitted – contempt.

Once again I had surrendered to the emissaries of the quotidian. Lexie and Celia burst upon us in frustration and outrage.

'He took me *right up the town*,' Celia raged. 'Right up through the traffic.'

'She didn't get her test,' Lexie quietly explained.

'Everyone Ah know got taken to the Waterside,' Celia

continued to rant. 'Where it's nice and quiet. So that's where Ah did all me driving. I think he took me up the town just for badness. He was as *crabbit,* Helen. Oh he was *horrible . . .*'

'A lot of them are bastards,' Lexie said to me with quiet intensity. 'They'd be like that. Especially with a young girl.' Language failing him, he turned away and drove his right fist violently into his open left palm.

'But sure you can have another go,' Helen soothed. 'You'll get somebody nicer next time. Somebody to take you round the Waterside.'

Celia refused to be mollified. 'But *everybody* gets their hill starts on Browning Drive . . . *everybody.* I'm sure nobody made *you* go up the town, Helen. Where'd they take you for yours?'

'The Waterside,' Helen was obliged to admit.

'*See?*' Celia turned to each of us for acknowledgement as an innocent victim. 'Nobody made *her* do an emergency stop in the middle of Foyle Street. Nobody made *her* go through those wee narrow streets. And in that massive big car.' Now she was berating her husband. 'I asked him to get me a wee-er car for the test. But nothing will do him only that massive thing.' Cheated, bullied, abandoned, Celia turned away in ineffable anguish.

'I've the tea on.' Helen slipped out to the kitchen.

In the sudden lull Lexie studied me suspiciously, no doubt wondering what I was doing alone with his sister-in-law at this hour.

Convention urged me to distract and reassure. 'Still drivin' the big Zodiac, Lexie?'

Immediately his pucker of concern relaxed. 'Aye,' he sighed, with the local studied indifference to coveted posses-sions, achievements and status. Contentedly patting his pockets for fags, he gave a dismissive shrug. 'Need the big boot . . . and room in the back for the weans.'

'She'd be sore on juice though?'

It was obvious that Lexie had never thought me capable of

such insight and shrewdness. New respect flared in his canny eyes. '*Drinks it.*'

Lexie and Celia were now established in my mind as the Maiden City's secret police, dedicated to upholding convention and stamping out pleasure. They even succeeded in blighting Christmas Day, which we had planned to spend hidden from families in the unorthodox bosom of Quinns' flat. The Quinns were to cook a goose (also thrillingly deviant) and we were to bring champagne and wine. Then Celia announced that she could no longer have her parents for the Christmas meal because Lexie's mother had fallen ill, so that Lexie and Celia and children had no choice but to go to her. Helen suspected that, in fact, they were dining with Lexie's new business associates – but accepted the responsibility of her parents, insisting that their presence would not spoil a wonderful day.

Marie was outraged and decided that, if she had to be in the company of parents, it might as well be her own. Marie's mother, who had been planning to go to one of her sons, was more than happy to stay at home if Marie and I were to share the meal. So instead of an independent Christmas it was the usual mess of obligation, conflict and rancour.

Marie's family home was in a terrace of tiny houses perched on a hill of alarming steepness so that first-time visitors were likely to experience, in rapid succession, feelings of precariousness, vertigo, claustrophobia and suffocation. But the terrace compensated with seasonal cheer. In every window was a tree with coloured lights and many front-room sills had cribs displaying Nativity scenes to passers-by.

Why did the decorations face the street? Conventions are meant to be observed not explained; to enquire would make me sound like a lunatic.

Mrs Nelis was another enigma, a bizarre blend of submissiveness and obduracy. She talked in a listless, defeated tone and moved in an apologetic sidle, body held to one side and head averted and lowered, furtive eyes always sliding from contact like mercury globules from an importunate thumb. Yet she had a powerful will which she frequently imposed. A favourite strategy, immensely effective, was to appear to accept defeat when resisted and then, when the apparently settled issue had been long since forgotten, suddenly return to the attack as though there had never been a debate, so that the opposition, appalled at the prospect of endless wrangling, would frequently yield with a sigh.

The Guinness saga was a perfect example. One of her axioms was that all male visitors must be given *The Journal* and a bottle of Guinness. After the first few visits I asked Marie to mention discreetly that I suffered from a deficiency shocking in a Paddy – I was not fond of bottled Guinness and would be happy to drink tea with the women. On the next visit Marie pre-empted her mother by saying, 'No Guinness now, Mammy,' and indeed I was offered only tea. But on the occasion after that, when I was absorbed in a *Journal* report on the court appearance of an after-hours car-horn-blower (Mr D.A.B. Lawler, defending: 'Hagan is not one of those harum-scarum people'), I suddenly looked up to find pressed into my hand a bottle of stout already opened and partly poured into a glass.

'Come in out of that cold and get a bit of heat at the fire.' Mrs Nelis now ushered us into the living room, where an intimidating blaze indeed roared in the grate. 'Aren't you as well out of that old flat in this bitter weather?'

Our flat was not large – Marie had her mother's taste for the bijou – but its living room was probably twice the area of the one in which we now stood. Indeed the flat's total floor space could well have exceeded that of the house. But of course space was not the issue. A house, however small, had mystical properties of autonomy and gravitas which made it superior to even the grandest of flats. Mrs Nelis had visited our flat only once, walking cautiously around it with half-suppressed smirks and giggles at the absurdity of living in such a place. Eventually she approached the window and gazed on the forlorn patch of grass at the back.

'Yees'll have to do something with that bit of garden.'

'It's not ours, Mammy. It goes with the ground-floor flat.'

Authentic shock and outrage immediately dispelled every trace of amusement. 'Not *yours*? Not *your garden*?' She looked wildly at each of us in the hope of a denial. 'Jesus Mary and Joseph, Marie, *what kind of a carry-on's that?*'

Her reactions were often unpredictable – and at the moment I was undergoing intense scrutiny.

'You're lookin' well-mended,' she announced at last.

Another axiom asserted that mature men should be fat (or, in her vocabulary, 'well-mended'). This may have derived from an upbringing in one of the poorest areas of Donegal, where corpulence indicated prosperity and a slim build sub-sistence income; it was significant that her adjective for 'thin' was 'failed'.

'I'm usually much the same weight.'

'Not at all. You were desperate failed-lookin' the last time you were here. But Marie must be feedin' ye. Ye're well-mended now.'

Satisfied, she went out to the kitchen and returned with a Jameson and a cream sherry. One seasonal consolation was the replacement of Guinness by whiskey. A glass was placed in my hand and *The Journal* dropped in my lap.

'Mammy, I want whiskey not sherry. I don't drink sherry.'

'Sure it's poured out, look.'

'Drink it you.'

'I've me own poured.'

Understanding the futility of argument, Marie accepted the glass of sherry but immediately set it down on the mantelpiece and went out to the kitchen.

'Did any of the fellas call in?' she shouted, pouring herself a large glass of Jameson.

'Sure I never see one o' them.' Mrs Nelis shook her head at me in disgust at filial neglect. 'Jim was in for a wee while with his two. They're as contrary, that pair.'

Marie returned with her glass and took a seat by the fire. 'Did they wreck the place on ye?'

'They've me eaten out of house and home. When they finished everything Ah gave them, they went into the room and opened one of the selection boxes Ah got for Liam's weans.' She appeared to brood on this outrage – but resumed on an entirely different subject. 'Jim was sayin' Mrs Brolly was taken bad yesterday.'

'Maggie Brolly from Chamberlain Street?'

'She was taken to Altnagelvin in an ambulance. Seemingly the woman isn't well at all.'

Ill health turned out to be the theme of the day, although in this Mrs Nelis was merely reflecting the local preoccupation with accident, disease and untimely death (possibly inevitable in small towns, where everyone's fate is minutely known). The festive meal was accompanied by dismal tales of serious illness ('Did ye hear that Sean McGinty has multiple sclerosis – he's still walkin' around grand but he has it all right'), medical bungling ('Altnagelvin sent her home and her appendix burst and she died'), and frightful carnage on the roads ('Phonsie Condron said he seen it and apparently the car was *halfed in two*').

At Christmas dinner a man was required to make only one comment (silence was another attribute of male maturity). I waited for a lull in the horror stories and nodded gravely at the turkey. 'Nice bird.'

Our hostess instantly brightened. 'Ye'd take another wee pick?'

'No. No thanks. I'm full as it is.'

'Marie?'

'I'd be fat as a fool, Mammy.'

Mrs Nelis began to tidy up, leaving us to struggle with our

enormous portions. Then, suddenly, she was at my elbow shovelling extra meat onto my plate. 'Take a bit more, look see. I'd never be able to get through a whole turkey on me own.'

Afterwards the heat and food and alcohol created a soporific silence. Whiskey was immensely welcome, although *The Journal,* in one of its rare foreign news stories, suggested that this craven dependence, the curse of the nation, would soon be no more.

RADIATION MAY
CURE DRINKERS

Small doses of radiation may be sufficient to turn habitual alcohol drinkers to water, claims Dr Lelon Peacock of the University of Georgia. The technique has yet to be tested on humans but experiments on animals have been 'immensely encouraging'. After 48 roentgens of gamma radiation a group of mice habituated to alcohol developed an aversion and preferred water.

Our pleasant somnolence was interrupted by a tremendous commotion in the hall.

'*Jesus Mary and Joseph, it's May McCool.*' Mrs Nelis leapt to her feet, seized the Jameson bottle and pushed it into my chest. 'Put that in the kitchen. Put that in the kitchen.'

I was stupefied and confused. '*What?*'

'Put it away somewhere out of the way. *May takes a drink.*'

After hearty greetings the visitor addressed her companion, a sullen fat boy. 'Show them what ye got, Noel.'

He opened the cardbox box he was carrying and displayed an enormous racing car.

'Och isn't that great,' Mrs Nelis marvelled.

'But sure we can't get it to go, Maureen,' May McCool wailed. '*Here.*' Brusquely pulling the car from her son's arms, she thrust it at me. 'See if ye can get that to go.'

With a pucker of authentic concentration, I turned the car over, examined the underside, prodded and twisted, removed and replaced the batteries. 'I'm afraid I'm not very practical. Not much use at fixing things.'

'Are you the accountenant?' As jazz musicians hate to play the precise notes of a melody, so many townspeople were reluctant to use the standard syllables of words. Addition and subtraction were equally common. 'Do ye know Ciaran Roddy from Blucher Street? *He's* goin' on for to be an accountenant too.'

'I can't say I know him.'

'Big fella. Curly brown hair. Very civil.'

'I don't know him.'

She seemed less disappointed than annoyed, as though I was perversely denying knowledge of a fellow professional I must surely have known. Retrieving the car abruptly, she returned it to the boy. 'We'll just have to take it back to the shop, Noel. Go you on over now and tell the rest of them Ah'll be back in a minute.'

When Noel gave no sign of wishing to leave, May placed a hand on his back and walked him out to the door.

Mrs Nelis leaned across. 'She's back on it, God help her. The husband left her because of the drink. And the children are completely neglected. I have to feed them many's a time.'

May returned, settled herself on the sofa and looked pointedly at Marie. 'Did ye have your dinner wi' your mother?'

'We did.'

'And proper order too. Maureen was sayin' ye were goin' to go somewhere else.'

'Now, May . . .' Mrs Nelis warned.

'Maureen, I just think it's desperate that she wouldn't have her Christmas dinner wi' her mother.'

'Sure I was goin' down to Brendan.'

'And he's another.' May's eyes rolled sightlessly. 'He's another one never darkens the door. I think it's desperate that none of yees would visit your mother. There's your mother sittin' on her own in this house the whole time.'

'Now, May, that's none of your business.' Mrs Nelis was becoming firmer. 'There's no call to be goin' on like that.'

But May, almost shouting now, turned to Marie. 'It's a wonder ye wouldn't think of visitin' your mother more often.'

'That *will do*, May.' Mrs Nelis was almost at her wits' end – for now the terrible inquisitor was about to turn on the *accountant*.

'You tell Marie to visit her mother. *You tell her.*'

Both Marie and her mother were on their feet.

'I'll have to put you out, May,' cried the mother. 'I'll have to put you out on the street.'

'I'll make us a drop of tea,' Marie said.

I too rose. 'I'll give you a hand.'

In the kitchen Marie buried her face in her palms. 'Those McCools ... what a crowd. They're all away in the head.' She groaned in agony. 'Jesus, I need to get out of here.'

'What about your mother?'

'I'll tell her some story.'

Marie had a curious relation to truth. She was a chronic liar though totally honest. Her lies were attributable, not to her core personality, but to the difficulties of enjoying youth in a society where the generation gap was two centuries wide. With her peers she was shockingly frank but with anyone older or in a position of authority she lied glibly, instantly, almost unconsciously. Some of the whoppers she told her mother made my hair stand on end.

There was another problem.

'Where can we go? The bars are closed.'

'Anywhere. Anywhere. Aren't there dances on?'

Mrs Nelis was in the hallway with her neighbour, now penitent and tearful, so it was easy to retrieve *The Journal* from the living room. Its teeming entertainment pages informed us that the Cameo had Maisie McDaniel and the Fendermen ('Ireland's only Hootenanny Stars'), while the Corinthian had Willie Bradley and his Woodchoppers ('The Personality Boys').

'What about over the border?'

'The Swinging Viscounts. The Premier Aces. The Mighty Avons ("King Larry and his Merry Men").' There was no response from Marie. 'Frank McLaughlin and his Old Tyme Band.'

'Oh God.'

'The band's specially augmented for Christmas night.'

'Oh *God*.'

12

After the claustrophobia of the overheated living room, the freezing night offered a tonic astringency and freedom. But freedom to go where? We could not even visit the Quinns for, as appalled as Mrs Nelis by the notion of Christmas dinner in a flat (an aversion which crossed the boundaries of gender, religion, age and class), Helen's parents had persuaded the Quinns to come to their retirement bungalow by the sea and, since this was over forty miles away in Portstewart, the Quinns were unlikely to be back. The public houses were also locked and shuttered and our own unheated flat was uninviting.

We were resigned to returning to Mrs Nelis when we ran across a merry band en route to a party in Róisín Coll's – the very Róisín Coll who had been a school friend of Marie's.

'Is that not the bully who sat behind you and used your pigtails for paintbrushes?'

'That was Celestine Barr. *She* married a Yank from the American base and went to the States. Apparently he beats her up so she's getting a touch of her own medicine.' Marie chuckled happily. 'No, Róisín was lovely. We did the Legion of Mary together.'

The true redeemer, hope, was born in our alienated souls. All we had to do was swing by our flat for a supply of alcohol and purple hearts.

Looking back from the distance of late middle age, the most mysterious youth phenomenon is the fanatical belief in, and craving for, parties. The yearning for transcendence was certainly desperate – but how did we convince ourselves that it was possible in dingy flats? In this case the venue was a house – though it seemed to be presently accommodating the entire under-thirty population of the town. It was even difficult to get beyond the front door. Animated groups blocked the passage all the way to the kitchen at the back, and along the stairs was a toilet queue whose top disappeared out of sight on the landing, while its bottom doubled back on itself in the already overcrowded hall. Yet no one gave any sign of being put out by the crush. Patience and good humour seemed to prevail even in the line awaiting relief.

'It's like queuin' up for communion at midnight mass in the cathedral.'

'More like queuin' for the Blessin' of the Throats in the Waterside chapel.'

'More like queuin' to sign on,' suggested a third, and a shout of laughter acknowledged this as the definitive comparison.

Holding a glass above her head, a young woman made her way along the hall with constant entreaty and apology.

'Róisín,' was all Marie could find to say to our hostess.

The girl was flushed and bewildered – but appeared to have enormous reserves of goodwill. 'God, isn't it desperate, Marie. I don't even know half of this crowd from Adam.' In renewed wonder her gaze followed the toilet queue up round the landing. 'Jeekers, I'll be glad to get to me bed this night.' Still shaking her head in amazement, she pushed her way upstairs past the queue.

Never had the portals of the infinite been so congested. It was surely obvious that few would pass beyond by this route. Nevertheless, no one was willing to leave. Yet another group had arrived and was pushing us into the house from behind. We had little choice but to move forward into the first available room.

A striking couple leaned on the mantelpiece in intimate conversation. The man, in his late twenties, was tall and well built with short jet-black hair and a sheen of tanned wellbeing which would have been dramatic at any time in this pallid, blotchy-skinned town but was especially egregious in bleak midwinter. The young woman was also tall but extremely pale, with a black roll-necked dress and severely rectilinear hair (its rigour a delight amidst the prevailing frothiness) cut above the ear on one side and chin length on the other.

This couple were exotic in every way. Yet the girl was actually waving to us with every sign of intimacy and gladness.

'Jesus, Helen, is that . . .'

Her new hairstyle defied my halting attempt at definition. Marie was struck dumb, looking from Helen's hair to the handsome consort and back again to the hair. She was not attuned to this new geometric age, where the curlicue had been supplanted by the straight line. I managed to continue only with difficulty.

'Is that what's known as a bob?'

'Not exactly.' Her mischievous tone made it clear that she wished to be interrogated further.

'What then?'

'An Asymmetric Isadora.' With a triumphant peal of laughter she turned to introduce her companion. 'This is René. Grew up next door to us on Northland Hill. He's a civil engineer in Uganda now.'

'We thought you'd be in Portstewart,' Marie managed to blurt out at last.

More laughter from Helen. 'We were ... but we couldn't stick it.'

'Is Neil around?' Marie's tone had a note of accusation and censure.

'He's about somewhere,' Helen cried in blithe disregard. 'I think he went with Dessie Duddy to try to find a bottle opener.' She turned back to René. 'Tell them the story about the elephant.'

René grimaced with becoming modesty but when Helen persisted began in a deep measured tone. 'Well I was driving along this bush road with an American nurse. I say *road* ... but it wasn't much more than a track. All of a sudden this elephant appears out of the bush in front of us.' René revealed a fine sense of timing by pausing now to drink from his bottle of stout. 'No space to pass it. No space to turn. Impenetrable bush on each side ... and if I reversed I'd have to reverse all the way for nine miles.' Obviously the memory was still affecting. He shook his head. 'I'm not sure which is worse ... a rogue elephant trumpeting or an American woman screaming.'

'A *rogue* elephant?' Helen gasped. 'You never said it was a *rogue*.'

'Oh yeah. Had to be shot after that.' René was impressively unperturbed. 'So no way out front sides or back. *What did I do?*' He looked at us as if in genuine hope of an answer. When none was forthcoming he dipped his free hand in an under-and-up swooping motion. 'Put my foot down to the floor and drove straight through its legs.'

Several surrounding groups had fallen silent to follow the anecdote. Even the returning Neil and Dessie waited respect-fully at a distance. Helen gazed with admiration upon this rare and exemplary phenomenon: a traveller, an explorer, an *adven-turer*. Suddenly I was assailed by the fear of becoming trapped in this town whose grey torpor cast such a spell on its children. Like wood spirits changed into trees, most of them remained forever rooted to the spot.

It was certainly time for a drink – but Neil and Dessie confessed the failure of their mission to find an opener. Gently removing the bottle from my hand, René turned and aligned the metal cap with the mantelpiece edge.

'You'll crack the tiles,' Helen warned – but he brought the heel of his hand smartly down. The cap flew off – and the tiles remained unmarked. To prove that this was no fluke he did the same with a second bottle and gallantly presented it to Marie. Then provided for the rest of the party.

'In Africa you learn to improvise.'

'Difficult to work out there?' I asked.

René answered this question with three of his own. 'Job spec? Work schedules? Plans?' After turning to place his bottle on the mantelpiece, he enacted a slow expressive mime, tearing imaginary documents to pieces and flinging the scraps to the four winds. Then he calmly retrieved his drink. 'And of course you can't depend on the natives. I had this character come to see me with a letter from an engineer on another site. Looking for work and delighted to have a reference. So I open the letter – and what does it say? If you let this fucker close enough to hand you something you've already made a serious mistake.'

Helen suspected exaggeration. '*René* . . .'

The engineer shared the common belief in repetition as the key to converting sceptics. 'That's exactly what it said. I swear to God. If you let this fucker close enough to hand you something you've already made a serious mistake.'

'That's just the Ugandans,' Dessie Duddy suddenly came in. 'The Ugandans are rubbish. The Ugandans are wankers. But the Kenyans are *aristocrats*.' Sternly he drew his bulk up for a moment, as if in pride at his own membership of a noble élite. 'Your Kenyans are hunters. Hunters and *warriors*. I was reading this novel about the Mau Mau thing . . .'

The music in the next room was thunderously turned up. René took hold of Helen and made as though to swing her off, impossible in such a dense crowd. Helen look startled but suffered his whim.

Desisting as abruptly as he had begun, René reclaimed his bottle and took a quick swig. 'You see, they live on this white stuff called *mealie meal*,' he said to Helen. 'Know why it has to be white?'

'Why?'

'So they don't eat their own fingers by mistake.'

Helen grimaced – but her reproof was mild. 'Oh René . . .'

Nor did disapproval cause her to turn away from the engineer. After the opening exchange she had barely given me a glance. Consummation, which should have strengthened the bond between us, seemed to have been entirely forgotten. Perhaps there was nothing personal in this. There is a gender difference in attitudes to the act. Men obsessively anticipate and recall sex; women enjoy it while it lasts. Assuming, of course, that enjoyment is possible. Penetration for a nanosecond would hardly make the earth move.

Whatever the nature of her feelings, my tenderness towards Helen was being steadily eroded by this blatant admiration for a neo-colonial supremacist boor. Standing at an angle to the rest of us, René was talking into Helen's face like a lover. Neil's response was to speak to Marie in the same fashion. My options were silence – or conversation with Dessie.

'Don't know how I'm gettin' the drink down me tonight,' Dessie said. 'Wild session over the border last night in Thran John's. You know it? Half grocer shop and half pub. The craic's usually good. Anyway, there was a whole gang of teachers . . . and Noot Doran. Teaches geography. Good gas – but a Pioneer. Drinking orange squash all night . . . but buying his round even so. Eventually he gets fed up with the price of everyone else's drink. So says he to me, Get me a quarter pound o' cooked ham wi' the orange. And every round after that he has a quarter of ham. *Jesus, is it any wonder Ahm broke?*'

'Haven't you collected your poetry prize money?

'Oh fuck.' Dessie covered his face with a splayed hand. 'See,

Ah got this letter addressed to Master Desmond Duddy and I was showin' it to Neil and sayin', How the fuck did they know Ah was a teacher? This is Neil: They don't think you're a teacher, ye stupid cunt, they think you're a child. So Ah read the rules again and it turns out the age limit's fifteen. Good job Ah showed that letter to Neil, eh? Ah'd a gone for me five-pound prize and been made a whole laugh of. Ahm still cackin' meself in case anybody finds out. That fucker Quinn was supposed to keep quiet.' Dessie turned accusingly to Neil.

Momentarily detaching herself from her engineer, Helen cast an anxious glance round the room and leaned towards me to whisper. 'René's inviting us back to his house.'

Apparently the portals of the infinite had moved to a mansion on Northland Hill. This did not strike me as a guarantee of transcendence – but the rest of the party were not prepared to abandon the quest.

At the door we encountered Celia and Lexie arriving. With a cry of delight Celia flung herself upon Neil.

'She's been on vodka and white all day,' Lexie explained, tolerantly smiling at his wife bestowing kisses on Neil. 'Usually she only has the one.'

There is always something frightful about the skittishness of the staid. When my final accountancy exam was over a group of fellow students waylaid me and insisted that I accompany them to a club. They liked me as little as I liked them – and yet were determined to bring me along, no doubt as proof of irrepressible *joie de vivre*. I refused the accountants then, but could do little about Celia and Lexie joining us now. Considering this pair's major disruption of Christmas plans, Helen and Neil seemed remarkably calm.

I could have hugged Marie when she asked, with just the right touch of impertinence, 'How's your mother now, Lexie?'

'*What?*' Lexie's tone was of slightly irritated but essentially benign incomprehension. He seemed to make an effort to recall and then said, in a condescending tone, 'Och sure that was nothing really.'

Once again the rigorous night delivered us from dross. After so much hot air the cold wind was a joy. Beneath a gibbous moon there glittered a rime of new frost and ice, and we paused for a moment of involuntary wonder, our breath the smoke from censers lifted to an inviolable altar of white.

'It's like a *bottle*,' Celia warned, seizing Neil's arm for support. 'Nearly went on me neck in these shoes.'

Also arm in arm, René and Helen followed the lead couple. In a looser but equally companionable pairing, Lexie and Dessie went next.

Marie took my arm. 'Let me link onto ye.'

'What was Neil whispering about?'

'How much he hates René.'

'And what do *you* make of the engineer?'

'A dreamboat.'

Detached in every way from the little terraces, Northland Hill was a wide tree-lined avenue which fell in a steep slope to the grounds of the Protestant grammar school and, below this, the river at peace in a majestic curve.

As a result of intermittent but hectic horseplay, Celia and Neil had fallen behind René and Helen. At the top of the hill Celia cried out, 'Remember we used to always slide here, René,' and launched herself at the engineer with a shriek too intense to be justified by jeopardy or high spirits or even both. René absorbed the impact and held her upright.

'*Celia*,' Lexie warned, glancing about him.

'My husband's as sensible,' Celia announced in a loud voice, leaning back in René's arms with a malicious laugh. 'Lexie's as sensible. Aren't you, Lexie?'

Nodding towards René, Dessie put his mouth to Neil's ear. 'Is that character a Prod or what? What kind of poncy name's René?'

Speaking from the corner of his mouth, Lexie explained to

the upper group. 'That wee girl's blootered.'

'It's T.J. McCormack he's worried about.' Celia indicated a substantial home across the street. 'Lexie's been to see T.J.'

So this was the lair of my arch rival, the town's principal Catholic accountant and the former employer of Barry Hinds. But its sombre red-brick façade gave nothing away.

'Tell them what he said to ye, Lexie.'

'It was kind of intimidatin' a wee bit ... ye know?'

'Tell them what he said to ye.'

The derision was surely unmistakable but Lexie either failed to notice or felt that his achievement was beyond mockery. His head was high, his chest was out, his voice was unequivocal and clear. 'Said Ah seemed to have me head screwed on.'

Marie hissed advice to Neil. 'That wee girl Celia needs a kick up the hole.'

He laughed indulgently. 'She's not used to drink.'

We moved down the hill slowly and carefully, clutching the old iron spear railings which fronted the gardens. The leading trio had stopped before the second last house, which must have been the sisters' former family home. Yet Celia was peering through the window with astonishing malevolence.

'You know it's a sin the way he's let our house go. Seemingly he's never lifted a finger since the day he moved in. Even the outside's falling to pieces. What's this he is, Helen?'

'Some kind of lecturer or writer. A historian, I think.'

'All he does is read books. It's a *sin* what he's done to that house.' Celia seemed to want to break in, drag out the negligent scholar and string him up from the nearest lamppost. She was one of those dangerous bullies with the resolution of a Caesar and the intelligence of a rabbit. 'It's an *absolute sin,* so it is.'

'It was the back garden I loved best,' Helen sighed. 'It used to be gorgeous in summer.'

This distracted Celia from thoughts of forced entry and lynching. She turned to nudge Neil playfully. 'Remember us sunbathing out there?'

Helen was recalling an even earlier time to René. 'Do you still have that tent? The one we stayed out in all night in your garden?'

'Of course *I* wasn't allowed,' Celia complained. 'Ah could have *strangled* our Helen, so Ah could.'

This rampant nostalgia excluded the rest of us – and drinkers not permitted to participate sink into grievance and bile. Fixated for some time on the stained glass fanlight, Dessie now shared his thoughts. 'Ah'd love to put a fuckin' brick through that.'

My gaiety was also dissipating. This august home, embellished with stained glass and ivy, put a different perspective on Helen's fashion dress and bob. Compared to the solidity of old money, high jinks in darkened flats were mere froth and spume.

Men are inclined to believe that penetration yields the secret of a woman, that carnal knowledge is total knowledge (an illusion perfectly captured in the Victorian use of 'possess'). But Helen was more of an enigma now than in her Lady Turquoise phase.

René's home did nothing to put us at ease. Situated on a corner, where Northland Hill met a side road running across the hill along the school grounds, it was almost twice the size of its neighbours and enjoyed a full frontage on each of the roads. In fact, the road intersection was dominated by the house's imposing pediment and door, which led us into a dark vault where a massive sideboard, sinisterly mirrored, faced a dead barometer and grandfather clock. Here time and weather had long since ceased to count. Indeed it was probably many years since the last jarring sound. Silence seems to grow in duration and intensity as one ascends the social scale; presumably in heaven it will be perpetual and profound. Every trace of rowdyism in the intruders was extinguished. As in stately homes, a wide staircase branched left and right but, where a stately home would have had a suit of armour in a niche at the fork, here there was a life-size statue of the Virgin with her arms open as if in entreaty and on her sorrowful features a rebuke for the revellers: Have yees no homes to go to? Sure there's no call for this carry-on.

Passing her with guilty steps and averted faces (Dessie was especially chastened by this unexpected encounter with the Heavenly Mother he had celebrated in verse), we made our way to the first floor and a drawing room furnished in the grand style of the hallway but humanised by a decorated Christmas tree at one end. Even so, burdened with clinking bottles, we felt like winos breaking into a crypt.

The conversation was suitably sober. Neil questioned Lexie on his new business venture. After many years as a breadman for a Protestant bakery, Lexie had become convinced that he understood better than his masters his Catholic clientele. Apparently Marie Antoinette had been right after all – the people wanted not bread but cake. Or, in this town, buns. The problem with the Protestant product was its quality. For instance, the cream buns were filled with real cream, whereas the customers in Katanga and the Congo preferred the artificial variety, 'dummy cream' as Lexie called it.

'That's true,' Helen laughed. 'Neil, your brother Kevin wouldn't look at fresh cream.' She turned to her husband for corroboration but, when none was offered, had to explain herself. 'I brought Kevin these lovely cream fingers from Limavady and he wouldn't even *look* at them.'

Lexie also understood mysterious patterns of seasonal demand. In an interesting process of compensation, the time of most intense mortification of the spirit was also the time of maximum indulgence of the flesh.

'See during the Women's Retreat,' he cried excitedly, 'they can't get enough a cheap buns. And especially in the Congo. They'd take the fuckin' arm off ye in the Congo, look see.'

'*Lexie*,' Celia had to caution.

But his profanity had broken the spell. René produced a

bottle of Powers and glasses and went to a sombre item of furniture that was now revealed to be a radiogram incorporating a record player. Unfortunately there was no contemporary pop, only classical music and a smattering of Sinatra and Nat King Cole.

The Powers was passed round appreciatively – until it reached Celia.

'Oh don't be givin' me any more drink!' she cried. 'Ahm as *giggly* after a few drinks. What am Ah not like, Lexie?' The question appeared to be rhetorical. 'Ah'd be as *giggly*.'

To the soothing strains of *Songs for Swinging Lovers* René took the floor with Helen, who placed her arms about his neck and laid upon his broad and capable shoulder her Asymmetric Isadora. Neil followed swiftly with Celia. Emboldened by whiskey, Dessie approached Marie.

'I suppose it might help to shift a few pounds,' she sighed.

'Do like me,' Dessie shouted. 'I'm on a seafood diet.' He paused to look round for attention. 'See food and eat it.'

Lexie and I were left side by side on a sofa, supported, respectively, by Arthur Guinness and John Powers. As I searched for some trite remark about his business, Lexie turned to forestall me. '*Listen*' – his aggressive tone was oddly intensified by the calm of his demeanour – 'Don't think ye have to say somethin' to me. I know ye've no time for the likes of me.' I made some sort of protesting noise – but he stopped me again. 'Ahm grand here . . . *see?* All Ah need is a bottle of stout and a fag.' He nodded complacently at his Guinness and cigarette, then took a satisfying draught and followed it with an equally pleasurable drag. Blowing smoke at the ceiling, he nodded contentedly. 'All Ah need is me bottle a stout and me fag.'

Already Lexie was undergoing the petrifaction of financial success. Money vindicates everything – beliefs, opinions, habits and of course sins, both venial and mortal, past, present and future.

The company of John Powers had to suffice.

And after this it grows hazy. A few tableaux remain – but little of the choreography which changed one into another.

Dessie, eagerly, to René: 'So there's great opportunities out there?'

René, legs apart in a relaxed but virile and authoritative straddle: 'Nah.' He shook his head and conclusively blew out cigar smoke. 'Africa's finished for the white man now.'

Lexie to Dessie: 'See those big fat weemen in Katanga and the Congo?' It seemed that he was still unable to credit the memory. 'They come out to ye in frilly nighties . . . or shout down to come upstairs for the money.'

'Would they . . . ?'

'Would they *what?* One time I was deliverin' a sliced pan and a bag a Paris buns. This big midden comes to the door in a dressing gown. Bring them out to the kitchen, son, says she. God, the kitchen was *mingin'* . . . the smell of it would really have turned yer stomach. Says she, ye're a lovely wee fella, son . . . and grabs me by the *how's-yer-father* . . . ye know?'

'What?' Dessie puzzled. *'By your cock?'*

'No!' Lexie shouted. 'By the fuckin' Paris buns.'

Lexie to René: 'Nah, ye wouldn't want to come back and start a family in this town. The teachers in this town are for fuck all.' He glanced around but did not lower his voice on discovering Neil close by. 'A teacher used to be somebody – but sure every slag in the town's teachin' now. And no wonder, eh? Fuckin' holidays they get. See if me or you took holidays like that . . . where would we be . . . *eh?'*

'On permanent holiday,' René suggested.

'Out on our arses. Too right.'

Objective reporting gives the impression of a narrator remote and detached. This was far from the case. Concerned at a gender imbalance which always kept two men off the floor, I went down to the landing where Mary's expression and outstretched arms now appeared to be a desperate plea for a dance. Unfortunately the plaintive Virgin belied her ethereal aura by weighing a ton. I had to make do with invoking her presence in the drawing room.

Narrator to Dessie: 'Recite "Our Heavenly Mother" for us.'

Dessie (rumbustiously): 'Fuck away off.'

Tired of the suavity of Sinatra, Celia rooted among the records and happily flourished a sleeve on which, above four Aran sweaters, there beamed the coarse hearty features of the Clancy Brothers and Tommy Makem. Soon Neil was swinging Celia in that boisterous revel known as a 'swizz'. Unable to maintain the hectic pace, the rest of the dancers withdrew.

Dessie cornered Lexie and René to tell them the story of *Badge 313,* a tough New York crime novel which begins with the discovery of a murdered teenage girl who has semen in every orifice.

Watching the swizzers with tolerant good humour, Helen explained to Marie and me. 'Neil and Celia have always carried on. From Celia was no age. They're never done teasing each other. Celia's still very childish in many ways.'

Marie's sudden exhalation was almost a snort.

'Are *you* never jealous?' I asked Helen.

Like Christ with the bewildered fishermen, Helen smiled serenely on us. 'It's just Neil's nature. He's very spontaneous and emotional.'

'Semen in every orifice,' Dessie was repeating angrily. 'A fourteen-year-old. That's New York for ye. Dirty fuckers, eh?' He challenged his listeners to contradict him. '*Dirty huers.*'

René replaced the Clancys with Nat King Cole, much to Celia's disgust. In this increasingly febrile madness only Helen retained her poise – pale and slender and numinous as a consecrated communion wafer. I yearned to dance with her, to hold her against me – but Marie took my hands and pushed me out onto the floor.

'That Celia one's a real sickener. She's teasin' the life out of Neil and the big eejit's lappin' it up.' Throwing her arms about my neck, she gazed hungrily into my face. 'I'm so glad to be with you ... *hmmm* ...' My features were slowly and minutely scrutinised by eyes in a face flushed and intent. Without warning she removed her arms from my neck and plunged them inside my waistband, imperiously thrusting down and moaning on achieving her goal. '*Your wee toot.*'

To be assaulted in public by a spouse was absurd. It was fortunate that my genitals understood and refused to respond.

'For Christ's sake.' I grimaced and glanced round.

'What's the matter with *you?*' Marie withdrew her arms and rolled her eyes at the corniced ceiling.

'*Honey.*' Approaching from behind, Neil laid tender hands on Marie's waist. 'I've hardly seen you all night.'

Marie angrily twisted away. 'Don't *honey me.*'

Neil gazed upon her in wise beneficence. 'You're not cross about Celia?'

'Just piss off, Neil.'

'Celia always carries on like that. She's only a child.'

'She's a married woman with two children.'

'She's a *child.* Lexie daddies her. Spoils her rotten. She doesn't know what she's doing.'

'I believe ye, Neil. *Thousands wouldn't.*'

'Listen.' Suddenly solemn, Neil pushed us over behind the Christmas tree and, after checking that we were not observed, addressed us in a low conspiratorial tone. 'I'll tell you something I never told anyone. Not even Helen. But you'll have to promise it *goes no further.*' Already his confidential tone was having a palliative effect on Marie. She nodded earnestly. 'This was years ago when Celia was a teenager. We were sunbathing in the garden ... *that garden*, next door ... and Celia started carrying on ... throwing water and so forth. So anyway, I went for water myself and she chased me into the kitchen and started a wrestling match against the sink. She was only wearing this bikini and I was in underpants. So of course I got a big rock straightaway ... and she kept banging against it and making it worse. Helen was lying out in the garden ... I was scared she'd come in and wouldn't know what to think. But you see what I mean about Celia? The wee girl has *no idea* what she's doing. She's totally innocent ... a *child*.'

This was a remarkable stratagem – attempting to establish innocence by supplying further evidence of guilt. It was so audacious that it nearly worked. Marie regarded Neil for a long time. But finally she snorted.

'It's you that's innocent if you believe that.'

Neil now tried to overcome her reservations by sheer enthusiasm, seizing her round the waist and swinging her clear of the ground.

Marie's scream was authentic and fierce. 'Put me *down this minute*. Put me *down*. Put me *down*.'

Neil did as he was told – but not before attracting the shocked attention of the room. Silent crestfallen faces regarded us. As so often, the season of goodwill was coming to an end in ill will.

Marie stepped away from Neil and snapped down her dress. 'Don't you grab me like that again. *Ever*, Neil Quinn.'

13

Weddings: long gruelling days in which you move from sobriety to stupor without ever passing through intoxication. Barry's nuptials were no different – and the one surprise was unwelcome. At the reception the judge backed me into a corner for hostile cross-questioning on the subject of his new son-in-law. His manner reminded me of my older schoolteachers – the same barely repressed anger at a world determined to flout the will of God's senior representatives in the community, the same brazen assumption of immediate and total subservience in a junior. He should have been informed that such impertinence was no longer tolerable – but I settled for protecting my partner's privacy.

Much damaging information could have been disclosed. All Dominic's cronies had gravitated to Barry. But Barry was not qualified to sign their accounts. Many clients worked to the calendar year, so that the first signatures were needed at the end of December. Barry had bustled into my office snapping his fingers and grimacing in apparently irritated forgetfulness.

'What's this was the name of that place . . . the place with the two-tone shirts?'

The moment he'd seen me wearing one of these Barry had demanded the name of the shop. I had put him off for as long as possible but, too insensitive to take a hint, he had badgered me until I told him. Since the Maiden City was not large enough for three men with the same shirts, it was fortunate that Barry's persistence did not extend to detailed planning.

'Was up in Belfast there but couldn't mind the name a that friggin' shop.'

When reminded, he cried out in dramatic remorse, rapped his skull with the knuckles of his right hand and, with his left, casually thrust forward a set of accounts, so that the bottom end rested on the desk for a signature, while the top remained firmly in his grasp.

'That's grand, Barry.' My grip on the bottom end was equally firm. 'I'll just look over these and do that in a minute.'

It was a key moment in the relationship. When our eyes met I caught the flash of malevolent anger. But I had him by the goolies – and he knew it.

'*Right.*' Peevishly he tossed the pages onto the desk top. 'In your own time . . . *you know?*' His parody of accommodating politeness was the very height of insolence. 'There's no rush at all. Just whenever you have a minute . . . *you know?*'

These accounts were in order – or at least contained no obvious fabrications. Barry thought me overscrupulous but I had no desire to journey round the country checking if builders had acquired new diggers or farmers new threshing machines. Like most professionals, I was content if the documentation looked convincing. Tax inspectors are no different. As long as *some* tax is being paid and the detail is plausible, they will not question returns. And when this is explained to clients, most appreciate that it is easier in the long run to appear to co-operate with the system.

But there are always a few, usually of the self-made variety, who cannot bear the thought of surrendering hard-won gains to the state and regard it as an accountant's sacred duty to ensure that not a penny of tax is paid. These are the clients to avoid – and not merely for reasons of caution. As much as enriching themselves, they enjoy suborning others – and, in particular, making fastidious professionals join them in the trough.

Eamonn Flanagan started in business at fifteen by having a half-ton of coal delivered to his parents' back yard, transferring it to sacks with an old shovel and distributing these to corner shops in a dilapidated pram with the hood removed. Now over fifty, he owned a coal merchant's, a building firm, two dance halls and, the local equivalent of gilt stocks, several pubs. Like most Catholic businessmen, he moved his money into the Irish Republic (it would be another thirty years before Southern banks with branches in the North were prevented by law from abetting this) and owned an extensive estate in a resort town just over the border. He could easily have equipped this second home by purchasing in the South but resented the much higher prices and insisted on bringing everything from the North, thus attracting the attentions of Southern Customs.

At our first meeting Flanagan explained his solution to this problem. 'There's this one character in particular was always givin' me bother. A big thick Southern huer ... from the back a the country somewhere. Probably turned down for the Guards ... that's how they end up in the Customs. Anyway, he'd sit on ees arse all day, wavin' everyone through – but the minute he saw me comin', up would go the big hand ... ye know? Then he'd stroll out, takin' ees time about it, and start tryin' to give me the third degree. So after a while Ah got fed up wi' this carry-on.' Suddenly confidential, Flanagan leaned forward and established eye contact. He was already grey-haired and florid but his eyes, although barely visible in narrow apertures (a characteristic known locally as 'tight eyes'),

gleamed with malice and guile. 'I get on the phone to Dublin
Castle. Jack Kavanagh, please. Och how're ye doin', Eamonn,
says he. Long time no see. Bit a craic about this that and the
other and then says I, A wee bit of a problem here, Jack, and
tell him what's goin' on. Says he, Listen, Eamonn, just leave
that with me. Just leave that thing with me ... OK?' An
experienced and skilful raconteur, Flanagan paused to create
suspense, actually beating his pockets for cigarettes and taking
time to light up. 'So next time Ahm goin' over the border out
comes yer man ... *runnin' this time* ... and a face on him, ye
know? So I wind down the window: What seems to be the
problem? Says he, What do ye mean goin' over my head to
Dublin Castle? Says I to him, Over yer head, son?' He
removed the cigarette from his mouth in a sudden animation
which partially rejuvenated his puffy features. 'Ah'll go so far
over yer head Ah'll be shitin' down on ye like a fuckin'
seagull.'

Laughter caused his eyes to disappear completely, as though
withdrawing for a private celebration in his head. For a time he
heaved contentedly, taking deep rewarding drags and shaking
his head at the almost unbearable pleasure of the memory.
Then, in abrupt resolution, he subjected me to a sober stare.
'Have ye got a minute?'

'Now ...?'

'Come on.' Springing up with surprising alacrity, he came
round the desk to lay a paternal hand on my shoulder. 'Want
to show ye somethin'.'

Decisive action after bonhomie is hard to resist. Before I
knew it, we were crossing the hall.

'It's only a step outside.' And he led me across the street to a
battered mud-stained Ford Consul.

'I haven't time for a drive.'

'No drive.' Raising a palm in reassurance, he went to the
boot and flung it open. Like wildflowers in a spring meadow,
bank notes of various denominations (and two currencies)

were strewn over all the available surface in colourful profusion. 'What do ye make a that, eh?'

Not for nothing was Flanagan known in the business community as 'Big Rattle'.

This piece of street theatre was meant to create several impressions: that the Flanagan wealth was a bounteous natural growth, like dandelions and daisies, which renewed and extended itself no matter how much was removed; that, in consequence of such abundance, the owner had no interest in counting or hoarding; that, to partake, it was necessary only to lean forward, plunge in both arms and gather to the bosom an exhilarating sheaf.

My own reaction was a sickening remorse at subjecting myself to such a performance. At least there was the self-discipline of refusing to enquire how much money lay before us.

He was finally forced to supply a figure without being asked. 'Usually twenty grand or so here.'

'And you drive around with that lying loose in the boot?'

'I take a handful when I need it.' He shrugged and blithely waved at the notes to reinforce the three impressions.

All were illusory. Not only entirely unwilling to give, Big Rattle would countenance no transaction which failed, as he put it, 'to turn a pound'. Although he had extensive stables and staff at the resort home, he charged his brothers commercial rates for stabling the ponies of their children. And anyone tempted to share in his wealth would get an unpleasant surprise. On the way back to the office he discussed the perennial problem of thieving staff and his recent apprehension of a barman with his hand in the till.

'Presumably you sacked him straightaway?'

'Not at all. Sure the next one would just be as bad. Naw, Ah took him out to the yard at the back a the pub. There was no bother after that.'

His sudden grimness should perhaps have alerted me. 'To

give him a telling off?'

'*Telling off?*' Flanagan hooted at such naivety. 'A lot of good that would do. *Ah gave him two thick ears and a couple a steevers up the hole.*'

The lovable rogue: a widely admired character type, possibly the Celtic ideal. Accountants meet many who aspire to the soubriquet. This accountant can only say that he has never found one to deserve it. I have yet to meet a rogue who inspired any liking, much less love.

The terminal decline of Flanagan's building firm brought our relations to a head (in this town building firms had the solidity and life expectancy of gnats). A dying business invites two scams: to remove as much cash as possible in the guise of nonexistent purchases and to boost its value by creating a paper sale to a stooge who appears to have sold it back later for an impressively large sum. It was entirely typical of Big Rattle to attempt both scams. Fortunately for me, he needed the transactions authenticated while Barry was still on his honeymoon.

Refusal did not disturb him. Indeed he was rather amused. 'So that's the way of it, eh?' He chuckled and simultaneously slapped both chair arms in the manner of a man about to rise for a pleasant undemanding stroll. 'Sure Ah only have to walk round the corner, son.'

'Where I've no doubt you'll find a warm welcome.'

This time he laughed out loud. 'Ye won't last long in this town.' Moving without agitation or haste, he got to his feet and nodded round at the walls. 'Ye shouldn't have wasted yer money doin' the place up.'

It was clear that he intended to take his time leaving and to inflict maximum damage on the way out. At the door he paused, as though just struck by a thought, and came back into the room. 'You know that partner of yours, he was round wi' me lookin' for a loan to get into this business.'

This was my first inkling of the source of Barry's venture

capital. 'I'm well aware of that.'

'Says I to him, Son Ah wouldn't touch the likes a that. Sure what would ye be buyin' only thin air?' He gestured to indicate the insubstantiality of the business. 'Wouldn't touch it, look see. *Wouldn't touch it.*' By now he was back at his chair. 'Oh, says he to me, Catholic businesses are boomin', there's great opportunities for Catholic accountants. The same boy can fairly talk, Ah'll give him that. Says he, There's great opportunities. Says I, Listen, son . . .' Gripping the chair back, Flanagan thrust his head forward in triumph. 'I heard frogs fartin' in long grass before.' Now genuinely finished, he made briskly for the door – but his last comment had pleased him so much that he paused with a hand on the knob to repeat it. '*I heard frogs fartin' in long grass before.*'

This was a difficult and trying time. The intention was to settle as much as possible before Barry got back – but working late and bringing folders home left little time or energy for resuming nightly meetings with the Quinns. And Marie had her own reasons for postponing resumption. She now attributed her recent weight gain to hefty three-course snack suppers – eating last thing at night was the worst one could do. Nor had she forgiven Neil his revelry with Celia. The man was the sexual equivalent of an alcoholic: a smile from anything in a skirt and he was out of control.

Eventually the Quinns called on us, Helen leading the way into our living room with a dramatic sense of high purpose. 'My husband is in the depths of despair, folks.'

And indeed Neil appeared to be intolerably burdened, slumping hunched into an armchair with his overcoat pulled tightly about him, brow puckered in perplexity at maleficent Fate. We patiently awaited an explanation – but this testimony could be released only after a smoke. He withdrew the packet and was slowly opening it when suddenly he jammed it shut again to blurt out. 'There's a young fella started teaching with us this year . . . Gabriel Murray . . . from Armagh. A lovely young fella ... sensitive ... an only child. Anyway, he comes in this morning ... first day of term ... goes into his form class and opens his desk drawer for the register. No register there. Just a big turd instead ... a big black human turd. So what does Gabriel do? Says nothing. Not a word to the class ... or anyone else. Just puts on his coat and lifts his briefcase and walks out of the school.' Now Neil fumbled open the packet, urgently grabbing a cigarette and lighting up, then throwing back his head to facilitate a long deep and desperate draw.

'It's Neil's first day back,' Helen explained.

'Winter term.' Neil expelled smoke in fierce despair. 'Fuckin' always lasts for ever. Nothing but darkness and freezing cold. Windows steamed up and wringing wet. The whole school driven mental. Fighting, horseplay, effing, spitting. And I've a third-year form class. Third years always turn nasty halfway through the year. Second half of third year and first half of fourth year – this is the worst. It's when their balls drop, Dessie says.'

'But isn't Dessie a comfort?' I suggested. 'Dessie and Tommy Peoples? The solace of like-minded companions?'

'Like-minded?' Neil jolted grimly forward. 'Didn't I tell you about the staff do? Dessie gets into an argument about fitness with this Gaelic footballer ... a big country fella ... teaches PE. Anyway, Dessie used to be a runner before he discovered the drink ... and he claims he can beat this character in a sprint. This is *Dessie*, at least two or three stone overweight. Outside and prove it, says the footballer. But it's pitch dark, says Dessie, ye can't see a styme. So then Tommy Peoples ... an older man who ought to know better ... Tommy says to them, Come out to the car park and we'll use the car headlights. Do you know the car park of the Ture Inn? You can well imagine it ... a big roadhouse over the border ... stuck out in a field. The car park's like fuckin' Passchendaele or somethin'. So everybody traipses out, cars are turned and headlights put on ... and these two big drunk men sprint like eejits across muck and stones. Dessie wins all right ... but crosses the finishing line on his mouth and nose with the leg torn out of his good suit.' Neil paused to consider the memory. 'These are my like-minded companions.'

The image of Dessie sprinting and falling had struck us all dumb. We gaped in horror as though he had risen before us bloody and tattered.

Neil inhaled again – but briefly – and suddenly got to his feet. 'Anyway, let's go to Mullen's for half an hour.'

Now it was my turn to look stricken. On the table before me was the financial history of a client with an appointment first thing in the morning. 'On a *Monday night?*'

Marie settled the matter by rising decisively. 'Sure you're only young once.' When she brought me my coat I was still staring in despair at the detritus of ancient financial transactions. She squeezed the back of my neck affectionately. 'Come on, slow coach.'

Desperate for any excuse, I pulled at my old heavy sweater. 'But look at the state of me.'

Marie threw back her head in a delighted laugh. 'Sure who'll be lookin' at *you?*'

'Mullen's will be empty,' Helen promised – and this was the case.

Accepting the obligations of instigator, Neil brushed me aside and insisted on buying the first round.

'If teaching's so terrible,' I said to him, 'why don't you get out of it ... do something else?'

'Exactly.' Helen gazed on me with satisfaction and gratitude – as though I had actually offered Neil an alternative career. 'That's what *I'm* always saying to him.'

Neil was sullen, intractable. 'What else could I do?'

The surly fatalism of the town never failed to exasperate. 'How do *I* know? What do you *want* to do? Become an engineer in Uganda for fuck's sake.'

'Aaaaaahhh ...' Helen laid a tender hand on Marie's sleeve.

'Isn't René just gorgeous?'

Marie rolled her eyes in a mock swoon. 'A big dote.' Then a sigh ... and a smothered laugh. 'In fact, I had a dream about him the other night.' Again she laughed. 'Too embarrassing to tell.'

This further inflamed a curiosity already fierce. Tribulations forgotten, Neil brought close to Marie a countenance avid, insistent, *on fire*. 'Tell us. Tell us. Go on.'

'*Tell us*,' Helen demanded.

I too had yet to hear the story. 'You'll have to tell them.'

Marie pondered impishly, enjoying the attention. 'All I can say is that I came in the dream.'

Already Helen was astounded. 'Women can't come in dreams.'

'They do in mine,' I said – but the Quinns were concentrating on Marie.

'All I know is that it happened. And what's so strange about that? It happens to men all the time.'

Neil shook his head in what appeared to be regret. 'I've never had a wet dream in my life.'

Marie nodded in my direction. 'Your man here has them all the time. Clatters me completely if he's facing the wrong way.'

Still attempting to absorb the revelation of Marie's dream orgasm, Helen received a fresh shock. 'You mean you *don't wear pyjamas?*' she cried at me. 'Neil always wears jammies in bed.'

Calmly I shook my head. She continued to gaze on me in speculative wonder. 'But what is it *like?*' Neil was murmuring with empathic tenderness to Marie. 'I mean, to come in a dream. Is it *different?*'

'Different,' she agreed, thinking hard. 'In some ways better ... and in some ways worse.'

'How ... *better?*' No doubt Helen was feeling deprived.

'Well ... because there's nothing actually in there you feel it more ... really *pulsing* ... you know?' Raising her right hand,

Marie formed her fingers into a cone and made abrupt lunging grabs like those of a hungry snapping turtle.

'And in what way *worse?*' Helen again.

Marie's expression was perfectly sober. 'There's nothing actually in there.'

Although everyone laughed, this was precise exposition. It also explained the difference between my own intercourse orgasm and the violent explosiveness of a wet dream. The lack of an interlocking organ had inevitable consequences for both sexes. In dream the snapping turtle found no purchase and the gun had no padding to absord the recoil.

It was one of those rare magical evenings with an apparently inexhaustible cascade of confidences, revelations, witticisms and insights. The incandescent hours to closing time passed like the flare of a match.

Tonight there could be no question of refusing to go back with the Quinns. Marie attempted to forestall supper but Helen would not hear of such a thing. Perhaps incensed at being overruled, Marie declined to eat and looked from Helen to Neil with a provocative gleam in her eye. 'How's Celia this weather?'

'Just the usual.' Helen ignored the subtext. 'She was up the other day with a new catalogue. She's always doing the rounds with a catalogue. I usually buy something from her – but you'd want to have seen the stuff in this one. Oh *Marie* ... you've no *idea*. Everything was as *dootsie*. You just couldn't look at *any* of it. So of course Celia was *raging* at me. We won't be seeing her for a while.'

Neil had been staring into his tea with an increasingly sombre and troubled expression. Now he put down his cup and turned to me. 'I need to speak to your wife.'

Could a liberal rationalist oppose a frank and full exchange of views? I shrugged accommodatingly.

'I mean in private.'

Once again I threw up obliging hands.

'We'll go into the bedroom,' Neil said to Marie.

Liberal rationalists champion free speech – but occasionally yield to sarcasm. 'Of course,' I murmured. '*Where else?*'

Neil could barely contain his righteous fury at this impertinence. 'Look, I need to speak to your wife in private. To clear up a few things. I can do it in a cold kitchen . . . in the hall . . . out on the street, if you like . . . or in a room with a heater.'

Along with Marie and Neil went the gaiety of the evening, its final manifestation a wink at me from Marie on her way out.

Into the sudden awkwardness and tension Helen blurted, 'More tea?'

'No thanks.'

'Eat that roll of Marie's. Sure it'll only go stale.'

I resented this notion of men as ever-ready waste-disposal units. 'I'm full, Helen.'

She began to tidy up, dragging it out – and spending a long time in the kitchen.

But eventually the cold forced her back to the gas fire. In silence we regarded its fulvous plaque, the usually comforting respiration now a reminder of the absence of talk. For once anger and resentment were not the problem. It was just that I could not think of anything to say. Or rather that every remark which suggested itself was liable to distortion and misunderstanding. In such a supercharged silence even the simplest of sentences would reverberate monstrously.

Helen began to shift, as if anxious to speak – and finally succeeded in doing so. 'Neil just wants to be sure Marie isn't still annoyed about Celia.'

'Oh she isn't. She isn't. She's not annoyed in the least.'

'Because there's really no need.'

'She's not in the least annoyed now.'

Helen seemed reassured – but then issued a heavy sigh. 'Christmas night wasn't the greatest of evenings.' She sighed again and turned to the fire. 'Did Lexie have a go at you on the sofa?'

Here was a chance to display the magnanimity at the core of my character. 'It was nothing.'

'I could tell by the look on his face. He's always doing that to people. Used to do it to me when we first met. He has a terrible chip on his shoulder. Though it's justified to some extent, I suppose. Daddy was paying for Celia at the convent, but when she was fifteen she started going steady with Lexie and making no effort to study for exams. Daddy was just *livid* with her. I mean, he pays for a grammar school education and she takes up with a *breadman*. And Lexie always knew he was regarded as not good enough.'

'Business success will reconcile him.' This was no vague reassurance but a confidently stated axiom. Money soothes many an unquiet heart.

We returned to gazing at the gas fire – but this time the silence was comfortable and calm.

By and by, Helen commenced another series of stirrings, their increasing frequency and febrility presaging a difficult new tack. 'You know,' she said at last, thoughtfully. 'I don't think those two are coming back.' Her tone was resolutely neutral – but its softness suggested absence of rancour and possibly even acquiescence. If she had accepted the disappearance of the others, what were the implications for us?

'Is that a problem?'

This time she laughed with unmistakable insouciance. 'No.'

I went to sit beside her on the sofa, though maintaining a distance of several feet. A further laugh seemed to indicate sweet comely confusion. Certainly there was no trace of distaste or alarm.

Even so, it was far from easy. The commotion of group encounters was too impersonal and frantic – but it helped to conceal individual volition. Now the slightest move would be cruelly isolated and magnified. How to traverse the space between us without it appearing a brutish attempt to jump on

her like a cleg? Initial moves ought to be bilateral and simultaneous, as though ordained by an implacable force beyond two
human wills. In the end Helen leaned towards me in a way that
was easy to reciprocate, so that the crucial first kiss was accomplished with a minimum of embarrassing ineptitude. The next
problem was our winter garb of heavy sweaters, shirts, jeans
and sturdy footwear. Again Helen was the perfect facilitator,
crossing her arms to pull her sweater over her head and disturb,
in the most enchanting way, her Asymmetric Isadora's purity
of line. I too removed my sweater and, proceeding in harmonious parallel stages (though each gently undid the shirt/blouse
buttons of the other), punctuated by the necessary reassurance
of kisses, we eventually got down to our underwear. Tonight
Helen was wearing yet another innovative bra and pants set.
This time they had a surprisingly cheerful brown-and-black
stripe and the material not only lacked a gloss finish but was
entirely without support features and filigree embellishment.
On her pale narrow body it resembled the swimsuit of a
child and, while youthfulness was undoubtedly invigorating,
I had no desire for prepubescence. Exposure of the cigarillo
butts provided a welcome reminder of maturity.

But when I slipped a hand into her pants, Helen gently lifted
it away.

There was no sanitary-towel bulge – but she may have been
a tampon user. 'Is it your period?'

'No ... it's just ...' Waving a hand in hopeless confusion,
she gave me a quick peck to reassert commitment. 'I just can't
tonight.'

The absence of the other two had put us under klieg lights,
so a measure of coyness was understandable. I too was reluctant
to remove my underpants, for although they were the greyish
tattered Y-fronts of Monday, on a Monday even worse
horrors could well lie beneath. Helen was a stickler for personal
hygiene and I had not had a bath since teatime on Friday. (Not
that I suspected a parallel problem – Helen's pants would

surely be immaculate as Mary's heart.) In any case it was pleasant to lie beside her in fond inertia, as though we had not stopped short but were basking in consummated afterglow.

Agreeable enough to begin with, this configuration eventually became chilly and cramped. 'We can hardly stay like this all night.'

Grunting mildly, Helen responded with another obvious fact. 'We can't burst in on them in the bedroom either. We'll have to leave them in peace.'

We lay together on the sofa, pondering.

Suddenly Helen sat up. 'There's an old camp bed in the junk cupboard . . . and a big travel rug in the sideboard.'

Before I could answer, she sprang from the sofa and pulled her blouse over her shoulders. A garment so flimsy it was semi-transparent, this could have given little heat. Her resolution was the true insulator. Pretending to an equivalent boldness, I followed her in Y-fronts and a hastily draped shirt.

In the hallway she yanked open a huge walk-in cupboard. A freezing mustiness assailed us.

Helen retreated a step. '*Jesus!*' Instinctively she pulled the blouse across her breast, a covering action with the paradoxical effect of exposure. As every mystagogue knows, radiance is always more dazzling when lightly veiled. We moved forward side by side, fearful but stimulated, like normally well-behaved children who dare to explore a forbidden cellar. An ancient light switch revealed a jumble of abandoned household implements, among them an ancient camp bed. When we each took an end it sagged, wobbled and squeaked and Helen's laughter had such ringing delight that I turned round to look. Her eyes, usually so bright and clear, had a film of yearning that had not been present earlier in the evening – or indeed at any time in our relationship. The adventure of the forbidden cellar had obviously wakened her desire. Like so many desiderata, erotic excitement is best created as an accidental by-product of some other process. Abandoning the bed, I took her by the waist and our mouths engaged with such natural intensity that I did not hesitate to draw her against my fully engorged cock, rejoicing in the flagrancy of the contact as much as the physical pleasure.

While I assembled the bed in front of the fire, Helen found a sheet to cover the mattress and a heavy tartan rug to go on top. Then she flung off her blouse and sprang in, humorously bouncing on the creakiness and drawing the rug back for me. The light was off but she had generously kept on the gas fire, so that its light glowed on her white skin like a glorious sunset on apple blossom.

'It's not a bit like a Monday,' I suggested.

She spluttered madly and collapsed, her face buried in a cushion. Helen often overreacted to drollery – but there are many worse faults.

Companionable laughter, complicitous darkness, concealing covers – conditions were certainly propitious now. Modern obsession with experiment and image should never cause us to underestimate the classic hidden form of the act. Blankets and night may add as well as subtract. The forbidden cellar is always dark.

And yet when, in the fullness of time, I tried to remove Helen's pants, she once again demurred – sympathetically, sorrowfully, even *tragically* – but with a firmness that would not be persuaded. This time the refusal was harder to accept. Both my expectations and militant member were higher than before. After consoling me with many pats and pecks of sisterly affection, Helen fell into a deep and apparently untroubled sleep. Not only was I now fully awake, there was no room to manoeuvre on the tiny creaking bed and the hairy rug tickled my body and face. Many thoughts contended for attention in my increasingly agitated brain – of a night-long vigil (I had never experienced insomnia before), of the client arriving first thing in the morning (I would have to go home first to fetch the relevant material), and, of course, of Marie and

Neil doing the nasty in a comfortable bed with cool hairless sheets.

Unlike healthy plants, paranoia blossoms in darkness. There returned the hypothesis, soon a certainty, that, as part of some bizarre and depraved pact, Helen had agreed to keep me distracted while Neil fucked Marie. Was there not the incontrovertible evidence of her refusal to consider disturbing this pair?

Sleep eventually came – but light, troubled and brief. By dawn I was a maddened bull tormented beyond any enduring. I leapt out of bed and began to get dressed.

Helen stirred sleepily. 'What are you doing?'

'What I should have done long ago if I'd had any sense . . . *going home.*'

'Come back in. It's early.' Early – but too late for coyness.

The direction I took made her sit up in alarm. *'You're not going to barge in on those two?'*

Marie and Neil lifted fearful heads, pulling sheets to their chins.

'What is it?' Marie whimpered.

'Get dressed now. We're going home.'

'But what's the matter?'

'I'm fucking fed up being fucking teased, that's what's the matter. *No touchie pretty girlie* – that's what's the fucking matter.'

Marie did not lack spirit but was intimidated by rational fury. For her, rage was emotional and inarticulate, a storm swiftly spent in screams, curses, flight, tears. In me she had encountered for the first time the white but controlled countenance, the long detailed list of indictments, the forensic accumulation and marshalling of evidence, the unwavering judgement and the punitive sentence. As soon as she read my expression her own face turned pale.

I took a step forward. *'Get dressed.'*

'Easy on,' counselled Neil – but without much conviction.

Terror-stricken, a cornered animal, Marie looked about desperately for somewhere to hide. 'I'll get dressed now. I will. But could ye just . . . like . . . could ye just go out a minute?'

I threw back my head in an incredulous bark. 'It's not as if it's something *we haven't seen.*'

Neil tried to speak . . . and failed. Marie was also incapable of speech now – but the mute entreaty of her anguish was more effective than any words. Suddenly I felt like a jack-booted commandant prodding a naked woman into a gas chamber.

'I'll wait for you,' I conceded at last. '*In the hall.*'

14

The working hours of Tuesday passed in a nightmarish vertigo of exhaustion. When I got home I could barely stay awake much less rant – but Marie still feared a resumption of wrath.

'You know Neil still couldn't do it,' was almost the first thing she said.

My attention, apparently extinguished, revived instantly. '*Still?* Not once? Not once *all night?*'

'Not even once. He couldn't get it up once.'

But was this simply a repeat of the excuse which had calmed me before? 'Why didn't you tell me last night?'

'*Last night?*' Her eyes rolled at the intolerable memory. 'When you're like that I shut up. You were practically *foaming at the mouth.*'

My guilt was swiftly replaced by fascination at Neil's continuing impotence. 'Did he keep trying?'

'Did he *what?* I never got a minute's peace the whole night. The sweat was lashin' off him but he wouldn't give in and go to sleep. And absolutely ragin' ... *past himself.* I was dyin' to laugh ... but he'd've *killed* me, so he would. He was at me the whole time. At me and at me and at me. I'm as sore with him workin' at me and pushin' himself into me.' Marie's squirm to indicate physical discomfort was unnecessary. Her eloquence was entirely convincing – and my rage for justice and equity appeased. The new gladness in my eye was misinterpreted by Marie. 'If you're thinking of making up for Helen now, forget it. I'm far too sore.'

Awareness of my own debility rushed back and expressed itself in a heavy groan. 'Honey, I'm too knackered to *move.* If Marilyn came back from the dead and pulled down her knickers I couldn't stir from this sofa.'

'Somebody'll have to make the tea though.' Well satisfied, Marie rose from her chair – only to bend over, wince, cross her legs ... and reluctantly sit down again. 'Oh God, Ahm as *sore.* He has me fanny *destroyed.*'

My weakened constitution attempted to support laughter – but failed.

In vain had innumerable songs warned us: love brings only pain.

And Barry returned from his honeymoon displaying no evidence of bliss. As my own experience had demonstrated, official occasions of joy rarely deliver. Nor was his mood improved by news of our parting from Big Rattle and others. It was hard to know which was more grievous for Barry – the loss of their goodwill or the loss of their money. At one time it might have been goodwill but now it was certainly money, for the newlyweds had purchased a four-bedroomed detached house in one of the private estates springing up along the river on the outskirts of town. The older estates, Hazelbank, Meadowbrook, Templegrove, had names suggestive of arcadian innocence and hence exclusion of riffraff – but in the age of heatwave colours, indirection and subtlety were no longer required. This new estate was known as Knightsbridge Park.

In Barry there now contended two imperious but mutually exclusive desires – to punish me for ditching lucrative clients and to dazzle me with the splendour of his new home. Over time the first desire waned while the second waxed strong. Eventually he issued an invitation I could scarcely refuse.

The mature shrubberies of old money had always depressed me – but the newness of Knightsbridge Park was not an exciting alternative. At regular intervals on each side of a gently curved roadway, immaculate detached houses gleamed in trim plots where saplings were strapped to stakes in beds so precisely circular they might have been punched by machine tools. Everything looked as though workmen had departed only a few moments before.

Inside it was the same – all the furniture and fixtures seemed to be just out of the packaging. Barry, brilliantly casual in an off-white roll neck and navy slacks, showed us round with a pride as unsubtle as the name of the park. Marie and I probably failed to marvel with sufficient frequency and vehemence – but there was one genuinely impressive feature, the picture window and astounding view. At this time buildings in Ireland were still designed to exclude hostile nature. We had never seen so large a window, much less one that displayed, still agleam in the last of the light, an already mighty river widening into its estuary.

Emer summoned us to the kitchen. She was now heavily pregnant and seemed to have put on weight besides, although this was cunningly disguised by a lime-green minidress in the waistless tent shape that was now all the rage. Looking harried and flustered, she served food that not only came from a packet but was the Vesta Chicken Supreme that had sustained me through the years of accountancy exams. The contrast with Helen's home cooking could not have been more extreme, and enthusiasm was once again difficult to express. In fact, everyone was ill at ease, even the normally ebullient Barry. Despite its relentlessly casual style (open-plan lounge scattered with easy chairs, kitchen with breakfast bar and stools), this home did not make its owners feel at home. The house hung about them like an oversized designer garment with the price tag still attached.

After the main course Emer seemed to relax. For the principal catering effort had been reserved for dessert. There was chocolate cake, trifle and lemon meringue pie. All were of high quality – though none was homemade.

When we returned to the lounge the river was lost in darkness but its presence still conveyed a sense of epic grandeur.

'Why such a large house?' I asked Barry.

He seemed to find the question surprising. 'For the children.'

'And how many of those will there be?'

Again he gave the impression that the answer should have been obvious. 'Five.'

Emer snorted. '*I* might have something to say on the matter.'

'But it'll be great for them round here, won't it?' Marie was certainly doing her best to be positive. 'I mean, it's as safe for them to play outside.'

Barry swung his arm in a vague arc of approval. 'It's perfect for children round here.'

We stared at logs blazing in a huge ranch-style fireplace whose bricks rose to the ceiling unencumbered by the fussiness of the traditional mantelpiece.

'That's a great fire,' Marie said at last.

Emer considered the remark before nodding solemnly. 'You need a good fire.'

Thus the conversation dragged along, banal, stilted, halting. No amount of alcohol could generate gaiety or ease. In the end there were two conversations. Barry engaged me on work while the wives soldiered on with small talk.

We escaped as soon as possible. Never so welcome the rigour of the inviolate stars.

'God Almighty!' I cried out to the firmament. 'Was it us . . . or them . . . or this park . . . *or what?*'

'*Them.*' Marie took my arm in instinctive gratitude and relief. 'Let me link onto ye. It was definitely them. Did you notice that they hardly said a word to each other? Apparently Barry's rippin' because he couldn't have a big house-warming party. Emer said she was too tired to cope with a whole crowd she didn't know. Sensible enough, really. She's not as stuck up as I thought.'

'Five children will certainly bring her down from her high horse.'

'Six, you mean.'

'*Hah?*'

'Counting Barry.' Marie began a laugh that modulated into a sigh. 'God love her.'

The note of compassion gave me pause. 'You're not getting broody?'

Now her laugh was unequivocal. 'God forbid.'

We walked along in silence, exhilarated by the bracing asperity of the night. Suddenly Marie jogged my arm. 'But I do have a bone to pick with you.'

'What's that?'

'How come Barry's in a big house and we're in a pokey wee flat? How can he afford that place?'

'He can't.' So why was he there? 'Probably he's desperate to prove to the judge that he's not a cornerboy. And getting up to his ears in debt to prove it.' I jogged her arm in turn. 'Do you want a house in Knightsbridge Park?'

'*Spare me!*' Marie shook her head afresh at the memory of the evening. 'What a waste of a Friday night.' Hideous details surged back. 'And all those *desserts*. Having to eat some of each to be civil.' She released a wail at the indifferent heavens. 'Ah'll be fat as a fool. Ah'll be a tub . . . a *big tub.*'

It seemed that Saturday would also end in dreariness, but after the evening meal, as we were shuddering afresh at the horrors of the previous night and wondering how to efface the memory, Helen led the way into our living room flourishing a handful of salmon-pink cards. Fate had resolved not only to reunite us but to lay on free entertainment and refreshments. Thanks to the sudden death of a bank colleague's mother-in-law, we had tickets for a supper dance in El Matador.

'Supper!' Marie cried in dismay, taking one of the tickets. 'Chicken in a basket at ten o' clock!'

'Dance!' I too peered at a ticket. '*Bridie Gallagher and her band!* Jesus is she *still alive?*'

Helen was not about to yield to such negative thoughts. 'Sure, at least it'll be a laugh. And it's not as if we have to pay.'

'And *El Matador*,' Neil added grimly. 'Just opened and just over the border. It'll be another Ture Inn.'

These roadhouses had been built for revellers frustrated by the puritan North's licensing hours. Each evening after the ten o'clock closing a merry crew piled into any available transport and drove across the border to continue carousing. However the proliferation of watering holes had made competition fierce and the larger establishments were now attempting to lure patrons earlier by offering live music and food.

But attractive design and ambience were not among the selling points. Traditional methods of providing variety and cosiness for drinkers – split levels, snugs, alcoves, nooks – had all been abandoned in favour of the new brutalism. El Matador was an enormous hangar with a bar along one side and a frightening expanse of tables stretching away to a tiny dance floor and stage. Nor was congenial service a priority: the tables were attended by an army of child waiters – the average age seemed to be eleven or twelve – with white faces entirely devoid of expression. Helen's attempt at cordiality might as well have been addressed to the cliffs of Moher.

'God in heaven!' she cried. 'What have they done to those children?'

'You're applying standards they don't have,' Neil

suggested. 'This is normality for them. This is their universe. I was giving a class dictation the other day and there was this sentence ... The French army encamped outside Turin. At least half a dozen of them wrote, The French army camped outside the Ture Inn. But that isn't the best of the story. Listen to this – *they were furious at being corrected.* For them the Ture Inn *is* Turin.'

A corpulent matron in a tweed dress and tight perm, Bridie Gallagher was hardly a smouldering chanteuse ('She's the image of Mrs McGilloway from up our street,' Marie claimed), while her band consisted of a drummer lackadaisically swirling brushes on his single drum and, entirely dwarfing an electric organ, a heavy white-haired giant, who looked like a retired police sergeant and every now and then furtively donned bifocals to peer at sheet music. As yet there were few dancers, though the child waiters were busy supplying rounds of incredible complexity and expense. But when the police sergeant swapped his organ for a piano accordion happy patrons flooded out onto the floor. Directly in front of our table two hearty young nuns enjoyed an uninhibited swizz. Whereas Helen had been appalled by the under-age waiters, Neil was outraged by dancing nuns.

'*Jesus,*' he grimaced, 'that's *disgusting*. Let's get out of here.'

I suggested that it was a shame to forgo the chicken but, although the food was already half an hour late, another twenty minutes elapsed before the appearance of baskets lined with magenta napkins arranged to form dramatic petals enfolding two tiny drumsticks in breadcrumbs. Demand for second baskets was immediate and clamorous – but the children remained deaf to entreaty, stonily adamant. Nothing seemed to disturb them. At the table next to us a grey-haired, purple-faced man flirted with a twelve-year-old waitress who waited in impassive silence for the wheedling to finish. 'Would ye not take somethin' yourself. Just a wee Babbycham?' Apparently unaware that the cigarillo in his left hand was on fire down one side, the aged suitor leaned drunkenly forward, his right hand dangling in front of the girl as though he were about to put it up her skirt.

Marie rose decisively. 'Let's go.'

It seemed like another wasted night but when the Volkswagen pulled up at our flat Helen turned to Marie and Neil in the back. 'You two can get out here.'

There was a moment of paralysed silence. I stared straight ahead – but my face burned with the sensation of being under intense scrutiny. No one could move from the back seat unless I left the car first. I got out on the pavement and turned. Marie and Neil stayed put. The unnerving sensation had not been illusory: everyone *was* staring at me.

I looked to the dispassionate stars for guidance.

'OK.' My calm tone concealed a desperate struggle for control. 'But none of this all-night business. Back to our own beds after.'

With averted head I pulled forward the passenger seat. Marie and Neil climbed out swiftly but carefully, sagacious eyes scrupulously fixed on the ground.

Terror and ecstasy of selection by the High Priestess – the chosen youth led to a secret chamber, where his mind is lulled by potions and attars while his body is anointed with unguents.

As soon as we crossed her threshold Helen commenced a perfervid atonement by pressing her lips and body on mine. 'I'm really sorry about the last time.' We fell onto the sofa and, while I was still attempting to come to terms with her fragrance, warmth and willingness, she had my belt open and zip down and was vigorously yanking my cock. This urgency was more disconcerting than coyness. Could such a hectic passion be authentic? Women were supposed to need lengthy foreplay. Marie would never go straight for cock. But just as I was behaving as if Helen were Marie, perhaps Helen was applying an approach suited to Neil.

Lovemaking is as subject to habit as everything else. Regular partners develop a routine, an apportioning of duties and roles, a style. As with skills such as cycling and playing tennis, a procedural memory is unconsciously stored. *We all have our own wee ways.*

Helen stood up, lifted her dress and drew down pants and tights. In wondering reverence I laid my palms on the tops of her bare white thighs. She brought her face close as if to whisper – but the remark was shockingly clear. 'I want to do it.'

A wave of vertigo passed over me. I lowered my face to her groin.

Wrong programme again. It was Marie who relished a cunnilingus *hors d'oeuvre*. Helen caught me by the ears and drew my head back up. Retaining control, she grasped my cock and guided it home. And before I could adjust to this astounding new force field, she was grunting and violently raking my back. But once again the instructions were explicit and calm. 'Let's get down on the carpet.'

One does not disobey a High Priestess. I moved to oblige – but was already in the grip of the divine seizure. Attempting to comply with the transfer, I shot my load somewhere between sofa and floor.

The High Priestess would have been justified in slitting my throat. But she seemed to be bitterly familiar with the unworthiness of male servitors. 'It's all right,' she grunted, not only silencing my babble of apology but actually offering to make tea.

As much as fear, shame inspires flight. I could barely wait to get my trousers zipped.

Returning home too early could have posed different problems – but Marie was sitting on the sofa alone.

'Neil's long gone,' she explained. 'He was terrified of you.'

Neil the hard man from the little terraces scared of a skinny-melinky-longlegs? 'Of *me?*'

'We had visions of you bursting in like a madman.'

'But how come I didn't meet him?' He must have hidden as I passed – a strange and disconcerting thought. But there were more urgent matters. Despite her attempt to look casual Marie had an unmistakable air of repletion. 'So he managed it this time?'

'He finally managed it.' Again the carefully offhand manner could not conceal a note of triumph. However, perhaps seeing dismay on my face, she added hastily. '*I* didn't come though.' Now she studied *my* features. 'And did Helen finally let you?'

'You could certainly say that.'

Marie waited for details – but finally had to break into my ruminant silence. 'So how do you feel?'

A new sensation, strange and terrible, was making itself manifest. '*Desolate.*'

Perhaps this was the first symptom of the heavy flu which was to lay me low a few days later – the most dispiriting sickness I have ever known. Ill health is always depressing but the low spirits are usually a reaction to the sickness rather than an integral part of it. With this flu, depression seemed as physical as shivering, sweating, debility and aches. And whereas these latter symptoms soon abated, the depression persisted and even intensified. I lay in bed consuming American thrillers with angry impatience, skipping descriptive passages and subplots, avid for a denouement which invariably disappointed.

Reflection, which the thrillers could not entirely hold at bay, suggested that the illness was in retribution for simultaneously overburdening my sexual, social and professional lives. Why had I entered into matrimony, settled in a dreary town, taken a buffoon as business partner, accepted a crippling workload, and fallen for the illusion of easy sexual pleasure?

Unaware of this disillusionment, the Quinns continued not only to visit but to beard me in the bedroom, where I lay in a pallid squalor of sweaty pyjamas and greasy hair. These people belonged to a distant lost universe of self-esteem, confidence, volition and hope, and the sole purpose of their visits seemed to be the flaunting of this distinction. Helen was especially insufferable, bursting in on me with a merry cry of 'How's the patient?' and proceeding to perch on the bed in a vibrant jauntiness that showed to advantage long legs now invariably exposed in a minidress and, on one Friday evening, exaggerated by startlingly jolly tights in a broad yellow-and-brown stripe. There appeared to be no way to prevent these intrusions. On one occasion the visits of Barry and the Quinns actually overlapped, so that, not only was it necessary to endure Helen immediately after Barry, but Marie told me there had been some kind of altercation between Barry and Neil at our door. Nothing could have better illustrated a small town's malign web of enduring and rancorous interconnections.

Beset by severe claustrophobia, I developed a plan to rid myself of Barry and escape from the town. It was obvious that Barry was overstretched and would soon face a financial reckoning. But while *his* debts continued to grow, *mine* were decreasing. By the time he reached crisis point I would be in a position to take another loan and buy him out. This could even be accomplished without guilt. Not only getting a profit on his original investment, Barry would still have a means of livelihood. His lucrative sideline of selling insurance could easily be expanded into a full-time activity. Familiar, assuasive and totally cynical, he was a natural salesman and would thrive on his own. Once he was gone, it would be a matter of maximising revenue and making judicious investments – already my knowledge of local business had suggested possibilities. Then goodbye to Barry, town and the Quinns.

As for Marie, if she could not bear to leave the Maiden City she would be welcome to stay. Often this seemed the most desirable outcome. To be rid of the entire bunch and depart in cash-rich autonomy! At other times the selflessness of her ministrations won my heart. Ruthlessly she pillaged the pharmacy for analgesics, anti-pyretics, decongestants, throat lozenges, soothing drinks and an innovative hotwater bottle covered in towelling on which cold feet could be warmed without burning the skin. Her nursing care was exemplary and tireless. She had even appropriated a thermometer and took my temperature at regular intervals, flicking the instrument with wonderfully professional violence before firmly lodging it under my tongue.

Frequently I was moved to maudlin gratitude in which I wished only to bear her away to the life she deserved. 'You know what I was thinking?' Marie was frowning at the thermometer but immediately looked up in concern. 'It's all this sex business that brought on my flu. It's all madness . . . *madness* . . . I don't know why I ever got into it. I should have been grateful for you.' Fervently I seized her warm hand in my own clammy pair. 'It's you I love, honey. Only you . . . you know that.' Enormous self-control was needed to keep tears at bay. In lieu of speech I squeezed her hand. 'And I'm tired of all this boozing and running around . . .' To judge by Marie's consternation, I might have been requesting a divorce instead of pledging eternal love. Desperately I shook her hand. 'I just want to be with you . . . and live with you . . . *and have a wee baby and everything.*'

My return to society was planned for a Saturday night. I wanted a quiet low-key evening but Helen first insisted on cooking a meal and then welcomed us as though to a gala, grandly dressed in a long dark skirt and an expensive-looking black blouse with dramatic leg-of-mutton sleeves.

'Your blouse is *gorgeous*,' enthused Marie, herself uncharacteristically muted in a floral shirtwaister.

'Just got it today in She. It's a mad buy really. Too see-through to wear out anywhere.' With a laugh of irresponsible caprice, Helen thrust forward her torso to prove the point. White skin was indeed clearly visible, as also a cutaway bra in black.

'She's gone clean mad on shopping,' Neil said. 'And rarely comes back empty-handed. She went up to Coleraine last

Saturday and I said to her, Did you get anything? No, she says, no nothing . . . just a wee top.'

'You never said you were getting all dressed up,' Marie now accused Helen.

'Don't be talkin'.' Neil removed from his mouth a long slender cigar. 'This woman's been trying out combinations for hours.'

'*Oooohhhh* . . .' Helen turned to punish this further ungallant betrayal – but Neil nimbly evaded her attack.

'That's about her fourth skirt.' Shrewdly Neil increased the distance between himself and his wife. 'And I don't know how many bras.'

Forming her right hand into a terrible claw, Helen raised it as though to rend flesh. 'I . . . am . . . going to . . . *murder* . . . my husband.'

Neil was already busy with glass and bottles. 'God I'm *gasping* for a drink.'

Grasping an opportunity to betray Neil in turn, Helen turned intimately to me. 'He hasn't had a drink since you've been ill.'

My astonishment was sincere. 'Not even a drop?'

'Sure who would I drink with?' Neil said. 'You can't drink with your wife.'

'Well *thank you*, darling.' Helen was deeply ironic but not truly incensed.

'And as for last night . . .' Neil rolled his head and for consolation drew on his cigar.

Helen was already helpless with laughter at the memory. 'You see, there's this retired Navy man moved into a bunga-low next to Mammy and Daddy. And he was lamenting about how the area's full of old people . . . and how he can't get spicy food anywhere. Apparently he got very fond of spicy food on his travels. So of course Mammy blurts out that I'm a great one at the curries. Oh Helen'll come down and cook you a really hot curry. And Celia and her husband'll come too. So the man jumps at the chance and says, I'll bring the wine.'

'*Hah!*' Neil removed the cigar from his mouth to accommodate a caw. 'Two bottles among seven. Glasses refilled about once an hour. Jesus, I was never so desperate for a drink.'

'So anyway, muggins here had to go down to Portstewart and cook a big pot of curry.'

'And you're cooking again tonight!' Marie cried. 'Helen, you *shouldn't have*. You should have *told us*.'

Not only unconcerned by this evening's labour, Helen was not upset by the gross ingratitude of the previous night. 'And the best of it was this . . . *most of them didn't even like the curry*.'

'*Helen!*'

'Celia had a terrible face on her while she was eating. You'd think she was having teeth pulled. Neil asked her outright if she didn't like it. What's this she said, Neil? What was it she said?'

'No I really do like it, she said.' Neil pursed his lips in imitation of Celia. 'I really like it, you know . . . but it isn't the kind of thing *I would eat a whole heap of*.'

Needless to say, we were lavish in our praise of Helen's sweet and sour pork chops and baked Alaska dessert. Afterwards we offered to wash up but Neil would not hear of submitting his guests to such drudgery. Instead, he proposed a drink in Mullen's. But by the time we arrived all the seats were gone and a three-deep crowd was fighting for service at the bar. Moreover, Helen had to keep on her overcoat to hide the see-through blouse. Marie suggested that we all go back to our place for gin.

When we were settled over glasses Neil suddenly fell silent and hunched forward to frown at the electric fire. Eventually he turned to me a pale intent countenance. 'Can I ask you something?'

'Sure.'

'Can I take your wife into the bedroom?'

My smile may have assumed a glaze. 'Why ask *me*?'

Neil turned his grimacing intensity on Marie. She shrugged helplessly, laughing and looking round to assess reaction. Helen and I were careful not to catch her eye. She laughed again and shrugged. 'I don't mind.'

Helen also laughed now, but abruptly and shrilly, swirling ice cubes and taking one into her mouth. Agitated but determined, Neil rose and approached Marie with the grave expression of a man taking irreversible religious vows. Marie permitted herself to be drawn upright and led out of the room.

'Well.' Helen released the ice cube into her glass. 'Here we are.'

My face was probably still fixed in the rictus of a smile. 'Here we are.'

Helen took a long bracing drink and, in a series of swift resolute movements, put aside her glass, rose to her full height and boldly strode across the room. Pausing before me for a moment, she touched my cheek with intimate fingers and then playfully disarranged my hair.

'Hello.'

'Hello yourself.'

Turning sideways, she gaily perched on my knees – a long-legged exotic bird alighting on a withered stump. Despite the slenderness of her frame, she was shockingly heavy. I took a hasty gulp of gin and set the glass aside.

'So how's the invalid now?'

'Better.'

Like a doctor probing for the sensitive spot, she leaned forward and laid a reverent hand on my bunch, actually looking down to follow her own gentle caresses. 'Is there anything the matter? *Hmmm* . . . ?' Her tone was absent-minded, languorous and dreamy. '*Hmmmm* . . . ?'

'Nothing's the matter.'

But something in my tone seemed to give her pause. She emerged from the trance to study me with sympathy and compassion. 'Don't you want to . . . *hmmmmm* . . . ?' Reaching underneath to take the bunch in her cupped hand, she hefted and squeezed with proprietorial interest. Like a child reassured by a favourite furry animal, she resumed her honeyed drowsiness. '*Hmmmmmm . . . ?*'

As unbearable stress will twist metal, anguish contorted my stony features. 'I just can't at the moment.'

She did not release her grip – but the film of longing vanished from eyes now cool and alert. 'You just *can't?*'

This empathy was encouraging. 'I don't know exactly what it is' – vague crippled gestures expressed the inadequacy of words – 'but I just can't at the moment.' To prove that there was no physical revulsion, I leaned forward to lay on her the hand of sincere sibling affection.

Helen pulled back and stood up, scrutinising me for a moment. Seizing the hem of her skirt in both hands, she yanked it firmly down several times.

'I'm *sorry.*' My eyes, as dolorous as those of Mary, implored her to be merciful.

She continued to study me. Then she took a step towards the bedroom. 'Neil!' Her tone was level, low, ferociously disciplined – but lack of response put an intolerable strain on her self-control. She took another few determined strides and let out a screech. '*Neil!*'

This time there came a strangled cry and after a few moments the door was opened by Neil in underpants, clutching his trousers.

Helen had to clench her teeth to preserve a semblance of calm. '*Take . . . me . . . home.*'

Neil looked from her to me. 'What the fuck's going on?'

With a bitter sob, I buried my face in my hands.

'*Take . . . me . . . HOME!*' Helen had traversed the frayed carpet square and when she brought her foot violently down on bare boards the entire flat seemed to reverberate. Recognising the effectiveness of this accompaniment, she took to emphasing each of the three words with a resonant stamp.

'TAKE ... ME ... HOME.'

Marie emerged, buttoning the shirtwaister over bare breasts. Coolly and quietly she questioned me. 'What happened?'

'I can't help it.' Convulsive sobs all but overwhelmed me. 'I can't help it. I can't help it.'

The hatred on Helen's face suddenly intensified, as though she had only now plumbed the foul depths of my fiendishness. '*Don't you see?*' she cried in loathing and frustration to her slow-witted husband. 'He has what he wants now. He has all he wants now.'

Though Neil almost lost his balance getting into his trousers, his progress was not sufficiently rapid for his spouse.

'Take me home *now!*' She went up to him and screamed in his face. 'THIS MINUTE!'

15

The idea of requesting permission to enter, of apologising for interruption, or even of entering with a measure of diffidence – all these were alien to Barry, who took it as axiomatic that his current preoccupations were of universal and abiding interest. Bursting into my office without knocking, he rushed across to sit in front of the desk and share his travail. 'That wee girl's on the phone again roarin' and cryin' out of her.'

'Emer?'

'What am I going to do with her?' Perhaps realising that this question, like so many others, had no answer, he turned to the turbulent heavens with his grievance.

This was a blustery unsettled day with rain that would neither pour nor abate and a wind apparently unable to decide on direction or strength. A sudden fierce gust flung drops at the window like a handful of grit.

'*What's wrong with her head?*' Receiving no answer from on high, he turned back to me. 'Married. First baby due. Big detached house in Knightsbridge Park ... and that wasn't fucking cheap, I can tell you.' Genuine incomprehension troubled his features. '*What's wrong with her head?*'

'What does she say's wrong with her head?'

For a moment Barry was too startled to respond. Then he made a dismissive gesture. 'That's just the thing. Nothing she says makes any sense. I mean, she says she's depressed and then wants me to take her to that thing in the City ... that black-and-white thing about married couples squealin' at one another. I said, are ye not depressed enough already or what? And if ye want black-and-white stay at home and watch TV. We've a twenty-one-inch set. And our living room doesn't stink of pish like the City.'

Barry paused to cast a resentful glance at the sky. Entirely indifferent to his plight, gravid slate-coloured clouds crossed the window at speed.

'And then she says she's stuck in Knightsbridge Park with no one to talk to. But there's a great crowd moved in there. Full of craic. Full of go. There's something on in someone's house every weekend ... and many's a night through the week. But Emer just wants me to stay in with her. The two of us sittin' lookin' at each other. Sure what kind of a night's craic is that? And most of the wives don't work, so they're at home during the day. I said, go and talk to them ... but no no no ... apparently that's no good either.' Barry brooded – and then came forward in sudden outrage. 'Fuck *I* wouldn't mind being down there all day. Know who's just moved in? Nora Fleming. Gerry Fleming's wife. That's a woman and a half, Ah can tell ye. Dominic lumbered her once. Fuckin' brilliant, he said. Like goin' intay a can a live worms.' Barry's usually glad features were ever more deeply vexed. 'Not that Nora'll mix with the rest of us. Far too snottery for that.'

It was probable that Barry had been rebuffed by this woman. Narcissism and lack of application prevented him from matching his mentor's success. In fact, although Barry worshipped the male Holy Trinity of Fly Boy, Seducer and Hard Man, he had never successfully emulated any of the three persons of God.

Our ruminations were interrupted by Roberta with tea and biscuits on a tray. Accustomed to independence and embarrassed by service, I had tried to discourage this practice. But Roberta had been so shocked and offended that I had had to give way. Now of course I was dependent on the indulgence and grew furious if the tray was even a few minutes late.

'Isn't that a desperate old day?' Roberta turned to the window with a mixture of outrage and apology, as though the rain was an unnecessarily harsh punishment for some dereliction of hers.

It was a measure of Barry's despair that he could not respond to the secretary. Briefly consoled by chocolate bourbons, he soon returned to his original question. 'What am I going to do with her?'

It was necessary to nibble and sip discreetly. Appetite in a counsellor is unbecoming. 'Barry, you're expecting too much gratitude from Emer. Remember that she's completely uprooted for the first time. It's not easy to adjust to married life and a new town. I haven't found it that easy myself.'

A classic counselling stratagem is to reveal an analagous trauma in one's own life. But this approach may be *too* successful. Enlightenment and hope blazed in Barry's eyes. 'Come you down and talk to her.'

Urgent work would have given me the righteousness and resolve to refuse – but I had only been reading a newspaper. Ever since the flu my concentration had been fitful and weak. Sensing a lack of conviction in my objections, Barry continued and even intensified his pleas – so that fifteen minutes later I was standing at the Hinds' home, while the man of the house drove away in relief.

'It's *you*,' Emer said in utter contempt as soon as she opened the door. Her hair looked unwashed and uncombed and she was wearing a dressing gown with half of the collar carelessly stuck in underneath. 'He's sent you down to deal with the mad woman, has he?' She turned away in dismissive disgust – but left the front door open.

There was little choice but to follow the pink mules she listlessly dragged to the lounge. Already she belonged to the dim shuffling people. 'I suppose you're going to tell me to pull myself together. That's all I ever hear from Barry. Pull yourself together, for Jesus' sake.' She withdrew twenty Embassy from her pocket and angrily lit one up, employing the cigarette as both comfort and shield.

'I offered to come down when I heard you were depressed. I've been depressed myself recently.'

'*You?*' She looked me up and down in disbelief. 'I saw you and Marie a couple of weeks ago with your friends. Crossing the Diamond you all were. Didn't see us in the car. But the four of you were all laughing and carrying on. I've never seen anyone looking so *happy*.' At this last fateful word she turned abruptly away.

'One of the problems with depression is that it makes everyone else appear confident and happy. Not only that, you feel they're being happy *deliberately* . . . just to humiliate you.'

This insight was gained from the experience of Helen breezily perched on my sick-bed. But Emer did not acknowledge it – or even turn her head from the picture window.

Everywhere else the day had a rackety discontented air but nothing could discompose the mighty river which lay at peace with its form and course, curving and widening like a scimitar and shining even in wintry light.

'What a wonderful view.'

At last Emer turned. 'Not for long. They're going to build more houses right in front of us. Soon all we'll see is people's kitchens.' She snorted bitterly. 'Barry of course never thought to ask about that.' She sucked desperately on her cigarette. 'And the money we're paying for this house. Barry was hoping my father would help us out – but he said he wouldn't give a penny to a cornerboy. Told me I'd made my bed and I'd have to lie in it.'

'So you can't admit to your family there's problems?'

'Daddy loathes Barry. Didn't want me to marry him. Expected me to have the baby and hand it over to nuns or something.' Rather shamefacedly, Emer now offered the Embassy packet.

'I don't smoke.'

'Then I suppose you'll be looking for tea.' The resentment was still strong – but weakening.

It seemed safe to sit down. 'I'm just after tea.'

Emer took the armchair on the other side of the fireplace. 'You've been well warned. Barry probably told you I'm a disaster in the kitchen.' While I groped for an answer she suddenly hit her stride. 'Now everything I do seems to be wrong. I can't understand it. One minute Barry's chasing me everywhere . . . insisting he's crazy about me. Then as soon as we're married he goes off me completely. Either he's driving round the country or if he's home he wants to drink with a crowd from round here.' This was a painful conundrum for Emer – but the obvious explanation would have caused her even more pain. Barry could value only what had already been valued by others and, since he never understood the reasons for high valuation, was doomed to disappointment as soon as he possessed the object of desire.

'We can hardly even go out to the pictures. He can't stand anything difficult or strange. All he wants to see is comedy thrillers. Preferably with Frank Sinatra or Dean Martin.'

Like so many wives before her, she was discovering that her husband's uncharted regions were not hidden depths but hidden shallows.

'Marriage is always a shock,' I suggested. In fact, the great life events of birth, marriage and death all defy anticipation. However rigorously we prepare, the reality is always unexpected and traumatic.

'Don't be talkin'.' She was beginning to relax and even get into the swing of it now. 'For a start, Barry never mentioned that he wasn't qualified. Or that he borrowed a fortune to buy into the practice. I just don't like to think about some of the people he owes money to.'

Tempting to ask for names and figures – but probably better not to know.

Emer rose to stub out her cigarette in an ashtray on top of an oriental lacquered table.

'New piece?' The table had not been there before and the acquisition of furniture revealed at least some interest in life.

'That'll be gone by next week.' For a shocking moment I thought she meant that the bailiffs were due. 'Barry buys and sells antiques when he's travelling.'

'He's a *terrific salesman*.' My tone was cautiously ironic. Making fun of spouses is a delicate business. Most partners enjoy it – but only up to a point. If the mockery is too harsh they become protective and aggrieved. 'Sells insurance policies like billyo.'

'He's always in great form getting out on the road. That's what he enjoys best ... getting all dressed up and heading out in the car.'

'I hope you see to it that he's properly turned out in the morning.'

Making a spouse laugh at her partner provides much of the pleasure of adultery with none of the wearisome complications. 'Don't be talking. *Let me show you something.*'

She rose with surprising animation and so obviously therapeutic was her impulse that my vow to refuse mystery viewings failed its first major test. The pink mules ascended the staircase with a step that, if not exactly joyful, was certainly light.

Our destination was a small unfurnished spare bedroom. From this height the river was even more splendid. Emer went to a built-in wardrobe and yanked open the door. Inside was a rack with a long row of buttoned shirts, each on its own hanger. 'The shirt wardrobe!' she cried. 'The first time I ironed Barry's shirts I folded them and put them in a drawer. He nearly went *mental*. Folding them causes too many creases. They have to be hung up here.'

We considered the wrinkle-free shirts. 'Must be twenty there.'

'Fifteen at the moment. And there must be always at least twelve.'

'So this is his secret.' My awe was in no way feigned. 'Could I get Marie to do this?'

'I doubt it.' Emer laughed – but then was suddenly uneasy, as though guilty at betraying her husband or realising the impropriety of inviting a stranger upstairs. Hastily she shut the wardrobe door and assumed a polite tone devoid of sarcasm. 'Are you sure you didn't want a cup of tea?'

'I'll have to be getting back.'

'Sure come down again with Marie for a drink . . . and bring your friends.'

We had not seen the Quinns since their last stormy departure. It was exactly like a marital row in which neither party will yield first. Any attempt to renew contact would be a kind of apology – and I was not disposed to apologise. Where was the offence that required absolution? Surely a man has as much right to decline as a woman. Not all males are brutes ever ready to mount. I too was a sensitive and delicate creature.

The ideal reunion would have been an accidental meeting – but the Quinns appeared to be avoiding Mullen's. After almost three weeks of deprivation Marie announced that she was not prepared to spend another weekend without company. If I was not prepared to go with her, she would visit them on her own.

So of course I went with her.

Neil was overjoyed, almost ecstatic, possessed by a rapture which would not admit reserve. 'I was dyin' to call on yees as often,' he blurted out, turning excitedly from one of us to the other. 'But Helen wouldn't hear of it.'

'Neil.' Helen was sitting bolt upright, head high and unmoving, coldly implacable.

Ignoring her, Neil babbled on. 'I want to apologise for getting you two into this whole business.'

'*Neil.*' This time Helen's tone was so imperious that Neil had to stop. 'I don't think it's *you* that needs to apologise.' She was resolutely refusing to look at me – but her hierophantic certainty was crushingly effective. The urge to grovel was overwhelming.

'It was the aftereffects of the flu.' Helen did not respond or relax. 'I'm still not completely over it in fact. Can't seem to settle to do any work.'

At last she issued a low sceptical grunt which seemed to suggest that, while the apology was pitifully inadequate, her tremendous magnanimity and forbearance obliged her to accept it as the real thing. Henceforth her attitude was of dignity grievously insulted but nobly intact. And, this evening as on many others, she took to flaunting her charms with a kind of disdainful remoteness, as though to emphasise the value of what had been rejected and would, needless to say, never be offered again.

To make the reminder more specific and the lesson more telling, the diaphanous black blouse was frequently on view – and, in a new enthusiasm for playfulness, she took to wrestling with Neil or skittishly perching on his knee. At these times she would often extend and stroke her long legs, frowning upon them with a critical severity which would surely have detected the slightest flaw had there been such a thing.

This simple strategy was entirely effective. Men may have moments of fastidiousness and asceticism but few can resist a prolonged sexual assault. Soon enough I was tormented by yearning and loss, whacking off with anguished intensity to the fantasy of unbuttoning a transparent black blouse.

Ever resourceful and ingenious, blocked desire discovered a new form of transgression. When we were drinking in the Quinns' flat I would pretend to go to the toilet and enter their bedroom to root for Helen's minimalist underthings among the couple's dirty laundry, a search made longer but also more mysterious and thrilling by their use of a bag with a drawstring instead of a basket. Soon the bag itself was an object of fetishistic worship. Sublime ecstasy of locating underwired cups and, the ultimate prize, filigree pants in which intoxicating fragrance overlaid intimate musk. Deep and hungry the inhalations — again, again, again, again — gusset eventually crushed against mouth and nose like an emphysema sufferer's oxygen mask.

Once the two forms of homage were vertiginously combined; I stole a redolent pair of lace pants and jacked off in them later.

Helen also drew apart from the foursome by socialising with bank colleagues and, in particular, meeting Leo Patton for an after-work drink in the City Hotel. Neil's annoyance at this development only served to heighten Helen's pleasure.

'Neil's convinced I'm planning to run away with Leo,' she'd cry, unable to decide which was more absurd — the jealousy of her scowling husband or the idea of a sexual liaison with her colleague. 'If you'd see the state of Leo. Bri-nylon shirts and a big belly hanging out over his trousers. I don't know how his trousers stay up . . . I'm always terrified they'll fall down.'

'Helen has a thing about bank types,' Neil explained in revenge. 'Went out with one for years before I met her. An incredible nancy boy. Never laid a finger on her. Went off home at ten o'clock with a rolled-up plastic mac under his arm.'

There was more to these meetings than punishing us and humouring lonely men like Leo. It transpired that Helen coveted promotion to a Belfast branch of the bank and was soliciting colleagues for information and support.

Neil was savagely scornful. 'As if they'll give a big job to a Catholic.'

'All that nonsense is over,' Helen insisted. 'Or if it's still going on it's only in shipyards and factories. People in banks are *civilised*, Neil.'

'Well, if you get it I'm not shifting.' Neil gave Marie a short but intense glance of solidarity and commitment. For of course Helen's eagerness to leave was a deliberate insult to the group.

'Scale One and he won't shift.' Helen addressed this to Marie and me. 'Stuck on Scale One and fighting with the head. Neil's career prospects are *just great*.'

Since the interview was early on a Thursday morning, Helen went up to Belfast on Wednesday to stay with an aunt. It was understood that we would meet on Friday evening to hear her news.

But on Wednesday evening a long peremptory ring on the doorbell heralded the entry of Neil. 'Would you come out with me for a midweeker? I just had a terrible day at work.'

Marie was moved by this unexpected and passionate summons. 'Just give me a wee minute.' Resigned to a quiet evening at home, she was wearing an old checked blouse and washed-out jeans.

'Come as you are.' Neil spoke from the true affinity which transcends appearance. 'Sure you're grand as you are.'

Even my occluded heart was touched by his need. And there was another intriguing factor. Although going out in a threesome was unprecedented, Neil did not even mention the missing fourth party. This omission, surely deliberate, seemed to indicate rejection, perhaps even betrayal. Here was a wonderful opportunity to administer to Helen some of her own nasty medicine.

Over the first round Neil expanded on his ostensible motive. 'I was taking a fifth-year class today and I said to this character, Don't you find the *Daily Mirror* sensational? Know what he said to me? He said, God aye, it's fabulous.' With a cigarette in one hand and a pint in the other, Neil was momentarily uncertain about which to apply. After a happy glance at each he decided on drink. 'The problem's not so much dealing with stupidity . . . although that's bad enough. It's the effect of being subjected to it day in and day out. Eventually you start to get stupid yourself. I'm so used to seeing misspellings my own spelling's starting to go. Now I can't remember how to spell the simplest of words. Today I couldn't think how to spell *occasionally*. And the staff's as thick as the pupils. We have this big Gaelic footballer who teaches PE. The one who raced Dessie in the Ture Inn car park. Big curly-haired character. Pig ignorant. Thick as champ. Every time he comes into the staffroom he boots a football right across it. Hard as he can, ye know? Thinks it's hilarious. And the saddest thing is that people like Dessie seem to agree.'

Though eloquent and forceful, these complaints were robbed of power by the gladness and warmth in Neil's voice – and by his obvious enjoyment of our intimate position. Mullen's was packed with midweekers, so the three of us, with Marie in the middle, were crushed into a tiny space at the end of a bench – a huddle which contributed to the atmosphere of conspiracy. There seemed to be an unspoken agreement to exclude Helen from the evening. Her name was never mentioned and, while I had the motivation and temperament for taking malicious pleasure in this, it was surprising to find the other two as steadfast in exclusion. But, of course, for the Irish Catholic temperament conspiring is the most exciting and natural human activity after sex. Indeed, for many it exceeds sex. And now *both* major sources of headiness were being *simultaneously tapped*. This was not merely a conspiracy but a *conspiracy of sex*.

Squeezed between two men, Marie was a constant physical presence to each. As soon as Neil or I moved there were exquisite frictions – and Marie's slightest stirrings were transmitted to one of us or both. So delightful was this proximity that every trip to the toilet or bar was an intolerable wrench.

At closing time there was no need to debate the next step. Neil accompanied the two of us home as casually and naturally as a son. The bench arrangement was difficult to re-create on a lightweight two-seater sofa – but the men were more than happy to turn sideways and perch on one hip.

Neil regarded me with disapproving pursed lips. 'You don't appreciate your wife enough.'

'Spouses are always undervalued.'

As Neil turned to Marie his countenance glowed with tenderness and wonder. 'Your wife is an incredibly beautiful woman.'

Marie suffered his adoring gaze for a moment and then looked away with a nervous cackle.

Without removing his eyes from Marie, Neil murmured hoarsely at me, 'Can I kiss her?'

My laugh was intended to be insouciant and blithe. 'Be my guest.'

Worshipfully he inclined his face to hers, presently taking hold of her shoulder the better to draw her close to him. After a time the hand on her shoulder dropped to her breast. Then he applied both hands to her blouse – but could not even undo the top button.

Marie observed his vain fumbling. 'Speedy Gonzales.'

Neil began to look cross. '*Fuck.*'

Throwing back her head, Marie released to the ceiling a mischievous peal of merriment. Then she finally revealed the secret. 'Those buttons don't open. It's sewn shut.'

Since the worn slack buttonholes had no longer been capable of restraining her abundance, the front of the blouse kept popping open and eventually Marie had to sew it shut.

'*Bitch!*' murmured Neil – but never was an insult uttered more fondly. Marie loosed off another wild peal. 'How the fuck do ye get it off then?'

'Like this.' Marie suddenly stood up and, in a single lithe

movement of startling fluency and speed, pulled the blouse out of her jeans, whipped it up over her head and flung it away across the room. It may have been the boldness and grace of the gesture or the novelty of seeing through another's eyes – but for whatever reason I was astounded and paralysed by her splendour.

Neil too observed a moment of stunned veneration. Then he began to tear off his clothes, revealing a body with the functional muscularity of a hardworking pit pony. And in contrast to my pale hairless frame, his dark torso was covered in fuzz which gathered into a rope leading down to pubic luxuriance and a depressingly formidable cock.

Simultaneously Marie removed her jeans and sat back on the sofa.

As soon as he was free of clothing Neil flung himself on her, wildly fondling and nuzzling and mumbling guttural endearments. Marie's eyes were shut but her hand vaguely reached out. I placed my own hand in hers and she squeezed it in tender reassurance before seeking my unit. This I swiftly made available and she stroked me feebly a few times before losing concentration or interest or both.

Uninvolved myself and with both the main actors unsighted, I was free to enjoy a visual feast in which Neil's juddering erection was the most remarkable novelty. But even the most committed voyeur will occasionally wish to participate. Tentatively I reached down to take hold of Neil's cock and immediately discovered the tragic limitation of the circumcised – the difficulty of back-and-forth movement without a facilitating prepuce. But there was no time to reflect on the wisdom of evolution in developing the foreskin. Neil's head jerked up so abruptly that for a moment I thought he was about to attack me for homosexual assault. It was merely a desire to reciprocate or, more likely, an *obligation* to return the favour, for after a few perfunctory yanks he turned away with a dismissive grimace. 'Nah . . . it's just like a rubber bendy toy.'

As he lowered his head once again Marie took hold of him and drew him up in a way that suggested readiness. With a groan of thralldom Neil obliged. Now that only his scrotum was exposed he was more like a pit pony than ever. I leaned across and gently cupped it. The response was immediate and vehement, though difficult to classify as either outrage or gratitude. 'Aw Jesus,' he shouted, *'someone's squeezing my balls.'*

Certainly it caused him to redouble his efforts – and if Marie was merely simulating pleasure, her performance was alarmingly good. Suddenly her limp grasp of me became purposeful. By nature fastidious and responsible, I would normally have worried about the messiness of uncontained ejaculation – but in the present wanton circumstances such concern seemed unnecessarily fussy. With a whimper of gratitude I closed my eyes and yielded to the ecstatic haemorrhage.

16

Was ever a springtime more gorgeous? For once the resplendence of nature was almost matched by that of mere women and men.

Like Van Gogh arriving in Arles, we were ravished and illuminated by the discovery of colour. The traditional palette, unquestioned for so long it had seemed like a given, was consigned to history overnight. Instead of beige, pink, brown, navy blue and dark grey, there were purple, yellow, orange, green and fire-station red. Even the drab male pulsated with brightness. Even Lady Turquoise blazed in heatwave hues.

Suddenly nothing was beyond redemption. Everything was capable of radiant rebirth. One egregious example: the woman's cardigan, ultimate symbol of dootsiness, was born again in a tight skimpy version which just reached the waistband, so that even the most modest lean or stretch exposed an inch of white flesh. It goes without saying that these fleeting glimpses were incomparably more enchanting than the wholesale flaunting of midriff later. And the shift in emphasis from minidress to miniskirt launched a new range of tops in a dazzling variety of materials and styles.

Marie exulted in the extra scope for self-expression afforded by pairing tops and skirts but, like so many bold spirits, was dogged by the plagiarism of those with less flair. No sooner had she acquired a red new-style cardie than Helen purchased the same garment in yellow. No sooner a purple waistcoat than Helen had it in bottle green. Though familiarity had tempered her outrage, Marie was far from reconciled. Often her patience was tested to the limit, as when she was excited by a Victorian-style blouse in unbleached cotton with broderie anglaise trim. Unfortunately the try-on caused familiar heart-break – it made her look 'all squashed up on top'. And the moment she regretfully replaced it on the rack Helen eagerly pounced. Marie was not only robbed of the garment but forced to acknowledge afresh Helen's increasingly important advantage of small breasts.

Times of radical change provide not only opportunities but threats. With big hair and high heels becoming increasingly unfashionable, Marie was in danger of having her limited stature simultaneously reduced at both ends. She did cut down on backcombing but was not prepared to adopt the new low-heeled shoes (another boon for Helen who was much taller than Neil). Instead she exchanged her now-tacky stilettos and sought an alternative style of high heel untainted by association with the vulgar fifties. Minimalist shoes largely composed of thin straps, these were elegant to look at but almost impossible to walk in. As always, Marie liked to 'link onto' me and now would often go over on one heel, almost yanking my arm out of its socket.

Losing an arm would have been a small price to pay. At the first appearance of spring sunshine Marie displayed a com-mendable determination to go about bare-legged. Here was one physical advantage over her rival. Marie had darker skin which took a tan quickly (though she was not averse to

assisting Nature with the occasional application of Tanfastic).
Unwilling to expose white legs disfigured by gooseflesh (she
was also much less hardy than the lower-class girl), Helen was
obliged to remain in tights.

Not only were present and future gloriously transformed,
even the torpid past began to glow. No longer a crippling
burden to be cast off, the past was revealed as a treasure house
waiting to be looted. Once more setting the example, Marie
took from her mother's house old earrings, necklaces, a
crocheted black shawl. But again the unfortunate innovator
was trumped. Helen's mother had a larger, more elegant and
better-preserved collection of accessories; the antique jewellery
was particularly impressive. And I was outdone by Neil. The
inability of the Quinn family to throw anything out, formerly
taken as evidence of squalor and sloth, was now seen to show
remarkable foresight and shrewdness. For Neil had access to
male wardrobes going back two generations; among the discoveries were a hoard of silk kipper ties, a three-piece suit in
dramatic brown butcher stripe and his grandfather's gold
watch and chain with a pendant of onyx in orange and green.
As so often with newly discovered gold, the watchchain was
immediately a source of contention. No sooner had Marie
remarked, in typically reckless generosity, that the chain
would make 'a gorgeous necklace', than Helen had ripped it
from Neil's breast and placed it round her own throat. More
excited than any of us by this pillaging of the past, Helen
attempted the most daring appropriation – her mother's fox
fur. The rodent head with pointed snout and glittering eyes
gave the bank girl an intriguingly sinister air – but Marie and
Neil loathed it so intensely ('Jesus that fucking thing gives me
the *creeps*') that unfortunately it was worn only once.

Helen occasionally relied on her own taste in the new
fashions but her independent purchases were rarely successful,
for instance a light-blue rayon minidress with a high waist and
billowing smock bottom that gave her the appearance of a

giant Victorian baby. While a girlish appearance was now all the rage, there was surely no need to go back to the cradle. But she had reliable taste in *haute couture*, an area where Marie never dared to venture.

Disillusioned with the bank after her failure to secure the Belfast post and distanced from her relatives by her radical new image, Helen had turned back to us in recent weeks and for her twenty-ninth birthday abandoned the intended lavish party in favour of an intimate dinner for four. Since it seemed absurd to burden a birthday girl with catering, Marie and I had offered our services as chef and genial maître d'. But we had no experience of formal dinner parties and had several pre-aperitifs to alleviate the preparation stress.

So it was that, with Marie toiling in the kitchen, I was both slightly inebriated and free from spouse attention when Helen arrived and removed her coat with a flourish to reveal a halter-necked dress in black jersey with a knee-length sheath bottom and virtually no back, exposing not only most of the skin surface but the full curve of the rear body to the waist and below. For the first time I understood the neglected beauty of the back. Neither static nor flat, as is often assumed, its subtle and sinuous undulations reconfigured endlessly, as the shoulder blades, lightly strewn with acne scars, rippled like the wings of a great spotted moth. Not only bewitching in itself, her appearance brought to shabby rented rooms an aura of the bejewelled and sophisticated glamour of the fifties, heretofore attainable only through glossy magazines and cinema screens. Now the glamour had sought me out and was smiling in readiness. The most saturnine ascetic would have drooled like an infant.

'Jesus,' I mumbled in ecstatic vassalage, 'you look *fucking sensational*.'

As Helen threw back her head in a merry peal of triumph, lambent rainbow hues danced in the necklace of heavy cut glass that encircled her throat.

Overwhelmed by an urge to submit and serve, I pressed upon her a bouquet of roses and a large box of chocolates. Perishable luxuries had seemed more appropriate than a sensible gift – a decision entirely vindicated by Helen's response. With a cry of delight, she stepped into my arms and laid her cheek against mine. Frightened to touch her naked back, I gently laid timorous hands on her waist. Such diffidence was unnecessary. Even after withdrawing, Helen continued to bathe me in undiminished effulgence. Flattery, the timeless and universal unguent, had softened her recent hostility. No one is immune to flattery – but Helen was especially vulnerable. She reacted to homage as sunflowers to sun; the tropism was involuntary, enduring and absolute.

Marie emerged from the kitchen drying her hands on a towel. 'My God.' This astonishment at the dress was too muted. Not only flustered by the demands of cooking, Marie was concerned that she had not had sufficient time to prepare herself. To me she appeared as immaculate as ever – but only self-perception counts.

'Isn't it *mad?*' Helen actually executed a jaunty half twirl. 'I only tried it on for a laugh but Neil forced me to buy it. Says he'll get a second job to pay the bill.'

Neil was happy to provide confirmation. 'My wife needs to be pampered. I'm going round the doors tomorrow selling bundles of sticks in a pram.'

'But oooohhhh . . .. how is it?' Marie addressed Helen with a concern which may not have been entirely sincere. 'I mean . . . *twenty-nine?*'

This was surely a number to chill any giddy young heart. Not only dangerously close to thirty, for a married woman to reach such an age without children was almost a criminal offence in this town.

Helen flapped her hands in blithe unconcern.

Neil regarded his wife proudly. 'She really doesn't give a

fuck.' Then he turned to Marie. 'You're looking very well yourself, dear.'

She was indeed perfectly delightful in a lightweight cotton minidress, where, once again dramatically breaking with tradition, primary colours swirled in joyous release from pattern's orderly grid (an effect known as 'the whirligig look'). But she grunted rather sourly. 'I'm *sure.*'

Helen brought to bear her unique vibrancy. 'Your dress is *absolutely gorgeous.*' Her favourite gesture – lifted arms, open hands, spread fingers – was this evening rendered even more dramatic by a metallic clash of silver bracelets on her naked white flesh. 'And thank you for the lovely presents.'

This served only to remind Marie that I had made the presentation without her – as though I alone had been responsible for the gifts. But her black and unforgiving look could not spoil my good humour. After intense work and many late nights the demands of the financial year end had been met and I had passed safely through into the lotus-eating days (for accountants April is the kindest month). My own accounts were also increasingly healthy. Champagne would certainly have been appropriate but in the end sparkling wine seemed just as good (despite encouraging finances, I was still cautious about spending – and even a bacchanal should be rationally costed).

The popping and fizzing were sufficient to enrapture an already grateful and high-spirited Helen. Unusually convivial and jocund myself, I described to the party my last major obligation for some time to come – the AGM of the City Golf Club this very Saturday morning. The annual accounts had been distributed to members and one peevishly demanded to know why expenditure on toilet rolls had doubled in a year.

'So what did you tell him?' Above exuberant bubbles mischievous light danced in Helen's blue eyes.

'That the members were obviously taking more roughage and we ought to applaud their new health consciousness.' Her laughter was gratifyingly immoderate. 'But I know what I should have said to the bastard.' My calm impassive pause forced the question.

Helen looked in my eyes. 'What?'

'Because members like you are full of shit.'

As though viciously kneed in the groin, she released a cry and doubled up. Yet she had the presence of mind to hold her glass out of harm's way.

One of the surest signs of intoxication is that the food recently craved and now on the table swims away into the distance, a redundant distraction. For this meal so carefully planned and executed, I remember no details of recipes, presentation or reception – only that we drank gin all through the three courses (at this time we had not learned to take wine with food). And my memory of the rest of the evening is a series of tableaux.

Helen, bracelets resonantly ajangle as her arms lifted in celebration to expose dark stubble in her pits: 'Isn't this just ... just ... *absolute heaven*. We'll have to get out of this town this summer. Just the four of us together. Away off somewhere lovely.'

Neil and I alone at the table, Neil leaning across in the manner of a fellow conspirator happy with the development of the plot: 'The chocolates were a great touch. Absolutely perfect. Helen's crazy about swanky chocolates.'

Marie and I in the kitchen, Marie regarding me with perplexity and distaste. 'One minute you claim Helen makes you sick ... and the next minute you're slobbering all over her.' Helen's uninhibited laughter drew Marie's gaze to the living room. 'God she's mad about herself.'

Helen and I renewing our secret toilet-trip trysts. But this time, instead of a brief guilty brush, we tarried in the bathroom with the door locked. At last I could move both my hands over her long naked back, a privilege bought with surely the greatest compliment a man can offer a woman. 'I toss off all the time thinking about you.' Helen released a wild whinny of triumph. 'Often in this very bathroom.' Another whinny – but this one was followed by a rattling of the handle and a peremptory banging on the door.

'I know the two of you are in there,' shouted Marie.

At a situation so exquisitely farcical, as good as a play, Helen and I simultaneously burst out into laughter. It appeared that Marie wished to entertain us with a lively caricature of the jealous wife. I opened the door with a ready grin instantly spattered by gin and tonic. Whoever was the primary target, Helen took most of it in the face and chest. The sight of each other's dripping faces heightened the absurdity to an unbearable pitch. In between shrieks of merriment we attempted to lick each other dry.

Neil appeared in the doorway – sober, grave, deeply concerned. 'Marie's run off.'

'How do you mean . . . *off?*'

'Away charging down the street somewhere.'

For a moment this too seemed absurd – a woman in high heels and a whirligig minidress careering madly through the town like some demented tropical bird. Then the danger of her situation became apparent. And, with this, the certainty that she was attempting to punish me by martyrdom. Not only tonight's fun terminated but lifelong disgrace, guilt and shame.

'Ah'll fuckin' kill her,' I shouted, charging out of the bathroom. Neil caught me by the waist and swung me back. 'Ah'll kill that bitch.' But Neil was remarkably strong. It proved impossible to break free.

'Are you going to calm down?'

When I sullenly agreed he released his grip.

'There's no point in you looking for her in that state. I'll go.'

For Helen this scene had been the delirious climax of the farce. 'You should have seen your face,' she cried. Helpless giddiness and bobbed hair in a tight-kneed dress – she resembled a nineteen twenties flapper at one of Gatsby's wild parties. If there had been any bubbly left she would surely have drunk it from a shoe. But even the tonic was finished and we had to dilute our gin with tap water.

When Neil did not return we assumed that he had found Marie and was consoling her in his flat and that there was no need to terminate our own revels. At some point we moved into the bedroom – but I remember little about this stage. Of removing the dress, which should have been a sacred ceremony tremulous with wonder and awe and for which I had already consecrated a special side chapel in memory, there is no recollection at all. To this day that dedicated chapel remains empty and forlorn. Instead, there is a memory of lovemaking, disastrous in a new way. The partial erection, with which I attempted to penetrate, invariably shrank and flopped out in the most humiliating manner. Helen hooted at this perfect coda to a farcical evening. Less amused, I eventually collapsed in disgust into deep sleep.

Towards morning there occurred a phenomenon which I would like to be able to identify as either a personal peculiarity or a common side effect of heavy drinking. After a late night of excess the profound slumber which ought to last to the following noon is frequently interrupted near first light by a lust of unparalleled ferocity and imperiousness – the sexual equivalent of the raging thirst which also breaks drunken sleep.

This feral need, our nudity, the darkness, the covers – all these made redundant the usual awkward preliminaries. Perhaps tradition was wise in reserving the act for primeval night, when the social conventions are all in abeyance. Perhaps, subjected to light, scrutiny, recording and analysis, it is now as banal as eating chocolates and the original demonic wildness has been lost.

Certainly I experienced for the first time with Helen the pride of detachment and control. It was the lucid excitement of the hired assassin. So great was my confidence in ability and discipline that I felt within reach of the ultimate prize – not easy self-gratification but the gratification of the other. Placing my lips against her ear, I murmured in the form of a wish what was surely inevitable. '*I want to make you come.*'

Presumption and arrogance of the disengaged! No human agent is remote from the human adventure. Helen's response exposed my laughable illusion of control. When she gasped, 'I *am* coming, I'm *coming*,' it was as though she had uttered the ineffable hundredth name of God. Duration, identity, bodily form – all the constants were annihilated in vertiginous paroxysm and effusion.

The received idea of male sexuality is that men desire only to jump on like brutes. In fact, I have always been heavily committed to both foreplay and afterglow (Marie was more inclined than I to make do with a quickie) and the lack of preliminaries in the night made me anxious to compensate with follow-through in the day. As soon as we awakened I reached across tenderly – but Helen sprang out of bed with a squawk of embarrassment. The social restrictions were back in force.

Yet the breakthrough could not be denied and the period which followed was radiant and replete. It was then that the cathedral of memory acquired its most hallowed side chapels and it is to these that I repair when I wish to contemplate and give thanks.

The delirium of that night was almost matched in subsequent encounters. Incredible oddity of the bank girl and accountant creating a beast with two spotty backs! Bear in mind that at this time the bank girl was a kind of secular nun. Brazenly rooting and rummaging in a bank girl's arcanum!

And then, in the course of one of our handovers, Neil leaned close to murmur ruefully, '*Helen likes your baggy cock.*'

My wee pink toot, ever an object of shame, had apparently impressed by the accident of retaining its prepuce. While abhorring male phallocentrism, I have to admit to enjoying inordinately the notion of a woman admiring my cock. Every day I gave thanks in my black heart to the bungling surgeon who had mutilated Neil. At least I was not so vain as to think this was why Helen went straight for the unit. It was just that directness was part of her style. Marie was languorous, dreamy, passive, fond of lying back with closed eyes to relish delicate attentions. In other words, she *let me* – and in a stingy puritanical era the granting of permission to trespass had seemed the height of female passion. Impossible even to conceive of a proactive woman like Helen who, within minutes of commencement, yanked down your zip, pulled out your goodtime and eagerly popped it in her mouth.

Not that Helen's style was superior. The game of favourites is for children only. Mature adults know that every excellence should be cherished.

However, the fact that Helen and I were both natural servicers caused problems (though not as many as for Marie and Neil from being both servicees). Helen sucked me regularly and voraciously but would never permit me to reciprocate. The psychology of this has been an eternal conundrum. Was it simply that the habit of servicing made her unable to accept service? *Unaccustomed* perhaps – but hardly *unable*. Was she saving cunnilingus for Neil? This too seemed unlikely. Embarrassment at her hooded clit? She no longer seemed embarrassed by physical imperfection (Marie was astounded by Helen's recent willingness to expose the spots on her back). The only remaining hypothesis is a misguided belief that the vagina is unclean and disgusting. It is hard to accept that a woman can suck donkey cock but be too squeamish to receive the equivalent favour. Yet the most likely reason does appear to be IUVS (Imagined Unclean Vagina Syndrome), one of the most tragic delusions ever to blight sexual relations between women and men.

It goes without saying that, however overwhelming the encouragement from Helen's lips, I always denied myself the pleasure of effusing in her mouth. Neil of course showed no such restraint with Marie. On at least two occasions she was obliged to swallow his impetuous ejaculate. Needless to say, he was never reprimanded for this. Allowances were always made for the one whose appetite was so imperious that he often ate from the pot and pushed a shining plate away for a fag while the rest of us were still salting our spuds. Ever contemptuous of the undisciplined and impulsive, it occurs to me in my twilight years that they may have the best of it after all. Smarter to shoot off and then shrug that you can't help it.

Despite lacking the necessary patience, Neil experimented with viticulture at this time and made his own Bordeaux at home from a kit. The wine was meant to be left for an absolute minimum of six weeks. After less than a month Neil not only broached the plastic container but siphoned its contents directly into his mouth. The bourgeois principle of deferred pleasure was unknown to him. And as alien as postponement was the notion of surcease. The assault on the Bordeaux took place at four in the morning and after a long night of conventional drinking. Though, weak as the wine must have been, it did inspire Neil to invent an intriguing new game in which one of the company was blindfolded and required to roam about seeking contact. Unfortunately what Helen encountered was not a mystery lover but her glass coffee table and, since she was naked at the time (the factor which gave the game its zest) and striding out with her customary boldness, the collision practically took her legs off at the shins.

But improving weather now offered the opportunity of outdoor pursuits. As though nature conspired to encourage love, spring was sunny and warm. On weekends Helen drove us to the most remote of the Donegal beaches and we would walk for miles to escape the lazy gregarious day-trippers. In the evening, instead of driving home like the others, we collected driftwood and Neil or I lit a fire. (Our different approaches to this were entirely in character. Whereas I would begin by building a carefully layered pyramid of paper, small twigs and larger twigs, Neil would impatiently torch a scrunch of paper and then rush around like a madman searching for fuel before the flame went out.)

Gathered round the blazing logs, far from the vulgar herd, soothed by alcohol, compassionate night and the murmurous sea, we vouchsafed many intimate revelations.

Regarding me with gratitude and admiration, Helen explained that, in fact, she was incapable of swallowing semen. She had a pathological fear of choking, as a result of a child-hood trauma when a brandy ball had lodged in her throat and her father had hurt and frightened her by shoving a big finger down to remove it.

'Ah!' I adopted a parody Viennese accent, joining the finger-tips of each hand as if for a delicate cage to trap subtle insight. 'Your father's *big finger*. Ja. Ja. I see. *Ja.*'

Helen gaily punched me. 'Fuck off.'

'It's just like eating oysters!' Marie cried, with a smugness that was scarcely justified. One swallow does not make a summer – and so far one had been the only result of requesting the equivalent of her indulgence of Neil. I had then suggested, rather waspishly, that she would permit Neil to do *anything* – but she replied, with equal sharpness, that she had been extre-mely brusque, even harsh, when the outrageous fellow implored her to let him watch her do a pee.

It would never have done to quibble on one of those magical evenings. I was happy to laugh along with Marie when she laid a hand on Helen's arm. 'You're just like my mother – she can never get even her tablets down. A wild bad swally, is what she calls it. Marie, Ah've a wild bad swally, love.'

Brilliant blue skies, gorgeous sunsets, roaring fires, dazzling clothes – how those days blaze with colour in retrospect. We were incredulous grubs who had changed into butterflies and cavorted in ecstasy over sun-drenched fields. Each had a partner but if other striking colours distracted us we would flutter with those for a time. And why not? Who would notice or care?

Weeks went by in a delirious pleasure haze which shut out the world.

Not for long will the grudging world consent to exclusion. Anxious to make up for lost time, complication, difficulty and rancour returned.

Marie awakened one morning with severe vaginal itch and discharge. She was furious, not so much at pain and discomfort or even potential medical complications, as at the shame of being afflicted with venereal disease. This stigma burned worse than the itch, bad though that was. Unwilling to go to her family doctor, she treated herself from the pharmacy for what she had diagnosed as nonspecific urethritis brought on by Neil's persistence and roughness. The Quinns were informed of the general nature of the problem though not its possible cause. Marie restricted herself to a measure of surliness in her dealings with Neil who, in turn, adopted a hangdog attitude which suggested an awareness of culpability. Naturally the sexual shenanigans came to an end. A shadow fell on the sunny meadow. The cavorting of butterflies ceased.

And one morning shortly after this, just as I had sat down at my office desk with *The Journal*, the front door shut with a mighty crash and Barry's heavy tread continued on up to my floor. Barry always looked in on the secretaries. It was obvious that something was badly wrong. He burst in on me, pursued by the Furies.

'Emer's bad wi' her nerves again. Really bad today. She's been bad ever since the wean was born but *today* ...' Terror and panic flared in his eyes. 'I could hardly even get out of the house. She was roarin' and squealin' out of her and hangin' onto me coat. Threatenin' to book herself into a mental home. Threatenin' to leave *me* with the wean. And maybe she *is* goin' mental. Know what she was sayin' to me? What am

Ah goin' to wear, Barry? What am Ah goin' to wear, Barry? I said, put anything on ye for Jesus' sake, what does it matter? This is her – But Ah can't think, Ah can't think, Ah can't think.'

For Barry, inability to choose an outfit might indeed be the most inexplicable lapse. In spite of his domestic crisis he was wearing a three-piece wool suit in bold Glen Urquhart check. Recently his taste had shifted from contemporary style towards traditional tailoring. Increasing corpulence certainly ruled out many current fashion options, but the check, instead of conferring the desired country-squire image, gave him the look of a music-hall comedian or a racecourse bookie.

'I said I'd bring you down to talk to her.' This was an announcement not a request. 'That was the only way I could get out the door.'

Emer's first words were equally to the point. 'I'd rather have cancer than feel like this.'

'You can't really mean that.'

'I do,' she shouted. 'I do so.'

Today she had exceeded her dressing-gown squalor with a man's sweater roughly pulled over a nightdress. Her pallid skin had an unhealthy sheen. A glaze lay over her eyes.

'If I'd cancer I might get some sympathy from Barry. He says it's all *notions*.' Her head went back in a harsh bark. '*Notions*.' Desperately she scrabbled for the consoling cigarettes. 'And when I try to talk about it he shouts, Would ye give me head peace. That's all I ever hear out of him – Would ye give me head peace.'

There was an interlude while she lit up and greedily inhaled.

'I suppose the nights are the worst.' I had always associated depression with insomnia and the terrors of the dark.

This misconception renewed her outrage. 'No, it's the *mornings*. The mornings are worst. It's the thought of a whole day to get through. I can't face a whole day. The mornings are *awful*.'

How could a beautiful spring day present an insurmountable challenge? Merely to exist was an astounding privilege. Even Knightsbridge Park was radiant.

'Can't you distract yourself with something? Read a newspaper . . . take the baby for a walk?' A spasm of fear convulsed me. 'And where *is* the baby?'

Emer gestured impatiently with the cigarette. 'Upstairs asleep.' Now aware again of solace at hand, she took a quick bracing pull. 'I can't make a decision to do anything. Can't even decide what to wear. And when I start something I can't stick to it. I give it up and start something else. And all the time there's this terrible guilt. I feel I should be doing something with the baby . . . or doing housework. Or doing Barry's washing and ironing. He throws a shirt and underwear in the wash every day . . . sweaters and trousers every couple of days. Golfing gear every time he comes back from golf.' Listing this throughput depressed her afresh. 'At the moment I feel I should be making you tea.'

'I'll make it for us.' Physical activity was a welcome distraction. I was beginning to feel jumpy myself.

Among the half-empty kitchen cupboards tea was not hard to find. There was milk in the fridge – but little else. How were they becoming so overweight? What did they do for evening meals?

'Couldn't you go to your parents for a while?'

As though believing it to be a talisman, Emer gratefully received the mug into two open hands. 'I've just been down with them for a fortnight. And I was grand while I was there. Mammy was great with the baby and did all the cooking. But it was even worse when I came back. Barry hadn't done a hand's turn the whole time. There was a mountain of dirty washing waiting. He didn't even wash his own underwear. Instead he bought a dozen new pairs of underpants and half a dozen new pairs of socks.'

The hint of humour reminded me that the most effective

method of therapy was poking gentle fun at Barry. But before I could move in this direction she burst out afresh.

'He spends money like that all the time. Money we don't have. I'm supposed to look after the money on top of every-thing else ... he says he gets enough of that at work without doing it at home ... but the more I tell him we don't have it, the more he runs out and spends. God only knows where it'll all end up.' She paused, tremulous, desperate, fighting back tears.

Obviously my master plan was working. As my own finan-cial strength grew, Barry was sliding towards the abyss. But Emer's anguish ruined the plan. When Barry went down he would take his family down with him.

'And he's got so *childish* about money. It's all tit-for-tat. He's gone mad buying clothes but if *I* buy anything at all he imme-diately rushes out and spends the same amount on himself. I bought a new minidress for my birthday ... I was trying to smarten up a bit ...and as soon as he found out he bought himself a jacket. A *cashmere* jacket. OK the dress was pricy enough – but it was my *birthday*. Birthdays are *different*.'

'What age were you?'

Could there have been a more tactless question? Even before she answered, her eyes filled with tears. '*Twenty*,' she whispered brokenly and yielded to a terrible silent weeping.

Until recently, with the careless indifference of the indulged, the four of us had been behaving as though the entire world was now an entry-free pleasure garden of the flesh. Even for youth it was not so. Here was a young woman enjoying no pleasure. Here was a beauty queen losing her beauty. Here was a butterfly with broken wings.

Cheery banal reassurance would have been an insult. I waited until she had dried her tears and regained her composure.

'Why has Barry gone mad buying clothes?'

Suddenly her eyes were alert and eager – though clouded by

doubt. The answer must have touched on something she was not at liberty to discuss. But at times of hurt the temptation to testify is overwhelming. Unburdening is not only therapy but revenge.

'It's this woman he's obsessed with. Just moved into the park. A big chesty English one. Her husband's a chemical engineer over with the Yanks. Where you used to work. Says he knows you to see. Anyway, she's only been in the park a month and she's taken over the whole social scene. She must be forty if she's a day but every time there's a blink of sun she's out prancing round in shorts and a wee skimpy sun top. Of course all the young husbands have never seen anything like it. They follow her round with their mouths hanging open and their eyes out on stalks.' Emer snorted in violent distaste. 'A real English one . . . you know? A real sickener. Too sweet to be wholesome. Oh isn't Emer such a beautiful name, she says. Beautiful compared to boring Sue. And never done inviting people round. Come over to our place for drinks and nibbles.' She paused for another derisive snort. '*Drinks and nibbles!* And it always ends up with her slow-dancing Barry till all hours. That's the worst of it . . . having to sit through that.'

'Can't you just leave them to it?'

'This is the thing – it's all couples. Barry wants me around because it'll look bad if he's on his own. And of course Barry can't stand to look bad.'

'But the baby?'

'She always says bring the baby along. I'm supposed to sit giving it a bottle while she slow-dances Barry.'

'And where is her husband through all this?'

'Baaugh!' Emer leaned away as if to throw up by the side of her chair. 'He's about twenty years older than her. Looks like a retired Betterware Man. A wee five-a-side moustache and Hush Puppies. He sits on the sofa making polite conversation. As if I was interested. And there's something *really creepy* about him.' She shuddered in a paroxysm of uncontrollable revulsion. 'He gives me the *absolute pip*.'

There was that replete post-story moment when narrator and audience ruminate together in silence.

Suddenly Emer added a coda. 'And last weekend she put on this special Italian evening. Spaghetti and everything. None of us had ever seen spaghetti except from a tin. So everyone was raving about it. And then she was slow-dancing Barry all night to Frank Sinatra and Dean Martin records. They're both crazy about Sinatra of course. And after it Barry says to me, You'll have to do a meal for them. As if I'd cook for that bitch! And anyway, he knows I can't cook. The *cheek* of it. I said to him, *You cook*.'

'Oh I don't know.' For the first time I frowned in disagreement. 'You could do an Irish evening. Scunner them with poundies and butter and deafen them with Clancy Brothers records.'

Emer shrieked in delight. 'I could put something into her poundies. *Poison the bitch!*'

'Take the husband out for a swizz. It'd probably give him a heart attack.'

'Uuuugh! I don't think I could even hold his hands for a swizz.'

'Then get dressed up and slow-dance the younger husbands.'

It occurred to me that a canny cocksman would have taken advantage of our current rapport. But even if I had been a cocksman and attracted to Emer, there would have remained the serious problem of a cock covered in cream. I too was being treated by Marie for NSU. These days my only partner was a Greek girl – *Chlamydia Trachomatis*.

And now the high spirits dissipated as suddenly as they had developed.

'That's why I bought the minidress.' Emer was once more in torment. 'But Barry said it was too short. . . . ridiculous for a married woman with a child. I said what about that big horse prancing round half-naked? Isn't *she* a married woman? How come it's all right for *her*? But of course Barry just walked off. If you say anything he walks off.'

In the defeated silence which followed I pondered the mystery of men who appreciate attractively dressed women but compel their wives to look drab.

Emer's brooding features twisted into a grimace. 'He never talks to me at all. And he's horrible to me now. As soon he gets up in the morning he farts. Practically right into my face.' No doubt this was Barry's revenge on overweening swankiness. Emer returned to sorrowful brooding. 'I'll have to say something to Sue.'

'I'm not sure that's a good idea.'

'But I'll have to do *something*. And Barry won't listen. What else can I do but speak to the woman?'

Before I could answer, Barry burst jovially back on the scene, obviously confident that Emer's problems were solved and bearing a contribution to the post-therapy winding down – a large paper bag whose greasy stains suggested fresh doughnuts. But as soon as he laid eyes on Emer, optimism changed to disgust. 'Jesus, have ye nothin' on ye yet? Could ye not put somethin' on ye for a visitor at least?'

'It's a very informal occasion,' I suggested – but neither was listening.

'I'll have to speak to Sue, Barry.' Emer's boldness made it seem that she had accepted advice – and the murderous look I received from Barry showed that he believed this to be the case. Every arbiter of marital breakdown gets caught in crossfire. I could have protested innocence – but the hatred in Barry's eyes did not dispose me to side with him.

'So this is what you've been talkin' about.' He nodded to himself with a horrible laugh. Then looked at Emer. 'You had to spread it to my partner.'

'I'll have to say something to Sue,' Emer repeated, though with less conviction.

'*Well.*' Barry threw up his hands in shocking brightness.
'First you destroy my professional life . . . now you intend to
destroy my social life. And you expect me to *take it?* You
expect me to *do nothing?*' He laughed in merry helplessness. 'If
you say something to Sue I just can't be responsible.' He shook
his head, already detached from his own future actions, though
as curious about them as any interested observer. 'I just
couldn't say what I might do.' He considered this further,
brightness fading. 'I'll give you a piece of advice though.'
Now he seemed to have developed a speech obstruction. 'Sue
looks after herself. If you want her to have any respect you'd
better clean yourself up . . . or put *some fuckin' clothes on at least.*'
He stood back and surveyed her with virulent contempt.
'Look at the fuckin' shape o' ye. Ye know what ye remind
me of now . . . *me mother.*'

This explained Barry's fear. His mother had suffered all her
life from mental illness, which was why her son had been
brought up by his grandmother. He was terrified of discovering that he had married his mother.

Emer retained her position, though visibly trembling. Then
she stood up with a strange cry and slapped Barry's face.

One of those who go white with anger, his countenance lost
its colour and his blanched skin appeared to tighten over his
skull.

'Fuck!' he suddenly shouted, striking the lounge door with
the paper bag which disintegrated, scattering doughnuts and
sugar. But this was not sufficient to calm him. He began to
pace with constant abrupt changes of direction, driving a hand
through his hair and casting wild looks about him. Eventually
he picked up a throw cushion and smote the wall with it.
'*Fuck!*' This seemed to afford some relief, for he set off on a
frenzied circuit of the lounge, at regular intervals slamming
the cushion into the wall with a violent oath. When he reached
Emer he paused in front of her with an expression of malevolent rage. She did not move – even when the cushion was

raised high. He seemed certain to hit her but settled for striking the wall to the side of her head. 'FAAAWWK!'

With no loss of intensity he turned to me. Again his intention seemed to hang in the balance – but it made no difference that eventually he flung away the cushion and stalked out of the house. In the instant our eyes met, the partnership was dissolved.

Emer had fallen back into her chair weeping and shaking.

Anxious to give Barry a long head start, I went out to the kitchen to make more tea.

When I brought it in Emer seized on the most trivial consequence of the scene. 'You've lost your lift.'

'I can walk. It's a beautiful day.'

This statement of the obvious was, in fact, a revelation. It felt more like the end of a long drunken night. Though it had been quite a while since our last drunken night. Marie was treating me with antibiotics as well as cream. Both alcohol and sex were forbidden now.

'Barry's right.' Emer said at last. 'I shouldn't have dragged *you* into this.'

'He would probably have hit you if I hadn't been here.'

She refused to face this possibility. Indeed the suggestion made her want to defend him. 'Maybe I've been too hard on Barry. He's been under terrible strain because of this debt business. It's probably even worse than I know. And the only way he can deal with it is to socialise all the time. He says he's been under pressure in work as well. Maybe he's going through some sort of breakdown himself. Have you noticed him behaving differently?'

Barry's recent taste for traditional tailoring was obviously an attempt to impress the Englishwoman – but Emer could have worked that out herself. 'The end of the financial year was hectic. Everyone behaved differently.'

The inconsistency of marital emotionalism is what makes arbitration so exhausting. First Barry had to be reviled as a monster; now it was necessary to sympathise with him as a victim.

Worse was to follow.

'You know what worries him most of all? What puts him under the most strain? He's scared you'll try to squeeze him out because he's unqualified.' My gesture of denial had the opposite of the intended effect. Obviously Emer had never till now suspected me of such perfidy. 'You won't . . . will you?'

'Of course not.'

But my powers of dissimulation were feeble. She read the intention in my eyes as clearly as if I had torn up the contract before her.

'Promise me you won't do that.' All her desperation focused on this. She turned on me a tear-stained imploring face. 'Barry would just die if he wasn't a partner. He couldn't stand the humiliation of going back to work for someone. He would just *die*. I know it. Not to mention what would become of me and the baby. *Promise me you won't do it.*'

Like a movie monster returning from apparent death, the dissolved partnership reconstituted itself before my eyes. 'Of course I won't.'

'*Promise me.*'

Freedom and disengagement are possible only in the inviolate heavens. Earth is not a pleasure garden but a treacherous morass. Wherever a foot is placed, it sinks in and is held.

Do we ever really have a choice?

'I promise.'

17

This was before the west of Ireland had attuned itself to the tourist trade. As yet it lacked restaurants with Seafood Symphony, coffee shops with carrot cake, municipal flower displays in old rowing boats, Heritage Trails, Venture Fun Parks with child-friendly environments, and Famine Experience Interpretative Centres with multimedia displays. It was not that there was no change but that change was driven entirely by local concepts of sophistication. For the publican, this meant neon-fronted lounges with leatherette benches; for other services, the substitution wherever possible of K for C (The Kute Korner, The Kottage, The Kosy Kafé); for householders, white stucco bungalows with a panel of crazy paving on the front wall, glass animals on the mantelpiece and plastic fruit in the sideboard bowl.

Neil was particularly offended by the scattered bungalows. 'The west's being ruined by this ribbon development.' Hunched in the front passenger seat of the Beetle, he seemed to feel personally responsible. 'They're too careless and lazy to bother with planning controls.'

Helen had wanted to holiday in Paris – but I was too obsessed with paying off my bank loan. Now, as we drove south-west through gusty showers and dreary market towns, this stinginess began to seem a terrible mistake. Helen too was subdued, no doubt burdened by the responsibility of having chosen the holiday home and stupefied now by the long drive (it was understood that no one else could sit at the wheel of her Beetle and, stung by the acerbity of her many refusals, I had vowed never to offer such help again). In the back seat Marie dozed discontentedly on my shoulder, waking only at Helen's altercation with her husband over his shocking consumption of Murraymints. These sweets had been bought to keep the driver alert, but Neil, quite unable to suck them at intervals in the manner suggested by the advertising slogan ('the no-need-to-hurry mint'), had crunched and swallowed one after another and was well on his way to finishing the packet. However the only consequence of Helen's fury was that *no one* felt free to eat the remaining few sweets.

Late in the afternoon we drove through a village, turned into a side road, passed a new hotel on a corner and descended a precipitous winding lane bordered with overhanging fuchsia, eventually rounding a sharp bend to come on our home for the next week. Unlike the ubiquitous sloping-roofed bungalows, the house was a low flat-roofed cuboid like a New Mexico pueblo. In fact, there was not a bungalow in sight. Commanding the hillside in isolation, the house looked out on a wildflower-covered declivity which led to a reed-fringed lake patrolled by four serene swans. Beyond was a vast silver strand and, beyond this again, a sea whose vividly coloured streaks exceeded even the most *farouche* abstract expressionist effects. On the left a mountain provided an encircling arm. On the right a darkly wooded island rose from the water and, inland but reassuringly far off, a farmhouse and outbuildings provided the only other sign of human habitation.

Rapture rose in our sour dough like a miraculous leaven.

'Isn't it *beautiful?*'

'Isn't it *gorgeous?*'

'We're *completely isolated,*' marvelled Neil.

Ravished, rapt, we stood in silence broken only by the noises of livestock from the distant farm.

'Listen to how the sound carries,' cried Helen, harkening intensely and then having to admit that it was not the mystical summons she imagined. 'But somebody should give that old sheep a good thump.'

As one, we turned back to the house. Behind, cloud shadows rippled over the mountain like sinuous fluke on a seabed. Above, excitable tiny birds darted and veered.

Already vindicated, Helen unlocked the door and, with a proprietorial flourish, ushered us into a room of irreproachable austerity and taste. Not only lacking glass animals, it had not even a mantelpiece to adorn. Instead, the space was dominated by a massive black range.

Marie made a face. 'Not one of those old things.'

'Wait till I tell you.' With a few strides Helen placed herself before the range and commenced an enthusiastic demonstration, yanking the damper in and out, spinning wheels and turning knobs. 'My aunt had one of these and she said taking it out was the stupidest thing she ever did. They're so *efficient* and *economic.* You have heat all day for both hot water and cooking. And the oven has a dry heat that's *perfect* for casseroles.' Snatching a metal lever from the top surface, Helen adroitly pulled open a door and then slammed it shut with a resonant clang. 'And of course you can make tea *any time.*' Now she seized an old kettle from the surface and, like a climactic clash of cymbals in a symphony, banged it down on top of a circular plate.

The brio of this performance left everyone speechless.

'You should have been a teacher, Helen,' Neil said at last.

'No,' I objected. 'One of those girls who demonstrate the

prizes on game shows.'

Always willing to laugh at her own excesses, Helen doubled up and leaned for support on the sturdy range.

The only problem was that one of the bedrooms had two single beds. Magnanimous in her hour of triumph, Helen proposed that she and Neil take this room and give us the double bed. Indebted and deeply appreciative, Marie insisted that the sacrifice be ours.

Neil was moved by the revelation of so much nobility and selflessness. 'We could change halfway through.'

'No no no,' Marie and I chorused. 'No no.'

Suitcases swiftly dumped in appropriate bedrooms, we set about exploring the little house. A rickety bookcase in a corner of the main room had wildflower and bird guides, a history of Connacht, classic novels in unusual American editions and a large dog-eared paperback of Bertrand Russell's *History of Western Philosophy*. In a drawer there was a long knife whose dark wooden handle was carved in the shape of an African god and, hanging on a wall, an elongated lugubrious African head in the same dark wood. It was obvious that the previous occupant/owner was not local, probably not even Irish. Helen could offer no explanation. She had seen an ad in the *Irish Times*, corresponded with a woman at a London address, forwarded money and received in return a set of keys and a sheet of neatly typed instructions.

'I thought it would be the usual hideous bungalow,' she said, 'though the London connection was what attracted me. I was *hoping* it might mean something different.' Never one to rest on laurels, she immediately addressed practical issues. 'We need turf. According to the sheet, you can get it from the farm over the way ... Mr Sammin across the fields. Neil, go you across and see about it and the rest of us'll make something to eat.'

Anticipating initial food problems, Helen had brought cold meat, salad ingredients and bread. When everything was laid out Neil returned to explain that turf could not be delivered till morning. Helen had prepared for this too and we washed down the cold food with beer (drunk from the bottles in the absence of glasses), Neil helping himself to an extra bottle in reward for bringing back news. Apparently the house had been built by an Englishman, a retired colonial official who had worked in Africa all his life. However, although the man had lived in the house for several years, the locals knew little about him. Then, a year ago, ill health had forced him to go to his daughter in London. Mr Sammin had no idea if he was living or dead.

Helen uttered an exclamation. 'You know what? I bet we could buy this place for a *song*.'

In silence we considered this astounding possibility. Of course my first reaction was to shy away from such an un-worldly investment – but I was anxious to make amends for refusing Paris and my promise not to get rid of Barry meant that money was available for other projects. I too was enchanted by the house and location. A flip through the history book had revealed that the island just to the north had once been the stronghold of Grace O'Malley, a sixteenth-century pirate queen who had dominated this coast, was reputed to have had an affair with Sir Philip Sydney and had travelled to London to negotiate in person with Elizabeth I. The spirit of an exotic colonist presided over house and land and that of a proud female buccaneer over island and sea. Here the timorousness and piety of our people did not hold dominion. Here we could surely be free at last.

Marie seemed to regard the purchase as already complete. 'All we'll need is a double bed.'

'Getting it down here would be a problem.' Negative possibilities seem to come to me as the leaves to the trees.

Marie had thought it all through. 'I could get us the loan of Dan Gallagher's lorry.'

At the removal of this final obstacle, Neil, who had been too excited to contribute, drank down most of his beer and helped himself to another.

'That's the last bottle,' Helen scolded – but without real concern.

There was always the hotel up the lane.

Here we were reacquainted with a familiar Ireland. The proprietor was a florid gombeen man whose loud bonhomie failed to disguise cunning eyes skulking in sockets like rats at the back of a culvert. On the subject of the colonist, his attempt to suggest intimacy and affection revealed the absence of both. Our landlord rose even higher in our estimation.

Later in the evening there passed behind the bar a youth whose casually arrogant manner indicated a proprietor's son and whose weak indulged features presaged gambling debts, wrecked cars and pregnant farm girls. When he saw Marie and Helen he took over the bar, leered nakedly down at them and attempted to strike up conversation when he came to remove empty glasses. Ignored, he took to exchanging loud pleasantries on the girls with the patrons at the bar. This too failed to elicit a response. Few things are more contemptible than the wastrel sons of autocrats. In any case we were genuinely absorbed in details of bank loans, redecoration, furniture, transport. When all the details were finally settled Neil proposed celebratory cognacs. No one else felt up to this – but so determined was he to mark the occasion that he ordered himself a large one.

We emerged onto the lane, moved afresh by the grandeur of the setting and excited afresh by our imminent stake in it. Seizing each of the girls by the waist, Neil crushed them against him and looked affectionately from one to the other. 'God I love you two. I love both of you. You know that.' He looked across at me. 'I love these two women. Aren't they *incredibly beautiful?*'

'Stunning.'

He continued to regard me, obviously wishing to extend

the avowal but finding it difficult. Loving accountants is never easy. Yet he was equal to the challenge. Releasing the women, he rushed forward to grab me by the waist, lift me off the ground and swing me round several times. 'And I love you as well . . . ye big miserable cunt ye.'

As so often, exaltation immediately faced practical problems. Setting me down, he turned to the others. 'Is there any drink in the house?'

It was wonderful to be able to justify his faith in me so soon. 'I brought a bottle of gin.'

'But there's no glasses,' Marie wailed.

Helen chuckled deeply and, when we turned to her, lightly agitated her bag to produce an unmistakable clink.

'You *didn't!*'

'*Helen!*'

'But there were hardly any customers. *They'll know who it was.*'

'I couldn't resist it,' she laughed. 'It was that hateful wee shite behind the bar.'

I was the only one yet to react. Helen turned on me eyes bright with daring and mischief.

'Pirate Queen,' I murmured, bowing my head in sincere homage.

But it had been a long day. Helen, Marie and I could scarcely get a single gin down.

'My eyes are closing.' Helen pushed away her unfinished glass. 'It must be the sea air.'

Neil finished Helen's drink as well as his own – and almost immediately left for the bathroom. After ten minutes Helen went to check on him, returning with a weary shake of the head. 'Boking his ring up.'

Far from creating awkwardness, Neil's absence in the morning showed that the women and I, rarely together for any length of time, could co-operate harmoniously on a domestic chore such as shopping in the Kwality Stores in the village.

This relaxed and convivial outing (rendered yet more charming by the local custom of apologising for high prices and rounding down totals) confirmed the promise of the previous evening. As well as drinking and communing with nature, we could enjoy menial tasks.

In the afternoon the three of us lounged companionably in the living room. Marie lay on an old wickerwork sofa with the wildflower and bird books. Helen stood at the window, entranced by inconstant sea and sky.

'Look at the different colours in the water ... purple and green.'

Going across to join Helen, I touched her lightly on the arm. 'Pistachio and damson.'

Helen frequently pretended that laughter had rendered her incapable of remaining upright and obliged to fall on the jester for support. I found it an endearing affectation – especially if she was naked at the time.

Marie seemed not to object to this intimacy. 'Those little birds are stonechats and wheatears,' she offered. 'And the wildflowers in front of us are butterwort and sundew.'

She came across to the window and stood on the other side of me from Helen – a move which could have been infuriatingly possessive. Instead, I had a sudden thrilling sense of being offered not merely two individual women, a prospect dramatic enough in itself, but a *pair* in which each accepted the other as a twin concubine. Neil would surely have put an arm around each girl. An accountant could never be so bold. We continued to gaze upon splendour, at peace with each other and the world.

No – the human animal can never be completely content.

'Ah,' Marie sighed, 'if only we'd thought to bring binoculars.'

Helen issued a lazy grunt of accord. Then the discontent passed and we surrendered once more. By and by Helen leaned an elbow on my shoulder. Marie seemed to draw closer. No god on Olympus could have felt more privileged than I.

An apparition out of legend made us all exclaim together. Approaching across the strand was a horse-drawn chariot in which a youthful blond charioteer stood up straight at the reins. Not the beautiful man-slaying Achilles but presumably a son from the Sammin farm with a cartload of turf.

The girls were at their most coy and skittish, determined to drive the youth's wits astray. But he retained his dignity and composure. And why not? He was a prince among his people. It was better for all that he had not succumbed. When homage becomes universal the wits of the worshipped are also driven astray.

The commotion roused Neil, ashen of countenance and querulous of mood.

'He's like a *bear* when he gets out of bed,' Helen cried. 'Let's just leave him to it and go for a walk.'

This was a further thrilling endorsement of the harmony our close-knit trio had forged. Taking an old straw hat from the bookcase, Helen gaily popped it on the back of her head.

'You're not going out in a *man's hat*,' Neil rasped.

Ignoring her husband, Helen pulled the brim over her eyes and roguishly pouted at me.

But straw hats are intended for a different climate. No sooner were we outside than the wind whipped it off and sent it bowling down the lane. My ineffectual pursuit was hugely enjoyed by the girls. Few things are more entertaining for women than the spectacle of men losing dignity.

Solemn feeling returned by the margin of the lake. Helen closed her eyes and released a sensual sigh. 'I *adore* the sound of lapping water.'

'Are they in couples?' Marie was studying the swans. 'Aren't they partners for life?'

'This is the sixties,' I said. 'Now they swap all the time.'

An inadvertent reference to our secret. Under cover of the joke, the girls exultantly laughed. They were again in formation, one on each side of me, and I was suddenly riven by the searing possibility of not merely enjoying both women but *both at the same time.* Just to contemplate this was staring into the sun. One woman is such an infinite universe of wonder. How could any mortal man explore two at once?

On the strand Marie kicked off her Dr Scholl sandals and waded into the sea. Helen immediately followed suit.

'Come on in,' Marie coaxed. 'It's *gorgeous.*'

These fleet Nereids might bear me off into the deep. Safer to remain on the sand and watch.

We wandered to the end of the long beach, the only evidence of human activity the drone of an engine from Sammin's fields. As we came abreast of the farm Helen revealed that a daughter of Nereus could still retain maternal instincts. 'Look at the age of that child driving a tractor. Can't be more than ten or eleven.'

Around the headland was another beach and a rocky foreshore with no fences or buildings – or any other evidence of man. Here a timeless inhuman force had absolute dominion. Both wind and wave seemed more determined, more indifferent and extreme.

The sky was the colour of elephant hide, with a black contusion overhead. Fate intended us to shelter in a cave – and there I would unite with each Nereid as the restless wind unites with the unquiet sea. From these unions of sea nymph and man would come mighty half-gods to astound the world.

Instead, we made a run for it, hampered by Marie's flapping Dr Scholls. Before we were halfway across our own beach, rain came down or, rather, across, driven by ferocious gusts into our bodies.

Once the fussy quotidian mind has accepted the certainty of a wetting and surrendered there is a wild pagan triumph in being soaked to the skin. We burst in on Neil fiery-eyed, shrieking with joy.

In no hurry to dry off, Marie dropped her sandals and ran to the window. 'My God would you look at that.'

Helen and I were more inclined to look at each other. We stood face to face, dripping, exalted, laughing. Her blouse and skirt adhered to her as tightly as cling film.

'That's on for the night,' Marie cried. 'What'll we do?'

Neil was at the table reading a local paper purchased with the groceries. 'How about a dance?'

Marie turned to him, running wet, radiant. 'A culchie dance!'

'There's Larry Cunningham in a benefit night for Sister Mary McNulty's Tanzanian Fund.' Neil's pause, apparently to permit a response, was play-acting. 'Or Philomena Moynihan and the Mohawk Showband.'

'YES!'

Helen was more circumspect. 'I don't want to drive in that rain.'

'It's in the village hall.'

'YES!'

While we changed out of wet clothes, Neil got a fire going in the range. Allowing the girls first crack at the bathroom, I put potatoes on to boil and unearthed a pan for frying chops. A tremendous atmosphere of industry obtained. Goddam it, we were pulling together as a team.

Such untroubled harmony could scarcely endure. Marie and Helen discovered that their hair-dryer plugs did not fit the sockets. This was especially traumatic because both of them were developing new styles. Marie was attempting to move to a completely flat, natural look and, in pursuit of the same new image, Helen was letting her Asymmetric Isadora grow out. Transitional hair is always problematic. The new look also demanded absolute straightness – and neither girl had absolutely straight hair. Without the close control provided by dryers the spectre of frizziness loomed.

The range fire was also at an awkward height – too low for sitting at and too high for lying towards. Ever resourceful,

Neil dragged in a mattress and used various pieces of furniture to prop it up at the required level. Soon Marie and Helen were stretched out in dressing gowns, heads to the fire and hair held straight in brushes. Not only was this a delightful tableau, the success in surmounting a serious challenge had had a terrifically binding effect. We were no longer individuals but part of a larger organism.

Only a genuine catastrophe would have dimmed the high spirits. Helen greeted her next problem as though it were a joyful surprise. Rushing from the bedroom, still in her dressing gown, she held up helpless hands with the digits splayed. 'Never do your nails before you put on your clothes!' Then, as if this were not enough, she added another of her delightful gaucheries. 'And my ring's all soap!'

Now mere rain would not deter us – or make less splendid our raiment. Neil wore his butcher-stripe three-piece and a nineteen forties kipper tie decorated with quaint racing cars. I sported a silk cravat and red paisley waistcoat. Helen was gloriously heatwave in a deep yellow blouse and orange suede miniskirt. Marie had a black miniskirt and a purple wrap-around blouse.

Getting up the rough muddy lane was the difficult part. Since she had lost valuable inches of built-up hair, Marie was more than ever dependent on heels. Her current pair were the highest and most minimal yet, providing virtually nothing by way of support. At every other step she went over, painfully yanking my arm and causing the umbrella to flail.

The village offered a classic choice – Owney's Dew Drop Inn, a temple of neon and leatherette, or the traditional austerity of the Ideal Bar. The clientele in the new lounge would probably have been nearer our age group – but the recent horror of the hotel made us favour the old. The latter establishment was so aptly titled it could well have been renamed the Platonic Ideal Bar. In its tiny wooden-framed window a prodigious litter of dead insects surrounded a pair of empty

Guinness bottles symmetrically positioned on either side of a cardboard John Powers box, as empty and bleached as one of the cattle skulls littering the strand. The interior had a dark wooden counter and wooden shelving with tiny compartments containing cardboard confectionery boxes, then a wooden partition and a door which led to a little bar where the only relief from sombre dark was a single high window of frosted glass and two brass signs nailed by the spirit bottles – FREE BEER TOMORROW and NO BLOODY SWEARING PLEASE.

The patrons, as old and traditional as the decor and jokes, were shocked into silence by the irruption of colour and youth. The contrast with dimness and decrepitude reminded me of Marie's tangerine dress irradiating the Crown snug. But now the female sexual power was doubled. Now there were two delinquent suns.

Of course it was only a matter of time. As I was ordering the second round a drinker in a cap who was slumped against the bar lifted a rueful face. 'If a man could only stick to the two pints.'

'If only.'

'*Hah?*' he grunted, as though at rude disagreement.

'The two pints,' I sighed tragically. 'More than enough.'

He turned to relay to the company this consensual wisdom. 'If a man could only stick to the two pints.'

General laughter was the signal for sustained interrogation – where would ye be from, what would ye do, how much would ye get in your hand?

'So you're an accountant,' said a tall man with yellow-tinged white hair. 'Good at the figures?'

'Not bad.'

'Well tell me this and tell me no more.' He furrowed his brow anxiously. 'If a hen and a half lays an egg and a half in a day and a half ... and allow ... how many eggs will the hen lay in a week?'

In accordance with accountancy precept I investigated the grey area first. 'Allow for what?'

He gazed gravely into his glass. 'The wear and tear on the hen's arse.'

The laughter was universal, loud and prolonged – but none was more merry than the high peals of Helen and Marie. They seemed to believe that they themselves were above being mocked – a smug illusion swiftly dispelled. When Helen proudly explained where we were staying her interrogator's mighty tusks of nostril hair shook in helpless mirth. 'The wee shack,' he cackled, 'the wee shack . . . heh heh heh . . .'

'It's a *beautiful* house.' Helen's outrage was intense. 'We intend to *buy* it.'

There was a shocked silence. The man next to me put his mouth to my ear. 'Jaysus, that big one's a tongue on her. You're as well off with the wee fat cutty.'

Marie overheard this. 'Less of the *fat*, if you don't mind.'

'But sure it looks well on ye.' Obviously one of those for whom voluptuousness would always be in fashion, he appraised the purple wrap-around with every sign of approval. 'Ye suit the beef.'

Nowhere among the company was the two-pint limit observed. Least of all by its advocate. Now he seized my hand and looked into my eyes. '*You're* an accountant . . . and *Ahm* a country fella.' He paused, as though expecting contradiction.

'Very true.'

'But listen to what I'm going to tell you.' His arm continued to pump mine. 'I'm as good as you . . .' This pause seemed to be especially meaningful. His arm came to rest. His eyes probed deeply in mine. '*And you're as good as me.*' Well satisfied with this apothegm, he released me and stood back. 'Isn't that right?'

'Exactly right.'

'Isn't it right what I'm telling you?'

'I never heard a truer word.'

But as I turned away he suddenly seized my hand again and shook it with renewed enthusiasm. 'No hard feelings now.

Don't get me wrong now.'

'No hard feelings whatever.'

His even more vigorous pumping was the signal for an out-
break of handshaking. Never were handshakes so frequent and
fervent. Marie and Helen were especially favoured and every
man in the bar attempted to buy them a drink. Mr Nostril
Hair even felt so generous that he tipped the lugubrious barman. 'Keep that change,' he shouted, winking broadly at
Helen, 'and bring it back when it's ready.'

When we attempted to leave, the girls' hands were held.
Only a firm promise to return the following night secured
their release.

'God my hand's *crushed*.' In the safety of the street Helen
stretched her afflicted fingers.

'Helen, I think the one with the nostril hair really fancies
you,' Marie cried.

The dancers were younger but no more fashionable than the
drinkers. Women had tight curly perms and dootsie pink
dresses with frilly collars. Men had short wavy hair and V-
necked pullovers underneath suit jackets; many sported rows
of pens in their breast pockets and there was even a case of a
tie worn out over a pullover. Contrast, the great enhancer,
was giving us another enormous boost. There could be little
doubt that we were the only genuine today guys in the hall.
But the conservatism did not extend to dancing. As we
emerged from the cloakrooms most of the company were
boogying enthusiastically to an up-tempo number called
'Wild Blood'. 'I don't hate my Papa . . . Papa had to go,' sang
Philomena, a pudgy freckled girl in a leather mini, tasselled
leather waistcoat and headband with feather. 'For Papa had
wild blood . . . he's not to blame. That wild blood drives a
man insane.' Male Mohawks in fringed buckskin jackets came
in on the chorus, 'There's no resistin' wild blood – like a storm
of wind and rain,' falling back again for Philomena's glad
surrender to genetic determinism. 'An' Ah can feel that wild

blood a–flowin' in *mah* veins.'

Perhaps emboldened by the Dionysiac message of the song, Neil seized Marie by the waist. 'You really do suit the beef.'

Would he never learn that any mention of abundance infuriated Marie?

'Fuck away off, Neil Quinn.' Her own wild blood a–flowin', she pushed Neil away and took Helen by the wrist. 'Come on, Helen! Let's dump these two and get ourselves some real men.'

Together they plunged into the mêlée and were immediately snapped up. In fact, so universal and overwhelming was the homage that the course of the night was irretrievably fixed. Neil and I had to stand by and watch as a succession of worshipful admirers swept the women gaily round the floor to jaunty Indian numbers such as 'Squaws along the Yukon' ('She makes her underwear/From hides of grizzly bear/And bathes in ice-cold water every day./Her skin I love to touch but I can't touch it much/Because her fur-lined carpet's in the way.') – and, in an unthemed, conventional slow set, outrageously pawed and squeezed them to the mournful strains of 'It Keeps Right on a-Hurtin', 'He'll Have To Go' and 'Tears on a Bridal Bouquet'. Only rarely did the women succeed in getting back to us between dances.

'Mine has three caravans in a field somewhere,' Helen shrieked. Never had I seen her so enraptured, flushed and bright-eyed with delirium. 'They're let right through the summer. And he's putting in two more next year. Talk about a good catch! Why do *I* get all the sensible ones?'

'You're welcome to swap!' cried Marie. 'All mine want to do is push themselves into me.'

'I saw that,' Neil snapped – but no one paid him any attention.

'And at least yours didn't have false teeth, Helen. This character was grinning away at me like that horse that won the Grand National ... what's this it was called?'

'*Come on!*' Helen grabbed Marie – and before they had taken a step, they were chosen again. Over the shoulder of her gallant, Marie mouthed Helen a message reinforced by displaying a bare finger: '*Your wedding ring.*'

Helen's wild blood had already advised her. She held up an equally bare finger. '*Took it off ages ago.*'

This was the high point of the evening – a speciality number involving audience participation.

> At around the time when drums began to talk
> There was a tribe of Indians they call Mohawk.
> They started a dance . . . it was all the rage
> With squaws and braves of every age.
> It was the Wigwam Wiggle . . . crazy Indian dance.

Philomena demonstrated the steps on stage and enthusiastically exhorted those below to join her. Soon all the dancers were rolling their groins. Even the bank girl was participating joyously, arms high in the air and the orange mini tossed from side to side in reckless abandon.

'God, Helen's in great form,' Neil murmured in awe. 'I've never seen her like this.'

> They did the Wigwam Wiggle every mornin'
>   and night.
> They did the Wigwam Wiggle . . . boy could they
>   do it right.
> Well, they wiggled up and down and they wiggled
>   to and fro
> They wiggled any way that their hips would go.
> It was the Wigwam Wiggle . . . crazy Indian dance.

Finally worn out, the errant wives staggered back, holding onto each other, completely helpless with mirth.

'Fuck,' Helen wailed, bending over. 'I think I've wet myself laughing. I'll have to go to the Ladies.'

'Oh God, so will I.'

Neil and I were to wait outside and protect them from

further admirers. But even a trip to the toilet produced high
adventure. Helen emerged in a helpless swoon, supported by
Marie.

'FUCK!' Helen fought debilitating laughter to mount an
explanation. 'All those old wooden doors look the same ...
there's no signs ... so didn't I *walk into the Gents* thinking I
was coming back into the hall.'

'It's easy done,' Marie agreed. 'And we couldn't wait to get
out of the Ladies. It's packed to the doors and the stink of
Pagan perfume would knock ye down ... *knock ye down*,
look see.'

Helen rallied sufficiently to continue. 'Come on ahead, they
said to me. Come on in. You're very welcome. Fuck, I was
never so *mortified*. I'll have to get out of here.'

As she collapsed again two men went by with a cheery
wave. 'Ye should have come ahead on in.'

'*Somebody get me out of here!*'

Without discussion, arrangement or awkwardness, Marie
took Neil's arm and Helen walked beside me. Since Helen
was still intermittently helpless, we soon fell behind. But the
rain had stopped and the sky had cleared and the silent night
was redolent with lushness and mystery. In the moonlight the
wet tarmac gleamed like obsidian.

'Every time I think of it,' Helen gasped. 'A row of men
standing with their cocks in their hands and me waltzing right
into the middle of them. The *stink* of the place, apart from
anything else.'

'There's worse smells than Pagan perfume,' I murmured
abstractedly. An evening on the sidelines had left me more attuned to the cold firmament than the warm human farce. A
belittling strew of stars reinforced the lesson of insignificance.
But as we turned off the main road the ditch bordering the lane
gurgled with sensual contentment; bedded in rich mulch, its
tangled profusion exultantly glistened. From further down, a
high musical laugh floated back.

'Someone's enjoying themselves,' Helen laughed in sweet ambiguity.

'They did the Wigwam Wiggle . . .' It was Marie singing – or attempting to sing through her laughter – and suddenly I understood that if the stars were frigid it was because of envy not disdain. Though too haughty ever to admit it, they would rather walk on the shining earth by a gurgling ditch to a woman's song. '. . . crazy Indian dance.'

'Marie was really good at the Wiggle.'

'You were tossing it around pretty well yourself.'

Her mouth rose to mine tenderly, inevitably. It was an odd paradox that detachment may have made me bold. Reaching under the suede mini, I firmly took hold of her damp genitals. (This may well have been the only occasion of beating Helen to the crotch.)

But, later on, detachment made me unable to come (though purple hearts may have been a contributing factor). Helen was even more noisy and uninhibited than usual – how the stars in their cold heaven must have shivered with deprivation and loss – but the more she shouted and swore, the more remote I became. It was nothing personal. I felt I could have pleasured every colleen in Ireland without approaching orgasm. A specific ministration was needed. Helen was startled by my request but agreed readily enough, even finding the idea appropriate to a uniquely odd night. Again, her style was completely different to that of Marie, who liked to coax pleasure forth with an almost imperceptible touch. Like a Victorian lady summoning a dilatory chambermaid with a bell rope, Helen commanded the attendance of pleasure with imperious yanking. Yet there was still no arrival. It began to seem as if I would never shoot a load again. One thing to be said for Helen – she was certainly no quitter. After a short rest she resumed with renewed determination and eventually there came, like the hoot of a still-far-off train, the first faint signal of approaching relief. My anxious movement was stayed by a suggestion as generous and selfless as any I have known.

'Just come over me,' she breathed – and any lingering recalcitrance was instantly dispelled.

This most purely personal of indulgences turned out to have a wider resonance. Neil was tremendously excited by the idea of Helen bringing me off. Presumably it was the fact of her cold-bloodedly servicing me – of becoming my whore. Then I was excited by the notion of Neil being excited by the notion of Helen being my whore. We were close to perpetual stimulation.

Although she would never admit it, not even to Neil, Helen too seemed to be sexually exhilarated. When we were in her bedroom the following evening it occurred to her that, since she and I had more or less the same build and height, most of her clothes would fit me. She begged me to try something on – just for laughs of course. The possible implications made me quake with delirium and dread. Were there strange uncharted depths in Helen? And had she sensed in me something weird I had not been conscious of myself? I was certainly aware of powerful forces astir.

Unsure if what I was experiencing was nausea or rapture, I donned a matching T-shirt and trousers in arterial red. Later such dressing would be commonplace for men but at that time the brightness and tightness were daring even for women. When I looked at myself in the mirror I knew that I had truly passed beyond to a region where normal conditions no longer obtained. Gravity, in particular, seemed no longer to apply. I felt weightless and empty. And volition abandoned me entirely. Assailed by waves of sick-sweet vertigo, I could scarcely move or speak. My only desire was for craven surrender, to be brutally used and degraded before being contemptuously cast aside. The ideal solution would have been for Helen to straddle me, encircle my throat in her hands and, with a violent jangling of bracelets, bring her pleasure to its climax by ecstatic strangulation. Instead, she settled for orthodox intercourse, though with herself supplying most of the drive. Despite being underneath *she* unequivocally fucked *me* – and, already drained of will, I was unable to prevent being also swiftly drained of seed.

What would have happened if she had realised the extent of her power? If I had worn a skirt and blouse - *or the backless black dress?* The consequences might have been incalculable. For passing beyond is indeed like venturing into outer space – there is a serious possibility that you will never get back. When Helen laid her hands on my brightly and tightly clad body I experienced the eerie tremor of an alternative destiny. I knew that instead of being a successful accountant, I could have become a great whore (though perhaps these vocations are not as different as they seem).

On the afternoon after this fancy-dress night we made our way along the coast to a third beach, even more isolated than the two before it and cut off from land by a sheer rock face.

Neil nodded towards the summit. 'That's where the Sammins come to make love.'

Helen looked up in rapture, as though expecting to commune with Cathy and Heathcliff joined on the heights. 'Why's that?'

'Because when you bring sheep to the edge of a cliff they push back really hard.'

Laughing, exhilarated, determined to explore the far end, we failed to notice the direction of the tide and discovered on our return that it had cut us off. Neil and I removed our trousers and waded across to the adjoining beach – but Marie and Helen would not be persuaded to try this. The water was still rising and the light was beginning to fail. The invigorating wildness of nature began to seem sinister. My joke about coming back when the tide had turned did not go down at all well. Tempers rose with the water level.

Neil saved the day by carrying each of the girls in turn on his muscular shoulders. Afterwards he claimed that Helen had held onto his hair, practically scalping him – but he was obviously well pleased at the success of the rescue, so much so that I began to suspect him of deliberately leading us into danger. Neil had an intuitive understanding of many team-building strategies which management gurus would formulate later – and in particular of the bonding effects of group jeopardy.

That night the harmony was at its most profound. We changed partners with the effortless fluency of dancers in a ballet. The hair-drying mattress had been retained in the living room (Marie and I had willingly squeezed onto the other single) and this evening Helen and I had our turn by the range, which I packed with turf and flung open in an uncharacteristically profligate manner. Our only joint climax so far had been an aberration caused by waking from dreams in darkness under heavy bedclothes. For our second we were wide awake from the beginning, unhampered by blankets or even sheets, naked in the collusive glows of moonlight and turf fire. It was not surprising that these circumstances provided us with another breakthrough. Although Helen still forbade cunnilingus, before we undressed she permitted me to press my lips to the gusset of her jeans. That coarsest of fabrics was like honey and mead.

And afterwards, instead of covering up in the usual hurried apologetic way, she strode confidently to the window and looked out in silence. Her pale body had always been charged with hieratic power. Now its source was revealed. Whiteness was in vassalage to higher whiteness. Helen was a priestess of the moon.

Quietly, respectfully, I padded across to her side. Her breathing was still deep, her breasts rising and falling like lucent seas drawn by the moon, her nipples lightly tinged with amethyst yearning towards the moon mother. Between her clavicles and shoulder blades were two bottomless dark hollows – like moon craters, except that they were alive and stirring gently, more unfathomable and profound than the abysses of space. To touch or even address her would have been gross sacrilege.

Eventually she resumed her human guise. 'Put the kettle on for tea.'

Even the return of partners, often trickier than the initial exchange, was accomplished with ease. 'Tea's made!' I shouted, beating the kettle with the iron lever from the range. 'First come first served!'

This was the occasion when Helen collapsed against me naked – and I was glad of my forbearance during her communion with the moon. Bounty seized is merely satisfactory; bounty received as a gift is sublime.

The other two emerged in dressing gowns, startled by their contrast with the primal innocence of the living room.

Marie cast a sceptical glance at my genitals. 'Is this a nudist camp ... or *what?*'

But it was obvious that they were pleased, and perhaps even moved, by a daring which suggested that shame was no more. The grandeur of the remote setting had fulfilled all its promise. We were free at last of timidity and convention. We were a marriage of four. We were finally beyond.

In a four-way marriage it is of course necessary to maintain the original two-way relationships and one of the most exhilarating aspects of the experiment was that, far from weakening the original linkages, it invested the familiar with the glamour and intoxication of the new. After an encounter with Helen, successful or otherwise, I always eagerly anticipated becoming reacquainted with Marie.

Morning was the time for these thrilling reaffirmations. A gentle touch on Marie's shoulder brought her to face me. But in her expression there was no expectancy, tenderness or light. Only darkness and resentment.

'I have the itch.'

For a long, joyless moment we regarded each other. 'Bad?'

'Bad enough.'

'Have you something for it?'

'No.'

'Can you get something?'

'Round here? *Without a prescription?*'

'Couldn't you see a doctor?'

She did not even deign to reply, already brooding on consequences. 'And of course Neil'll be looking for it again tonight.'

Surely it was obvious that the frolicking was over. 'Tell him.'

Marie twisted impatiently. 'I don't want anyone to know. And I don't want to have to speak to Neil. He would think I was blaming him.'

An understandable reluctance. To have to reject Helen now would be intolerable. 'What's the alternative?'

Marie waited for me to discover it – but was finally obliged to explain. 'We don't *have* to have sex every night.'

Once again she waited – and again was forced to be explicit. '*You* could say something.'

The enormity of this was too great to grasp. 'Wait a minute.' My brain refused to analyse the implications. '*You* ... want *me* ... to call it off tonight ... but without giving *the real reason?*'

Just when I had achieved a magical intimacy with Helen. Just when we were on the verge of the ultimate breakthrough. My tongue was almost in her redolent nectary. Intercourse is wonderful fun but for me cunnilingus may be the real con-summation. True worship requires a symbolic imbibing. It is necessary to consume the essence of the divine (if I had been a homosexual I would have made a marvellous lover). And just when the honey was within reach of my tongue Marie expected me to pretend to want to call everything off – to issue Helen exactly the rejection she would not issue Neil.

'You want me to tell Helen that I don't want to have sex

with her. That's what you want me to do . . . isn't it?'

Marie turned away in sullen pique. 'Not specifically Helen.'

'Well *who* then?' I looked about, as if in search of lovers to reject. 'Have I been humping Neil, for fuck's sake? *Have I been humping the sheep?*'

Not surprisingly, no agreement was reached and all day the issue hung above us like storm clouds. There were also real storm clouds, so that we had to abandon the afternoon outing – a hill climb on the bay a few miles south of our house. In normal circumstances the sanctuary we found would have been a thrilling discovery, for the Laughing Cavalier was an atypical new bar with a picture window on the bay. On this occasion Marie and I might have preferred traditional sequestration and darkness to modern exposure and light. With typical insensitivity to group mood, Helen cried out in delight and rushed to commandeer a window table. Her urgency was redundant. There was no one else in the bar, which, despite expensive and fashionable newness, had the unmistakable smell of death. The west was not yet ready for this kind of drinking place and the business was expiring in a slow agony as terrible as the lingering demise of a spouse (sometimes it is even more traumatic – proprietors are frequently more attached to a business than to a spouse).

The owner was a hugely moustachioed Dutchman with sagging features and discouraged eyes, intensely morose in spite of being surrounded by inducements to mirth. Behind the bar was an array of jokey cards ('Be Careful – Accidents Cause People', 'God's Second Name is not Dammit'), in the ice bucket lay tongs whose grips were the halfs of a set of dentures and on the bar top were a shilling and a half crown apparently forgotten by a careless customer but actually secured underneath. Patrons were supposed to tug at the coins and frown in frustration.

After ordering the drinks I felt obliged to oblige. 'Stuck on?'

The Dutchman roused himself. 'Bolted.'

Apparently still unaware of the lack of enthusiasm, Helen was marvelling at the bay below. 'Those rain clouds are changing second by second. You could watch them all day.'

Neil braced himself with a hefty swig of alcohol. 'Will somebody for fuck's sake tell me what the fuck's wrong?'

'*Nothing's wrong.*' But so feral was my snarl that Neil started in fright.

There was a long tense silence in which the bay continued its dramatic mutations unnoticed.

'I'll tell you what it is.' Marie's tone was grim. 'I have my problem again ... but my husband doesn't want to give up sex.'

'That's not true at all.' The disagreement was about choice of announcer and form of announcement.

'Here here here here.' Neil made gentle placatory gestures. 'Sure that's no problem. All you had to do was say.'

'That's what I told her,' I burst out. Marie's treacherous misrepresentation had denied her the protection of silence. 'Just say. A plain simple statement. *Just say.* But oh no. She wasn't capable of that. Couldn't speak up for herself. Tried to get me to say I didn't want it any more. Tried to get me to do her dirty work ... as usual.' Nominally addressing Neil, my eyes were firmly locked on those of Marie. Naked high-voltage hatred flashed between us.

Marie rose, not exactly in a blind rage, but swiftly and decisively and, without explanation, left the table, brushing aside Neil's attempt to restrain her. We followed her progress apprehensively, relieved to see her make for the Ladies instead of the exit.

Over the bay plumes and wraiths drifted against darker grey. Glumly we bowed our heads to our drinks.

'Go and see if she's all right, Helen.'

Helen looked at her husband as though he had taken leave of his senses.

We turned back to the clouds.

'Fucking rain,' Neil muttered, after a time.

'Maybe a picture window's not such a good idea,' I agreed. The despair and fatalism of the Gael seemed to be vindicated now. 'Maybe the original Irish bar designers were wiser than we thought.'

Abruptly tossing back his drink, Neil went up to the Dutchman for another round.

'Marie's a terrible softie,' I said to Helen. 'Can't say boo to anyone. All the dirty work has to be done by yours truly. But *this* time . . . to have to . . .' It seemed appropriate not to check the little catch of emotion. 'I've been enough of a bastard to you as it is.'

Helen's entire upper body came forward on a surge of supportive intimacy. 'You know that isn't true.'

'I've treated you atrociously.' I gazed down into my drink as if in its dregs were traced the very lineaments of shame. 'It's a disgrace.'

Now Helen too was trammelled in emotion. Her voice was low, husky, obstructed. 'You musn't say that.'

Neil returned with a tray bearing four strange drinks. 'There's an incredible range of things behind the bar. All sorts of continental stuff I've never heard of. Got us four different ones to try – Suze, Marie Brizzard, Poir Williams and Peach Schnapps.'

Plucky, stout-hearted Neil – still trying to restore the excitement of group exploration, still hoping we could drink our way to transcendence and glory.

Marie returned, composed and silent but unmollified. And unimpressed by exotic drinks. The tasting, which should have been joyously communal, proceeded without any sharing and with no comment other than a grimace from Marie. Desolate, Neil withdrew to the private pleasure of a Dutch cigar, forlornly drawing to himself a glass ashtray in the form of a crushed beer bottle bearing the legend Flat Beer Sold Here.

'It's probably just a wee touch of thrush,' Helen said

suddenly, in a consoling tone which did nothing to alleviate the tactlessness of the comment. Before anyone could respond she made it even worse. 'I mean, *I'm* all right . . . and Neil's all right. If Neil gave you something I'd have it too. And Neil baths or showers every day . . . I make sure of that.'

Neil threw back his head in a harsh bark. No one else spoke. Marie could scarcely credit that Helen was not only challenging the diagnosis of a medical practitioner but attempting to exonerate her guilty husband and perhaps even *impugn Marie's personal hygiene.*

'Thrush has a *white* discharge,' she said with the cold anger that is more effective than any blaze. 'This is nonspecific urethritis . . . not thrush. And showering has nothing to do with it. NSU can be caused by *roughness*. Neil is so *rough* all the time.'

In the process of demolishing Helen, Marie seemed to forget the collateral damage to Neil. Humiliated and broken, he hung his head in deep shame. Not even the entire box of Dutch cigars would have cheered him.

'That's why it's known as honeymoonitis,' Marie said. 'I have girls just back from their honeymoons in with prescriptions all the time.'

The termination of group sex was tolerable if depressing but the falling out of the wives was an unexpected and fatal blow. It destroyed the heart of our symbiotic organism. It tore the arse out of our team.

The rest of the day was subdued and dismal. We continued to drink, more out of habit than pleasure, and with little hope of restoring the old intimacy and excitement. Helen was especially withdrawn – Marie's attack seemed to have affected her deeply. And not even Neil had the heart to challenge the terrible apostasy of an early night.

The rain continued next day and we lay late to avoid it and each other. Eventually both had to be faced. Abandoning its campaign of fitful skirmishing, the weather had opted for all-out attack. Metal rods pounded the corrugated iron; rivulets ran off the roof edge; torrents roared in the drains. Equally invisible were the island before and the mountain behind. We were trapped in a low tent of dark grey.

Helen and I selected novels and retired to sofa and wickerwork chair. After failing to interest us in canasta, Marie and Neil resorted to draughts. A desultory pitiful enterprise, it eventually died of inanition. They took to studying the sky for portents.

Neil: 'I think it might have eased off a wee bit.'

Marie: 'The sky could be fairing up down there in the south.'

Neither reader commented or even looked up. Marie made a cup of tea as a way of attracting our attention.

'How about the Laughing Cavalier?' Neil was carefully casual. 'Try a few more weird drinks.'

'Why not?' Marie agreed. 'We can't sit here all day.'

So humble and desperate was her look of entreaty that I had to lay down my book. All three of us turned to Helen. For a moment it seemed that she had neither heard the suggestion nor registered our air of expectation. Then she raised her head, considered the rain, grunted – and went back to her novel.

We sipped tea, setting the cups down with great care, as though they were delicate phials of a rare and priceless elixir of hope.

'Go you three for a drink,' Helen said by and by. 'I'm enjoying this book.'

'We need you to drive.'

'Go to the hotel up the road.'

In relationships a trivial issue is often merely the medium for a crucial subtext – and a classic obstructive strategy is to talk as if there is only the trivial issue. The important thing was not drink or bars or even a desire to get out. It was the need to rekindle group spirit. Neil was asking Helen to *participate*. If we wished to emerge from the crisis we would have to pull together as a team.

There was a long difficult silence.

Neil spoke in a quiet tone – but with tremendous intensity. 'Jesus, I hate that superior attitude.'

Helen lifted her head and stared wildly about in search of the haughty creature apostrophized. Finding none, she turned back to Neil. 'I beg your pardon.'

'You heard me.'

'Neil' – it was obvious that she did not feel he deserved her enormous patience and calm – 'I'm simply reading this novel ... OK?'

'You know fine well what I mean.'

Marie or I should have intervened – but our own commitment to team unity was now less than total. We wanted Neil to gut Helen.

She flung down the book and sat up, combat-ready. '*Oh?*'

'That fucking attitude. It's the way you behave every time I want you to visit my family.'

'Neil, I really don't know what your family has to do with this. I have nothing whatever against your family ... it's just that their house is always bogging with dirt.' Helen turned to Marie and me. 'They're as civil, you know? ... really nice ... but they just sit there letting dirt pile up round them. It's so *unhygienic.* You're scared to even sit down.'

'They don't share your domestic standards,' Neil said. 'And why should they? *Why the fuck should they?* Their house is comfortable. It's warm. They're both perfectly healthy. Aren't they as healthy as us? *Hn?* Are they any worse off than us? *Hah?*' He had risen out of his chair. Helen turned in contempt from the aggression. 'Fucking *hygiene.*'

'Peeuff!' Helen dismissed him with a wave and lifted her novel.

Now that Neil was on his feet he was at a loss for something to do. Casting wild glances about him, he paced in inarticulate rage. Suddenly inspiration came. With a few determined strides he went to the window and snatched something which he bore to us in cupped hands. From an old web he had taken a fly, much enfeebled though still alive. Not a bluebottle but large enough – a substantial housefly.

He planted himself directly in front of Helen. 'Hygiene,' he snarled. 'I'll fucking show you hygiene.'

'*Neil!*' Marie screamed in terror but he paid no attention, eyes defiantly on Helen as he raised his cupped hands to his face and took their contents into his mouth. A violent shudder of nausea made me turn from the swallow.

'*Neil!*' Marie screamed again – and then there was silence.

Neil was still staring defiantly at Helen.

'Oh Neil.' Marie's tone was now anguished and tragic, as though she were addressing Socrates after he had drunk all the hemlock.

'Won't do me a bit of harm, dear.' Neil responded to Marie without taking his eyes off Helen, who was rigid and white-faced with shock. 'Won't do me the least bit of harm.'

Helen at last succeeded in finding words. 'There was no need for that.'

'Oh there was. There was, Helen. *There was.*'

Neil should have stopped with his *coup de théâtre* – for now Helen, who had seemed vanquished, summoned up deep reserves.

'Well, if you want to know, it's not just the hygiene. What I really object to about your family is their *complete uselessness.*' Helen certainly had gumption. A man who could eat live flies was capable of anything. 'All they do is sit about the house looking at one another.'

'And why shouldn't they? *Why the fuck shouldn't they?*'

'No reason at all.' Helen paused, not from mercy or doubt but the clinical fastidiousness of the master swordsman selecting the site for a clean kill. 'Except that you're just the same. You'd be happy to sit on Scale One in a lousy school all your days.'

Neil's teeth were clenched so tight that he could scarcely articulate. 'So? . . . *So?* It's my own fucking funeral, isn't it?'

'No, dear.' Effortlessly, voluptuously, Helen slid home the blade. 'Because *I* have to live with the financial consequences of that.'

Neil fell back a little – and for the first time in the engagement turned to Marie and me for support. 'Now we're getting to it. This is *really* what it's all about. Helen always knows *to the exact penny* how much more than me she earns. To the *exact fucking penny* . . . always . . . and never lets me forget it. I'm sure she knows what it is now. Ask her. *Ask her.*'

Needless to say, we declined this invitation.

'Someone has to deal with money,' Helen hissed.

'And when I told her that Brother Claud was retiring this summer, what's the first thing she said? *What was the first thing she said?* Go and see the new head about a Scale Three. Not even a Scale Two. *Scale Three.*'

'You'd never do anything if you weren't pushed.' But there was a new uncertainty in Helen's tone. In this passionate contest of fluctuating fortunes it was her turn to go back on the defensive.

Suddenly Neil turned directly to me. 'I'll give *you* an interesting titbit.'

Far from feeling privileged, I was shocked by the venomous contempt in that *you*.

'Did you know Helen's great plan for me? Her plan to make something of me? She expects you to take me on and train me as an accountant.'

Obviously he had broken some sacred agreement. Immediately Helen was on her feet and at her most fiercely subjugating. '*Neil.*'

'Tell him it isn't true.' Neil knew that victory was finally his and seemed untroubled at winning by foul play. With an almost nonchalant air, he fetched an overcoat and umbrella and went out into the rain.

Helen would not look at me. For a long time she remained on her feet staring after Neil. Then she turned abruptly and went into the bedroom, viciously slamming the door.

The tension suddenly released, Marie slumped forward and buried her face in her hands. 'Oh Jesus.'

Immediately she had to jerk up in fresh terror. Helen had re-emerged and was making straight for her. Marie cowered back with a strange animal noise. Without looking at either of us, Helen passed Marie, went to the sofa for her novel and returned to the bedroom, slamming the door even more savagely than before.

Was it possible that everything Helen had done in the last year had been scheming and dissembling to make her husband an accountant? Such calculating she-devils exist only in fiction and *film noir*. But the possibility that she had been manipulating me even some of the time soured everything. The High Priestess served not transcendence but worldly advancement. There was no escaping or recovering from this terrible truth.

We sat out the afternoon in uncertainty and dismay. In the end Marie suggested that I go and bring back Neil – but I could still hear his vindictive *you* and see the contempt in his eyes. My relationship with the other husband was as damaged as that with the other wife. The four-way marriage was dissolving in acid. Marie then offered to go – but I refused to be left alone with the dragon. And so we lingered, uneasy and fretful.

'How are you by the way?' I asked Marie at one stage.

'What do you mean?'

'You know ... *your* ...'

'Itchy.' She paused grimly. 'Itchy and sore.'

Evenings in the Wild West are often serene. Like a medieval warrior repenting of atrocities, Nature falls into an enraptured and mystical trance. Against radiant back-lighting, blue in the upper sky and turquoise-tinged lower down, a long smudge of rubbed-charcoal stratus surmounted a cumulus bank of peach pink.

Neil returned, giving no sign of drunkenness or anger but not apologetic or friendly either. Marie and I, who had already eaten, now felt free to enjoy a walk on the beach. The rapt backdrop had held and the only change was in the shape of the foreground cloud.

'It's an old man,' Marie said.

'But not local.'

'How can you tell?'

'No nostril hair.'

There was a certain relief in being released from passion. We were in no hurry to go back. Every so often Marie stopped to commune with the mutating cloud.

'Now it's a shark.'

Helen and Neil were drinking bottles of Guinness. What else was there for us to do in the evening? Habit is a quiet but effective enforcer.

Neil turned towards the calm sky, only now fading to night. 'What a setting . . . and what a balls we made of it.'

'There's no point in discussing that.' Marie's tone was surprisingly sharp. She seemed to have decided that the affair was over and to have lost the sympathy with Neil that had been its starting point and support.

'What difference can it make now?' Neil had a point. If everyone accepted that the episode was over and all passion spent then we could review it as calmly and objectively as historians discussing the Punic Wars. 'I'm sorry I ever started it.'

'We had our moments,' I suggested, 'as well as our problems.'

Neil nodded grimly. 'I could have worked with easier people.'

'I think Helen and I have to take most of the blame.'

'Speak for yourself.' Helen's viciousness should have been a warning.

'That's enough about it,' Marie intervened.

'No, it's all right.' It seemed to me that only candour and acuity offered a way forward now. Important lessons could be learned. I spoke with enormous humility and diffidence. 'You see, Neil and Marie are two of a kind. And Helen and I are two of a kind.' This was impromptu analysis – but it seemed to be hugely valid and useful. 'Neil and Marie are spontaneous ... warm ... not calculating in any way. Whereas Helen and I are calculating and cold. We're ...' What was the precise term? '*Cunts.*'

Absorbed in developing the next stage of the argument, I failed once again to remember that calm rational exposition is often more infuriating than insult or violence. With a strange high-pitched keening noise, Helen had risen and was coming at me wielding a heavy glass ashtray. Surprise and shock rendered me incapable of motion. The consequences might have been frightful had not Marie sprung to my defence, intercepting Helen and wrestling the ashtray out of her hand.

'Put that down ... *you stupid bitch.*'

18

Like many of those who go into business, I intended to spend a few hectic years building a fortune and many relaxed years enjoying it. But, as so many of the many discover, the second part of the strategy may be more difficult than the first. To begin with, the pleasure of wealth accumulation is hugely addictive and the reasons for making money are easily forgotten in the intoxication of the process. Then the trappings, acquired temporarily and perhaps even with contempt, are suddenly discovered to be indispensable. Finally, if the will to escape still survives there are children who have grown up accustomed to affluence but without the ability to provide it for themselves. Perhaps it is always so with deferment. One thing leads to another in a casual progression that seems as though it could at any time be effortlessly reversed. But when we try to retrace our steps, the way back is lost or cut off. The path of least resistance leads to the point of no return.

When Barry eventually invited me to buy him out it was

already too late – our children had bound us to the town and the need to provide. How such an overreacher escaped financial ruin will always be a mystery. Especially since Emer went on to develop an independent social life without independent means. I saw her occasionally at the AGM of the golf club, where she became Ladies Captain, but the confidences were never repeated or even mentioned. She had developed a carapace, as most of us do. If she had belonged to a later generation she might have left Barry but, like many wives of that time, she settled for separate friends and separate holidays and buried the misery under armour-plated worldliness.

It was probably Barry's separate holidays which provided him with life-saving powerful friends. Almost by accident he became the founder of the most exclusive club in town. In the late sixties he persuaded five other youngish businessmen, all married and prosperous, to accompany him on a fortnight's golfing holiday to the Great Western Hotel in Galway. A relaxed golf tournament proceeded in the afternoons and in the evenings there was heavy eating and drinking. So congenial was this experience that it was repeated the following year with eight men and the year after that with thirteen. Soon it was an institution and when the membership reached twenty the list was capped, which drove the many desperate applicants into an even wilder frenzy of need. From then on I was plagued by clients begging me to use my supposed intimacy with Barry to get them a place in the club.

A few months after our own less successful group holiday in the west the Quinns left for Belfast to further Helen's career. Relations had never recovered after the holiday so their departure was neither a surprise nor a blow. I never saw Helen again but Marie and Neil kept in touch and would meet for coffee or a drink when one of them was in the other's town – though even these brief encounters became more infrequent over the years.

When Marie died the Quinns were in New Zealand for the

wedding of their eldest son. I had a long anguished phone call
from Neil that was as harrowing as anything at that difficult
time. He himself outlived Marie by only a few years and after
his death Helen went to live with the son in New Zealand.
This would not have been a problem for her. No more
attached to culture and place than to her own past, Helen had
a tremendous gift for living in the present and rarely looked
back. It is unlikely that we will ever communicate again but I
sometimes think of a china tea cup raised by a delicate white
hand that once bore to those same lips my baggy cock.

The last time I saw Neil was at the wake of his brother
Kevin. I had not been in one of these tiny terrace houses since
Marie's mother died – and the garrulous unfamiliar wake
crowd made it even more claustrophobic. I was hovering at
the door of the front room and thinking of slipping away
when Neil spotted me and came over.

'Another gone,' he said grimly. 'Next five stand up.'

Nothing in his appearance belied this prognosis. He had
dull glassy eyes and the broken-veined puffiness of the heavy
smoker and drinker. Worse, the key to his virile authority –
the compact stockiness – was gone. Now he was round-
shouldered and dumpy. But who improves with the punishing years? No doubt he was just as shocked by my meagre
strands of white hair.

'That's the way of it,' I agreed. One of the advantages of
mature years is that banality can be invested with genuine
weight. 'Heart, was it? Fairly quick?'

'Instantaneous apparently.'

'Lucky fellow. That's what we'd all like.'

There was a respectful pause in which we paid homage to
the immensities.

'The world has lost a great scholar,' Neil resumed. 'A
leading expert on the Second World War.'

'So he kept up his interest?'

'Oh he did. He did.' Neil nodded across the room at an old

bookcase where heavy volumes not only packed every shelf but were jammed in above each and also piled high on top. 'Don't suppose you want a few books on the Eastern Front?' We considered the dusty legacy in silence. 'Or to go upstairs?'

'I never met Kevin. There doesn't seem much point.'

From the front door came a great commotion loud with expressions of gratitude and relief. We moved down towards the kitchen to make way for a priest and several women. One of the women went into the front room and shepherded the occupants out to the stairs. Another summoned those in the parlour and kitchen. When we were the only two left in the hallway the second woman turned to Neil.

'That's Father McGettigan for the rosary now, Neil. He said he had to anoint a woman in Ballymacgroarty, that's what kept him.'

'All right, Cissie.'

'I'll go, Neil.' I touched his arm lightly in commiseration.

'Stay where you are. I'm not going up to that.'

But Cissie soon reappeared with a determined air. 'They're waiting for you, Neil.' He looked at her without replying. 'Your sister's waiting for you to say the first decade.'

I laid a hand on his arm once again. 'I'll leave you to it.'

'No sure wait here. I'll only be ten minutes. I want to talk to you.'

The departure of the mourners had not made the room less oppressive. On the windowsill a Child of Prague faced out onto the street. Against the back wall, also facing the street, a china cabinet with a flower-engraved glass front displayed three shelves crammed with tiny ornaments and souvenirs. Above a bijou tiled fireplace the mantelpiece supported another line of similar items, the largest a lugubrious Irish donkey whose twin creels bore snippets of real turf. Increasingly evident was the smell of torpor – a heavy compound of musty fabrics, old books and stale cigarette smoke. Distraction was the only solution – but irrational fear kept me from touching the books.

Neil preceded the descending crowd and took me firmly by the arm. 'Let's go for a drink.'

'To the Rembrandt?' I suggested with grim irony. This was one of four bars nominally owned (but, more likely, fronted) by Barry – the Rembrandt, the Monet, the Vermeer, the Gauguin. Since Barry had no interest in art and these bars were said to have been purchased with IRA money, I often wondered if he had chosen the names to annoy his ex-partner. In the course of frequent city holidays Marie and I had become art lovers, addicts of galleries and museums and even collectors in a small way. If annoyance had been the strategy it was certainly effective. Every time I passed the Vermeer a blade pierced my heart. On these painful occasions it was necessary to remember the positive developments – Barry's three sons had turned out to be stupid, delinquent and fat.

Neil laughed bleakly at the reference to Barry. 'I was thinking of the Park Bar round the corner.'

Was this choice of humble watering hole significant? I was glad that he failed to associate me with the new BMW across the street.

'That Cissie character.' Throwing back his head, Neil groaned at the heavens. 'Not even a relative. A *neighbour*. But the minute the news was out she was in with us making tea and sandwiches. In her element, of course. Taking over the whole show. A bully. As soon as they lay their hands on a gun they put it to your head. She knew Josie would die of shame if I refused to say the rosary. And of course Josie has to live with these people afterwards. What else could I have done?'

'You had no choice.'

'They put a fucking loaded gun to your head.' Neil laughed bitterly. 'Kevin hated her of course. She bullied him any chance she got. He said she was like one of those Russian women who built tanks during the war.' We were moving at a relaxed pace and now Neil stopped completely. 'Can I tell you Kevin's great theory?'

'It would be a privilege.'

In fact, I was apprehensive about the youths outside the corner fish-and-chip shop. They seemed more surly and menacing than the teenagers I remembered. This was probably a subjective reaction but there was no doubt that the Maiden City had become more violent over the years. Few people now ventured into the town centre at night (and my own children would never dream of such recklessness). Mullen's had long since been abandoned by the professional classes and was now frequented by a gang with a leader who specialised in biting off noses and ears.

'According to Kevin,' Neil was saying, 'the key to the entire war was the T-34.'

'A Russian tank?'

'Five hundred horsepower, wide tracks that could manoeuvre in snow and mud, and best of all a revolutionary sloping hull ... fifty-millimetre shells just bounced off. This was how the Russians stopped the Panzers ... the first time anyone had. The Germans had to build the Tiger tank to counter it ... fifty-five tons, twice the weight of the T-34. Ever heard of the Battle of Kursk?'

'No.'

'Neither has anyone else. Yet it was the crucial battle of the war ... and the largest armoured engagement in history. The Germans had 2,500 Tigers, the Russians 3,500 T-34s. But the T-34s were outgunned and had to get in close. Basically they just drove head-on into the Germans. Tanks were ramming each other like dodgems. The ferocity was unbelievable ... no prisoners taken on either side. After twelve hours the Germans were stopped ... and they never advanced again anywhere.'

This epic encounter demanded solemn and silent consideration. 'So the designer of the T-34 won the war?'

'That was Kevin's theory. He knew every detail of the Battle of Kursk.'

'Why did he become so obsessed with that?'

'Because it won the war but it's never mentioned. The Brits and Yanks never give anyone credit but themselves. In fact 75 per cent of German casualties were inflicted by the Russians.'

So the brother had not been a crank but a lonely fighter for justice and truth – perhaps even one of the invisible thirty-six just men.

'And that's how our Kevin spent his days.' Neil seemed suddenly disheartened. 'A miserable enough existence, I suppose.'

'No worse than many another.'

This response was sincere. In youth life had seemed to me profoundly banal. Later it was revealed as banally profound.

The Park Bar was in a terraced house on the same scale as the Quinn home and consisted of one small narrow room with two stools at the bar and tiny twin tables next to a stack of beer barrels. One of the stools was occupied – but the tables were free.

'Kevin came here every Saturday night for four bottles of stout. Every Saturday night for years. Decades maybe. And always exactly four bottles.' Reflectively Neil sipped his own double whiskey. 'Then one week he wouldn't go. Wouldn't go and never went again.'

'What happened?'

'Someone said something to him. We could never find out who or what. But it was the end for Kevin. After that he had the four bottles at home on a Saturday night.'

Even in a culture of self-circumscription this was extreme. Neil fell to ruminating. 'We're all shuffling forward in the queue,' he suddenly said.

'Does the heart thing worry you? Have you had a check-up ... tests?'

Something of his old ferocity burst out. 'Helen has me tortured about health. But I don't read health articles or watch TV health programmes. I won't give up the fags. I won't go for tests.' He sat back in implacable defiance. '*I won't feel my balls.*'

The Park Bar was not meant for private conversation. I had a feeling that the barman and single other customer were listening. Certainly they were silent now. We applied ourselves to the whiskey.

'And how is Helen?'

Neil emerged from absorption with a start. 'Fine. The usual. *Fine*. She's coming down tomorrow for the funeral.' This last sentence was rushed out as though in answer to criticism.

Just as hastily I got in my own excuse. 'I've an AGM tomorrow, so I can't make the funeral. That's why I came tonight.'

Fortunately Neil was still concerned to explain Helen's dereliction. 'The youngest girl's playing in a concert tonight.'

'I see someone beat Helen to it.'

'*Hah?*'

My remark was meant to be teasingly obscure – but Neil's bewilderment and apprehension were excessive and embarrassing. 'Some woman in the South is the first female bank manager in Ireland.'

Now his relief was equally extreme. 'Helen never got as far as she expected. But she did well enough. Well enough. If we hadn't had the five kids we'd have been grand.'

Once again he drifted off.

'And yourself?' I asked.

'*Ach.*' A violent dismissive gesture.

'Still teaching?'

'I'm in a place up the Falls Road. But it's much the same. Much the same.' This time I refrained from interrupting his reverie. 'Remember Tommy Peoples and Dessie Duddy? They came to the wake earlier.'

These sonorous names were like legends from the Middle Ages or the Wild West. Incredible to think of them still walking the earth.

'Of course they're both out of it,' Neil went on. 'They were always fly boys. Dessie's just got out on invalidity ... supposedly something wrong with his hip, though it seemed fine to me. And Tommy got early retirement years ago. Dessie was saying he made the presentation to Tommy – Mr Peoples is officially retiring today ... but in fact he retired twenty years ago and just forgot to inform anybody. A corny old joke – but true in this case. Tommy was always a lazy huer. Feet up on the desk and *The Journal* out – Get on with Exercise Six. Many a one's put their time in like that – but I could never do it. Never cheeky enough, I suppose. So here I am still beating my brains out while the fly men golf and booze.'

This truth was so unpalatable that it took the rest of Neil's whiskey to wash down. There was nothing for it but to go to the bar for two more – though it would mean leaving my car in an area where BMW was said to be an acronym for Bust My Windows.

The single patron on a stool continued to talk to the barman as though I did not exist. 'See fuckin' businessmen? Never done moanin'. Always cryin' about somethin'.' Was this for my benefit? It seemed unlikely. I had never seen the man before – and the truths he was expounding were universal. 'Know George Breslin?'

The barman twisted slightly from the optics. 'Big George? The coalman?'

'This is me to him: How's business, George? This is him: Don't fuckin' talk tay me, sure amn't Ah up tay me balls in debt. Alls Ah sold this week's a couple a hundred bags. Isn't that plenty, George? That's all right tay say ... but Ahm payin' out wages the whole time, says he. Ah need tay let somebody go off the lorry ... but sure Ah don't wannay do it.'

The barman handed over my change and resumed his leaning posture. 'Fuckin' Santa Claus, Big George.'

Neil received the fresh double with sincere gratitude. 'I had a bit of a bad patch this year. Thought I was losing it completely. Well I *was* losing it. Managed to pull myself round in time. All right now ... *touch wood*. But for a long while there

. . .' It took a bracing sip to give him the courage to continue. 'For about three months it was really grim. I hadn't a word to throw to a dog. I just felt like saying to every class, Go on home, there's nothing I can tell you, I have nothing to tell you, go on home now. And when I did try to teach . . . even things I'd taught a million times . . . I'd forget and get mixed up and start to panic. I had to go over even the simplest things a dozen times beforehand . . . just to be sure of them. And always nervy and jumpy and sweaty. Jumpy all the time . . . *you know?*'

In fact, I did not know. Anomie rather than jumpiness was my affliction – my bane not the days but the grey silent evenings. Professional competence had never been a problem.

'I couldn't remember how to spell anything . . . not even the simplest words . . . not even words I'd been using every day for thirty years. I'd turn to write something on the board and realise I couldn't spell it and break out in a sweat.' Describing this seemed to reactivate Neil's symptoms. He fumbled desperately for cigarettes and relaxed only after several deep inhalations and a long drink of whiskey. 'It was fucking ridiculous. In the end I could hardly sign my own name. Couldn't even sign my own name on a cheque.'

'What caused it?'

'Who knows?' His features puckered in concentration. 'I took it very bad about Marie.'

This was the one area I did not wish to explore. 'I know that.'

'It was like losing a spouse for me too.'

Obviously Neil had retained his proprietorial claim on Marie. He always liked to pretend that, although they had grown up in the same area at the same time and were obviously perfect for each other, Maleficent Destiny had used all its ingenuity to keep them apart. In fact, Neil would never have married Marie even if they had been together every day

290

of their youth. What had interfered was not Destiny but a social imperative. Intelligent working-class boys like to marry posh girls.

'I don't want to discuss that, Neil.'

'I suppose you're with someone else now.'

It was good to be in a position to reject such impertinence. 'No.'

Of course well-meaning acquaintances had brought me into contact with available ladies of suitable standing. Several had turned out to be intelligent and attractive. Yet these meetings were always absurd. We felt obliged to acknowledge each other's achievements and status and to converse in a polite up-lifting tone. Exactly what lovers never do. Or, at least, what Marie never did. Maybe love has to be born in the sublime idiocy of youth so that it can always dismiss the solemn encrustations of adulthood as a joke. For Marie, I was never the successful accountant – always the eejit who shot his load in his good-suit pants.

It was time to assert my own claim. Who had loved and lived with the woman for thirty-five years? 'There's no replacing Marie.'

Seeming to realise that he had gone too far, Neil finished his glass and blundered awkwardly to his feet. 'Take another?'

It was a sort of apology, almost a plea. Though I had now largely given up drinking – it only made me morose – I could not refuse.

Slumped against the bar, Neil looked like just the sort of wee man who would frequent such a place. While worthless trash like Barry flourished, noble souls were beaten down.

'Maybe I *should* have employed you as an accountant,' I suggested when he returned with fresh drinks.

'Could you see me as an accountant?' He snorted grimly. 'That was Helen's idea. You know she never forgave me for letting that out. Not to this day. She claims that of all the vicious things I said that was the worst.' He pondered, troubled. 'And it's true it made her out to be some kind of calculating monster. Whereas she really enjoyed the whole business. Probably more than any of us. She's too repressed to start anything herself ... so when she's pushed into something ... not that she has been since. All through that year she was spending a fortune on expensive underwear. She'd be wearing these beautiful things every time we met you two ... just in case something happened. There was this matching three-piece set ... in bright green with yellow polka dots ... bra and pants and this wee wee slip ... about this size.' Ruefully he measured off a centimetre between forefinger and thumb. 'And she discovered this stuff called stretch lace ... as nice as lace but without the bagginess. She had a beautiful set in that material ... with wee holes in it' – adding quickly, to dispel any suggestion of peek-a-boo or open-crotch vulgarity – 'wee holes all over, you know ... just a bit bigger than pin pricks.' He sighed heavily and consoled himself with a long, deep drink.

The moment seemed to freeze. And this is how I will always remember Neil – his face deeply trenched, greyish-yellow, the colour of my father's big toe nails. Even the smoke above his head seemed to freeze. Like stretch lace – but dirty, ripped, tattered, irremediably aged.

Eventually he resumed. 'But my favourite was a combination I came up with myself – flesh-coloured stockings, a cheap black suspender belt and plain white pants. Helen didn't understand it at first ... but she came round ... and eventually it was *her* favourite too. The deliberate mismatch was the whole point of the thing.'

There was no need to explain. The genius of the concept, immediately apparent, was to capture the heartbreaking realism of lack of money, time and taste. Artifice may intrigue and amuse – but only authenticity tears the heart out by the roots. The thought of rejecting opportunites to gaze on this practically tore my old heart out now. And how gifted Neil had been! Instead of suffering a nervous breakdown he should have won fame and fortune as the Degas of lingerie.

'When did she wear that?'

As I probably was to him, Neil was now entirely transparent to me, his only function to serve as a conduit to Helen. Is this why ageing contemporaries get together? To provide each other with long channels into the past?

He did not reply. We were both back in the past now, enchanted afresh by the rustles and slithers, the murmurs and sighs of ravishment, the dazzling effulgence of youth unveiled. Youth can never see itself – but how it blazes in retrospect! The dingy cramped bar, the late hour – time and location fell away. We had stumbled on paradise – the only paradise attainable, paradise lost. Certainly there is none in the future. No shining threshold beckons us to the light. Only darkness and silence lie beyond.